ILLUSIONS

Books by Donald Honig:

SIDEWALK CAESAR

WALK LIKE A MAN

NO SONG TO SING

DIVIDE THE NIGHT

JUDGMENT NIGHT

THE LOVE THIEF

THE SEVERITH STYLE

ILLUSIONS

Donald Honig

ILLUSIONS

1974
Doubleday & Company, Inc., Garden City, New York

PS
3558
.05
I43

Library of Congress Cataloging in Publication Data
Honig, Donald.
    Illusions.
    I. Title.
PZ4.H773Il   [PS3558.05]   813'.5'4
ISBN 0-385-08912-0
Library of Congress Catalog Number 73-10859

For my Mother and for Sandy

The writing of this book was made possible, in part, with support of the Creative Artists Publication Services Program of New York state.

ONE

The bicycle was stolen, the shirt on his back was stolen, even the smoke-trailing cigar in his mouth was stolen. The past half hour's egregious dishonesty filled him with exhilaration and his knees pumped high as he pedaled with a certain lunatic joy through the warm California sunshine which by virtue of its bland perpetuity and lazy benevolence had sired an industry and helped spawn a culture which had been condemned as the apotheosis of all that was decadent and corrupt in the nation.

His lips expanded in a roguish grin around the rakishly angled cigar which he had taken smoking, and still moist from its owner's mouth, lifting it from the ash tray on the adjoining table in the cafeteria while its owner sat preoccupied with a newspaper. Frank had watched the man unpocket it, divest it of its cellophane wrapper, set it between his teeth and light it, and a few moments later rest it on the ledge of the chipped four-cornered glass ash tray. Frank thought it would be a fine thing to top off his breakfast with a cigar that had probably cost as much as the breakfast had. So when he was ready to leave he sent deft fingers to the next table and lifted the cigar from the ash tray, slipped it between his lips with the casual ease of ownership and left, his cheeks swelling opulently as he exhaled with great panache.

Pumping his bicycle, he grinned at the sun-heightened colors around him, colors that shot from the gleaming two-toned cars racing past, colors which seemed to explode from everywhere, from gardens and billboards and store windows and from the garish costumes of affluent, perpetual summer. None of it, he knew, could be re-created 3,000 miles east. New York summers were grimed and sullen and torpid, estivating in the blasting incandescence of concrete and steel. Here the oppressive heat never seemed insane, was a yellow not a white heat, radiating broadly from the sky and not, as seemed in New York, from blistering and wrathful fires below.

Drops of perspiration lay on his forehead, his brown, longish hair was damp, sweat patches darkened his armpits. But in spite of the pulsating heat he continued to run the bicycle with a joyous energy, smiling at nothing, though not vacantly; good-naturedly, an expression of amiable tolerance, his body swaying rhythmically as his legs churned the bicycle forward through the traffic. Not even when that youth had yelled, "Hey, that's my bike!" did he feel anything more than zestful, mischievous excitement. Last week, when he stole the shirt from the department store, he had felt some uneasiness; but today was different, today was a day of sweet, emboldening confidence, so that he knew he could lift a smoking cigar from under a man's very eyes and get away with it. He felt invincible in this particular sunshine and even had the wild and dynamic urge to keep pedaling, up into the Sierras and through them and east over trails and passes that had been carved by the trundling and epochal forty-niners. The motion of his legs and the infallible spin of the tough thin wheels seemed in perfect harmony with the fecund yellow air and with the unfettered quests and designs of his imagination.

He had hunched like a racer when the youth started chasing him and begun pedaling maniacally, scattering people as he went, yelling at them to clear a path and then simulating a siren's wail with his voice, sticking to the sidewalk because that seemed the most incongruous course. After turning several corners he obeyed still another impulse and whipped the front wheel and pedaled into the supermarket. It was perfectly explainable: he wanted to put pressure on the approach and have the automatic door sweep back as it might before a potentate. It amused him as he cruised the stocked and spacious aisles that most of the people walking there with their shopping carts gave him nothing more than incurious glances—further evidence of man's evolution as an emancipated and emancipating creature. Finally an aproned clerk, some authoritarian relic, some enchained and abysmal toiler, told him that bicycles were not permitted in the store, whereupon Frank headed for the sensitized corduroyed approach to the automatic door—the rear one this time; thanks to California's ubiquitous automobile culture there were parking lots everywhere and hence alternate entrances and exits—and for a second time the door fled before him and the potentate reappeared in the indomitable sunlight.

He stared curiously now at a marching crowd of young people on the sidewalk. There were perhaps a hundred of them. They were a shuffling, restive tangle of jeans and sandals and beards and long hair and vesturing placards, with other signs stapled to sticks and held aloft, and with various chants and slogans erupting impulsively from them. He stared back at them over his cigar as he bicycled past, mildly curious. They were from the university, he knew, where he himself was a sometime student. He had heard of a mass meeting scheduled for the campus that afternoon, but had paid little attention.

Later, he paused at a red light, balancing himself on one leg, panting. As the light drew itself out he noticed the motorist next to him staring with dull, mildly disapproving eyes. Frank tapped the handlebars.

"This is my anti-pollution device," he said.

The man looked at the bicycle now, studying the sleek frame and thin tires and raised, uncomfortable-looking seat. Then his flat, noncommittal eyes returned to Frank.

"Stick it up your ass," he said tonelessly.

Frank removed his cigar. "I happen to be an ordained minister," he said sternly.

"Well then," the man said as the light blinked green and he began to accelerate, "in that case you can kiss my Presbyterian ass."

The car ripped away with the rest of the traffic. Frank began pedaling slowly, scowling now.

When he reached his neighborhood, where people knew him, he was stared at with a mixture of disinterest and curiosity as he pedaled along the street. He waved genially to several stolid faces, his own broad smile undaunted by the utter passivity with which he was observed. For this was a poor neighborhood, an uneasy blend of low-roofed industry and peeling, age-stricken stucco houses turned the color of oxidized metal, and the poor at that moment of the twentieth century were sullen and pent and inscrutable. It was a neighborhood whose dwellers were at once unalike and affinitive. They were a mixture of insolvent transients

enduring ignored and inwebbed lives, or were the grounded
poor, defeated and annulled, left to welter in their delineative
streets.

He had been living here since his arrival in California, now
more than a year. He had one room, upstairs rear. Most of the other
residents of the cheerless, two-story rooming house were transients, nameless people who appeared and disappeared, with their
variety of colors and strains and breeds and accents, their shabby
clothing and glances of estrangement, their imposed privacy. He
did not like Los Angeles, with its incredible distances, the anomalies of its people and its culture, and most of all because it
was the background, the sometimes opulent background, for his
unfulfilled, vaguely defined aspirations. The neighborhood where
he lived, however, was reminiscent of that where he had grown
up in New York. And it was not far from the university, where
he went occasionally to sit in on a lecture and of which he fancied
himself a student. Nor was it far from the Tabernacle where he
preached his sermons, preaching to many of the same sort who
lived in this house, on this street, people whose faces were engraved with wild vacuity and despair and defeat. At first he had
been uncomfortable with them, with such people who would come
to the Tabernacle and climb the wooden stairs and sit on the
narrow benches and listen to him with such rapt, mindless attention. He felt at times in the beginning that eventually they must
suddenly surge forward and devour him with their limp, fallen
jaws. That was what he had grown to notice about them more
than anything else—those lower faces, sagged and jowled and
knobbed and wrinkled, orthognathic and prognathic; the slack
lips, parted and inarticulate, like the mouths of enthralled children. He soon realized how desperate and enchanted they were,
transported by a mild, innocuous madness, listening to the spurious oratory of a stranger twenty years younger than the youngest
of them, and then parting with their thumbed coins and folded
dollar bills when it was over and leaving in an almost chastened
silence.

He brought the bicycle into the hall and leaned it against the
wall. The landlady appeared. She was in her late thirties, trim,
with dyed red hair. She was wearing tight blue jeans and a blue
workshirt rolled to the elbows. She had small, life-wearied eyes

and a thin slash of mouth. She was an abandoned woman—her husband had disappeared some years before—but she was tough and sturdy and dealt efficiently with the unpredictable assortment of humanity that came to spend their nights under her roof. Occasionally he slept with her, particularly on rainy nights; on rainy nights he could expect her to use her pass key and enter his room, naked under her housecoat, and slide into bed next to him. She was a grim, tense bedmate who clenched her fingers in his hair and often caused him pain. She was always gone when he wakened in the morning and the episode never alluded to when next they met, the bulk of their relationship muted, the mistrustful landlord and the blithe incongruous tenant who would inevitably one day vanish without a word.

"What is that doing in here?" she asked, slowly bringing her hands to her hips—she seemed always to put her hands on her hips when talking to a man, as if this were some attitude or posture of self-defense.

"It's a gift," he said, relighting his cigar, now a mere stump.

"A gift for who?"

"You."

"I don't ride a bicycle."

"Then give it to Louis," he said. That was her brother, a mongoloid of indeterminate age who stalked the premises with staring emptiness, wearing overalls and a sailor hat and clutching a rubber hammer.

"You stole it, didn't you?" she said.

"That's unworthy of you, Mrs. Andrews," he said.

"Reverend," she said, her emphasis on the word a dry blend of cynicism and sarcasm.

He grinned at her. It was a winning smile, an asset that had helped him through many difficult and embarrassing moments; it was the guile of the affable rogue, the shallow and devious charmer; nothing of very great moment was to be won with such a weapon, but in commonplace situations it was irresistible.

"Take the bicycle," he said.

"Why don't you give it to one of those derelicts who come to your meetings?"

He smiled again and began heading upstairs.

"You have a letter," she called after him.

He recognized immediately the handwriting on the envelope. He smirked. As ever, this was the neater, more thoughtful, more legible penmanship; it had style and precision. In this case it was a revelation of character, because Paul himself exuded those traits, down to the very fingertips that controlled the pen that shaped those impeccable vowels and consonants.

The letter was brief, concise, conveying its message on a single page, partially dehumanized by the tidelike flow of the calligraphy. Their father was ailing. It was nothing specific, Paul said, but whatever it was it seemed to embody a petulant negation of life. "He is depressed, pessimistic, and in pain." All at once now? Frank thought. The old man had become jaded and cynical years ago, another battle-scarred radical who had scaled the peaks and found them to be desolate, who had seen his cherished dogma crumble like so much dead parchment. Nothing spoiled so thoroughly and irascibly as an old radical stripped of his illusions. Ben Dublin had placed his faith in people and ideology, making vulnerability monstrous and disillusionment inevitable. He had been too inflexible to adjust or adapt; repudiation had been sudden and total—and what did one do with a strenuously used half lifetime which had gone nowhere?

Paul was not asking him to return, though Frank believed such a request was implicit in the letter. He reread it now, sitting on the edge of his bed, the cigar stub in the corner of his mouth, his eyes squinting in the smoke as he stared down at the page, the flawless handwriting. The letter was succinct, dispassionate, a cool summation. Frank discerned his brother's fine strength and clarity and maturity in it. He was truly fond of his younger brother (they were separated by less than two years), despite the many divergences in their personalities. Where Frank was gregarious and extrovert, Paul was reserved. Frank's impetuousness was contrasted by Paul's sense of care and discretion. Frank was still footloose, unsettled, while Paul was moored, adjusted. Their shared years of adolescence had been harmoniously spent and not until Paul had come here, to California, to college, had there been a substantial separation between them. The separation, the paucity of letters during those years, saddened and vexed Frank. And then the sudden, violent death last summer of Paul's wife Janine had buried him even deeper within himself, until he had become (Frank learned this from his father) almost reclusive.

So Ben Dublin had cleaved through his sons, endowing Paul with intellect, with the peculiar somberness that sometimes characterized the father. Frank was suffused with the father's generating force and willfulness, but without the discipline, the purpose. Frank had inherited the strong baritone, the public speaker's voice which Ben Dublin had used like a club on Union Square crowds in the thirties during those maturing days of Depression and Hitler and Spain. That voice, Frank's voice, even before he was born, that voice harnessed to the raging energy, cutting a swath the son would feel compelled to follow. We would have gone with your father to the ends of the earth, some of the old radicals told him; we were all for making the whole thing over again, shoving it up and making it over again, because of your father. The sight of these old men, shrunk and fat and gray, their depleted energies floating in nostalgia, bleared eyes searching for their place in history, was a cynic's justification; listening to them remembering meetings and marches and petitions and causes and speeches and letters to the editor and articles in forgotten magazines with names like *People* and *Justice*, was like hearing the tales of children's games, of rafts on the river and gambols on the green.

But the aura around his father had always been different. Ben Dublin had never deteriorated into a maudlin remembrancer. In fact there was a kind of glamorous worldliness in his repudiation, his disenchantment, his disdain. It made him more interesting than his former comrades who still secretly nurtured their old futile naïvely honed designs on the world, who shuffled around today with the dignified self-righteousness of unheeded prophets. His father was different not merely because he had been only minimally duped, but because he sneered at them today, at all of the fist wavers and table pounders and petition signers of his youth, including himself; his father possessed what was rare and pleasing—the capacity to belittle the most dedicated and zealous efforts of his young manhood.

Frank would press from his father reminiscences of the radical thirties. There were wild and bloody stories to be told, but Frank was most interested in the mass meetings, the crowds in the streets and parks and halls, how one orated to them and raised the foam from them. There was no technique, he was told. It was not as cold-blooded or as calculated or as sophisticated as that. The relationship between speaker and crowd was a very fundamental one. You stood before them on the platform or the stump or the soapbox and they either listened to you or they didn't. It was you, alone, versus the crowd—and versus was the word, Ben said, because even if they liked what you were saying you still had to say it so it permeated and "inspired" them and made them feel as though you were speaking through their throats. It was you, alone, with your words and your voice and your presence and your fervor and your own mad recklessness and something else, something crucial, without which no public speaker had a chance; something called charisma or personality or magnetism ("No, Frank, not sincerity."); something that made the speaker a visionary or an oracle in the eye of the crowd, which made him everyman and deity at once; it was addressing a crowd and at the same time transcending it, transfiguring yourself in its eyes as you directed your voice to the universe. And something else. "What?" Frank asked. "To believe it yourself at the time you're saying it." "But—" "No, it still isn't sincerity." "Hypocrisy." "You're not listening," his father said. "But to believe it—" "To be willing to die for whatever you're saying at the moment you're saying it." "But how can you do that to yourself?" Frank asked. "It has a name," his father said, and went on: "No good, or no evil either, can be accomplished without it. Fanaticism."

So it was the man who had been, the man he had never actually known, rather than the disillusioned, monumental sneerer and pessimist he had grown up with, who had cast the spell. He would stare at his father—still a formidable man of six feet four inches, some 240 pounds, bald now except for tufts of white hair around his ears, still with enormous hands and forearms and biceps, still with the thunderous baritone that lay in his throat like a sheathed weapon—would stare at him and try to re-create through imagination the old battles and furies, the fanaticism. Ben was tired now, disenchantment enjoying the consolations of age. But the old man's vision of life had seemed always to give him a certain perverse comfort. He viewed contemporary radicals with the same jaundiced eye he did their predecessors. They must eventually go the way he had gone, he contended. Though Ben had gone further, at least to the extent that he had never bothered to deny the old and persisting story of the embezzlement of thousands of dollars in political donations for which he had been caretaker. The money had disappeared from the Party's office in 1939, right after the signing of the Nazi-Soviet Pact. "That was the beginning of the end for me, that pact," Ben said. "And the end of the money," Frank said. "Oh, that old canard," Ben said, dismissing it with a wave of the hand. "What about it?" Frank asked. "There are some people who think I took it," Ben said.

But he can't really be that sick, Frank thought now. I don't want him to be sick. It's too soon for that. What is he now—upper sixties? Of course he took that money. He's too shrewd and intelligent not to have taken it. What were they going to do with it anyway—just piss it away on a hopeless campaign so some pinko hack could drag himself around the city and make dreary speeches to a lot of simple-minded fellow travelers. The candidate they were going to back, Ben said, was a young lawyer, an earnest young ass who waved his finger from side to side like a metronome when he spoke, who couldn't have been elected on a Farmers Forever ticket in Kansas, a fact which the Party readily conceded but which they said was not important. The important thing was to air the issues. In the midst of the Depression, there they were, Ben said, raising money to pour down the drain so some futile imbecile could air the discredited issues of a lost cause. Gestures. Gestures. Ludicrous, futile, insane gestures. Naïveté's last gasp as the sun set for World War II. Selling a Marxist line to save the country from the nitwits in Duluth and Dubuque who knew without even having to use their brains that the New York intelligentsia had been taken. I have to hold my head with both hands now when I think of it, Ben said.

I'll bet that money's still there, Frank thought now, holding the stub of cigar between his fingers and staring at it abstractedly. There were always those locked drawers and chests. A house was really a very large and secretive place, especially with accommodating basement and attic. Or it could be buried in the yard, or hidden in a wall or under the porch steps or in the trunk of a tree.

"You'll never find it," Ben said. It was a rainy day, a Sunday,

a day perfectly attuned for a treasure hunt. Frank and Paul were
in the attic, rummaging through trunks and boxes, exhuming old
clothes and hatboxes and shoeboxes and books and papers and all
the rest of the stored-up residue of a lifetime. Suddenly their
father was lounging in the doorway, neither amused nor annoyed,
staring at them. "We had nothing to do," Paul said. "We thought
we'd look for it." The guileless admission killed the lie, the denial
that had leaped to Frank's lips and he stared at his brother in
astonishment. They were ten and twelve then. "Give us a clue
then," Paul said. "I just did," their father said. "I said you'll never
find it." Then he went away. "Why'd you tell him?" Frank asked
as they faced each other, still crouched over an open suitcase, the
rain scattering against the small attic window. "He knew, didn't
he?" Paul said. So they stopped looking for it. Their mother never
referred to it; she simply did not know. "The money disappeared
one day from the office," she said. "That's all I know about it."
Nor was their older sister Helen better informed. "I've heard
the story," she said. "But I don't care one way or the other." "But
it's twenty-five thousand dollars," Frank said. It wasn't the wealth
that he was interested in then (he could do things with ten or
twenty or even fifty dollars, but twenty-five thousand was beyond
comprehension, beyond spending), but the thrill of believing it
was there and the excitement of searching for it.

Looking at the letter now brought back speculations about the
money. The belief that his father had taken it had never been dis-
lodged from his mind. The old friends, the faded old men who
would have followed his father to the ends of the earth, had always scoffed at the idea of such a betrayal. Someone had broken
into the office one night and taken the money. A right-winger,
they said. It had been in the newspapers a few days before that
they had raised the money for a congressional campaign in 1940.
Right-wingers had read the story and one night forced the lock
on the door of the office on East Twenty-third Street. The old-
timers were convinced of it, even though Ben alone knew where
the money was hidden, even though Ben had been delaying bank-
ing it; Ben who for weeks had been trying to convince the Party's
Election Committee of the futility and absurdity of throwing the
money away on such a campaign, Ben who for weeks had been
brooding about the unspeakable Pact. The investigation had been

somewhat perfunctory; the Party felt the police were not overly energetic in this particular case. There was little official sympathy expressed. In fact there were still men today telling those who would deign to listen that the candidate had been so formidable that political enemies had colluded with the police to cripple the campaign by stealing the money.

The noise from the yard distracted him now. He rose from the bed and went to the window. The mongoloid was lying amid several upended garbage cans, one leg under the spilled bicycle, the other over. He was making plaintive, squealing noises. His sister, the landlady, appeared, passive, punctual, virtually automated into the role she had been performing for a lifetime. She kicked aside the cans, then lifted the bicycle with one hand and with the other helped her brother to his feet. She said something to him, then looked up to the window.

"You and your lousy bicycle," she said.

He raised his hand, palm out.

"Blessings," he said through the screen.

TWO

He decided to go to the campus and watch the demonstration. From his occasional trips to the classrooms he had noted the abundance of combustible emotion and was lured by the possibility of violence.

He walked slowly through the sunshine (the mongoloid had disappeared with the bicycle), hands in rear pockets, resting on his buttocks. The letter, the recollections, had made him nostalgic. It was nearly a year and a half now, a barren and pointless span of time following an impulsive and purposeless departure from home. "I've got to follow my demon," he told his father. "Well, send us a letter once in a while," Ben said. He had been working in Manhattan as a shill for a Florida land-development company (subsequently indicted for fraud), speaking in the ballrooms of third-class hotels to groups of specially invited lower-middle-class people after two free cocktails had been served, and after the showing of a half-hour color movie in which the invited guests watched bulldozers turning the sun-drenched Florida earth and model houses being built while a sound-track narration described "the miracle growing before your very eyes." Frank spoke for ten minutes, opening with two stale jokes and then sliding into information about down payments and mortgages and equity and tax shelters and all the other blessings of property ownership, and then a team of salesmen with peppermint on their breath filtered through the wary guests who were beginning to feel guilty about the free cocktails. So he left this cul-de-sac job, left his furnished apartment on the East Side, said good-by to his family in the Capstone section of Queens, and went away, buoyed by the thought that this was incontestably the time to be doing what he was doing, taking from this inspired thought both assurance and justification. There was no plan or goal or destination. Rather he was like a child who goes about lifting the edges of tablecloths in hopes of finding a coin.

He took a bus to the Pennsylvania Dutch country and found himself, on impulse, trying to get work as a carnival barker. He insisted upon demonstrating his technique even after being told there were no openings, standing on a barrel and shouting to an empty midway on a dreary drizzly morning. "You'll be sorry you didn't hire me," he said as he went away. "Sure," a fat, pebbly-eyed man said, "you'd look good in a derby." He drifted into the Midwest, cheerful, optimistic, relieved of boredom and stagnation, excited by the fecund and indestructible heartland. He tried to palm himself off as an auctioneer, found out (was told) he was totally incompetent for such work. "Bullshit," he said. "I worked the New England circuit for three years. Why, I've sold more mattresses and . . ." "Bullshit to you," a man said. "You're not allowed to sell mattresses. Nobody sells mattresses at auction." So he went on to Chicago, after several more rebuffs. He resented it, the stolid inevitability of a city, the only place where he could sign in and live and find employment. He was compartmentalized, a specialist: a city person. He found work in an insurance company, sitting at a desk in a bland, common vacuum, living in a furnished room on the South Side. One night he walked into the local Democratic club and sat through the meeting, listening to the speeches. A primary was pending and the speeches were heated. Later, he got to his feet and asked questions and participated in a noisy debate. At the end of the evening he offered himself as a compromise candidate for the State Assembly. At that point someone asked him who he was.

He hardly had to look at a map to know where he was going next. It was inevitable and inescapable, and it carried the authority of history. By geography and by tradition, as sure as the leap of the wind and the roll of the river, he was going to California. Because for more than a hundred years his countrymen by the millions had been doing it, in the name of hope and gain and change, desperate and zealous and ambitious, by foot and by wagon, by bus and by plane, up and over the tumultuous Rockies and down into the last place, to the westward margin of the continent where it all stopped and congealed and shaped its sprawling, eccentric, variegated growth.

There was nothing else to do but go to a photographer and have a set of glossies made—a mixture of smiling and contemplative poses—and then visit agents and casting directors and the other people who inhabited the front echelons of the national fantasy. He invented a dossier of credits and experience, but even the simplest of his fellow aspirants knew he was a fraud. Kindly people told him he was wasting his time, others either would not see him or else told him bluntly to go away and not come back.

His sense of despair and depression became heavy, as he realized that California—paradisiacal, sun-dynamited California—did not hold the answer either, that he had come to the ultimate place and still not discovered whatever it was he had set out to discover, to prove. He had left home with the sure sense that something pivotal was going to happen; he did not know what or when or where, felt simply that all he had to do was set out and allow it the opportunity and it would occur, that it was all a matter of making himself visible, available. He began to take sober and despairing notice of the poor, the lowly, those on the flatlands of society. He realized that the gravitational law he was trying to buck was a powerful and callous one that would not be repealed by myths and simplistic rituals. He became frightened. He was adrift in a hugely uncaring world and did not know what to do, being infused with self-discoveries and insights that were running on the same tides as confusion and helplessness.

In addition to sporadically attending lectures at the university, he had been working nights in a drive-in restaurant under a flamboyant neon sign, carrying hamburgers on trays which he hooked onto the lowered windows of automobiles, living on a small salary and tips. It was during this period that he met the preacher, the man who called himself Friar Norman.

He was walking home from work late one night when he saw the man sitting on the sidewalk in a stuffed chair that someone had thrown out, as relaxed and comfortable in the ruined and broken chair as though contemplating the walls of his living room.

"Keep the TV down please," Frank said. "It's late."

The man eyed him stonily, with a misanthrope's steady, disdainful gaze.

"That's the least clever remark I've heard in the last hour," the man said. He had a drunken expression but contented, and his voice was comfortably sluggish. "The last son of a bitch who passed asked me if I knew my house had been stolen. Another asked how much the sidewalk rented for. Californians are natural humorists. They're great at shadowgraphs, too, what with all the sunshine out here."

Frank had stopped. The man was of indeterminate age, anywhere between forty and sixty, thin, slack, used, poorly but not shabbily dressed, wearing desert boots. The fingers of his left hand were covered with gaudy rings. His thick black hair was combed straight back. He had the canny air of a small-town pool shark; the center of any small gathering, the fringe of any large.

"You look like a refugee from a moving van," Frank said.

"Kindly preface your remarks as to whether they are going to contain humor or not," the man said. "I don't like to laugh unnecessarily, nor do I want to miss anything that's funny."

"You're drunk."

"Would a sober man be sitting on the street in somebody else's garbage in the middle of the night? Ask yourself. You're a bright young man. Ask yourself."

Frank folded his arms and contemplated the man, amused.

"You live around here?" he asked. It was a neighborhood of garden apartments, its monotony broken by several young acacia trees.

"No," the man said. "But I saw the chair. Despite its infirmities it's still better than anything I've got in my room. And anyway, this California is a land of displaced pilgrims. Where are you from?"

"New York."

"New York," the man said, nodding with a certain wistfulness. "A village northeast of Philadelphia, founded by the Dutch, conquered by the English, subverted by the Irish, and saved by the Jews. Are you Jewish?"

"No."

"Neither am I. I'm a drop-out from the Franciscans, if it's any of your business."

"It isn't," Frank said, starting to walk off.

"Wait. Just wait a second. Listen. Are you interested in a wonderful business opportunity?"

"Sure," Frank said. "The best commercial advice always comes from bums sitting in the street."

"No bum," the man said motioning negatively with his hand. "I'm not that. I may be drunk, but I'm no bum. I'm educated enough to be a bum, but still I'm not. I'm *other* things. Do you know the Halcyon Tabernacle on Mindinao Street?"

"No," Frank said. "I can't say I'm acquainted with that landmark."

"Well, that's mine," the man said. "I'm the spiritual leader there, and I have my followers. I have a very active sectual life. Excuse the crudeness, please. At the Halcyon Tabernacle I am known as Friar Norman."

With reluctant curiosity, Frank listened.

"Two nights a week," Friar Norman said, "on Wednesdays and Fridays, between thirty and forty beaten and abandoned people show up at the Tabernacle. I talk to them and we sing hymns together and we pray together and they go away comforted."

"And your reward is in making them happy."

Friar Norman closed his eyes for a moment and solemnly nodded.

"In other words," Frank said, "you're a charlatan."

"Not quite. I don't promise them anything. It's a religious service by definition only. What's the difference, as long as they're comforted? Take an allied field: psychology is all psychological."

"But you do take money from them?"

"I live by their generosity. I give them my time and my compassion, they give me their money. Nothing unscrupulous about it. But now I have to leave them, my little flock. I have a business opportunity in Sacramento, something non-sectarian and prosaic, but full of promise. I'm looking for a replacement, someone I can introduce to my people and say, Here is the man who is going to stand in my place and continue the good work. What do you do for a living anyway?"

"I'm a student at the university."

"You're a little old for that dodge, don't you think? What do you do for a *living?*"

"I sell hamburgers."

"Honorable, honorable. You're on the right track."

"Speaking of the right track . . ."

Frank offered him a dollar before leaving.

"I told you I'm not on the dole," the man said savagely.

"Then screw yourself," Frank said, walking away.

Several nights later he appeared at the Halcyon Tabernacle. He did not know why, really. It was his night off, a Wednesday, and through idleness and curiosity decided to look for the place. He could hear the singing from the street; it had a gray, thin sound, as if the singers were uncomfortable with the rising of their own voices. The neighborhood was poor, with frame houses and run-down taverns and a bus terminal; the succor of evangelical fervor seemed logically situated. He stood on the sidewalk looking up at the lighted windows above an empty store. *Well I'll be damned,* he thought. He went inside. A red crepe paper arrow ran along the wall the length of the staircase, pointing finally to a door with flaking gold lettering that read: HALCYON TABERNACLE. FRIAR NORMAN.

The lackluster room was about forty feet long, perhaps twenty wide. There were rows of backless wooden benches. Light bulbs burned overhead inside of diamond-shaped glass fixtures. The walls were bare except for a forty-eight starred American flag tacked up behind the lectern, which stood on a wooden platform.

Frank lounged against the rear wall, looking over the bent, aged heads and sagged shoulders at the man on the lectern. Friar Norman was talking quietly to the congregation about the rigors and infirmities of age, the ordeal of the spirit, the trial of the soul. He was compelling in a controlled, almost self-effacing way. The man in his milieu was effective. His homilies were laced with commonplaces, platitudes, clichés, backed nevertheless by a certain candor and artlessness which, while not converting the cynic would at least have disarmed the scoffer.

Frank remained standing against the wall as the people filed out at the end of the meeting, which had concluded with a silent prayer. Then he walked to the lectern, where the Friar leaned, waiting for him.

"I have to be in Sacramento in two weeks, come what may," the man said.

"But this isn't a candy store," Frank said. "You can't just sell it to someone else and walk out."

"You think it's me, don't you?" the man said. "Well, it isn't.

They don't care who's standing up here, just so long as it's some-body who talks to them. It's a communal thing. It's *their* place. It's the only place where they feel they belong. You have to be able to talk for an hour or so—with time out for hymns and silent prayer when you run dry—and show sincerity and compassion."

"But I don't know much Scripture."

"There's a book called the Bible. Do you know how to read?"

"But will they accept me? After all—"

"Just *talk* to them," the Friar said, banging his fist on the lec-tern. "They'll listen to anybody who has a heart and who regards them as human beings."

He was not unfamiliar with the approach. In Capstone there had been a man called Brother Spackle who had run a similar place, who also had preached on street corners at one time, chalk-ing long messages on the sidewalk as he talked. Frank had always been mesmerized by the man, had in fact in children's games sometimes played a parodic "Spackle," improvising sermons and speeches, to the delight of his friends. Spackle of course had been a fire-and-brimstone type, impassioned and explosive and omi-nous, promising limitlessly and threatening direly.

So he agreed to pay Friar Norman three hundred dollars, took over the lease for the big room, and was introduced at the next meeting as the new friar, Mr. Dublin, fresh from an eastern semi-nary. "Remember, my friend," Friar Norman said, "not too much fire. They're coming here to be comforted, not saved."

He took to his new role with ease and confidence, and he liked it: liked standing on the platform, leaning on the lectern with folded hands and talking to the stolid depleted faces that looked at him not with hope (they didn't believe in that any more, there were limits to that), nor with expectation, but with the same vacuous credulity with which they stared into their television sets, heads cocked to a side with interest or else from impaired hear-ing. Generally he eschewed histrionics, controlling his hands, modulating his voice, using verbal italics sparingly. He established his dominion by virtue of his position of authority and their mild, passive dependence. Occasionally he became enveloped and con-stricted by some inner frustration and would shout at them, raise his voice and strike the lectern with his fist and make their eyes blink, and he felt a giddiness then, a sudden surging need to shout even louder at the dead impenetrable faces, but then forced himself to suppress the desire, the need, and stood under his own restraints. They came slowly to their feet when he asked for the hymns, fumbling for their spectacles as they tried to manipulate the worn, paper-covered hymnals. He thought of children when they sang: regimented, detached, obedient (some confided to him —when, infrequently, they did speak to him after a meeting—that they came primarily for the singing). They lowered their heads in silent prayer when he called for it and he stared at them and wondered what was going on in their minds, whether they were indeed praying (and if so, for what) or merely sitting there mute and insensate, with vague wandering thoughts. And then they went away, shuffling and bumping at the doorway as he stood at the lectern watching them drop their money into the Liberty Bell bank on the table at the door (the bank was lined with velvet because Friar Norman had believed the sound of falling money to be crude). When the last of them had gone he walked the length of the room and emptied the bank, put the money in his pocket, turned off the light, locked the door and went home.

He realized between eighty and one hundred dollars a week from the Tabernacle, enabling him to become a part-time employee at the drive-in, where he now took to wearing dark glasses, though not in typical Hollywood affectation but because he did not want to run the risk of being recognized by someone from the Tabernacle.

There were times when he became terribly bored, when he was not even listening to the sound of his own voice, when he felt as though he were almost spiritually part of the congregation. *They're pulling me down with them,* he thought. *They've been sitting there for a hundred years. They're all going to outlive me.* Because they were so responsive to talks on pain and sorrow and loneliness, their dead winkless eyes narrowing perceptibly, their mouths tightening; because they no longer had a life force to expend and exhaust, no appetite, no metabolism, no expectation, no craving: they were simply there, impassive and indestructible, survivors of a thousand doomsday pealings. And yet he needed them, and for that reason damned them.

The petty thievery grew out of twin branches—boredom and need. He had finally quit the job in the drive-in and was periodically short of cash. (After leaving his job he had felt it necessary to rent a flashy convertible for two hours and go to the drive-in and tell his former colleagues—people he knew he would never see again—that he had come into a six-figure inheritance.) Time hung heavily on his hands and he wandered about the city, challenged and bedeviled by its great distances, making unflattering comparisons in his mind between this city and the one of his birth. He became adept at leaving behind unpaid dinner checks in good restaurants, at stealing books and food and articles of clothing.

One afternoon when he went to the Tabernacle to paint the lectern, Frank found two young men knocking on the door.

"Yes?" he said coming up the stairs.

"Are you the preacher?"

"I am."

They could not have been more than twenty, were relaxed and slouchy, dressed in T-shirts and jeans and sandals. One had a clenched fist silkscreened on the front of his shirt. They had short, trim beards reminiscent of Elizabethan courtiers. Their hair was long, shoulder-length, calculatedly free and shaggy, as symbolic on this day of recorded history as the clay-plastered, feat-heralding hair of primitive warriors was upon another; as indicative of caste as the unshorn locks of Frankish kings, the tufted heads of savages, the tonsured skulls of ecclesiastics. And on this day of recorded history such thatching filled the popular mind with the threatening contemptuousness of iconoclasts and nihilists and social deviates, was no longer alone the style of traditional bohemians and artists.

They were not religious people, but they respected him all the same, they felt compelled to tell him. One, with hard, earnest eyes said that the theocrat's place in society had been modified but was not yet obsolete. Frank smiled tolerantly. They were telling him this, giving this balm, because they wanted something.

"I don't believe in organized religion," the youth said. "But I do believe in faith."

"That's what we have here," Frank said.

"What do you have here?"

"Organized faith."

The youths were uncertain, then they smiled, boyishly through their beards. Then one folded his arms.

"We want to rent your hall," he said.

"For how much?" Frank asked. Amused, he noted the quick blinks of surprise from them, these worldly and cynical radicals. They stared at him for a moment: because not why they wanted to rent his premises, not for whom, not even when: but for how much. He wanted to say to them: It's plainly evident who you are and takes no great perception to know what you're going to talk about. It's as plain as though you were wearing sandwich boards.

"We can't pay more than twenty-five dollars," one of the youths said.

"When do you need the place and how many people will be here?"

"The night after tomorrow. We hope to have about seventy-five people. We're holding a meeting, you see. It's not a mass meeting. We don't want a big meeting, but just to get together in one room the various committee people . . ."

"We can assure you there won't be any trouble."

"I'm not concerned about that," Frank said. "The things that are important in this less-than-sumptuous meeting hall cannot, I assure you, be damaged by human beings."

The youths glanced at each other.

"One favor," Frank said.

They stared at him.

"I would like to attend your meeting."

"Well . . ."

"After all," Frank said, smiling, "I wouldn't let my Tabernacle to people in whose message I didn't believe."

After the next evening's regular meeting a plainclothes policeman appeared. He waited for the place to clear and then approached Frank.

"Do you know who you've rented your room to, Mr. Dublin?" he asked.

"What do you mean?" Frank asked.

"You've rented your room to a lot of scum from the university. A lot of left-wing, Communist scum. There's no law against it, but I just thought I'd tell you."

"How do you know about it anyway?"

"Never mind."

"You mean to say you've infiltrated them and have an informer in their group?" Frank said. The idea amused and excited him.

The policeman scowled. He was obviously displeased, either with the transparency of his department's machinations or with the audacity of Frank's presumption.

"Never mind," he said.

"I hope you're not objecting," Frank said. "In fact, you should be pleased. If you mistrust these people, then the more public discussion they have the better it is, the easier it will be for you to know what they're talking about."

"This is not a public discussion, it's a closed meeting."

"The windows will be wide open. You'll be able to hear every word."

The policeman regarded him with an utterly vacuous gaze.

Frank laughed. "It's a conspiratorial world we're living in," he said. "You see . . . even a man of God . . ."

"I just wanted to make sure you knew who you were renting your room to," the policeman said.

"A house of worship is open at all times to all people."

"Don't horseshit me," the policeman said, a look of resentment flashing into his eyes. "I know what kind of 'house of worship' this is."

Frank tried his widest, warmest, most disarming man-to-man grin. He shrugged his shoulders. "It's a living," he said genially.

He stood at the door watching them file in, the men with their free-growing hair and beards, the women with their waterfall tresses and militant faces. They all looked so young, to the extent that he felt older than his years and estranged, the only one in the room not privy to a certain secret, excluded from the unity he sensed among these young people. Being outnumbered and estranged (particularly on his own ground) aroused in him a vague, sullen hostility that seemed to emphasize their youth, their drive for individuality, and he consoled himself with the idea that he was too much of an individual to indulge in individualism. Wide gulfs and unyielding differences did not exist only between the generations, but within them too. Increasingly people were individualizing themselves, assuming new postures and identities. The world had suddenly become so complex and involuted as to have spawned a surplus of experts and authorities who could not be refuted. People had become impatient with tempered transition and conversion, with the natural sculpture of time. It was a day of sudden change and displacement, with all the attendant violence, contention and acrimony. There were avalanches of fear and resentment, crowned by the anomaly of a favored generation passionately declaring itself free and unique, laboring with petulant self-righteousness and grim ecstasy to assert what they were free to assert.

Many of the youths chose to sit on the floor around the walls even before the benches were filled. With cool, detached curiosity, Frank studied the so far strangely quiet group that was gradually filling the room. Some of the women were wearing colorful serapes over their sweaters or blouses. Male headgear included slouch hats, black berets, Dutch sea captain caps, Australian bush hats; also Apache-style headbands, worn by men as well as women. There were soiled and tieless white shirts, and sweatshirts and colored T-shirts and leather vests over bare chests, and jeans and khaki chinos; virtually all apparel interchangeable between men and women. They were shod with sandals, loafers, sneakers, and some of the women were barefoot. Frank stared most interestedly at the feet of these latter, as intrigued by bare feet in public as he would have been by bare breasts. Here was the new foppery, as self-indulgent and self-conscious as the old; an impure coxcombry at once blatant and simplistic in its repudiation of tradition, and at the same time as vain and conceited as a Regency drawing room.

One of the last to enter was a slight, rather short, unprepossessing young man. He wore the obligatory clothing—a green T-shirt and red-striped white trousers. His hair was full rather than long and made his head appear enormous, giving the impression of terrific cranial capacity. He wore silver-rimmed glasses, imparting a scholarly mien to his earnest Semitic features which were the patent consequence of thousands of years of continuous inbreeding; the face alone a composition capable of inciting latent hatred in those who determinedly saw in it the threat of the alien, the usurper, the historical trouble center; another irritating mem-

ber of this aggressive minority which was at the same time few
and unconquerable, obvious and abstruse. Frank watched the
youth advance toward the front of the hall, mount the platform
and stand behind the lectern, sober and preoccupied.

The others waited, watching the youth, very much at their
ease. Missing was that tense, charged expectancy Frank had noted
in audiences upon similar occasions. *Of course*, he thought. *They
know what he's going to say.* The youth began speaking, without notes, also without preamble, instantly into the substance of
his talk. Frank saw immediately why this unprepossessing person
was at the lectern. This youth with the scholarly and offending
face, who would be inconspicuous in mundane situations, who
was perhaps diffident with strangers and helpless before simple
practicalities, was complete heir to an oral tradition, from the
forums of ancient Rome to the backwoods homilies of Baptist
preachers. He spoke with fire and anger, riveting his listeners and
filling them with restive animation. His voice was high, sometimes
shrill, his gestures brusque and contemptuous. His millenarian fervor elicited chanting slogans and sudden raisings of clenched fists
from the youths before him.

As he closed, the youthful chiliast raised his fist and answered
the slogans shouted at him with his own, responsive shouting.
He was perspiring and his eyes behind their silver-rimmed lenses
were dilated. Frank stared at the youths, all of whom were on
their feet now, chanting and shouting. He was astonished by the
energy, the life force that had suddenly filled his dismal and impotent room where the old people sat like headstones and listened
to him drone. He felt a sumptuous surging impulse to run to
the lectern and take hold of this force at the crest, to speak to such
an antiphonal group, to hear the counterblast of his own words.

The chiliast shouted to them a time and a place, exhorting all
to be there, and concluded with a raised fist, shouting:

"There are no followers! We are all leaders!"

He stood at the lectern, gazing upon the quiet room, his eyes
roaming over the empty benches, his mind rolling back into the
past hour when the youths had been there. He grafted himself
to the silence as intently as a scholar might standing alone in a
moon-white Colosseum, though it was not hints of classical echoes

that Frank was straining for. He saw before him on the charged
air of the meager Tabernacle the full-blooded bodies and eager
faces of a restless, profoundly motivated generation, proud in their
beards and their beads and their rags, promulgating their ingenuous and unsuspecting ideals and programs with almost
canonical absoluteness.

"There are no followers! We are all leaders!"

"Bullshit," Frank said quietly.

There was a regular meeting scheduled for the following evening, but when he woke up in the morning Frank realized that
he did not want to face his starers, his hymn singers, that night.
In fact, he felt he never wanted to see them again. He had the
peculiar feeling he might shout them to death if he did. So he
went to the Tabernacle with a hand-lettered Meeting Canceled sign
to hang on the door.

He found the policeman sitting outside of the Tabernacle in
an unmarked car. Together they went upstairs.

"What did they talk about?" the policeman asked as they
mounted the stairs.

"Didn't your spy tell you?" Frank said.

"Now look—"

"All right, all right, I was only joking. You fellows have no sense
of humor."

The policeman stared at him—threateningly, because the man's
face had utterly no expression.

"I guess you do have a rough job," Frank said, taping the sign
to the door. "I sympathize with the police. I really do. It's a thank-
less, abuse-ridden job. Underpaid, too, all things considered."

The policeman waited. He was wearing an open-necked sport
shirt and slacks.

"I'll bet this is your day off," Frank said. There was the merest
flicker in the man's eyes. "You're doing this on your day off, aren't
you? God, you must really hate those kids."

The policeman neither affirmed nor denied anything. Perhaps
it was no longer possible for him to do either. He stood mute with
the indomitable perseverance and brutal unpredictability of the
law, of authority; a cold insentient fidelity sustained by a level
icy rage; as capable of laying down his life in service of a stranger

as he was of dispassionately manhandling some hapless offender; whose occasional demonstrations of kindness were looked upon as monumental because they seemed so uncharacteristic.

"They talked about capitalist imperialism and liberation," Frank said. "The liberation of oppressed minorities."

The policeman's face remained bureaucratically immaculate, as changeless as a photograph.

"You a capitalist?" Frank asked. "A slaveholder?"

"Look—" the policeman said, an undercurrent of tension in his voice.

"If not," Frank said, "then you have nothing to worry about. Because those are the guys they're after."

"You going to let them use this place again?"

"They didn't ask."

"Will you let us know if they do?"

Us, Frank thought. The multitudinous, impersonal, hidden *us*; vague enough and vast enough to encircle and subjugate anything; an *us* so ubiquitous and infallible as to have its place in mythology.

"I don't know if I would do that," Frank said.

"Why?"

"Would you want me to tell them about you?"

The policeman's face remained expressionless, as though there were not the slightest preoccupation in his mind. His next words could have been affectionate or murderous, for all his face showed, for all his voice intoned. He wet his lips, and the corners of his eyes twitched for just a split second.

"When was the last time this place was checked out by a Fire Inspector?" he asked.

THREE

He was brooding about that letter again. Even as he neared the campus, in one detached and insulated corner of his mind he was brooding, not so much about the letter really as about the chief consequence of his having read it: the money. Of course it was thirty years since the old man had taken it, and it was probably all dissipated by now. At less than a thousand dollars a year, simply at that modest rate, it would all be gone. His father had always worked, however, up to his retirement a few years ago. Frank knew of a few thousand in savings, and there were social security checks, but—could his father have retired with any sense of comfort if he did not still have that money? The old man had never earned much, certainly not as much as he could have, given his abilities and intelligence. It was almost as if after his political disenchantment he had developed a mistrust of his own intelligence. His trade for the last thirty years had been carpentry and he had worked only when he felt like it or needed to. It was quite possible that in one of the many cabinets he had made for the house the old man had built in a sliding panel or some such secret place in which the money was cached. Of course he still has it, Frank told himself as he walked with full, fast strides in the direction of the campus. He was aware of the crowds of students surging in the same direction as he, many of them in the streets, impeding traffic, swinging their placards; more and more of them, a thronging relaxed self-assured crowd, not without its clowns or humor but not entirely good-natured either.

Of course he still has it, Frank thought again, doggedly, obsessively. He never spent anything, never owned a car, never traveled, and the house had been paid off long ago. Paul had gone to school—on this very campus as a matter of fact—on a scholarship and worked part time, while he, Frank, went to a city university

and worked summers at a job in Coney Island exhorting people
to step up and try their luck throwing soft stuffed baseballs at
bottom-heavy wooden bottles. So there was no way to account for
$25,000 except to assume it was still there, which he believed com-
pletely because he was dealing with obsession not fact; still there
because there had never been gambling or whoring or any vices
or excesses that might have depleted the money. There was just
the man, holding frugally or prudently or vindictively to that
money which had been accumulated from the coins and dollars
contributed by a long-disintegrated group of 1930s radicals too
innocent to believe that one of their own had, could have, taken
it and betrayed them; or maybe something else, maybe a dogmatic
alacrity to ignore reality for the opportunity to level yet another
accusation against people, a system, they abhorred.

And then he stopped thinking about the money. There was a
broad expanse of lawn fringed with japonica hedges, the approach
to the campus, and it was filling with youths. Several automobiles
were parked on the black-topped driveway that wound toward the
buildings and on each of the automobiles one or two young men
had climbed and were shouting speeches or slogans or instructions. There was a distinct festive air to the gathering, orches-
trated by a group on the grass around a guitar player, singing
folk songs and clapping rhythmically.

It was moving into convocation now, person by person, almost
as if accidental, unplanned, by fragments and components
manifesting what it was, what it would be. One of the youths on
an automobile was shouting through a megaphone, telling everyone to go to the crest. "Professor Kifner will speak at the crest!"
he shouted.

A crowd of other people, non-participants, watched from across
the street with patent and outspoken disapproval.

"Don't know what an honest day's work is, the sons of bitches,"
said one, a short, surly man with a punched-around face that wore
an expression of experienced malevolence, like an oldtime railroad
detective's.

"I heard the Commies put LSD in the drinking water here,"
said another. He was in his late twenties, husky and shouldery,
with the beginnings of an old man's fat belly and fleshy jowls. A
plaid shirt hung straight down over his workpants. His hands were

on his hips, his arms squared out. "I don't say I believe it," he said through thin, tough-guy lips. "But that's what I heard."

"Nonsense," a thin, intense young woman said. "You're saying they're not responsible for what they're doing. They know what they're doing," she said knowingly. "This is all carefully planned."

"It's their parents' fault," an old woman said to no one in particular as she walked by, passing like some meddlesome Iris.

Frank looked at her and nodded severely to her revelation, then grinned as she went on repeating her message to others.

"These fucken kids are going to burn down the country and nobody is going to do anything about it," said a tall, expensively tailored white-haired man in a voice as righteous as a declaiming minister's, speaking to everyone and to no one.

"That's right," the short surly one said. The white-haired one glanced disdainfully at him.

"Get out of the street you bastards!" the white-haired one suddenly shouted furiously, raising his arm and shaking an attaché case at the youths. "The streets are not your personal runway." Those youths who heard and deigned to respond did so by grinning at him or raising clenched fists. One cupped his hands around his mouth and yelled back at the white-haired man,

"You're old, you're old, you're old!"

"Freaks," someone said. "A bunch of goddamned freaks."

"They're abusing their privileges," the white-haired one said bitterly and moved away, walking slowly, glowering at the youths across his shoulder with all the supercilious contempt of pride and station.

"Look at that," the husky one with the incipient belly said. "How do those faggy bastards get girls? Look at them, the filthy faggy bastards."

"You call them women?" the short surly one said scornfully.

The husky one glanced contemptuously at him, underlip bunched as if formulating a response, rode his eyes briefly up and down the other, then turned away.

"Some of those broads are beautiful," Frank said quietly. He was standing just behind the husky one and now he saw the thick powerful butcherboy neck wrinkle and the head pivot like some implacable turret and found himself confronted by a pair of hot contentious eyes that seemed to be trying to distinguish between insult and innocence. He studied Frank for a moment with the baffled, hostile confusion of the benighted, then turned back around, resuming his role of grim and venomous spectator.

An exquisite blonde passed, a girl more suitably designed to be—one would have thought—Queen of the Roses, but here wearing a pair of faded cut-down jeans, her full, ripe breasts swinging freely under a baggy polo shirt. Next to her walked a slim, ascetic, wild-bearded youth shaking a tambourine and chanting the Hare Krishna.

"That fellow must have something all right," Frank said and even as the husky one began to whirl—there was a glimpse of one murderous eye—Frank was moving, taking quick lateral strides away, grinning mischievously.

He crossed the street and joined a group heading across the grass. At once he had a sense of their peculiar sodality. There was a palpable candor about these people that was almost serene. Simply to enter their ranks was to become one of them, accepted and trusted. They were the spectacular army of irregulars, the battalions of barefoot saints who had been marching these past years under broiling southern skies and in the streets and upon the campuses and across the television screens, shaping the contours of events. Planning and charting his own foredoomed designs over the recent years, he had largely ignored them. They were a noisy fringe, he felt, seeking enormous responsibilities for which he did not believe they had the capability or the comprehension or the simple staying power to cope with; a band of Jonahs who would in the end prove to be as digestible as everyone else in this voracious society.

Some were marching with militant stride, eyes alert and humorless mouths petulant; some were shambling forward, arms swinging loosely; while the bearing of others suggested the utmost sobriety and dignity. Steadily they all moved up the long gently sloping incline. He became increasingly aware of an air of participation, of shared experience. Man's predisposition toward clannish behavior with all its fears and provincial devotion was never far beneath the surface. He could sense these young people exulting in their rare and sobering concept of union, the idea of loping toward a corridor in history; united by an idea, a protest, and most of all an opponent, an antagonist vast enough and vague enough to cohere a mob of the most singular dissidents.

Frank followed the crowd toward the crest, toward the buildings that stood bright and strong and architecturally sound beyond the grass and a line of impeccably manicured hedges. Here and there he saw a campus guard. They did not look particularly imposing this day, standing alone in their own slim bastions of authority. It was not that they were not capable, nor was it because they were vastly outnumbered, but simply as if they were people honoring some obsolete tradition.

One young man was darting through the crowd wearing a red plastic pig mask, shouting, "People power!" over and over. Some of the crowd laughed and applauded, others clearly did not appreciate the act.

"He's the son of a bitch that's going to be on television tonight," someone said with disgust.

Here and there were small knots of people arguing and discussing and debating, some heatedly, some quietly.

"There's a lot of resentment on this campus," a girl said to Frank as they happened to fall in step together.

"Why?" he asked.

She looked at him curiously. She had a soft, pretty face.

"Because there's not enough resentment," she said.

He waited for the smile he was certain was coming. There was none.

"Yes," he said. "We've been much too passive."

"Are you a student here?" she asked.

"Graduate student," he said. "Political science."

"Do you know Kifner?"

"Yes."

"What is he like?"

"He's beautiful," Frank said.

"Everyone says that," she said wistfully.

A man with a plastic-covered press card pinned to his shirt was talking to a slouching, bearded youth.

"What are the issues?" the reporter was asking.

The youth replied in a quiet, even voice: "Where the fuck have you been for the last 190 years, man?"

Swinging in his grandfathers' balls, you nitwit, Frank thought.

Two girls were handing out mimeographed handbills that announced, with appropriate exclamation points, that a demonstration was going to be held.

"Isn't this a little redundant?" someone asked them.

"We've got to reach the uninvolved and uncommitted students," one of the girls said.

"Fuck the uninvolved and uncommitted students," said a sullen youth who had 'God Is Young' painted on his white T-shirt.

Upon the roof of another parked car a person with a drooping Wild West mustache and Bill Hickok hair was proclaiming that they were not young but were indeed the oldest people in the world.

"We have satori!" he shouted, and was rewarded with applause and shouts of "Right on!"

Again Frank saw the person with the pig mask darting through the crowd, and then another with a bandana tied round his head like a pirate of the Spanish Main, and he shot another glance at the Hickok person exclaiming satori from the roof of the car, and he felt a great silent laugh explode inside himself. He began deliberately to look for the grotesque and the outlandish, and they were easy to find: people wearing American flag shirts, men with T-shaped D'Artagnan mustaches and goatees, white men with explosive Afro hair styles, a girl with a golden headband and an ankle-length white garment, and he could hear guitars and tambourines and bongo drums. He felt as though he were standing in a carnival in the very Middle America that was so despised and derided here, looking at the exhibits and the booths and listening to the barkers. A Ferris wheel would be magnificent here— to centralize the speakers, one in each rotating gondola, each having his moment at the summit, orating in steady descent until he disappeared, to be replaced by another and another, revolving on and endlessly on.

"Look," he heard a girl say. "Isn't that cool?"

Under a tree he saw stacked dozens of cafeteria trays, next to them a sign stapled to a stake driven into the ground: TAKE ONE IN CASE OF PIG VIOLENCE.

"Do they expect violence?" Frank asked the girl.

"There'll be a lot of heart-broken people if there isn't," she said cheerfully; then added, reprovingly, "of course they won't be the ones who get clubbed. There simply isn't enough resolvability here."

"Resolvability?" a passing youth said, overhearing. "That sounds like an Establishment word. Stick resolvability up your ass."

Frank laughed.

"What's funny about that?" the girl asked.

"Nothing," he said, suddenly poker-faced. "That fellow needed a haircut, that's all."

He paused to look around. He had some elevation now and he could see the demonstrators still advancing up along the winding driveway and across the grass, a formidable forward-moving convergence, constant and implacable, as many still coming as had already come. He felt a terrific exhilaration, looked briefly, with spontaneous exultation, up to the bright sky expanding infinitely in the sunlight, then closely at the passing faces around him, the earnest, generous, scowling faces of supplicants and tyrants, absurd and naïve and splendid, each of them independent and self-molded, sprung from adolescence as abruptly as rocket fire to become the surging prepotent galaxy of their generation.

The grass ahead was littered with discarded handbills, some lying flat, others crumpled. There was less crowd motion now, groups were becoming more compact. Ahead, erected in front of the suave modern lines of an administration building, was a speaker's platform with people standing or sitting on the grass before it. The raised platform commanded a great expanse of lawn where the demonstrators were gathering. Frank heard someone point out Kifner, and he pushed forward, curious, anxious to catch a glimpse of this man of whom he had heard so much for several years, to at last see him in person. He had seen pictures of him, of course. Paul had an album full (including some candid shots of the professor lecturing in class) and there had always been one of Paul and Janine and Kifner framed and hanging on the wall over Paul's desk, perhaps taken somewhere nearby, under one of these trees, with those very buildings in the background. Frank had had to be impressed—if grudgingly—with Kifner, because Paul had been, and Paul was seldom wrong about people. Ben Dublin, however, had been unimpressed, even disturbed; writing to his younger son at the time Paul was attending this university: "Don't become a goddamn Marxist out there what-

ever you do. Better a rapist or a drug-addict. Steer clear of radical
politics and stay on the prosaic high road of reason and sanity.
Build a foundation of success and not a morass of regrets. Kifner
is a cunning faker and villain." Paul's response partially placated
the disquieted father: he was not in the least interested in Kifner's (or anyone else's) politics. In fact, Paul wrote, this was perhaps one of the reasons for the affinity between them. "I am his
respite from politics," Paul wrote. "Believe me, he is as insightful
and provocative about literature as he is about politics. This is a
genuine friendship, wide-ranging and not narrow. The radicals
who crowd around him are constantly challenging or flattering
him. He is mostly bored by them. He consumes them all, the way
a fire does moths. He relaxes himself with Janine and me. He has
said so himself." The professor came to their off-campus apartment for dinner, soon after Paul and Janine were married, Paul
wrote his father, describing the unforgettable evening in great
detail, the menu, the conversation, what the great Kifner wore
and said. "He's found himself a father figure," Ben said disdainfully. "And whom does he pick but the chief asshole olympian
paterfamilias theoretician of the sanctified Left." And Frank said:
"What are you worried about? Paul is one hundred per cent apolitical. He's too intelligent to fall for that nonsense." Ben laughed
sardonically. "The more intelligent, the more vulnerable. Look,
I know all about that son of a bitch Kifner. He's mesmerized by
his own inanities. He's a vicious amoral politicizer who's capable
of convincing intellectuals that Leningrad is a city named after
one of the Beatles. You laugh. You don't know these bastards.
I do." "You should," Frank said chidingly—"you were one of them."
Ben scowled at him. "Fuck you—son," he said. But Paul did not
become politicized. He remained aloof from the university's fo-
menting political wing. He was more interested in the civilities
of Hazlitt and Lamb and the literate sophistication of the essay in
general. Nor was Janine differently oriented. Their common
ground, the thing that originally brought them together, literature,
remained their primary obsession. Janine had published poems in
the university paper and in several Midwestern quarterlies, dreamy
abstract snippets of free verse that were quite good, and she was
convinced she was into a career; while Paul worked at mastering
the essay, which he felt was the most direct and effective way of

communicating ideas (Kifner concurred, insisting that all other literary forms were too sluggish and ambiguous to be effective in contemporary culture). During his final year at school Paul's letters continued to be filled with references to Kifner and he even sent the professor's latest book to his father, to be read "more for style than content"—which Ben sourly described as the Collective Writings and promptly tore apart in his powerful hands. "It's a teacher-student relationship," Frank said, to placate his father. "Which means it exists mainly in the eye of the beholder. He had a crush on his teacher when he was in the fourth grade too. Believe me, it will go to seed when he leaves there." But it didn't. On a visit to New York to lecture, Kifner called to invite Paul and Janine to dinner. "He's been divorced for four years, you know," Paul told his brother. "His wife and kids live in Hawaii and he's very lonely. For all his friends and all his fame, he's very lonely." Frank reported this to his father, but Ben remained unregenerate. "If he ever brings that son of a bitch here there'll be murder," he said. "Listen," Frank said, "I thought you were retired from politics." "Yes, I am," Ben said, "and there's a fine and disgusting reason why, too." Frank felt his father was exaggerating a situation. His brother had too much good sense and independence ever to become another's satellite. But it all became academic when, soon after Janine's death in Scotland, Paul turned inward and there was little talk of Kifner or anything else.

Frank pushed to the front of the crowd and stood on the grass about ten feet from the rostrum. It was large enough to accommodate four hardbacked chairs which had been carried from one of the buildings and placed there. Three of the chairs were occupied by solemn-faced young men, apparently student leaders, their virtually identical beards giving them an almost comical, vaudevillian appearance, as though they were there to be victimized by the antics of a low comic. A fourth person was standing at the edge of the rostrum in studied isolation, away from the single stalk of microphone, shuffling several sheets of paper with an air of great preoccupation.

Frank felt a private, involuntary smile as he stared appreciatively at Stephen Kifner. The man was in his upper forties, of medium height, round-shouldered, rather heavy in the middle. His hair was gray, sprouting across his strong squarish head in thick bristles. His high-boned, somewhat Slavic face was unhandsome but distinctive, with a strong nose and broad mouth. He did, however, project a compelling physical presence, a strong and austere masculinity. He possessed a bearing that suggested a certain inviolability, a privileged aloofness that would not brook encroachment or easy familiarity. What had provoked Frank's smile was Kifner's neatly barbered hair and clean-shaven face, his immaculate brown suit and fresh white shirt and tie; a sartorial anomaly among this singular congregation of unconforming adherents and votaries, who revered him nonetheless, and who evoked a palpable air of expectancy merely at seeing him step to the microphone.

There was no introduction. They all knew who he was. He stood at the microphone without looking at them, his eyes on his notes. He did not look up until he began to speak and thereafter did not again refer to his notes. His voice poured through the microphone with the ease and fluency of the experienced speaker. It was a strong, trained, skilled orator's voice. It dropped over the crowd like a noose, alternately taut and slack. They listened, rapt and attentive, as if he had just marched down the slopes of Sinai. When he raised his arm to gesture he shot six inches of white cuff. The sun flashed and burned on his tie clasp as if he was transmitting signals to the universe. Applause and shouted slogans from the crowd were frequent, at one point those sitting on the grass rising to their feet in spontaneous leaps to bang their hands together and look at their neighbors and nod approvingly, as if responding to shock waves released from some titanic center of energy. He was intense, caustic, sarcastic; he was boldly, almost arrogantly assured. Sometimes he spoke angrily, hurling challenges and making prophecies; and then, like an approving elder, praising them for what they had done, were doing.

"We have done much," he said, his voice carrying resonantly through the warm, sunned air, through his thronged listeners the way a wind pursues its path into a forest, touching every upright tree and blade of grass, flawless and permeative. "But the progress we have made, the upheaval we have caused, the vibrations we have sent out, constitute only the beginning—which should be a frightening revelation to the upholders of this social and political system."

"Everything in this society continues to move with increased acceleration—automobiles, trains, airplanes; not to mention hypocrisy and oppression and sloth and dehumanization—everything in this condemned society continues to move with increased acceleration, except progress and reform and tolerance and compassion, which grunt along with glacial inertness. We have too long been dominated and subjugated by the vicious and corrupt triangulation of military, industrial and governmental power!"

He built to these last words with cold and terrific effort, emphasizing with incremental anger and contempt, concluding with a jabbing finger that shot at the crowd like a bayonet. The crowd response was at once virile and jubilant. Feeling emotion billowing in him like foam, Frank joined in the shouts, throwing up his fist and shouting, "Right on!" his eyes fixed upon Kifner with a momentary glitter that was almost maniacal. He quickly brought his fervor under control, however, and detached himself from the noise around him and studied Kifner as intently as an assassin, as if trying to read a message in the man's eyes. There was an electric energy rampant in Kifner's body at the moment that Frank could fairly feel; the man on the platform seemed for a split second capable of the miraculous—capable of it because the shouting, gesturing crowd believed it. Then the shouting subsided.

"They criticize our tactics," Kifner said sternly, glaring imperiously at his listeners, giving each the feeling they were the subject of his gaze. "They say we are disruptive and destructive. But we are merely their product, their learned pupils. They speak loftily of the necessity for peaceful dissent while they unleash upon us every form of violence, up to and including murder.

"Remedies and tactics become obvious when the response to peaceful appeal is arrogant dismissal. How long can one shout into a deaf ear? The seats of power are occupied by dangerous warlords and power brokers and they cannot expect to contain a force that is at once in the summer of its expectations and the winter of its discontent."

The end of the speech brought loud, sustained applause from the crowd. They were now a deeply permeated and highly aroused mass of people, having been told what they wanted to hear from the man they wanted to hear it from. Kifner had spoken for twenty-five minutes (Frank had timed it) and with subtlety and skill manipulated and directed and seeded the sensibilities of his audience; his speech had been almost symphonic in structure, building toward not merely a conclusion but a series of thematic resolutions and a crescendo that left the air charged with emotion —which was natural, Frank felt, since the primary substance of the speech had been emotion. He approved of the technique. You did not employ dialectics with a crowd; you strove for emotion, which was the most effective way of molding and possessing a disparate assemblage of people, who then manufactured their own logic and shaped it to establish such facts as they determined were indeed facts. The process was then completed with the transmutation of fact into dogma.

Kifner left the platform at the height of the applause and shouting, like an engineer walking away from a rumbling generator whose valves and levers he has just finished adjusting. He walked quickly, not looking back, a coterie at his heels. Frank's first instinct was to run after him. Being Paul Dublin's brother would give him entree. He did make a move to follow, but was diverted by something else: the platform. It was empty. He pushed through the crowd and with a solemn sense of ceremony climbed the few steps and stood before the microphone, surveying the slowly dispersing crowd. It was a heady feeling, standing before so many people, the cheers and applause still vibrant in the air. He fingered the microphone's long, warm, metallic stem and stared into the filaments of its potent little speaker, an oration marshaling in his throat.

An earnest little debate was taking place behind him on the platform, where two young men and a young woman were now standing. The subject of the debate was the four empty chairs.

"We ought to leave them here, as a symbol of protest."

"But we brought them out."

"That isn't the point. If we leave them here it will be a symbol of protest."

"How do you know anyone will understand what it symbolizes? They might think it just laziness or carelessness."

"Look, not every revolutionary gesture has to be blatant."

"Somebody will get the message. And anyway it's not important what people think, it's what you achieve."

"But if we leave the chairs here it'll only be the workers who have to cart them back."

"But it's important to make some gesture."

"Why don't we carry back two chairs and leave two?"

"But still, the workers . . ."

"I hate to say it, but on this campus they're very Establishment."

"But we can lose them forever if we—"

Frank did not wait to hear the question resolved. A disturbance had broken out near a building about a hundred yards away. Many of the students began running in that direction, an exhilarated excitement in their faces. There was shouting now at the scene of the disturbance, not angry or turbulent shouting but rhythmic rather, chanting, sloganeering, punctuated by sudden bursts of cheering, as though things were occurring in stages. Then he heard the sound of shattering glass, followed by a triumphant lift of voices.

Frank got down from the platform and joined the hurrying youths who were passing in an increasingly accelerated current. Walking quickly, he joined them. Everyone was converging on a focal point that was just ahead. The shouting and cheering and chanting were blending into a raucous fabric of noise. The pending dissolution of discipline and reason was fairly palpable on the air now, replaced by a swift, animate sense of impetuousness and excitement. Young, vibrant energies were being released in an atmosphere of bursting valves and smoking orifices.

"What's happening?" Frank asked someone.

"They're taking the library," he was told by a youth who did not look at him but whose eyes kept straining ahead, his lips expanded in a wildly enthusiastic grin.

There was more shattering of glass and now Frank saw a red flag being waved over the crowd. A half-dozen youths, faces fixed with malicious determination, overturned a small foreign car, sending it tumbling over on its side, two of its tires suddenly grotesquely in the air. This effort was rewarded with a cheer, and a slim young girl with flowing hair ran out of the crowd with a can of spray paint and wrote LIBERATED on the roof of the car. Shouts of "All power to the people!" crackled through the air.

The library entrance was clogged with people. Some were pushing through the crowd and running inside. One youth with long spilling hair climbed up onto the pedestal of an august Founding Father-type statue and, with one arm hooked around the statue's granite neck, began yelling, "Down with capitalist imperialism . . . down with fascist racism . . . down with technocracy . . . all power to the people!" His face was grim, fanatic. A girl ran up to him and handed him a flower.

Frank advanced to the steps of the library, pushed and bumped by the surging crowd. Then he saw everyone drawn back from one open space where a small American flag was burning, the onlookers chanting, "Burn, baby, burn," and clapping their hands. There was a drugged, ominous sonority in the chanting, the mindless obedient quality of ritual.

The library's lower windows were smashed; behind them Frank could see people darting about inside of the building. Faces appeared at the broken windows, exhorting others to join them; but the great majority were content to remain either vocal supporters or merely spectators.

"I knew this was going to happen," a middle-aged professorial-looking man said to no one in particular, looking around with a bereaved expression.

The youth clinging to the statue was still shouting slogans, louder now than before—he was receiving less attention—his free arm raised with clenched fist, holding the flower, looking like some feeble and perverted representation of the Statue of Liberty. Another was mounted upon the overturned car, straddling legs planted on the door, shouting: "One solution: Revolution!"

Frank looked around with animated, fascinated curiosity, reading the growing agitation in the faces around him. He felt a peculiar, scintillant expectation, as though he had stepped into an anteroom of destiny. There was a shining excitement and eye-glitter and self-pleased sophomoric grinning everywhere. The vocabulary of the shouters remained fixed in an incantatory series of slogans and catch phrases that soon became as ritualistic and as lusty as the shouting of spectators at a sporting event: a series of conditioned verbal reflexes soon without freshness or meaning.

A photographer was standing on a small rise, legs apart, just lifting his camera, focusing on the crowd around the library entrance. Suddenly a girl was hurrying toward him. She was short, porky, her buttocks grinding in tight-fitting jeans, her breasts jouncing under a drab colorless blouse, her dark hair hanging straight out from under the brim of her flat-crowned Western-style hat. She went directly up to the photographer and suddenly aimed a solid kick into his groin. The camera dropped from the man's hands and swung pendulously from the leather strap around his neck as he doubled up and sank with agonizing slowness to one knee. The girl turned and hurried away; several people saw what happened, but no one made a move, toward either the girl or the photographer.

In spite of the incident of the kicked photographer and the over-turned car and the broken windows, in spite of the shouting and the sloganeering, the crowd still was not a mob, its mood reso-lute but not hostile, its interest piqued by the antics and provo-cations of a handful.

Then someone yelled: "Here they come!" There were shouts —some fearful, some cautionary, some oddly elated—announcing the arrival of the police. The crowd responded most immediately with moody, wary, watchful silence. For several moments not a voice was heard, hardly a sound beyond the shuffling of feet on the grass. Smoke from a burning wire trash can rose straight as a pillar into the bright windless air.

They were advancing through the small trees on the far side of the library, moving with a steadiness at once uncompromising and inexorable. Their façade of impersonality heightened their menace; they were outsiders coming to participate: unquestioning and unanswering intruders entering upon the stage of a well-played scene. They were the more menacing and sinister for not having been noticed before, for the suddenness of their appear-ance. Coming with such stony force made each seem individually stronger and more hostile and implacable than they in truth prob-ably were: moving forward with the sanctioned, automatous effi-ciency of men on salary and under orders. Their uniformity of dress—crowned with gleaming blue helmets—gave them a chill, elitist look. The three-foot-long clubs in their hands each had the dread inevitability of a Chekhovian pistol.

An officer, wearing motorcycle goggles, a holstered pistol on his hip, spoke through a megaphone, ordering the crowd to dis-perse. A middle-aged man, wearing suit and tie, cupped his hands around his mouth and asked everyone to do as they were told.

Some of the crowd began drawing back as the phalanx of police moved steadily forward, clubs poised upright in the air like unlit torches or laid restively across open palms.

The first rocks came from behind Frank; they had to have come from fairly far behind because they fell in rather extended looping arcs. He saw several strike the grass in front of the police and some others drop in among the men. Then one of the policemen was struck and fell, one hand covering his face. Someone cried out: "Kill the pigs!" More rocks and some bottles too were hurled at the police. There was one moment of fixed and terrible clarity when the falling rocks' soft impact on the ground could be clearly heard, one last revocable and unclaimed moment before the poised, pending collision became inevitable. Then the police charged, running straight toward the crowd, moving with an incredibly soft, almost graceful swiftness, looking somehow less fierce in their running than they had in their stoic, symmetrical marching. Suddenly clubs were rising and falling and rising again in a melee of crazed batons. There was a frenzied scattering of people. There was screaming and cursing and shouts of defiance: and somewhere in the cacophony was the voice of reason gone mad with pain and despair. Several people were on the ground now, stretched out or in various sitting or kneeling positions, dazed and shocked and hurt and confused, some of them bleeding about the head. A youth running with a thick sheaf of handbills was struck from behind and fell amidst his scattering literature. A second policeman ran up and raised his club in a *coup de grâce* gesture and with a teeth-baring grimace brought it whacking down upon the youth's back.

Frank drew back slowly, warily, bumped and jostled by the panicking crowd. He tried to keep his eyes on the police, but that was becoming more difficult now as they had begun to spread out in pursuit of individual targets. He heard the wail of sirens as police cars and vans came up the driveway. Now people were running around him in mindless panic as though they were being strafed from the air, ducking and darting as if being menaced from every conceivable direction. Their faces looked like the faces of people fleeing natural disasters in the movies, frantic, stampeded, eyes glaring for refuge. Frank whirled to try and see everything that was happening, to see everyone who was crisscrossing around him, pursued and pursuer. His eyes dilated and for a moment he stood breathless before the chaos being generated by the controlled, taciturn fury of the police who seemed released from all their combinations, who were running with heavy dogged determination, the sun blazing on and off of their badges, their unappeasable faces sternly fixed. He watched one club a youth to the ground with a single lateral swipe and keep running, hardly having broken stride. Again the effect was cinematic—the police were too fierce and efficient to be real, to be breaking bones and drawing blood; the apparent absence of emotion or anger was chilling. Suddenly a barking dog came running with the undeviating swiftness of a torpedo, charging through the madness with wildly glittering eyes, trailing a leash after it.

Frank hurried past the platform, the microphone still there tall and thin and indestructible, a gaunt, lethal witness, backed by two empty chairs. He saw several youths winding up and throwing rocks and bottles toward the police, the missiles being hurled with an almost reckless disregard for target. One bearded youth with sunglasses had a handful of small stones and was running up throwing one after another, his long corduroy shirt swinging around his body with each effort. There was an incredible mid-air collision of rock and bottle resulting in a stinging overhead crash and shower of glass splinters. A policeman was struck full in the face by a thrown rock and went down and rolled over on his back, blood pouring sumptuously from his nose. A youth was crawling across the grass, blood streaming down his neck, his eyeglasses hanging crookedly across his face off of one ear. A couple were running in tandem, the man's arm protectively around the woman, their heads ducked into raised shoulders. The burning trash basket had been thrown over, its smoking contents strewn upon the grass. Some people were simply standing and watching as others were struck down around them, as if mesmerized into some sort of protective incredulity. The shouts of pain and anger continued to be penetrated by the toneless wails of sirens that sounded like some bizarre orchestration for what was happening.

Frank hitched his trousers, moving through it all with a feeling of becalmed infallibility, staring at the harsh, frenetic scene as at some gaudy pageant, captivated, fascinated, with a spectator's sense of vicarious participation. The sound of heavy clubs making

hard contact with human bones was sometimes very near. He
pushed people away, he moved briskly, sometimes jumping to
see over the head of some obstructing person. People continued
to dodge and scatter around him, first in one direction and then
another, the strength, resolution and purpose they had possessed
as a crowd now gone, fled from them in the act—the necessity—
of becoming individuals once again, chased and menaced and
clubbed by the ubiquitous police whose faces continued fiercely
passive under their helmets. The scene passed beyond the dimensions of reality for a moment, into an almost soundless, sa-
tanically choreographed dream of distortions and histrionics, of
muted pain and brutality: victims all, slayers all. A policeman
came near, red-faced, panting, gulping air through an open, extended lower jaw, glaring around, pounding his club restlessly
into his hand, blouse pulled and bunched over his belt; then
abruptly ran again as though he himself were being pursued.
Frank watched him chase a running girl toward the driveway and
when close enough to strike drive his club as hard as he could
between her buttocks. The girl screamed and the policeman had
to leap over her tumbling body.

A youth ran past with a wild grin frozen on his face. Another
stumbled out of the crowd holding a bleeding forehead, moan-
ing, "Oh God." A sobbing girl blurted: "How can they go home
tonight and face their families?" Wherever he looked now, Frank
saw shocked and incredulous faces. *All this in a few minutes,* he
thought. *It hasn't been more than a few minutes.*

Then he saw a policeman starting toward him. The officer
was tall, lean, with a receding chin that looked eroded by meanness. Frank began backing away. He raised a clenched fist and
gestured toward the policeman, then turned and started to run,
taking long strides, his fists pumping. There was a calm, almost
serene expression on his face that belied the excitement and reckless joy he felt at the moment, as though he were experiencing a
zealot's fantasy. He leaped over a piece of hump-backed sculpture
on the grass, taking it with the poised infinite grace of a hurdles
jumper, looking for a moment like a flying appendage to the sculpture, arms spread for balance, free and rapt in space, and then
touching the ground with feet running so immediately it was as
though they had been pumping even as he had been afloat in thin

air. He ran past the library, wheeled suddenly and continued along a row of low hedges. He threw a look back over his shoulder and when he saw he was not being chased he grinned foolishly and slowed to a trot, then leaped easily over the hedges and let himself slump on the grass and lay on his back, panting, more with excitement than from exertion.

A girl was sitting nearby, hugging her legs, which were covered to the ankles by a long colorless muslin dress. She was staring blankly at him, biting her underlip.

"They arrested my boy friend," she said tonelessly. "He wasn't even doing anything. First they clubbed him down, then they dragged him away by the arm. He wasn't even doing anything. Philosophically, he's a pacifist."

He closed his eyes, trying to compose his breathing.

"Why does this society provoke such violence?" the girl said plaintively in a wandering voice, moving her head dumbly from side to side. Then she rode her eyes slowly along his prone, sky-facing body. Her eyes came to rest on the quite perceptible bulge in his pants. She said, not reproachfully but curiously,

"Is it frozen with fear, or is this how you get your kicks?"

FOUR

1

"*Her body is being brought in by lorry.*"

The policeman—or was he a constable?—had just returned to the room, the door to the anteroom left slightly ajar behind him. He was extremely solicitous and apologetic, in both demeanor and voice. He stared at Paul with round, faultlessly blue, guileless eyes. (Paul had never seen eyes like that in the face of a policeman in Los Angeles or New York.) The man's uniform was a nondescript blue; he was bareheaded, his thin reddish hair neatly combed and parted. He was holding an unlit brier in his hand. Over his shoulder there was a clock on the wall and next to that a picture of the Queen.

We wakened at the outlandish hour of six o'clock in the morning and I remembered staring with a most critical feeling at the asymmetrical carpentry of our walls and ceiling where they conjoined most irregularly; or was it age that had caused it, in this traveler's inn in the shadows of the wild and bloody mountains? In any event, the ceiling was crooked and the wall was crooked and the floor sloped and even the small window was aslant, and I did not like it, though Janine said the place must be a hundred fifty years old at least, and decrepitude was part of its charm. She always had this romantic affinity for places where the sleep of time and countless dreams were a mood in the very timbers; places where people centuries dead had talked and dined and slept and loved and looked with boundless exuberance to the fair promise of the future. She would rhapsodize before an abandoned, grass-hidden shack as a scholar before an Angkor Wat; would try to guess the age of hoary trees or place the time when this grim boulder tumbled from that glowering mountain; sit pensive at places where the flight of the wild wind went unheard and the passage of time left no wake. This bent toward romanticizing ancientry was natural with her, I suppose, an outcropping of those impulses to write poetry, which I so treasured in her. I remember saying to Kifner, early on, that we wanted to live like anchorite and anchoress, in an urban Walden, and he laughed and said that was impossible, that any of that sort of thing was impossible today, much less an urban Walden. The insular shack by the pond and the cottage by the lake were irrevocably dead and lyrically buried and anyone who tried to revive that style today would end up a social parasite. (He could deromanticize a dream quicker than any man I knew.) Nevertheless, I had intended to find with Janine an orderliness and a quietude, and follow our aspirations with all the harmony I could.

It was tough and rocky, this clansman's earth, this mountainous land of sudden and startling beauty and uncompromising mood, where blood feuds had raged like eternal fire and vengeance reached from the grave and leaped through the centuries, hardening the rocks and chilling the mountain waters and casting gloom through the glens. At seven o'clock in the morning we began hiking through the chill inhospitable dawn toward those mountains which seemed to scowl at man, which stood like contemptuous vaults of history and legend over the puny mortality of their seekers. There was little conversation; I knew her poet's sensibilities were responding to the stark and frowning beauty of Glencoe, that she was trying to infuse herself with the grimness of its history and delineate the smoke of its ghosts, that her mind was keenly dreaming even as she strode ahead in her dubbined boots and heavy woolen socks, her rucksack strapped over her small, feminine shoulders. And I, for my part, was hardly desirous of conversation that morning. From seven o'clock until noon we walked over short tough grass and iron earth into the Sphinx-face of the mountain, past icy peat-brown streams that tumbled over the rocks, as indefatigable in their courses as the stars. Our boot soles barely made prints as we walked through cool sunlight and valleys of cold shadow. We climbed past slashes of gullies and small gnarled trees and up over the rocks, up, up into the tombs of giants.

"She was—? She was—?"

The policeman again, still with compassion, sitting now, staring at Paul from across the desk, pen in hand. Paul's gaze moved, to the window, across the streets of this village and to the mountains beyond, which were leaden now against the day's dying light, an unholiness in them now as their vast shoulders awaited the descent of the black cape, standing forever as they had to the eyes of shepherds and crofters and lairds and chiefs and kings a thousand years ago. The mountains, the village, this room, the soul of Paul Dublin: a mutuality of quietude. The telephone had not rung in an hour. It was a rural police station, as a rule not a place of crises or emergencies or tragedies. What had happened today was probably the most excitement in years. He heard discreet voices in the other room, with their slight burrs. "*Amateurs. Pity.*"

At one-fifteen in the afternoon she fell. How can I be so precise about the time? I don't know. I must have looked at my watch, or maybe I saw hers because I believe that it stopped when she struck, recording the moment of her death. I did not immediately rush back down the trail when she fell. If there had been the chance of finding her alive I would have, but that fall was a good three hundred feet straight into a swarm of rocks edged enough to slice moonlight. I stood for some moments, staring into space, hearing from afar the splash of water, feeling chilled and naked and alone in all of this and all of the rest of the world; of the mountain, of the rock, of the bitterness of Glencoe. A lone bird flew overhead, as random as a piece of wind-tossed black velvet.

I was not even the first to reach the body. Two Englishmen, hikers, were already there. They were father and son, their ruddy, genial faces appropriately solemn. The son, who was about twenty, claimed excitedly that, "I just happened to look that way at that moment and saw her in mid-air, looking like she was suspended by a rope, and for a second I thought she was, because of the way her arms were raised into the air, but then she began to drop and I knew . . ." They became embarrassed when I told them who I was. They were lingering about the body when I got there, coming close and then drifting away again, obviously not knowing what to do about this thing which had so unceremoniously dropped into the middle of their holiday. Unaccountably, I felt sorry for them. And I wished they hadn't been there; I very much

*wanted privacy, to be alone with the body. And Janine? She was
lying on her back, in a slight crevice formed by the juncture of
two giant gray boulders of Glencoe. She quite clearly had many
broken bones; there was a drape to her body that could not have
indicated otherwise. There were small cuts on her forehead and
on the bridge of that small, perfect, haughty nose. She had
bled profusely from the mouth, which had a smeared, child-in-the-
jam appearance. Mercifully, her eyes were closed, but there was a
furious, impotent frustration in her face, as if while falling in thin
air she had been clawing and struggling and filling with rage for
what was happening, had happened, was going to happen.*

"My wife," Paul said. "She was my wife."

"Ah," the policeman said softly, pausing for a decent interval
before writing on the paper in front of him.

"If it would have rained this morning, we wouldn't have gone
out."

The policeman nodded sympathetically, keeping his eyes upon
what he was writing.

"How long have you been in Scotland?"

"Three days," Paul said. "We landed in Edinburgh, then rented
a car and drove here. My wife wanted to come to Glencoe."

2

It would slip in and out of mind, occasional and unsummoned,
every detail and nuance as crisp and sharp as that Scottish morning had been. He never tried to resist or dislodge it, of course;
he was enduring too much solitude and silence to want to dis-
courage even the most disquieting companions of the mind. And
anyway the memories were integral to the very solitude and silence he had chosen for himself and he had no desire to obturate
his mind to them. He was capable of sitting for hours in utter
stillness at his desk downstairs in the old frame house where he
lived alone on the fringe of an undeveloped section of the neighborhood where he had been born and raised, where the rich and
abundant years of childhood lay spent, and to where he had returned because this was at once the most simple and most complex of places for him.

He sat now at the desk, which was positioned like a command post, looking out upon the expanse of ground not yet hacked and smoothed and overlaid with concrete; the last spacious parcel of Capstone earth still looking as memory had always known it: too rocky and irregular for choose-up games of baseball, weed-covered and strewn with such debris as tires and inner tubes and oil cans and spring-bristling easy chairs and soiled mattresses and broken glass, as if a surreptitious ocean rolled in the night and disgorged its flotsam and jetsam over this ground.

He watched the woman coming along the street, walking now on the dirt where the sidewalk ended, pacing her shadow through the warm noontime sunlight. Mrs. Hanratty strode forward with a rolling, almost belligerent motion. Unconsciously, he put down the pencil he had been holding in his hand, placed it neatly along the edge of the blank white page and leaned forward on the desk.

She was about fifty, widowed a dozen years, working as a twice-weekly domestic and cook for his father. She did not like Paul; he knew that much, in a vague, uninterested way. Detached, incurious, he watched her pass the last house on the other side of the street with that determined, belligerent stride that sometimes characterized the prematurely widowed woman who has resolved not to be bent by calamity. *She could be coming to tell me he's dead,* he thought. It would have to be done that way, since there was no telephone in this house. His last visit to his father had been depressing. The old man was not well, had been dispirited, melancholy. Ben had spoken of pain and death, sardonically of man's "dustiny," then dismissed it all with a drop of the hand. His inner strength seemed markedly diminished. It saddened Paul (and alarmed him enough to write a letter about it to his brother in California).

"He wants to see you," she said when she had come in. They were sitting downstairs, on the plain, spartan chairs in the parlor. One of the things that annoyed her was never being invited further into the house than the parlor. It was not that she suspected him of concealing anything—it was the insistence upon privacy and formality that irritated her, who considered herself an adjunct to the family, who had sent him twenty-five dollars when he was married and who had cried for him when his wife's body had come home from Scotland nailed into a wooden box.

"I just saw him," Paul said.

"That was three weeks ago," Mrs. Hanratty said.

Three weeks?

"He's worried about you," she said.

"He is?"

"Yes," she said, the word slowly protracted and ironic on her lips. Her eyes were fixed upon his face. She was a thin-lipped, sharp-eyed woman with a colorless face. She had a terse, measured way with her words, which seemed to be honed as their wary syllables fell one by one from between the twin razors of her lips. Her plain brown hair was tied back in a bun, her invincible Irish face proud and tough in its impassiveness, her large bosom propped and proud like the chest of a field marshal.

"He's curious about what you're doing," she said.

"I have my work."

"He says he hasn't seen any of your articles lately."

"They're essays," he said testily. "And anyway, I'm working on . . . something different."

She stared at him.

"Personal work," he said.

"I wasn't about to ask," she said.

He looked older, she thought. There was a deep, soft sadness in his eyes, a heaviness in his shoulders. For a single man living alone, however, there was a neatness not only about his person but about the house as well that intrigued her. But he had always been that way, somewhere between prim and proud, a sharp contrast from the shiftless brother and the sister, both of whom Mrs. Hanratty considered to be worthless and beyond redemption. Paul was not nearly as definable as they, and so to be resented.

"He misses his children," she said dryly, staring at him.

"He never did before. He's always been very independent."

"The years do bring their changes."

"Has he by any chance seen a doctor?"

"I've suggested it. But he said that time always beats the doctor to the door—whatever that's supposed to mean."

She continued to stare at him. Suddenly, abruptly, out of this staring, she said, "I think he's got cancer."

"What?" Paul said, taken aback.

"In my opinion," she said.

"What the hell do you know?" he said angrily. "You have some nerve."

Mrs. Hanratty remained unruffled, poised.

"My husband died of it," she said, "and my father died of it."

"What are you—some kind of ghoul? What do you do—flap your wings and land next to somebody and nest there until he dies of cancer?"

The woman's thin lips clenched for a moment, though her staring eyes never faltered.

Paul slumped in his chair, covering his face with his hand. He shook his head slowly from side to side.

"Christ," he muttered. "All this death."

3

His father was not alone when Paul arrived that evening. Ben was with an old friend, Harry Desser, proprietor of a long-established Capstone stationery store. Desser was a slight, gray, desiccated-looking man who had aged into shabby, nervous anonymity. He wore a set of poorly made dentures which made his smile appear excessively jovial and skeletal. When he wasn't smiling or engaged in conversation, his face would settle into a morbid and solitary expression, giving him the appearance of the most abused and unheeded of prophets.

Desser was peculiarly animated when Paul entered. He crossed the room, hand outstretched in welcome.

"We were just talking about the good old days, your father and me," he said.

"It's one of the things that keeps us young," Ben said sardonically, his strong voice a pained rasp as though it had to corkscrew up through his throat. He was sitting back in a soft chair, shoeless, his white-socked feet crossed at the ankles, his arms at rest on the sides of the chair. His blue denim workshirt was open at the throat, exposing white curly chest hair. His face had an almost serene pinkness, softened further by tufts of feathery white hair that seemed gently pasted to the sides of his otherwise bald, domelike head. A water glass half filled with bourbon, the bottle next to it, stood on the end table next to the chair.

"I was telling your father," Desser said after he had ushered Paul into a chair and taken a stance in the middle of the room, "we had principles in those days. We were organized, dedicated. We knew what our cause was. We had *discipline*. These radicals today," he said with a disdainful sweep of his hand, "they don't know what discipline is. They put on a pair of red socks and grow a beard and think they're radicals, eh, Ben?" he said, turning to Ben with a broad, hopeful smile.

"Sit down, Harry," Ben said quietly.

"We were ready to put our lives on the line," Desser said, taking a seat on the edge of a chair. "We believed in something and weren't afraid to fight for it. We went to Spain . . ."

"*You* went to Spain," Ben said.

"The proudest thing I ever did in my life," Desser said to Paul, soberly. "I was no hero, mind you; but I was where the shells were falling. I got my little wound in the thigh and I'm damned proud of it." Turning to Ben, Desser, with his sad eulogist's face, said, "A lot of good men died there, Ben."

"Idealists," Ben said without inflection, picking up his drink. Paul scrutinized his father's face, searching there for the sarcasm which had not been evident in the older man's voice.

"A few years ago," Desser said to Paul, "I visited Europe with my wife—for the first time since 1937—and *refused* to step foot in Spain. That's because I came from a different school. The difference is, we had a set purpose in my day, a fundamental set of principles and a solid program for the betterment of mankind which we believed in and adhered to. There is very little intellectuality among the radical movement today—which is why they're so prone to meaningless violence. In the thirties we had the cream of the intellectuals with us; we realized there was more strength in brain power than in muscle power. And that's how we got things done."

"Bullshit," Ben said irascibly.

Desser smiled nervously at him, then went on.

"Today the radicals are too fragmented. Every day a new cause grows out of the ground and they discard yesterday's to pursue today's. That's precisely the way to achieve nothing, to bring the wheels of social progress to a standstill."

Desser sat back now, pensive. Apropos nothing, he sighed.

"I was thinking just this morning," he said. "I passed that old store front on Grant Avenue near the American Legion hall and suddenly I was called back almost thirty-five years. Ben, do you remember the meeting we had there—you were speaking—and the Legionnaires broke in calling us Communists and started a riot."

Ben nodded, sipping from his glass.

"Those lousy bastards," Desser said. "They came in like a bunch of storm troopers, calling us Communists—"

"Which we were," Ben said politely.

"But it was different in those days, Ben. A man had a right—a goddamn *duty*—in those days to be as radical as he could. People were starving, one third of a nation was—you know—out of work."

"So the Legionnaires came in," Ben said, suddenly animated, putting down his drink and leaning forward, his voice suddenly strong, vibrant, his eyes severe, searching. "I was standing up on the stage, speaking from behind a lectern and a water pitcher, trying to raise the bleak spirits of a defeated proletariat, when suddenly the door broke down and in they came, in their Belleau Wood uniforms, big-bellied and red-faced and righteous. 'Commies!' they cried. 'Nazis!' we cried back. (A few years later when they did the same thing to Bund meetings we called them patriots.) And they proceeded to wade into us and knock us sprawling across our little wooden folding chairs. I was the last one, because I was holding high ground up there on the stage. Four of them came at me. I picked up a chair and brained two of them as the chair splintered in true Hollywood style and went flying. Then I kicked another in the balls—he walks with a stoop to this day—and grabbed the fourth by the hair and put my big fist halfway down his throat. Then I stood there with my hand over my heart and sang the 'Internationale' until the police came."

Desser gazed at him, puzzled.

"I don't remember that, Ben," he said quietly, apologetically.

"You don't?"

"We all ended up on the floor; including you."

"Paul," Ben said turning to his son. "How many times have you heard that story?"

"Two hundred and twenty," Paul said.

"And you're weary of it. And it bores you. There," Ben said, pointing at Desser. "I've lived longer than you have, Harry, and I've learned some things. You've got to start *changing* the endings, so that even when you begin regaling the company with an old chestnut they'll still pay attention, curious as to how it's going to come out this time."

"It's tinkering with history," Desser said.

"History your ass," Ben said scornfully. "Who gives a good goddamn for history? Most history is just the memories of old men and they're entitled to do as they please with them. Next time the story comes up I'll end it with me converting the Legionnaires to socialism. Stop sulking, Harry; you have your wound in Spain and nobody can take that away from you."

"I seldom speak of my wound," Desser said stiffly.

"You speak so often of your wound that I look for bloodstains on the rug after you leave."

Desser smiled uncomfortably at Paul.

"Your father always was a good joker," he said. "I only wish he'd get serious again. We've never stopped needing men like him: more so today than ever."

"Thank you, Harry," Ben said with a solemnity that surprised Paul.

Desser prepared to leave. He shook hands with Paul, then most affectionately with Ben, who remained seated.

"Be well, old comrade," Desser said. Ben smiled wanly, inclining his head ever so slightly. Turning to Paul, Desser said, "Pardon the ravings of two old revolutionaries."

"Not at all," Paul said.

"We get sentimental . . ."

Ben roared with laughter. "Sentimental revolutionaries!" he cried with savage delight.

"Some of us still believe in the good fight," Desser said petulantly. A moment later, seeming to regret the emotion in his voice, he pleasantly bid them good night and left.

"By all means, change the endings," Ben said, lifting his glass again and draining it. "If you were dull and deluded and ineffectual, if you have regrets, and if there is no other way of catching anyone's ear, then by all means, change the endings. 'We had the cream of the intellectuals with us.' As if that in some way sanctified us. Did you ever hear such horseshit? Oh, we had them with us all right, and they sucked up the Party line like so many babies with so much Pablum. One was inspired by the ingenuity of their rationalizations and the profundity of their naïveté. So intelligent . . . so sincere . . . and *righteous*."

Paul sat across the room, a faint smile on his lips. He liked it when the old combative spirit was at prowl in his father.

"Why am I cursed with such imbeciles?" Ben said, shaking his head. "Harry Desser, Revolutionary. Oh, he went to Spain all right. Didn't know his rifle from his pecker. Some fast-talking Marxist got hold of his ear and off he went. *And* got shot all right, not in the thigh though, but in the ass, which he won't admit. Thinks it's undignified."

Ben poured himself another drink, took a long swallow, smacked his lips, and put the glass down.

"Babbling idiots," he said. "Imbeciles. It's depressing. Shit. You should have come a half-hour earlier. *Vietnam* was on the agenda. 'What right do we have there?' So he asks me. What right does the sun have to come up in the morning? What the hell do I care about Vietnam? I don't trust myself to make an opinion. 'But what right do we have to intervene in a civil war?'" Ben said, mimicking Desser's earnest voice. "'Well, Harry, what right did *you* have to go to Spain and intervene in a civil war?' 'That's different.' It's always different. When somebody comes up to me and proves that one and one make three—*that* will be different. Are you drinking?"

"No," Paul said.

Ben made a disparaging sound.

"It must be heartwarming," Paul said, "having your disciples around."

Ben grinned at him, slowly, appreciatively. Then the grin faded and he stared at his son.

"I miss you, Paul," he said soberly.

"I guess it has been three weeks," Paul said.

"It isn't the three weeks; it's the half mile. I don't miss your lunatic brother, because it's three thousand miles and I know he

can't negotiate that any more than he can write a letter or
make a phone call. But you. A half mile away, and I never see you.
What are you doing with yourself anyway?"

"Writing."

"You haven't shown me anything for quite a while."

Paul sat silently, sealed by a sudden patina of reserve.

"I know," Ben sighed. "Never ask an artist about his work."

"Hanratty says you've been ill."

"Does she say what's wrong with me?"

Paul paused. "No."

"It's just a ploy to get you here. Play on the son's sympathy."

"Sure?"

Ben made a face. "I don't know," he said. "You know I don't
like doctors. I don't think I have any more pain than a man my
age should."

"You've lost weight."

"It's that bitch's cooking."

"I think you're probably lucky to have her," Paul said.

"You have a woman?"

"No."

"Hanratty says the place is neat as a pin. Doing it yourself?
Well, you always were that way. Everything just so."

"Everything," Paul said.

His father had aged. Paul stared at him with cool, detached
interest, studying the old man's face—that old familiar parent
face that had seemed impervious to the incursions of time, locked
imperishably into memory like a portrait, had changed finally under the sure and subtle inflight of the slowly unwinding years;
time, in its passage, brush-stroking the terminal portrait. The
once keen blue eyes lay back in the old man's head now like
drained vials, a veiled hostility in their gaze. His big body seemed
deeper in the chair, engulfed, the strong arms on the rests in neat,
listless arrangement. Gone was the proud, independent strength,
the bruising restless energy, tempering the terrific eagle image of
parent, father, replaced by a slow and spent body at rest in a chair,
a tired, engraved face staring with pulse-beat monotony in the
descending shadows of the nearby lamp.

"You're going to have to get out into fresh air more often,"
Ben said. "You've crossed the line from grieving into brooding. May

I say this? I don't want you to become melancholy, a recluse, an eccentric, a local character. We have enough of those already in this neighborhood. I might even be considered one myself by now, for all I know."

"I'm not a hermit yet," Paul said.

"It's the 'yet' that concerns me. You're not leading the life of a normal, healthy young man. I know you've suffered a loss. But it's been a year now since Janine's death."

"I'm aware of that," Paul said testily, clearly annoyed.

"You want to know something?" Ben said. "I knew it would break you. When I heard about it I was twice-crushed, because I knew how goddamned sensitive you were. Your brother is capable of shrugging off something like that. But not you. I knew you were capable of brooding upon it indefinitely."

"Then you should be glad," Paul said. "If you knew I was going to be broken, and I have been broken, then you wouldn't have known how perceptive you were if I didn't break."

"I'm sorry if I sound callous, but I see you so infrequently that I have got to try and make an impact. You ought to listen to me. I'm much closer to the ground now than I am to the stars. I've shrunk an inch, you know," Ben said with a wry smile. "Measured myself the other day. Now *there's* something that really gives the ego a good crack."

Paul smiled faintly.

"I have to leave," he said.

"Stay awhile."

"I have to get back."

"Why don't you have a drink?"

"No," Paul said irascibly. "Dammit, don't you see that I've got to get back?"

"No, I don't," Ben said. "But if you put it like that, then I'll say I do. You were never unduly melodramatic."

"Thank you," Paul said, rising.

"So, here I am and there you go," Ben said. "Or perhaps, here I go and there you are."

"I'm sorry."

"What for?"

"I'll come again soon," Paul said.

"Do," his father said.

4

Paul hurried home through the dark, bland summer night. Vandals had broken a half-dozen street lights along his route, plunging some streets into almost total darkness, illuminated only by the private yellow lights of the quiet houses around him. He was unmindful of these things, however, as he pressed forward, his eyes riveted to the sidewalk, his lips moving as if in conversation with himself. Then, abruptly, he stopped and turned around, frowning into the darkness. He stood still for several minutes, so absolutely immobile that a cat slipping from beneath a parked car walked past as if it were alone in the night. He fixed his eye upon a street light at the far corner, watching the insects swarming and flitting around its bulb, the light sending a swath of deepening shadows through the magisterial old oaks that raised clouds of summer leaves to the night. A warm, vagrant breeze passed and the leaves swayed with a susurrant depth-of-night rustle. "Janine?" he whispered. He peered inquiringly into the unanswering night. Then, suddenly, he grinned self-consciously. He lectured himself, mildly, amiably: he hadn't really heard her, because she had not been there. Of course not. That was impossible. It was true they had communions, but always in the privacy of the house, and the communications always followed a certain pattern of silence, reflection, before dawning slowly, very slowly, sometimes over a span of hours, before he felt the full, intoxicating permeation, and even then there was no audible sound, no voice, simply the arrival of something that had been inward borne for some time. One of the reasons he accepted its authenticity was precisely because there were no voices on the air, no mysterious footfalls in the dead of night, no faces reflected in pools of water. It was all quite acceptable and reasonable, with nothing supernatural or auto-suggestive about it. (It amused him sometimes, because he had always been the "logical" and most coolly reasoning one in the family, the most intellectually responsible.)

He continued walking. Further ahead he could see burning on the night the red and blue neon signs in the window of a side street tavern and could faintly hear the discordant sounds of a throbbing jukebox.

And then he was startled to hear the sound of his name whispered, tensely and suddenly, almost into his ear. He stopped, annoyed not only by the intrusion but at having been startled and deprived of his repose for an instant. He looked around with a querulous frown and into the face of his brother-in-law, Philip Werner. Philip was standing in the shadows, pressed against the thick trunk of a tree in an obvious attempt at concealment, the distress in his face fairly glowing in the dark.

"Paul!" Philip whispered a second time—as if confirming to himself Paul's presence.

"What are you doing there?" Paul asked.

"Shhh," Philip said mysteriously. He took Paul by the arm and maneuvered him a step or two behind the tree. "Helen is in that saloon," he said.

"So?"

"Look," Philip said. "Look." And he put his hand on Paul's chin and turned his brother-in-law's face to a side. Paul immediately shook the offending hand away. Now Philip pointed across the street toward a narrow alley that separated a low, one-car garage and a frame house. Paul was about to ask—out of mounting impatience—what this was about, when he saw the orange coal of a cigarette suddenly dilate in the darkness; then he was able to distinguish someone standing in the shadows at the mouth of the alley, a person drawn back in patient, watchful stillness.

"What about him?" Paul asked.

"He's a kid," Philip said. "About eighteen. I know him from the neighborhood. He's a smart-ass kid."

"Philip—" Paul said, his voice strained.

"He's waiting for Helen."

"How do you know?"

"How do I know?" Philip asked, a slight hurt in his voice, as if disturbed that anyone could after all these years question him where his wife was concerned, that anyone could still doubt his credibility in these matters; hurt because the one thing he could expect at the very bottom was that he knew what was happening: he wanted that much at least, that much concession to his manhood.

He was a slight man, of medium height, with a worn and harassed look. His eyes had an almost perpetual expression of intense,
pondering perplexity. He was a man of few initiatives or surprises
and seemed to have an obsession about not offending people,
being quick to agree and slow to argue; it was an irritating quality.
Because of the relationship, Paul found himself having to be civil
to a man whom he considered totally ineffectual, for whom it
was impossible to muster any sympathy.

"I've been watching him," Philip said. "He doesn't know I'm
here."

"I don't quite understand what you're doing. Helen is in the
tavern, that kid is standing there, and you're standing here. What
are you trying to do?"

"She'll be out soon. Then you'll see. He's going to accost her."

Paul did not care, not about any of it. It was just another petty,
sordid back-street episode involving his older sister, another episode in an ongoing pattern which had remained constant as long
as he could remember. These things were part of his existence
since childhood. The sister, five years his senior, had been doing
things with boys which as a child he had known vaguely were
wrong or daring, knew by instinct because he was still too young
to know any other way, adapting by instinct the moral judgments
that were part of the air he breathed. She had from childhood
possessed an uninhibited sensuality that made his eyes linger on
her with sullen, involuntary scrutiny whenever she moved about
the house with impudent sashay in her slip or her pajamas, even
when he was too young to understand any of it. She had a blithe,
unself-conscious invitatory way about her. At ten and eleven and
twelve one knew she was a woman, not simply girl or female, but
woman, with precocious mammary glands and burgeoning sensuality which was being held in abeyance, lush and inevitable,
which would spring one day into full bloom, so that the transition
from child to woman would be blinding and accomplished seemingly not by time but by desire and decision. When he was seven
he heard from a playmate that his sister sucked off boys in the
schoolyard, but he did not know what that meant. When he was
ten and she fifteen he knew she was going for rides in automobiles
with men twice her age. He understood more then. Every male
in the neighborhood seemed to have a chattel mortgage on her.

Older boys came to him and asked leeringly if he saw his sister naked and what she looked like. He absorbed her reputation and all the obscene innuendoes that went with it, while his heart burned with resentment toward the older boys and then toward his sister too. He thought it would end when she was married, and for a while it did. But a few years later it began again, even though she was a wife and a mother too now. So it was an old story, old and ongoing through marriage and motherhood, by sheer attrition no longer a scandal, to the extent that in spite of seventeen years of marriage she was known to some men still as Helen Dublin.

So it was with patent indifference that he stood there in the soft unruffled summer night next to this tense, pathetic, ineffectual man who was his brother-in-law, who in the beginning of their relationship and for years afterward had effected a certain stiff, avuncular tone toward him because the man, Philip, was the older and it seemed proper, until the older man finally realized that neither of his young brothers-in-law regarded the spread of years as having any significance, that they were none the less, nor he the more, for it. How long Philip had been standing there Paul could not guess; the man was capable of feats of endurance —doubtless a derivative of his extreme docility—and could have been pressed against this tree for hours if necessary. While Philip in his years of experience stood utterly still and mute, across the street the youth had begun to demonstrate restiveness by the constant dilating glow of his cigarette.

The silence was broken by the passing of a curve-backed old man pushing an ancient baby carriage piled high with newspapers. They watched his slow and infinite passage across the street, listening to the whining creaking of the wheels. He was a familiar figure in Capstone, he and his carriage, which by its box design told of its years, sufficient for the infant who had lain in it originally to be himself a grandfather now. He passed finally, laboriously, an eternal, solitudinous figure in the neighborhood, passing with his carriage and his accumulation of papers and years and secrets, into the night.

"Phil," Paul said, tentative, restless.

"Wait," Philip said. The urgency in his voice kept Paul rooted. Now Paul realized two things: the music from the tavern's jukebox had stopped, and the music had come from the same record, being played over and over.

"She always plays that record," Philip said.

Helen appeared then, opening the tavern's screen door, saying something over her shoulder as she went that elicited a burst of raucous male laughter. The screen door slapped shut behind her, and she began walking in a direction away from the three lurking males. At once the youth moved. Paul saw him leave his corner of darkness as the beacon of cigarette light suddenly sailed through the air like a miniature meteorite and splashed sparks in the street.

Philip moved at the same moment, away from the tree, wordless. He and the youth walked parallel routes on opposite sides of the street; Helen was on the same side as Philip. Reluctantly Paul joined the strange, silently stalking progression, following his brother-in-law by some twenty feet.

The youth closed the gap between himself and Helen with nervous haste. He stepped into the street and began crossing diagonally toward her. He passed through a pool of light and Paul saw him—tall, lanky, slack-spined, thin arms swinging; wearing ankle-high suede boots and blue jeans and a free hanging blouse with the raised collar covering the back of his neck. He loped toward her and in a soft, inquiring voice called her name. She stopped, turning around. Philip went into the street then, moving to intercept the youth.

"Leave her alone," Philip said, raising his hand and pointing a finger.

Paul stopped, watching the youth, who had also stopped, wide in mid-stride, one foot advanced, the heel of the other about to leave the ground, his face turned toward Philip, startled and apprehensive, not quite sure what to make of the intruder, whether or not the man portended a threat and if so whether it would be physical, legal, or moral. *Wait outside the bar for her*, Paul thought, knowing what the youth had been advised by someone wise in the ways of the neighborhood. *Tell her you want to walk her. Put your arm around her. If she lets you touch her tit, you're in. Take her someplace—the park, anywhere. She loves it anywhere.* Philip was the only one in motion, walking with his pointing finger toward the suspended youth whose face was fixed with uncertainty at the idea of having to make some judgment, some decision based on nothing more than inexperience and incipient panic. Helen remained frozen, half turned, watching.

Suddenly the youth spun around and began to run—he apparently had been that uncertain, that insecure about the whole thing (was perhaps even glad for this opportunity to escape, to withdraw, not to have to face up to being a man to a thirty-five-year-old nymphomaniac). He ran with long, awkward strides into the darkness of a side street, his elbows pumping like pistons. Philip went after him, running with his own short scuttling steps, like a man mimicking the haste of a woman.

"Phil!" Helen cried. Then, seeing her brother for the first time, she yelled, "Paul—stop him!"

Paul went after his brother-in-law, not running, but walking quickly, irritated now with his involvement in a situation he should have resisted and avoided. *This has been going on for more than twenty years,* he thought as he walked self-consciously after the two running idiot figures. *French farce in the middle of the street, late at night. What am I doing here?* He looked back once resentfully at his sister; she was standing just outside the rather melodramatic descent of street light, in her short skirt and her sweater, gnawing pensively on her thumbnail, a tawdry whore-figure of the night who by all the abominable ironies of fate happened to be his sister. *Insatiable,* he thought. Consequences did not mean a damn. A public circus like this would have utterly no consequences, would by morning be an indistinguishable part of a thousand other nights. It would happen again—what in the ordinary life would be a schism of solemn proportions would here be less than a seam: would happen again tomorrow or next week and continue in this mindless and sordid pattern until she was either too old for desire or too old to be desired.

He heard a thudding sound up ahead and when he turned another corner saw Philip sprawled across the sidewalk, lying amid a thick scattering of newspapers, the upended carriage next to him. The old man was standing some ten feet away, as if the violent collision between the running man and the carriage had blown him back in fright. He was gazing vacantly at Philip who now struggled into a sitting position. Philip's trousers were out at one knee, the torn flap hanging slackly. He looked up at his brother-in-law, not angry or embarrassed or sheepish, but with an expression of great earnestness.

"I collided with the wagon," Philip said.

The old man nodded dumbly, with a kind of weary sageness, as if this were simply another inevitable thing in a long life of trial and indignity.

Paul looked at the carriage, this ancient thing he had known in Capstone all the years of his life, that had always been busily active somewhere about the neighborhood day and night, as inviolate and indestructible as its owner, from whom it seemed indivisible: a relic, an antique, a thing that none but the old man had ever touched—lying thrown over on its side now, exposed in all its ancient shabbiness, looking no longer like relic or antique, but junk.

Paul turned his back and walked away.

Helen was still standing where he had last seen her, the thumbnail still abstractedly at her teeth.

"He fell over something," Paul said. "He's all right."

Now she clasped her hands lightly under the strong thrust of her breasts.

"I don't even know that boy," she said.

"He knows you," he said dryly.

"He thinks he does."

"It's just about the same thing, in this case."

She seemed never to age, at least not to his eye anyway. Her breasts seemed as vibrant and desirable now as when he had first seen them, nearly twenty years ago, when he had accidentally walked into her room while she was dressing, and he could remember to this day, this moment, the burning flush of his face and at the same time the high-pitched laughter as she turned and noted his embarrassment and yelled gaily at him, "Hey, evil-minded!"

"What are you staring at, Paul?" she asked.

His eyes rose and fixed upon hers. For a moment he believed that she knew what he was thinking, that she was remembering not only the small boy walking in and seeing her naked breasts but that she was also aware of the impact it had made upon him; that out of a lifetime of sordid and prurient moments she was able to remember this one and always remembered it most vividly when they were together. But then he realized this was nonsense, that the taunting and impertinent look in her eye was nothing more than her normal expression.

"Where does it end, Helen?" he asked.

"Who knows? Maybe right back at the beginning."

"What is that supposed to mean?"

She smiled faintly, provocatively, he thought. He felt the impulse to strike her; the palm of his hand began to tingle, as if in anticipation of landing the blow.

"This is a goddamn disgrace," he said.

"No it isn't; it's just part of my life, that's all," she said with a brief, ironical smile.

"I don't know why it should bother me, since it's been going on forever."

"I don't know why it should bother you either, since your mind is just as dirty as the rest of them around here."

"I don't know what you're talking about."

She arched an eyebrow for a moment in a way which infuriated him.

"Don't you?" she said.

"I just want you to leave me alone, that's all," he said.

"You were the one who came running up."

"I didn't come running up. I was walking home, trying to mind my business."

"Oh well," she said with a shrug, "don't fret. A kid brother is supposed to be a pain in the ass." She reached out affectionately to touch his cheek, but he jerked his head back. She dropped her hand and studied him for a moment. "Your problem is," she said, "you're intolerant."

Suddenly he laughed, falsely, harshly.

"What's the matter?" she asked.

"Nothing," he said. "I was going to give you a lecture. I must be losing my mind."

5

He paused a half block from his house. Had he left a light on? The living room windows downstairs were squared brightly against the night, blinds tightly drawn. It was unlike him to have done something like that. In this dark, sparsely populated corner of the neighborhood the lights burned with particular conspicuousness. As he neared the house, his eyes fixed upon the lights, he suddenly stopped again and stood absolutely still, his body leaning slightly forward in anticipation of his next step, his eyes filling with brooding inquiry, apprehension.

Like some floating black garment, a shadow had crossed the window. He stared, biting down lightly on his underlip. He waited. It did not reappear. The knee-high grass around the house pulsed with the languorous sounds of summer. A breeze passed on high, moving aside the leaves at the very peaks of the trees. With building tension, he waited. There was no question in his mind that he had seen something. Often he left the house while deeply preoccupied, forgetting to lock the door; but he did not now consider the possibility of a larcenous entry. His mind had leaped ahead to something else.

He did not believe in her actual physical, audible, air-breathing, carpet-indenting presence inside the house, but did consider the possibility of something spiritual having been loosed there, tangible enough to have come between window and light and thrown a shadow. *But there's a limit to how much you can accept,* he thought. *Or ought to be.* There were rational explanations for everything, but not for this. This was a frontal assault on his sanity. He could go inside and find her there or some evidence of her (or something) having been there, or he could find nothing. Neither prospect was comforting, nor was the idea that he might have seen a shadow cast by his own mind.

He realized he was afraid. He could taste the perspiration on his lips. There was a telltale sweat gland above his upper lip that excreted whenever he was afraid. Well, why shouldn't he be? His head moved up and down in barely perceptible nods, in a sort of mesmerized admission. *The dead of Glencoe are most restive,* she said. *That's why I want to go there and write the poem, to try and infuse it with that kind of eternality, to try and capture the quality of it.* He knew that something had begun to overcome him at his father's house, so that he had had to leave. And why had he stopped on the way home and whispered her name to the night? *Was it spoken by me or to me?* This was the first time she had ever impinged upon him outside of the house.

She got away from me right in the beginning. I think that was when it really started. After all the red tape and the polite and discreet British voices and compassionate pats on the shoulder, after signing all the forms and documents and feeling incarcerated and infected in my own soul, there was this monumental foul-up, and she got away from me, who was so recently dead it was as if she were not dead at all. When I got to the airport she had already been dispatched. Somehow, someway, they had managed to mishandle and misship a coffin. The embarrassment was, to fall back again upon that word, monumental, in that composed, demure way in which only the British can be embarrassed. (They already were walking around with this somber air of culpability, since it was, after all, one of their mountains she had fallen off.) They traced the blunder to some baggage men, who had thought —God knows what they had thought. Hours passed before it could be determined upon just which plane she had been sent. (Everyone courteously referred to "she," except the baggage men, who referred to "it.") I sat there while they went at the task via telephone and telegraph, their embarrassment growing by the minute, more shy and unruffled British mortification. First the Empire, then this. Every apology laced with the words "dreadful" and "inexcusable." Then I heard someone say: "I believe she's going to India." I could almost hear her saying, her refined, finishing-school voice quite tense and petulant: "How could you let such a thing happen? How could you? This is disgusting!" *The heat of her temper had a certain level beyond which it never went, no matter the magnitude of provocation—again a quality infused by those small, crisply elegant, invisible-from-the-road schools she went to in New England, whose campuses seemed always to be dripping with autumn leaves.*

The itinerary was Rome and the Middle East, with India the terminal stop. Perhaps it was then I began making the subtle and persuasive associations, linking the first units of the terrible, multicellular obsession. In my frame of mind it would have been understandable. It all became enmeshed in self-arranging certitude, the pious and the supernatural and the mystic; it was as if her dead and disembodied self was floating by some occult design through consecrated skies where the high and lonely winds were like the lips of God; coming down finally in that ancient and alien land as if in answer to some summons that had been issued the moment her falling body had been incased in thin air.

They got her back finally, of course, while I sat alone and had too much time to think, had too many visions of Hindu holy men chanting the Vedas on the runway of the New Delhi airport. So it got inside of my distraught and vulnerable and overly receptive mind then, during that unbelievable day and a half when she continued incased in thin air making that willful journey back and forth, while unspeakably apologetic airline personnel kept asking me if I was comfortable. For thirty-six hours I sat, at the airport and in a hotel room, not sleeping at all, waiting for her to complete her journey, while outside dark clouds blotted the sun and discharged their thunderous loads of rain over Edinburgh's cobbled streets. That was when I read her spiral-ringed notebook, where she wrote the rough drafts of poems she was working on. She never allowed anyone to look at them. Work In Progress. I understood, of course, was the same way with my own work. I sat and read the lines over and over, stared at them, so dazed and incredibly alone I barely remember doing it. Paging through the notebook, reading the words she had crossed out, the deletions, the corrections, the humanizing marginal comments to herself, the misspellings which were part of the charm of her writing (those expensive schools had taught her how to walk and how to talk but not how to spell); seeing in the corrections how her gift employed and refined itself, seeing all of the exposed wiring of her imagination, watching how her mind groped and sifted through language, how it searched and strove for precision and vividness, the silken loom of the intense and overheated laboratory itself where the apperceptions were so painstakingly synthesized. And all the while I held in my hand her pencil (it had been lodged in the spirals of the notebook), which was scarred and crunched from being clenched between her teeth during those long, pondering, mind-searching hours of composition.

About a month after I had returned home the letter came, addressed to Janine. The publisher had seen her poetry in the quarterlies and had been duly impressed. Was there perhaps a collection in the offing? So I replied. She would have been so pleased, I wrote

*(she had spoken of it often enough), and indeed had been plan-
ning to devote her life to poetry. But what made me say that a
posthumous collection was a distinct possibility?—particularly
when she herself had said there weren't nearly enough poems yet
to form a decent collection. I referred to a sheaf of unpublished
work, among it her best. The publisher expressed interest. (I suspected them of perhaps a ghoulish motive now; the posthumous
work of a poetess who had died so young would be in the most
tragic tradition of the form and doubtless draw special attention.)
I told them further poems would be forthcoming, when I had had
time to go through her notebooks and papers. Again, why did I
say that, when what remained was in so unfinished a state?*

*Getting back to my own work, the first piece I wrote was a
rather romantic article about the Civil War dead, the more than
half million soldiers killed in that war. I found my theme in a book
that referred to the conspicuous paucity of memorable achievement in American literature in the closing decades of the nineteenth century, as compared to all that had been done before. I
attributed it to the slaughter of a generation. Indulging in romantic fantasy, I put the rhetorical question: What would America
have been like had the half million dead been permitted to live
their lives and mature their designs and expectations? I equated
the high-mindedness and heroism of so many in those armies with
the qualities of their unfulfilled destinies. Poets went to death in
storms of grape and canister and to burial in roadside graves instead of in the cool shade of country churchyards, leaving a literature shorn of its honors, poignant in its silence. Did an American
Shakespeare or Dante perish in a racket of muskets at Cold Harbor,
was our Sophocles or our Homer blown to pieces by the guns of
Gettysburg? Let it be said, I wrote, that many who vanished into
war's consuming flame were men of might and grandeur, that
their deaths saddened the wind and aged the earth and diminished the living. Let us continue to pay homage, I wrote, to songs
never sung and words never penned, to unleaved boughs and
withered roots, to the curious stillness that will ever haunt our
past.*

*This was a preamble to what soon followed. I was spending
much of my time indoors, in the old house I had bought on my
return. (I did not return to our Manhattan apartment; it would*

have been impossible for me.) Since I knew my life was for a long time going to be hermitic, I wanted a house, a place I could move about in without feeling claustrophobic. (She had a life insurance policy and this was the source of the money, and even this I symbolized and made part of the raison d'etre *of the entire pattern.) I had neither been waiting for nor anticipating any abstruse incursion upon my mind, but soon after finishing that article about the truncated work of the prematurely dead, I felt my mind being toyed with by scraps of imagery. At first I dismissed them as merely vagrant wanderings of the imagination. After all, my state of mind was loneliness and depression; poetic sprouting seemed natural. All manner of people turn to poetry as a cathartic. But soon I began to put them to paper (there was a relentlessness about them until I did). I tried to be objective about this. I tried to be rational. I would put them away for days and weeks, then return to them, trying to achieve as much objectivity as I could. But the similarity, in thought and sentence structure and imagery, to Janine's best work was unmistakable. It was harrowing. Even then I rejected any supernatural explanation; I was not looking for one; my mind did not work that way. I was not an animist, nor did I believe in such things as ESP or extraterrestrial communication; in fact, I refused even to read about these phenomena. I accepted the lines as having been shaped by some completely logical and explainable psychological urgency; again, considering my state of mind, the anomalous was quite natural. (I had written poetry in college, but these new lines were much more mature and proficient than anything I had ever put my hand to.)*

The lines continued to come into my head, usually late at night, after I had been sitting idly for several hours. Automatically I would pick up a pencil and begin writing them down. I felt like I was taking dictation. The substratum of my intellect began absorbing some unsettling possibilities, slowly, assiduously; absorbing them so thoroughly that they achieved an insidious compound inside of me. At these times, during the writing, I felt Janine very much with me. I tried to rationalize and dispel that, too, but there was no denying the sense of permeation. There were sudden, diamond-bright gleams of language, pulsing, fullborn, complete. There was no grappling with ideas or phrasing, as I always experienced with my own work. Her poetry came straight to the page with an ease and fluency that were contrary to the natural labors of creation, all of it so alien to me, my perceptions and sensibilities, that I had to cast logic to the damned and accept what I saw.

Of course we had been very close and deeply in love and filled with mutual understanding and respect. Whatever it was, supernatural, illusion, madness—I chose to accept it and finally to believe that it was Janine filtering through the mesh of reality to communicate to me those lost lines which would not be lost.

6

Paul stood on the porch outside of the front door, listening, feeling oddly like a stranger at his own threshold. The porch was not elevated but was built at ground level like an unwalled extension of the house; it was stark and chairless; the faint, outer radius of a street light draped the far railing. A cricket was sending a rhythmic, inquisitive beat from out of the grass. Then it stopped. The abrupt silence made him turn his head, his eyes pinched at the corners. He stared mistrustfully into the dark, then turned back, contemplating moodily the entrance to his house.

Without making a sound, he opened the door. The light met his eyes and he gazed into it with peculiar reverence. Coming from the living room, the light illuminated the hallway and the lower steps of the stairway that climbed into the second floor darkness, painting the balustrade in spectral sticks against the wall. He closed the door behind him, guiding it to with his hand to preserve the pristine silence. He lifted his chin slightly, as if emboldening himself for an unpleasant interview. Then he went slowly along the hall, consciously softening his footsteps on the hall carpeting, his shadow riding over the framed Japanese prints on the wall. At the opening to the living room he paused before turning to step in, as if trying to time to perfection his entrance. He could see the leather-covered armchair and the glass-topped end table and part of the sofa, the large Brueghel on the wall in its wooden frame, the dark blue carpeting.

He stepped inside.

"Jesus Christ, you gave me a fright!"

At once he felt rage and surprise and relief, for a moment

unable to speak, waiting for the shock of not seeing what he had expected to to subside.

"Frank," he said incredulously.

"What are you trying to do," his brother said, "give me heart failure?"

"What the hell are you—?"

"I got in a few hours ago. From L.A.," Frank said. "By bus," he added distastefully.

Frank got to his feet. He had been lounging in a stuffed chair, reading a paperbound book. He smiled at his brother, obviously pleased with the effect of his surprise.

"Unpredictable as ever, hey?" Frank said.

"As ever," Paul said.

Frank had a look of robust health, tanned, strong, heightened by the rakishness of his grin, the ease of his posture. He was wearing khaki trousers, an olive mock-turtle sweater, his well-rounded biceps filling out the short sleeves. His feet were sockless in a pair of down-at-the-heel moccasins. A scarred suitcase lay open in halves where he had been sitting.

Now he came forward and took his brother's hand. After the handshake Paul threw his arm warmly around Frank's shoulders.

"I'm glad to see you," Paul said.

"The door was open, so I just walked in."

"I was to see Ben tonight."

"How is he?"

"He's—"

"Listen, don't say anything about my being here. I want to walk in tomorrow and surprise him. How is he?"

"He's not well. He's . . . listen, sit down. Sit down. For God's sake, it's been over a year."

"Hey, you look a bit peculiar yourself," Frank said, dropping himself onto the sofa.

"Well," Paul said, sitting slowly on the edge of the leather chair and clasping his hands between his knees, "it's just that . . . when I saw the light I . . ."

"You thought it was a burglar." Frank laughed. "And it could well have been you know—leaving your door unlocked like that."

"I saw Helen and Philip, too, tonight."

"And how are they?" Frank asked with a perfunctory show of interest.

"Unchanged, unchangeable," Paul said.

Frank leaned back expansively, crossed his legs, slipped a long thin cigar between his teeth and began to talk of himself, filling in his absent months for his brother with broad, conversational strokes. He was deliberately, skillfully vague about how and where much of his time had been spent. He referred to various places, his "travels," his "adventures." "But I won't bore you with details," he said several times as his memory raced over some particularly ignominious experience. For the most part, he said, he had been working in Los Angeles, at a job (he did not say what, nor was he asked) that had thrown him into close contact with "the people"; mostly young people, he added. Unquestioned by his brother, uninterrupted, he went on. It had been "enlightening," he said. Great and tempestuous things were happening across the country; he had seen evidence of this new, raw strength, this movement, wherever he had been: the East, the Midwest, California. It was surging, inevitable, explosive. A dividing country was headed toward revolution; the potential for social reform was terrific, the current ideas presented man with his most decisive opportunity since the birth of Christianity. He "knew," he had been on the "inside." It was no longer possible to be apolitical or disinterested. There was a generation afoot now unlike any other in the nation's history: intelligent and resolved and selfless; they were tough-minded saints, with an olive branch in one hand and a length of dynamite in the other. "Bullshit," Frank said, "is out. Truth and justice are in."

Then he realized that his brother's interest had wandered. After a half hour's rambling monologue, his voice running non-stop, Frank saw that Paul's silence had not indicated attentiveness, but rather abstraction, preoccupation.

"You haven't been paying attention," Frank said.

"I have," Paul said.

"I'm telling you important things . . . things that have made me travel three thousand miles."

"I thought—"

"That I came back because of the old man? Well, that, too—partially. But another reason is because I wanted to be where I could be most effective . . . where I knew people and was familiar with the lay of the land, so to speak."

"Effective at what?"

"I've just been telling you," Frank said impatiently.

"I know all those things, Frank. I read about them."

"But I was in the middle. I've seen it in action."

There was a brightness, an alacrity, in his brother's face that Paul regarded with wary curiosity.

"Things are changing now with almost blinding speed," Frank said. "Look how many of the old verities—once regarded as absolutes—have already gone asunder, been modified, or discarded altogether."

"What in God's name were you *doing* out there on the west coast?" Paul asked with an incredulous smile.

"Catching up," Frank said. He finally lit his cigar, then sat back and smiled with satisfaction—that smile of roguish affability which seemed to call for the jester's scepter, which was manly and disarming, but which was too easily expanded for Paul ever to put his faith in its sincerity. "Surprised, are you?" Frank said. He was pleased with his brother's reaction. "Well, let me tell you. I wasn't rolling around out there leading a picaresque life. That I can assure you. I was coming to life, getting with the wave of the future—and believe me, brother, it's a tidal wave. And it's not only here in America. There's a universalism to this movement, something that transcends nations and continents and languages and cultures. I tell you, Paul, the old world and all its jaded arrangements are going out."

"To be replaced with what?"

"By the best there can be for mankind; the absolute best," Frank said. "Let me tell you, the problem has always been one of leadership. That's the way I see it. People have never gotten proper leadership. The ordinary individual can do nothing, even if he is enlightened. In fact, the more enlightened the poor son of a bitch is, the more despairing he'll become, considering the history of this planet. Only the extraordinary individual can bring about change—by recognizing that each man is a representative of some element of society, that every man counts, that they're all different and yet have some common denominator, that every man is a goddamn perceptive arbiter of injustice. The thing to do is to throw a harness over that indignation and shake it into rage."

"Are you hungry?" Paul asked.

"What?"

"Do you want something to eat?"

Frank sighed. "You know," he said, "when the upheaval begins, we're going to be on opposite sides of the barricades."

"No," Paul said. "I won't be there at all."

"You and your fucken ivory tower. By the way, I saw your friend Kifner on the coast."

"Did you talk to him?"

"No, but he talked to me—and a few thousand others."

"Oh. He likes to do that," Paul said dryly.

"I think he's a great man."

"Do you?"

"Me and a lot of others. They worship him out there. Do you still hear from him?"

"No."

"You ought to keep in touch."

Paul was staring at him steadily now, expressionlessly—an old and familiar look that Frank knew indicated a polite parting from the conversation.

"What do you have to eat?" Frank asked.

Later, after a meal had been consumed, they sat at the kitchen table, idling over coffee.

"Yes," Frank said, "I was stunned. It was a shock. Unbelievable. I liked her very much . . . sorry I didn't get to know her better. Listen, I felt bad about not getting back for the funeral."

"I missed you," Paul said.

"I'll visit the grave. Where is it?"

"About ten miles north of Philadelphia."

"Oh. Maybe I'll have some flowers sent. Would that be all right?"

"If you like."

"Christ, when you got married I was three thousand miles away. Then . . ."

"You never seem to be in the right place at the right time."

"I am now," Frank said.

Later, they were upstairs putting sheets on an old army cot that had been left behind in the house.

"Frank," Paul said, "I can't ask you to spend more than the night. I'm sorry."

Bent over, busily tucking the ends of the sheet into the mattress, Frank said,

"A woman, huh?"

"No," Paul said.

Frank looked up, stared thoughtfully at his brother.

"Something's troubling you, isn't it?" he asked.

Paul said nothing. He was holding a pillow lengthwise against his thighs, staring down at the empty spread of white sheet.

"It's all right," Frank said. "I'll find a place tomorrow."

"You can stay with Ben."

Frank grinned. "I'm sure I could," he said. "But I'm afraid my ideas would give him apoplexy. But listen, I don't want him to know about any of this. It's between us for the time being, okay?"

"Believe me," Paul said, "I won't say a word."

FIVE

Frank's return to Capstone began, symbolically at least, on the day of the campus disturbance. He realized that something had happened to him during that tempestuous afternoon, knew it to the very depths of his volitant and unpredictable self, knew that he had been exhilarated beyond any previous experience, that he had reached a watershed in his life.

Leaving the campus, he went directly to the Tabernacle; there, he stood at the lectern and to an empty room orated as he had never done before, slamming the lectern with his open hand and shouting an extemporaneous speech at the rows of vacant benches, going on for hours, with the fury and fortitude of a zealot. His theme: injustice and hypocrisy in America and what should be done. He ended by shouting to the now dark, echoing room: "Injustice is the foundation of revolution!" Then he looked around and said, conversationally, as if to a companion, "I like that."

The next day he bought newspapers to read the accounts of the campus disturbance. Headlines referred to a student riot. The stories, he felt, were slanted to put the onus for the trouble on the students. The police had been called in to control a surly and unruly mob. He called one of the newspapers, to protest their interpretation of the events, saying that if the police had not been called there would have been no trouble. The newspaperman asked who was calling. "The Los Angeles Seven," Frank said after a moment's thought. "You sound like one half of a football score," the newspaperman said, and hung up.

He studied the pictures in the papers of the scattering students and club-swinging police, peering to see if he could find himself in any of the crowd scenes. Later he bought a bottle of cheap rye and sat in his room, sipping from the bottle and thinking over and over about what had happened yesterday, reliving the excitement

through zestful memory. Even more vividly than the blood and
the violence, he saw Kifner on the platform, speaking and gesturing, a dynamo of challenge and ultimatum, still after twenty-four
hours able to feel the man's voice crackling through the crowd
like charges of energy. He lay back on his bed and closed his eyes
and saw thousands of angry faces and restive bodies swelling up
in his mind, poised and waiting with splendid fury.

He finished the last of the rye at seven o'clock and went out
for dinner. He was wobbly, had trouble locking his door; then he
turned, took several inattentive and ill-considered steps and went
headlong down the flight of stairs, bumping and tumbling in a
slack, boneless heap, coming finally to a sprawling stop at the
bottom, feeling giddy and unhurt; but there was blood running
from his head. He sat on the bottom step, holding his wound,
giggling. The mongoloid appeared and covered his mouth and
laughed into his hands. "Fuck you," Frank said to him. "Thou art
the Establishment." Then the landlady came, stared at him with
that weary and menacing tolerance possessed by the lords of transient houses and took him by the arm and bandaged his head.

After he had eaten he went to the Tabernacle (late enough
for the old people to have been there and gone) and stood again
at the lectern, surveying the empty hall, this time quietly, feeling
the pain squirming querulously in his head, a dull fury in his eyes
as he reflected upon the clutter that had been, that was, his life.
He watched with sullen suspicion as the four youths came through
the door. He recognized three of them from the meeting that had
been held there; the fourth was a slight, bearded young man,
reserved, wary, observant, who hung back in self-possessed taciturnity, his hands in the pockets of his soiled and threadbare pin-
striped suit jacket that looked even shabbier with his black T-shirt
and baggy chinos. They wanted to use the room again, tomorrow
night, for an important meeting. They were sullen, terse, almost
hostile, as if they had had all illusions thrashed out of them. One
in fact did have a dark bruise along the side of his neck. Frank
gave them permission to use the room. As they were leaving one
asked what happened to him. Frank touched the bandage with
his fingertips for a moment. "A policeman's club," he said. "Yesterday, on the campus."

"You were there?" he was asked.

"Yes," he said, "to the everlasting shame and envy of all those who were not."

"They'll have their chance," the bearded one said softly. Frank stared at him; their eyes locked. There was whimsy and madness in the eyes of the other.

They held their meeting the following night. The rhetoric was impassioned but dreary, predictable, the emotion flowing out of vacuum-packed chambers of liberal indignation. There were calls for petitions and marches and demonstrations and the formation of committees and committees to select other committees. Frank sat in the front row, the bandage still on his head. Many of the youths shook his hand and he solemnly acknowledged their professions of solidarity. A girl kissed his bandage and told him he was a beautiful human being.

At the conclusion of the meeting he asked to address the assemblage. He was received with respectful attention. They would be unable to meet there any more, he said. His Tabernacle, a place of God, a roof under which the weary and the lonely and the spiritually bereft could meet, was to be closed down by the police "by virtue of municipal technicalities." "They warned me not to open my doors to you a second time," he said. "I told them my doors were never shut to anyone, and in particular to the espousers of the cause of peace and justice." He received a warm burst of applause. Then they left, all except three: the one with the bruised neck, another, and the slight, bearded youth, who again held back, standing at the perimeter of the conversation, watchful, self-contained, like an auditor. "They could arrest you," Frank was told.

"I know that," he said. "I fully expect it. It wouldn't be the first time."

"You can't let that happen," he was told. In spite of the mass gatherings, one said, there were too few numbered among the hard core, those who were willing to sacrifice for what they believed in. He must not allow himself to be arrested; to disobey laws that were unlawful, he was told, was to pay obedience to a higher, more urgent law.

He left with them, solemn in a sudden fraternal bond. They had a car. Frank sat in the rear seat with the bearded one, who sat back in the shadows, profile set against the passing lights of the city. Frank glanced at him occasionally. The two in the front seat became voluble; they made threats and promises (the one with the bruised neck had been struck by a policeman at the campus), they cursed at the drivers of big sleek automobiles, glared at policemen. There was a mood of defiance in the car. "We've got to do something," the one with the bruised neck said. "We've got to do something or I'm going to go crazy."

The other one in the front seat turned around and said, "Either there's a revolution or there isn't." Now a sense of purpose, of grimness, and—most palpably—self-righteousness, was fixed.

They stopped at a vacant lot and the two in front got out and went into the darkness for some minutes, while Frank and the bearded one sat wordlessly in the back seat. There was almost a regality to his companion's silence, Frank felt; it was the taciturnity of one who did not deign to speak: not brooding or sullen or introspective; simply a soft and consuming silence that Frank knew intuitively was not to be impinged upon casually.

The other two returned to the car with several rocks in hand, got in and drove again. Now there was a tense air of mission and they cruised in total silence, in and out of the late-night streets. They were in the outskirts of the city now, passing through somnolent residential areas, the two in front staring at the bungalows and landscaped lawns and small palm and acacia trees with patent hostility. Then the one in the front passenger seat said sullenly, to no one in particular, "This is where it all comes from you know. This is from where the poison begins to seep." Frank became aware of something, turned his head. His seatmate was staring at him with a wry, ironic smile. Uncertain as to the import of that smile, Frank stared curiously until the other turned back to his secret, inscrutable staring, wrapped in inviolable silence.

"There," the driver said, slowing the car, pointing his finger at the building on the corner. It was a bank, modern, flashy, glass-walled.

"Slow, slow," said the other in the front seat. "Stop." The car came to a halt in the middle of the street, abreast of the bank. The two in front looked warily around at the dark streets, which were empty and unthreatening. The one in the passenger seat opened his door and, holding the rocks, got out. He moved away from the car, the door swung out behind him. He stepped up onto the sidewalk and stood there. After looking around again, he suddenly swung his arm back and hurled one of the rocks. It flew too high and bounced off of the concrete just above the plate glass window, clattering harmlessly to the sidewalk.

"Jesus Christ, Freddy!" the driver yelled in exasperation. After glaring back wildly over his shoulder, the youth on the sidewalk hurled a second rock. This time it went driving straight into its own hurtling reflection in the window which immediately went asunder with an irascible explosion and set off a loud nagging jangle of alarms.

The youth whirled around, the unthrown rocks dropping from his hands, and raced toward the car. He curved his back and bent his head as he prepared to dive into his seat, but in his haste and maybe panic, too, misjudged the height of the roof and crashed into it with his forehead. He staggered back, his eyes swimming out of focus. "Get in! Get in!" the driver screamed as the dazed youth swayed back and fell against the open door, as the alarms continued to roar with mean-souled metallic fury. Frank got out, grabbed the youth, pressed his head down and with the same motion pushed him into the car, throwing the door shut after him. The car was already starting as Frank leaped back in, pulling the door closed with a bang. "Get me to a doctor," the injured youth gasped, slumping, his head dropped forward into his hands.

"Sincerity," the slight, bearded youth said to Frank later. "That's what you saw. Good intentions in action. Worth about one pinch of dog shit." He chuckled, an odd, mirthless sound, deep in his throat.

They were sitting in an all-night diner, drinking coffee. The other two were gone, had driven off after a round of solemn handshakes and show of clenched fists. The diner was quiet, its fluorescent lighting bright, hypnotic, gleaming maniacally on the polished chrome that seemed to be everywhere. The only other customers were several chicanos sitting in another booth. The counterman was sitting on a wooden stool behind the counter, reading a newspaper.

"It was still a risk," Frank said.

"Slight," the other said. His name was Arthur Seavery. He was not taller than five-six or -seven, small boned, almost delicate.

His beard was short, dun-colored, though the way his face seemed to slide into it made it appear much larger; his hair was long in back but trimmed over the ears. His eyes were gray, with a level, scrutinous gaze, as if searching for some exactitude. He held his coffee cup in his small hands as he sat hunched close to the table.

"The risk was probably greatest for you," Seavery said. "Those two come from affluent families, you know. Bail would be posted, good legal representation provided. The charges would be dealt with in the least severe way. Playful college boys. That sort of thing. Now you. I don't know anything about you, but you seem to be a man without means. You'd be in the shithouse."

"And you?" Frank said. "What would happen to you?"

"I would survive," Seavery said. "I've learned to."

"So why did you go along, if it meant nothing?"

"Every experience means something; more to some than to others. For me this was little more than a skirmish; for those two —a memorable episode. They'll be able to act like veterans at the next caucus of their debating society, bullying the little radicals with references to dark accomplishments. They'll sleep much better for it tonight; a contented sleep. And a good night's sleep will help them in their studies, help them toward their degrees and subsequently toward the good job after they graduate, and then the wife, and then the house in the suburbs, in which they will sit in their own fat, concerned with real estate values and worried about blacks moving in, and from time to time become nostalgic about their days as revolutionaries, when they were helping to build a better world. And meanwhile, what have we done for them?" he asked indicating the chicanos. "Nothing."

Frank sipped his coffee, watching Seavery over the rim of the cup.

"There are gestures and there is action," Seavery said. "A gesture makes interesting reading in the newspaper and is very good for fund-raising and public meetings. But action . . . action is something that reaches people and puts rage into them. Without that rage people are nothing, utterly nothing. It's as simple as that. Do you know what you have to do to reach the rage in people?"

"What?" Frank asked.

Seavery smiled, a vague, almost paternal smile that lit his eyes. "A lot," he said.

"Let me tell you," Frank said. "The one thing we lack is leadership. My experience tells me that we'll go nowhere without it. What kind of Movement can we have that doesn't have leadership, organization, cohesion?"

"Go to mass meetings and demonstrations, you'll get all the leadership you want. They'll tell you when and what to sing, where to march, and what time your bus leaves. Now *that's* leadership. Look, there are dangers in working with a large group. We *have* been infiltrated from time to time, if you must know. I could tell you some stories about that. People have been killed," Seavery said flatly, pausing for some moments to let the enormity of his statement register. "So we've changed our tactics. The smaller the group the better. Small and mobile groups, shifting from place to place, city to city. A Midwest campus one week, California the next, New York the next, Washington the next. Speed, mobility, anonymity. Guerrilla warfare. It's the only way now."

"But we can lose everything we're fighting for if we don't have leadership at the proper time. There'll be chaos . . . it will all slip away."

"Leadership will emerge when we need it," Seavery said.

"Were you there yesterday? Did you hear Kifner?"

"Yes. Kifner. Now he's a man of enormous value. People believe in him. I think about Kifner. I think about him a great deal. He means so much to so many people," Seavery said quietly, staring pensively out the window.

"He got that crowd going yesterday," Frank said.

"He'd be the first to deny that."

Frank laughed. "Naturally," he said.

"How sincere are you?" Seavery asked, looking back to him. "I mean about what we grandiosely refer to as the 'Cause,' or the 'Movement.'"

"I don't have to answer that," Frank said.

"I didn't mean to be impertinent. I know you've been clubbed, I know you've defied the police and lost your meeting hall. But look, this is a very high-staked proposition and people have got to know if they can trust each other. If I'm to meet you again somewhere I want to know that you're going to be the same man."

"I wasn't radicalized yesterday, to be polite with you," Frank said.

"I'm sorry if I've insulted you. Did I insult you?"

"Were you trying to?"

"No. Look, you're not really a minister, are you? I mean you were never ordained anywhere."

"You can call it what you want. I'm out here trying to help people. I don't have to justify myself to you or anybody else."

Seavery smiled. "I *did* insult you," he said. "I guess a man of the cloth—"

"Look," Frank said heatedly, "don't give me that 'man of the cloth' crap. I'm not confined by any sectarian bullshit. I do and say what I think is right. Obviously God is not going to solve all our problems. I believe in people having faith," Frank said, enthralled by his own words, feeling as though he were traveling at some terrific velocity, "but I also believe in people doing everything they can to correct social injustice."

"Even to the extent of breaking some of God's laws?"

"God's laws have become so corrupted and misapplied that they've become man's laws, and therefore subject to breakage in every way, shape, manner and form."

"I'm sorry I never heard you preach," Seavery said, smiling.

"You just did."

"Well, I'm glad to see you're your own man, Frank."

"I'm glad you approve of me," Frank said sarcastically.

"Still insulted," Seavery said shaking his head. "What will you do now? I don't mean tonight."

"I don't know. I might head back East."

"That's probably a good idea," Seavery said.

Later, they were at the counter paying their checks. A burst of laughter came from the chicanos in the booth. The sound made Seavery whirl around and look at them, a scowl suddenly crossing his face. Seavery's change in attitude was so abrupt and so evident that Frank looked at the men in the booth, certain they must have done something to offend his companion. But they seemed totally unaware of the bearded young man who was glaring at them with an anger mounting rapidly into ferocity.

"What do you have to laugh about, you stupid greasers?" Seavery said, directing the question to the group in the booth, but saying it softly, so that none of them heard him.

"Hey," Frank said.

Seavery took several steps toward the men, his rapt, furious gaze fixed upon them.

"Greasers!" he suddenly shouted.

"Hey," Frank said, reaching to take Seavery's arm, but the latter shook his hand away.

The counterman looked up, his eyes moving wildly in his head.

The group in the booth—there were three of them—were silent now. Two, facing Seavery, were looking at him with expressions of surprised incredulity, not yet offended; the other was turned around in the booth, his mild, mustached face passing from surprise into hostility.

"Don't laugh!" Seavery cried. "Get mad! Don't you realize what they're doing to you? Get mad—you stupid greasers! You dumb spics!"

Now Frank grabbed him and pulled him back.

"Hey—shit—hey!" the counterman yelled, pounding the countertop with his hand. "Cut that out."

The men in the booth rose simultaneously, their eyes filled with sultry resentment. One was quite tall, the others rather short.

"That's it," Seavery said, smiling maniacally through his beard. "Show some fight. You sit there and laugh while they shit on you and make whores out of your stupid spic sisters. Don't you have any goddamn rage?"

"Shut up," Frank said, wrestling Seavery toward the door, manhandling the slight, smaller man with comparative ease.

"Get him out of here," the counterman said.

"He's drunk," Frank said over his shoulder to the chicanos, who were out of their booth now, moving slowly forward, the tall one leading the other two.

"They have nothing to laugh about," Seavery said, panting, trying to swing free of Frank's grip.

"Goddamn it," Frank said tersely. He had to let go of Seavery now as the first of the chicanos came near, the tall one, black hair gleaming under the glaring fluorescent lighting, eyes fixed not upon Seavery but on Frank, the unoffending one, the appeaser, because he seemed to be the more rational, the more responsible, and thus—sequential to the singular logic—the one most culpable; and Frank perceived the look in the man's eyes and read it for exactly what it was.

"No fighting," the counterman said adamantly, raising his hands in the air.

Frank hit the tall chicano. The blow caught the man in the mouth and he staggered back, reaching out behind him with his hand, groping in thin air for a moment, then falling between two stools, an expression of utter amazement on his face. The other two charged Frank. He shoved one into a booth, then hit the second very hard, putting him down on the tile floor with violent suddenness.

"Get outa here!" the counterman yelled.

Frank opened the door and, pushing Seavery ahead of him, hurried out. They crossed the street and stood there for a moment. They could see the chicanos standing in the diner, the tall one holding his head with both hands.

"You're crazy," Frank said. "What did you do that for?"

"Why?" Seavery said furiously. "You stupid son of a bitch, you ought to know why. The next time somebody humiliates them or tries to shit on them maybe they won't take it. Maybe they'll remember and reach back and use what they used tonight. Jesus Christ, they sit there in their barrio and pluck their goddamn guitars and let everybody dump on them."

"That's a marvelous lesson in civics you just gave them," Frank said as they began walking.

"It's the best lesson," Seavery said sullenly.

"You want to help these people, not antagonize them."

"What I want to do is wake them up. That's what I want to do," Seavery said. He stopped. "Don't you see," he said to Frank who had also stopped, a few paces ahead, facing him. "Now they know you don't just charge straight into somebody who's stronger. They're going to learn that the best way is to stand in the shadows and put something into the bastard's ribs."

They walked again. From time to time Frank glanced at his companion. Seavery had a certain repellent fascination; a man in rags who spoke ardently of bringing great change; physically unprepossessing but somehow formidable; a creature of brooding and contemplative silences as well as abrupt, calculated violence: visionary, zealot, madman; claiming to be part of something, though most likely wanting to become the thing itself.

Then they were sitting on a bench in a children's playground, amid a stillness as hushed as vespers, surrounded by the tender innocuousness of swings and seesaws and climbing bars. Seavery was sitting forward on the front slats of the bench, his thin back curved, his narrow bony shoulders hunched.

"It isn't going to be easy," he said, "nor is it going to be pleasant. What we're going to have to do has got to be classic and heroic, it's got to go slamming into the minds of thousands of people, with enough violent impact to arouse them so they in turn are able to arouse thousands of others. I've been working on some ideas and I think I'm moving toward just the right one," Seavery said, speaking with quiet, controlled intensity. Frank was at once wary of and captivated by the man's utter seriousness. Suddenly Seavery looked at him and asked, "How far are you prepared to go?"

"What do you mean?"

"I want to know how far you're prepared to go for something you profess to believe in. Now, listen to me. There are people who are prepared to go the distance in this thing. They're tired of having their grievances talked to death and are ready to go into action. And I must tell you, they're serious. They're awfully serious. Are you?"

Frank peered searchingly into Seavery's face.

"I mean," Seavery said, "to the extent of planting a bomb, or— if it comes down to it—killing someone."

"Yes," Frank said, because it was simple and easy to say it to this veritable stranger sitting on a bench in a children's playground in a corner of the night in a vast and alienating city.

"After all," Seavery said, "when you realize that you're in a war, your perspective on human life alters, doesn't it? It alters in two ways: increased reverence for the rights of those whom you would aid or defend, and total contempt for those whose deaths would help you realize your goals. And in a war of this nature, Frank, there can be some very unlikely victims. It isn't easy to kill someone, but if it's a person whom you think deserves it, well, that makes it somewhat easier. But suppose it's someone against whom you *don't* have any hard feelings?"

"Then why kill him?"

"If his death can help the Movement?"

"But I assume you're talking about someone who is on our side."

"Forget personalities. I'm talking about tactics now. I'll hypothesize. Suppose someone assassinated a venerated world leader—the Pope, for instance? Suppose it was proven to be the work of a Jewish conspiracy? What would happen? You know very well what would happen. Now, suppose you hated the Jews. Mightn't you have the Pope assassinated and arrange to have the blame for it thrown on some Jewish group? There are any number of variants. Assassinate some popular political leader and pin it on a group of militant blacks. Or kill a prominent black leader—and watch the ghettos catch fire. If you hated blacks that would be your thing, because every time the blacks riot there is less and less tolerance for them among whites. Work the blacks up into a sufficiently murderous frenzy and the army will come in and slaughter them. As I say, there are many variants. Shoot the right man, at the right time, then point your finger. I'll guarantee a hell of a lot of momentum for your revolution."

"This is all very cynical," Frank said.

"We're at war, Frank," Seavery said softly. "We're a handful against millions."

He's testing me, Frank thought. *Trying this crazy theory on me just to see my reaction.* No one could be serious about such a scheme. For a moment Frank felt a highly gratifying burst of disdain for this slight young man and his grandiose plan for foaming the blood of mobs. Seavery was much too clever and contemptuous; also, he seemed to be more at home with words than action. After all, it had not been he who had been clubbed at the demonstration, nor he who had thrown the rock through the bank window, nor had he lifted a finger against the chicanos after inciting them. He was a malcontent, an agitator, one who shot flaming arrows wildly and unaimed.

"So?" Seavery asked. "What do you think?"

"It has possibilities," Frank said.

"You're altogether too cautious. But if you understood people as I do, you would see it is actually very logical. Just remember this: any crowd can be turned into a mob with the greatest of ease. They move with one mind, and that mind holds no mysteries."

Frank saw Arthur Seavery once more before he left California. It was several weeks after their first meeting. Frank had been spending most of his time sitting in his room or in libraries reading about what was variously called the New Politics, the New Left, the Movement. He read books and magazine articles and pamphlets and Movement newspapers. Slowly but resolutely he convinced himself that the world was permanently reshaping itself, and that in the vanguard of these new configurations was a generation with the devotion of apostles and the grim determination of fanatics, attributes possessed by no other group in an increasingly lax and lazing world. He believed, too, that these activists were at the moment so scattered and fragmented and unco-ordinated that they themselves did not, in spite of their resolution, fully recognize their own inevitability, nor were they aware that they were transcending themselves. Lack of effective leadership was the single doubtful thing in their almost irresistible force. This latter was the point he drove home to himself beyond all others.

He met Seavery quite by chance, at a meeting of radical students on the campus.

"What finally happened to your hall?" Seavery asked.

"I told you, the police closed me down," Frank said. The truth was he had simply abandoned the Tabernacle, had not gone near it (nor given it a thought) in weeks.

"So what have you been doing?"

"Thinking."

"Destructively, I hope," Seavery said. "Which is the only form of constructive thinking there is today."

"I'm going back to New York soon."

"That's a good thing."

"And you?"

"I'm going underground for a time," Seavery said. He did not elaborate. "But we'll meet again," he said. "We've booked passage together into the future."

Frank's first reaction at seeing the old house again after more than a year was a sudden, sinking depression—so exuberantly high had been his sense of personal change and conversion. The house was a stolid and steadfast anchorage in the past: frame, roof, chimney, porch: so immutable, so eternal, so formidable in its antiquity, that for a moment it evoked in him a feeling of retrogression. Not only this house but the entire street gave the impression of being fixed in history, potent with bones and ghosts; all of the houses and the tall old shade trees and the stout shaggy hedges: like a painting in which the leaves moved and the seasons revolved; all of it still there, constant and self-renewing, as unchanged and unchanging as if its stability derived from being stared upon by the sun and the stars.

He went up the porch steps, smiling now in anticipation of springing his surprise. Finding the door unlocked, Frank let himself in without making a sound. Inside, he heard his father's voice. He was disappointed—he had been hoping to find the old man alone.

He stood in the hall, just off the living room, listening. Ben was talking quietly, a carefully modulated gentleness in his voice. He seemed to be trying to soothe someone, was saying that things would adjust themselves, that one had to be patient. *Clichés*, Frank thought. That was unlike his father. *He's talking to either an imbecile or a child.*

There were louvered half doors decoratively at either side of the living room entrance, and Frank now moved stealthily forward and squinted through one of the slats. He saw his father sitting back in a chair, gesturing with an open hand, speaking to a slim young girl whom Frank did not immediately recognize, then was astonished when he did: it was his niece Lorana, his sister Helen's daughter. How old was she now? Sixteen, probably. She had grown and matured considerably since he had last seen her. The oldest of Helen's children, Lorana had thus far proven singularly unlike her mother. She was shy and sensitive and somewhat introverted, a dispirited victim of the most virulent kind of unhappiness—domestic disharmony. She had always been a sweet-natured child of whom both her father and grandfather were inordinately fond (as the first child and grandchild, she had been the recipient of unstinted and undiluted love). She was staring attentively at her grandfather, soft-eyed, listening more with respect than conviction as the old man tried to explain without condoning or accusing, trying to at least palliate the incurable and irreducible. Frank shook his head. He had grown so accustomed to his sister's peccancy that he hardly thought it worth discussion.

"We can't change her," Ben was saying now.

The neighborhood would go out on strike if you did, Frank thought.

"It's an illness," Ben said.

"I know," Lorana said. "It's called nymphomania."

"It has nothing to do with her love for your father or for the rest of you."

She loves cock more, that's all, Frank thought. The neighborhood twat. The biggest manhole in town. Miss Quick Hump. Sadie Spreadlegs. The old plowgirl. The fastest gums in town. The senor eater. Lady Fuck'nsuck. —Capstone's flip references came pouring in on him. It had always made Paul silently furious and bitterly ashamed but left Frank, then and now, philosophical.

"But everybody in the neighborhood knows about it," Lorana said. "Men call the house. They call on the telephone all hours of the night, asking for her. Something happened again last night. They came home late and were fighting and arguing; they woke us up."

"You have to be patient, you have to understand," Ben said.

"But I don't understand."

"I know," Ben said quietly.

"I don't know how long I can stand it," the girl said. "I don't love her any more . . . I'm . . . I'm ashamed of her."

Frank sighed. He wished she would go away. He looked around, his eyes alighting upon the big old floor clock at the end of the hall. Did he ever look in there? he asked himself, rubbing his chin speculatively, the thought suddenly entering his mind, bending aside his other preoccupations. *Time is money.* A venerable old cliché. His father had a whimsical contempt for venerable old clichés; he could well have hidden it there, as his private joke. The clock hadn't worked in years; it was conceivable it was stuffed with twenty-five thousand dollars. The thought made him tremble; he had almost to physically resist the urge to go to it now and open it.

When he heard his niece preparing to leave, Frank slipped into the kitchen. He heard his father walk Lorana out, still with soothing words, say good-by, then close the door and return to the living room. As Frank was about to leave the kitchen and burst in upon his father, primed with the excitement of his surprise, the telephone rang—in the living room as well as on the extension next to him in the kitchen.

Shit, he muttered.

He heard his father pick up the telephone inside. Frank grimaced disgustedly as his father said, "Hello, Harry." He immediately recalled Harry Desser, that dismal little man, ineffectual fool and sycophant; his father's eternally remembering comrade from days the old man wished eternally forgotten.

"Yes, Harry," his father said. "No, no, of course not. It was a good, old-fashioned exchange. Nonsense; you didn't offend anyone."

Discreetly, Frank lifted the receiver next to him, hearing Harry Desser's apprehensive, sycophant's voice in a disembodied metallic babble.

"I got the feeling," Desser was saying, "that I somehow offended you."

"Not true, Harry," Ben said.

Frank shook his head. *Yes,* he thought. *For once say yes, tell the truth, and you'll be rid of the dreary son of a bitch forever.*

"Some harsh words were spoken," Desser said.

"No," Ben said, "there were no harsh words. The heat of debate, Harry, the heat of debate."

"I didn't want to appear like a poseur."

"You didn't, I assure you."

"Sometimes I let my nostalgia overwhelm my common sense."

Ben chuckled indulgently.

"Nevertheless," Desser went on, "things that need saying should be said."

"Bullshit," Frank said.

There was an immediate, puzzled silence on the line.

"What was that?" Desser asked.

"I think somebody's on the line," Ben said.

"You're not being tapped, are you, Ben?"

"Don't be foolish."

"Tap tap tap," Frank whispered. "You are being tapped tapped tapped."

"Somebody's on the line," Desser said excitedly. "Who is that? Who's on the line?"

Raising his voice several octaves, Frank said, "These are the souls that try men's time."

"Who *is* that?" Desser asked.

Then, in his normal voice, Frank said casually,

"Hey, Pop."

"Christ," Ben said. "Frank? Is that you, Frank? Where the hell are you?"

"Frank?" Desser asked.

"Buzz off, Harry," Frank said.

"Where are you?" Ben asked.

"Los Angeles. Say, I seem to have cut in on you guys."

"Los Angeles?" Desser asked. "How are you, Frank? How's the weather out there?" he asked, raising his voice, as people who are unaccustomed to speaking on long distance were apt to do.

"It's snowing," Frank said. "Can't you hear it?"

"Frank," Ben said, "where the hell *are* you?"

"In the kitchen," Frank said, and gave a loud yell.

"In the kitchen?" Desser asked puzzledly as both phones simultaneously went dead in his ear.

They met in the hall.

"You son of a bitch," Ben said loudly, grinning. "Where'd you come from?"

They shook hands, then embraced and rocked in each other's arms, with the awkward self-consciousness of big men, slapping each other on the back and laughing with strong masculine affection. Frank felt immediately in the embrace how much strength had been drained out of his father during the recent passage of time; Ben's back and shoulders seemed so much smaller, and for the first time in his life Frank did not feel dwarfed or diminished by his father.

They went into the living room and sat facing each other while Frank described and detailed the months of his absence. It was a prosaic story that he contrived for his father, one of respectable behavior and responsible activity: he had worked briefly as a salesman for a Chicago publisher, then gone from there to Los Angeles (". . . with a letter of recommendation that trembled with superlatives. I'm sorry I didn't save it.") where he had taken a job as assistant manager of one of the larger book stores.

"I've found my vocation," Frank said. "The retail end of the book business. I tell you, it's the most absolutely exhilarating thing. You know I've always liked being around people, and here you have a chance to do it and be part of the cultural apparatus at the same time. I tell you, just being around books is such a wonderful thing; it brings an inner serenity, like being in a church. No shit. I never thought I could feel that way about anything. It's what finally brought me back . . . along with the urge to see you, of course. I've decided I want to open a bookstore."

Ben listened without comment. Frank tried to interpret his father's reticence: Was the old man thinking that this was just another impulsive, hare-brained scheme? Was he impressed? Pleased? There was no way of telling, and when there was no way of telling what your own father was thinking at what was, for you, a crucial moment, then it was not very promising.

"I haven't sprung it on Paul yet," Frank said. "But he'll love the idea, I'm sure."

"You've seen Paul?"

"I spent the night there . . . sort of dropped in on him."

"How does he seem to you?"

"How?" Frank asked, considering for a moment the unexpected question. "He seems kind of . . . distracted."

"He's still brooding over what happened."

"It's been about a year now, hasn't it?" Frank said.

"He won't ever talk about it. He absolutely refuses. I think that's bad, very bad. He's becoming more and more introverted."

"Well, he never was the life-of-the-party type."

"He was always a good, warm, sensitive boy."

"This world is no place for sensitive people," Frank said.

"Were you here when Lorana was?"

"Yes."

"Talk about being sensitive . . . that girl has more sensitivity in her little finger than her mother has in her whole carcass. I would like to take your sister's neck and . . ." Ben said, lifting his hands, holding them up for a moment in angry, impotent frustration, then letting them fall disgustedly. "She's making that child miserable. I hate to see it. Do you know that girl is the only human being in the world who takes the slightest interest in me? She's here all the time. And not as an obligation, but because she *wants* to. She's intelligent, sensible . . ."

Poor old guy, Frank thought, even as he smiled and nodded to his father's talk of Lorana. Big, rugged, cynical, tough-minded Ben Dublin had got old; the fissures in his once infrangible rock-soul were beginning to show. He had aged into loneliness, to the extent that he was now sentimentalizing, talking about the visits of his granddaughter as though those visits were divine acts. It was sad, sad, to see all of that strength and pride and independence gone, lost in the soft, insidious drifts of time.

". . . worth all of them," Ben said. "She's worth the whole carload of them, that kid." It made him look older, and tired, this melting at the core, this emasculation of the spirit. "It's so easy for a girl to go wrong in that kind of environment."

"She'll be all right, don't worry," Frank said. "But anyway, getting back to . . . what do you think of my idea?"

"I like the idea of you settling down. I don't know how feasible opening a bookstore would be, but I'd be happy to see you start stabilizing yourself."

"There would be problems."

"Naturally."

Frank paused, watching his father, trying to gauge the old man.

"Trying to get a new business up off the ground entails a multitude of problems," Frank said. "Things like finding just the right location . . . things like that. Doing it right. The primary problem, of course, would be financing," Frank said, looking at his father with wariness and a growing feeling of suspense. Ben gazed back at him with a blandness that Frank found vexing and impenetrable. "It's most difficult these days to obtain financing. It's certainly not the great age of the small businessman. That's the nub of the problem."

Ben nodded.

"Financing," Frank said.

Ben stared.

"Money," Frank said.

"Sure," Ben said sympathetically.

"I don't think the banks would be very co-operative. After all, good intentions don't atone for a poor track record. And I don't have any wealthy friends I can call on."

So, Frank thought, there it is. Laid out on a pillow of black velvet, presented as artfully and humbly as possible. He was trembling from his own deviousness; it was something which would happen every so often, when he was mounting some especially momentous lie or presenting a proposition unusually flagrant in conception; it was as if some inner seismograph for measuring deceit could barely contain what it was recording, releasing subtle vibrations into his every nerve and muscle.

"The idea could die a-borning because of lack of funds," Frank said. "It would be a pity if it did. This is the first time I . . . I've done a lot of the things I wanted to and now it's about time to drop anchor, so to speak."

"I'm glad to hear that," Ben said.

"But what good is it if I can't raise the money?"

"It wouldn't be any good at all, I suppose."

"I guess in your younger, more radical days, this sort of situation—a young person unable to rise in the world because of financial inequities—would have really burned you up."

"It's still painful," Ben said. "You don't have to be an ideologist to have human feelings. That's a style of thinking reserved for radicals."

"I see. Well, I guess that's that."

There were several moments of silence. Then Frank saw his father's face begin to shed years as the old man's eyes narrowed shrewdly, followed by a slow, wise smile of enlightenment. Ben tilted his head to a side and nodded knowingly, his smile expanding now to an expression of almost malicious delight.

"God," he said, "I must be getting old. *Now* I see what you're up to. Jesus Christ. A father should never for a moment forget a son's obsessions."

"I don't know what you're talking about," Frank said.

"The hell you don't," Ben said genially, pleased with his own discernment, belated though it was. "You've still got that money on your brain, that old load of money which is supposed to exist, like Captain Kidd's treasure."

Frank despised himself. He felt like a fool. He damned his transparency.

"Well, does it exist or doesn't it?" he asked impatiently. "Once and for all, for Christ's sake."

"Bookstore my ass."

"It's true. It's a great idea."

"You had me going for a moment," Ben said, laughing. "What the hell *would* you do with so much money?"

"I'm telling you—go into business."

"Is that what you traveled three thousand miles for—another crack at it?"

"Oh shit," Frank muttered.

"Your persistence is remarkable: one idea, one obsession, no more, no less. Listen," Ben said, "let an old man have his secrets, and his leverage, too. If it wasn't for the myth of that money I'd *never* hear from you."

"That's not true," Frank said, hurt.

"Ahhh, it is so true," Ben said, more in despair than bitterness.

Frank slouched in his chair and sulked.

"A bookstore," Ben said with needling disparagement. "You."

Frank closed his eyes.

"Oh, cheer up," Ben said.

"You know something?" Frank said. "I'm beginning to get on my nerves."

SEVEN

"The theme of the Movement should be, 'Redress inequality and injustice.' I don't believe in slogans, as a rule—people tend to queue up behind them and let the slogans do their thinking—but nevertheless I feel *that's* a good one: concise, succinct, pertinent. Don't you think?"

Yes, he or she or they, will think, Frank said to himself with a sardonic smile, listening to Charlotte Breitman's voice floating out through the open patio doors onto the mild summer air. That voice: it had not changed, neither in its unfledged innocence nor its beautifully precise enunciation; disembodied, all of its carefully shaped and modulated vowels and consonants sounded as if they were being ushered through rows of polished teeth, with the unexpected, almost arbitrary emphases suddenly freighting word or syllable, as if to lend profundity to her skittering sentences. Within hearing but still out of sight, Frank roamed the garden, pleased by the familiarity of the impeccably trimmed grass and hedges, the rose bushes, the scatterings of purple violets, the intricately vined and brightly flowered latticework bower with its narrow marble bench where he had sat with her when they were young teen-agers and she read to him from Cummings and Eliot in that voice of airy unquenchable enthusiasm. Several bumble-bees were droning on the inert, sun-impacted air, darting in what seemed almost geometric patterns of flight. With its abundant shade trees and flowers and trimmed shrubbery and tall privet hedges to insure privacy, it had no parallel in the community (her landscaping bill, she once told Frank, ran her close to two thousand dollars annually). He felt quite at home here, walking the crushed fieldstone paths, looking up at the fine old two-tiered white house. Their families had been friends, and he and Paul had spent a good deal of time here with Charlotte. He grinned now

in recollection of some of the things he had done here. Because
Paul was always the more mature, the more serious, Frank had
felt obligated to provide the contrast: he was the one who leaped
from the garage roof into a hammock, who raced through the garden with a butterfly net shouting the sighting of some never-
before-seen specimen; which in turn impelled in Charlotte the
obligation to "inform" and "refine" him, while Paul watched with
wry amusement. And so, when she could make him sit still, it was
poetry in the bower and discussions—or rather, lectures—on
political science and sociology and history, with occasional deferring asides for approbation or corroboration to Paul who would
be nearby stretched on the grass with a book.

"People can no longer wait for the generosity of fate," she was
saying now. "They've relied for too long on that, and now disappointment has led to disillusion and disillusion to the rebellion
we see in the world today. Deprivation endows one with a most
realistic look at the world. People are now alert to the *details* of
the social structure. What we're getting today is a fusing of
idealistic realism and realistic idealism. Don't you agree?"

You bet your ass, baby, Frank thought, standing just off the
patio now. Two chairs stood pulled back from the filigreed iron
table, a pair of empty teacups on the tabletop next to a sterling
silver teapot with a spout like a swan's neck. So there was one person in there with her, probably a man, and doubtless he agreed.
They always agreed with Charlotte; there would be no point coming here otherwise.

She often said she felt guilty about being rich. When Frank
suggested to her the obvious remedy for this curious affliction, she
said no, that to divest herself of her money and property would
be of no value to the cause of Revolution, that in fact such a
gesture would probably have an inverse effect in that the money
and property would eventually return to the oppressors; at least
now it was concentrated in hands that would use it for the greater
good. So she continued to write modest checks to groups and individuals of whom she approved, paid occasionally for the printing
of handbills, contributed to full-page ads, to bail-raising funds,
campaign chests. None of this was unnatural for her. Her parents
had been active in the Socialist Party in the thirties, associated for
a time with Ben Dublin. Her father made a fortune in Queens

real estate and was remembered fondly in certain circles for allowing a Socialist debating group to use rent free an empty store in a
building he owned in the Astoria section. When Charlotte was
sixteen her father died, leaving her a fortune in cash, securities,
and real estate. Five years later her mother became senile and was
now living in a Miami Beach sanitarium, writing bombastic weekly
letters on various subjects to her daughter. Charlotte had been
inculcated early with her parents' zeal for social reform and political action, as a teen-ager speaking before radical groups, distributing leaflets, working indefatigably for foredoomed fringe
candidates. In spite of the basically conservative nature of the
community, she remained in Capstone after her mother was institutionalized, feeling she could be more effective here than
among more politically congenial people, who, she said, spent the
greater part of their time passing unanimous resolutions. She also
loved the spacious white house on the crest of a tree-lined street
where she had grown up, and which she was reluctant to leave.
When she was twenty-three she married a man named Hacker. He
was a bachelor, twice her age, a corporation lawyer, and a tough-
minded intellectual. He claimed to be apolitical, but the truth
was he felt it pointless to discuss issues with his young wife whose
left-wing zeal he considered (at first) charming and quaint, a
product of "intellectual baby fat." His reticence about the things
she held dear led Charlotte into giving him lectures on "political
awareness" and "social reality." Initially amused, he listened
politely, not taking any of it seriously. She accused him of having
"closet" political opinions when he began to object to her sending
campaign contributions to obscure left-wing candidates, and he
finally exploded when she told him she was planning to entertain
in the garden several dozen children from a black ghetto. He told
her to "please have the niggers cleared away" by the time he came
home. She accused him of being a fraud. "How can you call black
children 'niggers,'" she said, "and not have politics?" He neither
affirmed nor denied anything; he simply chose not to engage his
wife in discussions of this nature. Soon after that, her belligerent
participation in a civil rights demonstration led to her arrest for
obstruction and she spent six hours in jail before her husband reluctantly posted bond. After her release she became active in penal
reform, writing and publishing at her own expense a pamphlet on

her experiences in prison and distributing it at public meetings in
Capstone. She opened her house to a meeting of local ex-convicts
(LEC), most of whom had been away for bookmaking or petty
larceny or car theft, and solicited their suggestions for penal reform. She told them they were all victims of an oppressive, in-
equitable society, and they agreed. The movement held only one
meeting, however, after she discovered a half-dozen pieces of expensive pewter missing from the living room, cigarette burns in a
sofa, and that someone had defecated on a Persian rug in an upstairs bedroom. Later she abandoned penal reform and headed
for the Deep South to work in black voter registration drives,
doing much good and even courageous work in Mississippi; once
her station wagon was burned and upon another occasion she was
forced to watch helplessly while two black co-workers were beaten
senseless by a crowd of local toughs. She left the civil rights
crusade entirely when the antiwar movement began to gain momentum, and when she realized that such a movement, if it could
be kept galvanized and viable and pertinent, could lead to the
revolution she had always dreamed of. By this time her husband
was gone and Charlotte had a Mexican divorce decree framed on
her library wall and was living alone in the large house except for a
sleep-in coal-black middle-aged Dominican woman who wore
starched white uniforms.

"The *problem*," she was saying now, "is how to make a revolution with a middle-class proletariat, how to make them realize
they're being exploited, that their labor is being corrupted and
that their standard of living is being maintained at great cost to
the underprivileged people around the world, from Nicaraguan
banana workers to South African diamond miners."

Frank stepped onto the patio now, enchanted with the view inside, his eyes riding from the cut-glass chandelier to the wains-
coted walls to the black leather easy chairs and the opulent
carpeting. A corner hutch held porcelain figurines and expensive
pewter vessels. He knew this room well; on rainy afternoons
they used to sit here, he feeding jokes into those sober discussions
she so frequently foisted upon Paul, the tenor and content of
which always bored and alienated him.

"My God, a ghost!" Charlotte cried when she saw him.

Frank grinned, coming through the back-swung doors. He opened his arms as she rose from her chair and hurried toward him. He closed his arms around her and held her affectionately and kissed her on the cheek. Then she stepped back, holding his hand.

"You've put on weight," she said.

"The hell I have," he said, slapping his hand into his middle. Then he said, "Are you doing the garden today, or is that your revolutionist's uniform?" She was wearing a baggy cotton sweater and blue jeans that were snug around her round buttocks. She was barefoot. Her blond hair hung straight down her back in long thin strands.

"Don't get smart, long-lost brother," she said. "When did you get back?"

"A week ago."

"A week! And it took you until today to walk this far?"

"I've been busy, love, busy," he said.

"Where are you staying?"

"I've got a room."

"Not with Paul or your father?"

"No, love. I need privacy."

"You sound mysterious," Charlotte said. Then she said, "Oh," and turned around and led Frank by the hand into the center of the room.

A young man had risen at Frank's entrance and was waiting patiently to be introduced. He was short, sturdily built, with a pleasant though rather tensely set face, as though prepared for profound debate. He had fair, shoulder-length hair and a fringe of beard.

"Curt," Charlotte said, "meet Frank Dublin. He isn't really my brother, except in nostalgia."

The two men shook hands, exchanging frank, uncompromising stares for a moment. There was a tension of instant dislike.

"Curt and I were discussing the Movement," Charlotte said.

Frank sat down, taking possession at once of the chair and of the room: a big fresh dominating presence now irrefutably there, completely at his ease. Curt remained standing, supplanted now and obviously uncomfortable, anxious for a quick, graceful exit. He kept his eyes on Charlotte with a look, Frank felt, of mild contempt. *He knows a dilettante,* Frank thought, watching the young man with a sly, conspiratorial smile.

"Curt is a person I'm quite fond of," Charlotte said. "May I, Curt?" The young man nodded; Frank caught his eye for a moment and they exchanged glances—Frank's amused, the other's still mildly contemptuous. "He has just returned from what I rather melodramatically call the front lines. He was with a group picketing a Welfare Center in Spanish Harlem; in the heart of the *barrio*," she said, rolling the r's with great gentility.

"How exciting," Frank said dryly.

"It was," Charlotte said quickly. "Curt and his group were in a certain amount of peril. The Welfare people were against them, the police were against them, and even the people of the barrio were against them. The people were afraid there might be trouble and the Center be closed down."

"In other words," Frank said to Curt, "nobody took you seriously."

"It takes more than . . ." the young man began, but Frank cut him off.

"Spare me," Frank said. "I know the rhetoric."

The young man's eyes moved quickly to Charlotte.

"I'd better be going," he said.

Frank watched her walk Curt out to the patio. Outside, he saw her slip the young man a folded-up piece of paper, then shake his hand and wave him off.

"Still donating, eh?" Frank said when she returned.

"You shouldn't have mocked him like that," she said, sitting in a chair and slouching, curling her bare toes into the rug. "He's a dedicated young man and is doing good work with his group. Anyway, you're back. For how long?"

"Permanently."

"I'm glad. What were you doing in Los Angeles?"

"Oh, nothing," he said with studied casualness. "You know, surfing on Malibu, romancing starlets, dreaming in wide-screen technicolor at poolside. A perfectly idyllic, decadent life."

"Bullshit," she said. "You were probably a carhop, selling containers of fried shrimp to teen-agers in convertibles."

"And what have you been doing?"

"You know what I've been doing. I still have my 'causes,' as my ex-husband was fond of saying, with mild disgust. And I wish you wouldn't give me that patronizing smile."

"I can't help it."

"You ought to begin doing something constructive with your life. You have *so* much energy and intelligence . . ."

"What would you have me do?"

"Frank, even to *ask* such a question. In these times. Didn't you see misery and unhappiness when you were traveling? Didn't it bother you at least a little bit, ever? Wasn't there ever a moment when you wished the world could be a better, more just place?— Because if there was, if you ever had that one twinge of dissatisfaction, then you should search it out inside yourself and build on it."

"And march around holding up a sign—like your friend?"

"He's doing *some*thing. He's—"

"He's doing nothing. If anything, he's a symbol of futility. The Movement is flooded with people like that. In fact, they are no longer the Movement, if you must know the truth. Neither he nor you are relevant any more."

"Frank, that's impertinent."

"Your only function now is to provide a smoke screen for the people who are doing the real work."

"That's *most* goddamn impertinent. I've been active all my *life*. I've given time, money . . ."

"And one husband; but to what effect, sweetheart? Where are the great reforms sweeping the land?"

"This sort of progress is gradual."

"I know, and it gets swallowed up immediately and you're right back where you started from."

"Coming from someone like you, who's never lifted a finger, this is presumptuous and arrogant," she said heatedly.

"If you knew how few people are doing the real work, you'd be astonished."

"What *real* work?"

"Jesus Christ, you preen yourself on your achievements when all you've ever done is sign a lousy petition or march in a demonstration on a sunny day or slip fifty dollars to a clod like that kid."

"I'm not pretending to be Joan of Arc; I'm simply working to the best of my abilities."

"Well, it isn't good enough; not when there are people doing more."

"Who is doing more?"

"Oh, never mind. Skip it."

"No, you were saying something."

"I don't want to talk about it."

"Frank—" she said impatiently. "You've said things . . . cast aspersions . . . on something I happen to be quite deeply involved in and feel very strong about."

"And know nothing . . . really nothing, about."

"Now I resent that." She shook her head from side to side as if expressing great compassion. "Oh, you outsiders," she said. "How little you know about what needs to be done. How easy it is to sit back and remonstrate and ridicule and criticize."

"Some people know what needs to be done. And are doing it," Frank said quietly. She fixed upon him a look of wary curiosity.

"Charlotte, do you know why I went to California?"

She shook her head.

"No, I wasn't idling in the sun, and I wasn't selling fried shrimp in containers either. I've spent a whole year meeting with key people, talking with them, planning with them, working with them, plotting out a very complex and sophisticated program. Do you know what's going on, what's *really* going on?"

She was staring intently at him.

"Charlotte, do you know there are tiny communes scattered through the Sierras where people are stockpiling arms and learning techniques of urban guerrilla warfare?"

"I've heard rumors . . ."

"I'm not talking about rumors. Do you know that we have small affinity groups on every major campus waiting to go into action? I'm not talking about people marching with placards or sitting down in the middle of the street: I'm talking about people getting ready to put their goddamn lives on the line."

"And you're part of it?" she asked with guarded interest.

He had been sitting forward while speaking; now he leaned back comfortably and crossed his legs with a certain satisfaction.

"This is beyond belief," she said with an incredulous smile.

"Why do you think I've taken a week to come around to see you? I've been busy as hell establishing my contacts here. And believe me, no matter how trusted one is, making these sort of contacts is a delicate business."

"Frank, this is absolutely amazing. I'm positively speechless. You were always so detached and cynical about these things."

He sat back, pleased, allowing himself to be contemplated.

"How big is it, really?" she asked, lowering her voice in deference to what he knew and she did not.

"Very."

"How much can you tell me?"

"I've told you too much already."

"I'm nothing if not trustworthy," she said, piqued.

"Do you condone violence?" he asked now.

"In the cause of revolution? That's a very broad proposition. I suppose a . . . a violent revolution is preferable to a non-violent non-revolution."

"You sound indecisive," he said, fixing her with a lingering, inquiring look that flustered her. She smiled self-consciously.

"Frank, I'm just not *used* to discussing revolution with you."

"You'll get used to it," he said.

"How much of this have you told Paul?"

"Very little."

"Frank, why don't you try to bring him in? He would be a wonderful asset."

"This isn't his sort of thing."

"I'm concerned about him. He's been so . . . so . . . *inside* himself. He just can't seem to open up. I invite him to dinner all the time, but he doesn't come," she said ruefully.

"Paul has to work out his problems in his own way, in his own time."

"But how can he, when he responds to nothing, to no one? Oh, I know what it is; but it's been a year since she died. If he's still in mourning, then it's beginning to get morbid. And anyway, if you must know something . . . and I'm not trying to be unkind . . . she was never right for him in the first place."

"They were in love," Frank said.

"No, I can't believe that."

"Don't want to, you mean."

She stared at him, a beguiling candor in her face.

"I was always fond of Paul," she said. "I never tried to hide that."

Frank uncrossed, then recrossed his legs, his fingers idling around the collar of his black crew-neck sweater.

"I want to help him," she said.

"It can best be done by leaving him alone."

"I suppose," she said abstractedly.

"In any event," Frank said in a strong changing-the-subject voice, "I've told what I came to tell. And all in confidence, of course."

"Of course," she said, her attention returning. "What will you be doing; I mean that you can talk about?"

"Seeing people. Honing the edges of preparation. Waiting for the tide to crest. In these matters timing is all-important."

"You'll keep in touch with me, won't you?" she asked.

"Of course."

"And think of me as something more than a spectator."

"By all means," he said.

EIGHT

Frank felt the meeting with Charlotte had gone well. He was pleasantly surprised at how readily she accepted his tale of political transmutation; after her few moments of incredulity, which he had expected, there had been nothing but unquestioning acceptance. (But it was really not that artful a bit of persuasion, he told himself at a later, more objective moment; after all, she had spent a lifetime listening to the words of the self-anointed, and her style of unidirectional zeal bred its own vulnerability.) Finding that young man there had been an unexpected stroke of fortune. Being able to deprecate the efforts of someone else was always an effective ploy; if done with the right amount of lofty disdain it gave people the idea that they were close to the active and influential "inside," a delusion that generally cost them perception and perspective.

He felt he understood Charlotte perfectly. His "conversion" had excited her, given her ego a massage, and further certified the importance of everything she believed in. And not only were they working on the same side now, but he, as the one supposedly involved in the higher echelons of the Movement, had the position of supremacy. He was convinced she was ripe for manipulation. The deeply committed activists he had observed were invariably victims of their own zealotry, yielding much of their intellect and objectivity to high-voltage emotion and consequently were vulnerable to dissimulation. For these people there was nothing more stimulating than the idea of a conspiracy, or the hint of some violence designed for the greater good of mankind. Violence in the name of their cause was venial, titillating them the way others were excited by De Sade or books of medieval torture, because more than justice or progress they wanted vindication.

He had deliberately waited a week before coming to her that first time, knowing it would initially pique her conceit, then her curiosity, finally leave her totally credulous. He found it no effort to speak convincingly about the things she wanted to hear. It was no challenge at all to talk with facile eloquence about ending war and poverty and hunger and disease and injustice; the perversion of language was a most comfortable and genteel form of abuse.

His true feelings about the matters he so expansively discussed with Charlotte had settled into ambivalence. Of one thing he was convinced, however: sharp and crucial change was coming to America. It had to come because it was the will of the young, and the will of the young was a force of nature. Paul of course disagreed. On one of the occasions when a reluctant Paul allowed himself to be drawn into these discussions with his brother, he told Frank, "This is a most unlikely generation to make a revolution. I'm afraid their hatred and disgust are aimed at people rather than institutions, which gives you petulance instead of passion. And since they themselves have so much in common with the people they profess to abominate . . . well, I'm afraid you'll have to wait, or look elsewhere for your social drama." Frank attributed Paul's blindness in the matter to his shuttered existence. An absolute belief in the beneficence and the inevitability of change could not be minimized; was, in fact, crucial. In the perseverance of its dedication, it was similar to the quality of faith once reserved exclusively for that old, now eroding institution, religion: unless you brought your God with you into the church, you would never find Him there. The hard-core people of the Movement had that kind of faith, Frank felt; their expressions of it were not limited to speeches and lectures and debates; they were committed in their lives, down to the most prosaic detail of daily living, to an idealism and integrity of style and value and ethic, believing that continued and unfaltering adherence would create revolutionary change. But Frank knew, too, that it was only a matter of time before there occurred a fusing of that faith and strength with some responsive opportunity which would force the collision of the old and the new. The chemistry awaited only the synthesis, the chance incident that would incite the upheaval which would unite students and oppressed minorities and those "workers" so dear to the heart of any revolutionist into a single rampaging convulsive mob boiling with unreckoning fury. What his role would be then, he did not know. But he would not be part of the mob: that much he knew. He had been that all of his life, and to be a speck of anonymity in the midst of surging drama was simply failure of another kind. The wild and undisciplined mob would have to be led, and only those willing and able to assume that responsibility would be able to provide it. It was incredible that the idea of a raging, sacking, destructive mob could be exhilarating; it was like a throwback to primitive man, in whose head swarmed not rationale but imagination, who invented God and laid the foundations of civilized society. But mobs created the signposts of an epoch and the men who led them completed the historical correlative. And in today's impulsive world reality was close upon the margins of the dream, like the blotted sun burning the fringes of a cloud. The very nature of the dream, its keen glitter of possibility and its pinprick of anticipation, stimulated Frank into feeling that these were indeed exciting times to be alive in, rare times: for today the spirit matched the idea.

As far as Charlotte was concerned, however, he could not wait indefinitely for fate; eventually he would have to do something to substantiate himself. Mere talk would soon run thin. Her anticipation was growing with each conversation and would soon evolve into expectation. She was becoming more susceptible (though she refused to let him move into the house with her, despite his suggestion that they "consolidate"), and he felt that the right stroke of luck or action could swing her completely toward him. It would be more comfortable, he thought cynically, to plan a revolution from the finest house in town than from a furnished room.

Several nights a week he came to dinner in the fine white house on the crest of the hill, and talked revolution while sitting at a mahogany dining table covered with an enormous hand-made appliquéd cloth, eating meals on Rosenthal china, served by the coal-black hands of the Dominican woman; and after dinner they sat on the patio and admired the garden by moonlight while he smoked a thirty-cent cigar, and talked of the destruction of oligarchies, the subversion of nations, the liberation by blood and thunder of hundreds of millions of people. Sometimes, sitting on the patio late at night, cooled by fragrant breezes, a cigar in one hand, a snifter of brandy in the other, he felt almost as though they were discussing achievements rather than some vague storm of the future. One night he said to her, "Charlotte, I'm delighted by the way our minds have met in these matters. Working together, I feel we can do any damn thing we set out to." And then, with calculated whimsy, "Don't be surprised if I fall in love with you." She reached across the patio table and covered his hand with hers. "Darling," she said, "that's what the Revolution needs most of: love . . . love . . ." *Dammit*, he thought later as he walked home alone to his furnished room.

Occasionally he wondered whether he was handling the situation correctly. Even though that magnificent abstraction, Revolution, was her most ardent preoccupation, perhaps there was too much talk of it. It was possible that he could eventually pass into her mind as another abstraction, a person identified with an idea, and little more. He could not forget that, revolutionary or not, she had still been raised in wealth and was as self-centered as most who had enjoyed that privilege, that the "democracy" of the rich was sometimes too sumptuous to allow for definitions, that their conversion to popular causes could, like the free-thinking of fallen-away Catholics, revert with inexplicable suddenness. Too often they were elegant furnaces that needed their fire imported. Over and over he heard some insignificant clod praised in the most effusive terms simply for mouthing the weariest cliché or most vacuous platitude. He himself received these encomiums and gauged their worth according to the abundance of their utterance.

One afternoon, while walking in the garden, she suddenly said to him, "Frank, do you remember, when we were children, your saying someday you would marry me—and not because you loved me but because I was rich?"

"I don't remember that," he said, his face flushing.

"You did," she said.

"Look, I said and did a lot of crazy things when I . . ."

"Don't be so serious," she said chidingly, shaking his arm.

"I'm very serious today," he said.

NINE

"Don't look so glum," Ben said. "It's a small enough favor. I would have done it myself, except that I don't trust myself behind a wheel any more."

"I'm not complaining," Frank said.

"You've been uncharacteristically quiet."

"I'm concentrating on driving," Frank said. "I haven't been behind a wheel in ages," he added, moving the rented car through the expressway traffic.

"You should be pleased that your father possesses sentiment of this nature. It's a sign of character."

"I thought you didn't like cemeteries."

"Does anyone *like* cemeteries?" Ben said irascibly. "I'm going because I'm sentimental, because it's an obligation, and because I haven't visited your mother's grave in years."

"In years? Very sentimental," Frank said, throwing his father a quick sardonic glance.

Ben glowered at him, then stared straight ahead again, pulling forward on the checked cap that covered his bald head. Even on this warm, sunny morning he was wearing a sweater and a tweed jacket and heavy twill trousers.

The cemetery came into view, a gently rising knoll of soldierly stones, with a scattering of mausoleums and trees. Ben stared impassively at it, as though contemplating some barely audible insult.

"Christ, she's been gone a long time," he said quietly. "Some days I miss her terribly, other days I can't even remember what she looked like."

"Yeah," Frank said. He was embarrassed, hoping his father would not go on in this vein.

They left the expressway at the next exit, going down the ramp onto a service road which led toward the cemetery.

"I hear you've been spending a lot of time at Charlotte Breit-man's," Ben said.

"That's right."

"What's she up to—still planning to overthrow the govern-ment?"

Frank laughed uneasily.

"The only good that would come of it," Ben said, "is that if her scheme ever worked, she and others like her would be the first to be dragged off and shot."

"Oh, she's not so bad."

"A fool."

"I thought you liked her," Frank said.

"I do, to a point. Anyway, you can't entirely dislike someone whom you knew as a child."

"She's not as frivolous as you think."

"Is that so?" Ben asked, giving his son an amused look.

"She's matured. I mean it."

"Is that so?" Ben asked again, in a suggestive tone now.

"Oh, come on," Frank said, annoyed.

"Atta boy, Frank."

"I could do worse," Frank muttered defensively.

"I suppose. Christ, she's rich. But of course you know that. Paul could have her in a minute, if he wanted. Not that it would be such a good idea. She talks too much."

"I tell you, she's not as nonsensical as you think."

"Is she interested in you?"

"I'm really not thinking along those lines."

"Bullshit," Ben said quietly. "Not that it wouldn't suit you. I can just see you strutting around that garden in tweed knickers."

Frank laughed. "Swinging a croquet mallet," he said.

"Except, my boy," Ben said soberly, "if she marries again, it won't be to a pauper. Socialism can be very antisocial."

"She's not a snob, if that's what you mean."

"I don't mean that. What it is, is a completely different per-spective. A rich person is a snob the same way a priest is a virgin —it's a peculiarity accepted by everyone as being part of the pro-fession."

"What an analogy."

"Some priests are virgins," Ben said, shrugging.

They drove through the cemetery's iron gates and then into the narrow, one-way lanes that wound through the grounds. The rows upon rows of stones and carved seraphs were delineated sharply in the morning sunshine. Here and there one or two people stood head-bowed before a grave. They passed one funeral, a sparse handful of people gathered together on the grass.

"It's like coming back to an old battlefield," Ben said, staring moodily around. "When you're there originally you feel such emotional violence, such wrenching involvement; and when you return there's this unnatural serenity. Here, make a left up the hill."

"You remember where it is?" Frank asked.

"I have a homing pigeon's instinct."

Ben told him where to stop. When they got out, the slamming of the car doors sounded inordinately loud on the quiet air. Frank walked ahead up the narrow cement path toward a plot of ground shaded by several small trees. Then he paused and waited for his father. He felt a strange, bittersweet pang as he watched his father come up the path. The old man seemed to age a little more each time he saw him. The strong proud shoulders had a pronounced roundness and the once-crisp, confident stride had slowed. He was losing weight and his clothes hung loosely.

They walked together. Frank recognized many of the names on the stones. His mother had belonged to a church group which years ago had purchased this burial plot for members, and time in its passage had slowly filled it.

"It was a good thing she had foresight," Ben said. "Getting buried is no longer as easy as dying."

They cut away from the path and walked several yards across the grass between two rows of stones. Then they stopped. They stood silently before the grave, staring at the stone, reading the incised letters. The site had become overgrown.

"I've been neglectful," Ben said. "I ought to buy some yearly maintenance. She was always such a tidy person . . ."

Then Frank noted the old man staring at the rectangle of ground next to the grave.

"That's my bed," Ben said. "You'll find the deed in my desk, when the time comes."

"Oh, come on now," Frank said, forcing a smile. Ben gave him a look of tender understanding, seeing in his son's face the anxiety, the sudden, almost subliminal reversion to child-fright, the fear of the dark. And for a moment the parent felt a curious twinge of guilt, for being old, for being ill, for evoking disquiet in his son.

"Sure," Ben said, his tough old face breaking into a soft-lined smile. "It's way, way off." He paused. "Nevertheless . . ."

TEN

Frank had taken a room in a large, rambling old house on a dead-end street one block in from Grant Avenue. The house was run by a Mrs. Van Dyke, a florid-faced seventy-year-old widow who had been letting rooms to a local, non-transient clientele for more than thirty years, or since her late husband Buster fell off the roof at two o'clock one morning in a state of alcoholic hilarity, a broken neck ending at once his cry of delirious delight and his life. Mrs. Van Dyke, faithful to the memory of her affable, prodigal man, was always pleased to say that he had departed this world in his prime, with a shout of joy and a certain amount of style.

She was not particularly happy about letting a room to Frank; her preference had always been older men—the gray, dimly abiding old bachelors and widowers of the neighborhood, who lived quietly on pensions and nostalgia—but their number was dwindling, and so with half the rentable rooms in her two-storied house having open doors, she was forced to bend policy to necessity and give Frank a room.

The room was simply and adequately furnished. There was a double bed with a rusted bedstead and a wrought-iron headboard, a bureau, a table, two straight-backed chairs, one comfortable easy chair, two lamps, and a bright orange rug. Meals were available cheaply in Mrs. Van Dyke's dining room downstairs. Since the rent was scaled to accommodate the modest incomes of the old men, Frank found it quite reasonable. Nevertheless money was a constant worry and he had to budget frugally. The few hundred dollars he had brought back with him from California did not last very long and he had to borrow several hundred from his father and from Paul. And then he was able to achieve a major financial success, talking Charlotte out of five hundred dollars which he claimed was needed to help spirit "three invaluable Movement people" out of the country and into Canada. Later, he contrived for her a tale of a midnight departure from the radical environs of the East Village and a suspenseful automobile ride to the Canadian border and then word of a safe arrival in Montreal. It was the first money he had been able to pry loose from her and she had given it willingly, but he realized he could not overplay his hand here and that any further requests would have to be dictated by absolute need.

Frank was sitting in his room reading one evening when his brother-in-law appeared. Philip Werner looked more harassed and perplexed than usual. He was a man unable to disguise what he was feeling. Nevertheless he mustered a weak smile. He unwrapped a small potted plant he was carrying.

"I've been meaning to come by and wish you luck in your new quarters, Frank," he said. "Here, here's a little house-warming gift." He placed the plant on the bureau.

"You're very sweet, Phil," Frank said, staring at the plant, a nondescript thing of leaves and dirt in an orange pot.

"You have to water it."

"I know. Sit down. I'm afraid I can't offer you anything to drink; there's nothing here."

"It's all right," Philip said. He sat down on the edge of one of the wooden chairs. Frank, shoeless, sprawled out on the bed, crossed his feet at the ankles and clasped his hands behind his head and stared blandly at his brother-in-law. Philip clasped and unclasped his hands several times, stared at the floor for a few moments, then let a deep sigh.

"I've been wanting to come by and talk to you," he said.

"Well," Frank said, "here you are."

"It's about Helen," Philip said, looking up.

"Good old Helen," Frank said cheerfully.

"You know the story, Frank," Philip said dolefully. "I don't have to pull any punches with you. Well, it hasn't changed. I'm desperate . . . absolutely desperate."

"What can I do?" Frank asked. His reaction—which he tried to conceal—was one of indifference. Unlike Paul, he had never been particularly interested in or scandalized by his sister's behavior. (As a boy, he had even, in a perverse way, reaped some satisfying notoriety from it, when he was pointed out by older males as Helen Dublin's brother.) He could never quite understand the acuteness of Paul's shame and bitterness. When once he told his brother that there were a dozen girls in Capstone worse than Helen, Paul said bitterly, "But they're not our sisters."

"It's come into the house now . . . the children are becoming aware of it. Lorana can't stand it. The girl is sixteen now, Frank. She knows what's going on. This is a terrible thing for her . . . what kind of influence . . . it can warp her . . . distort everything. She's a sensible girl . . . a good girl . . . but to feel such shame at such an early age can be very damaging . . . knowing that boys just a few years older than she . . ."

"Are screwing her mother," Frank said flatly.

"Yes," Philip said, almost defiantly. "She's too young to cope with it. I've tried to explain to her . . . but what logic do you use on a sixteen year old who's heartbroken and ashamed?"

"Have you spoken to Helen?"

"Have I spoken to Helen?" Philip said as if he had just been asked the most incredible thing. Then his voice softened. "Of course. She cries and promises to reform . . . and she means it, Frank. She doesn't do these things maliciously or spitefully. That's the tragedy. She's sick. You know that as well as I. But she doesn't *try* to help herself. I thought it would play itself out as she got older, but it hasn't . . . it's become worse. Phone calls come in from men at all hours of the night. Sometimes Lorana picks up the phone. She's talking about leaving home. She can't take it any more. My family is going to hell and I don't know what to do."

"Look, Phil, this is my sister I'm talking about, but you've got to take a strong stand. Give her an ultimatum. If she doesn't stop it, throw her out."

Philip looked incredulous at the suggestion.

"No," he said quietly, his voice for the first time very firm and sure. "That's not the answer. I won't abandon my wife . . . she needs me."

"Then if you won't—or can't—do anything," Frank said, "what do you expect from me?"

"I don't know," Philip said, shaking his head, his voice suddenly empty of conviction and emphasis as quickly as it had filled, replaced by a soft, somber despair.

"For Christ's sake, Phil," Frank said irritatedly, "your problem is an ancient one. It isn't something that's just popped up. You knew when you married her that Helen had a problem with her central heating system."

"What do you mean?"

"That she was a hot number," Frank said bluntly, exasperated.

"It isn't true."

"All right, think what you want."

"I tried to talk to your father about it, but he was more concerned about Lorana."

"She's always been his particular favorite," Frank said.

"That's why I thought he might try to help, since you might say that Lorana is the real victim of all this. But all he said was that there was nothing he could do about Helen, but that if Lorana wanted to leave she could come live with him."

"Well, that's something," Frank said.

"It doesn't help, it doesn't stop Helen. I told him that. Your father has no respect for me. He thinks I'm an ass."

"Nobody respects a cuckold."

"Look, my only crime is I love everyone, my wife, my children . . . I'm trying to hold together a home and a family. I told your father . . ."

"My father is dying, Phil," Frank said quietly.

Philip frowned. "He is?"

"If you weren't feeling so sorry for yourself, you'd have noticed."

"I hardly see him . . . I didn't know. Are you sure?"

"Pretty sure."

"Does Helen know?" Philip asked.

"I don't know what Helen knows."

"This might sober her up."

"Why should it?"

Philip fell silent, subdued by the thought of death. He got up and walked to the window and stared out at the quiet summer's night that lay over Capstone, at the small houses with their scattering of familial evening lights. After several minutes of moody, pensive staring, he turned away from the window.

"Well . . ." he said pointlessly. Then he sighed. "It's not an easy life, is it? What's this you're reading?" he asked, noting the stack of books and magazines on the table. He began leafing through some of the magazines, then examined the books. "Since when are you into this sort of thing?"

Frank had been watching him with amused interest.

"You'd be surprised at the things I'm into, Philip," he said.

His brother-in-law looked at him puzzledly.

"What sort of things?"

"I'm not at liberty to tell," Frank said, crossing his arms casually over his chest, tilting his head slightly to a side and staring at Philip with an expression of subtle mischief.

"Not at liberty to tell what?"

"Not at liberty to tell what I'm not at liberty to tell."

"Are you trying to bullshit me?"

Frank smiled.

"According to this," Philip said, jabbing the stack of literature with his finger, "you've become some sort of Communist or something."

Frank laughed.

"Then what?" Philip asked.

"I happen to be into some things that are best kept secret," Frank said, pleased at the interest and curiosity he had evoked in his brother-in-law, and at the same time annoyed with himself for being pleased at the idea of trying to impress a person of this caliber.

"Secret?" Philip said, modulating his voice in deference to the word's import. He lowered himself onto the chair and stared intently at Frank. "What are you up to, Frank?"

"Philip . . ."

"You can trust me."

"It isn't a matter of trusting or not trusting; the question is much simpler: *Why* should I tell you anything?"

"About what?"

"About what I'm doing."

Philip was gazing so frankly at him, with such impertinent, irrepressible curiosity, Frank had to keep from smiling. For several moments the man was absolutely overwhelmed and tongue-tied by his own intense, querying interest. Then he glanced at the stack of literature.

"A man can guess," he said. "I'm not so much of a fool. I know you've been hanging around Charlotte Breitman's, and everybody knows what *she's* up to; and now that I see what you're feeding into your mind . . ."

"And what's your grand conclusion?"

"You're into something political."

"Brilliant, Phil, brilliant."

"Wait. Just a minute. You're into something political, and if you don't want to talk about it, then it's radical. But maybe you're fooling yourself. There's so much of this today that it's no longer radical. Why, I've got friends at the plant that are talking radical . . . about how the company is screwing them, how the union is screwing them. We ask what happens to our dues, how much is in the strike fund, and we get a big runaround from the shop steward, from the union, from everybody."

"And what does anybody do about it?"

"Nothing."

"There's your answer, Phil. Everybody knows something is wrong, but nobody does anything about it."

"But people are doing things. I read about these radical groups, throwing bombs and setting fires and things like that. *They're* doing something."

"Do you approve of what they're doing, Phil?"

"Do I approve? Let's say that I don't *dis*approve. I think people are beginning to get tired of being dumped on. Look, I might not like some of these radicals . . . the way they look and dress and that sort of thing . . . but who else is making a move to change things? You got to give them credit for that. People who go first are always crazy . . . that's the way it is in the army . . . but the rest of us would still be living in caves if *some*body didn't try to change things."

"That's right, Phil. You see things very clearly."

"Tell me what you're up to, Frank. You can trust me."

"How do I know you're not a police informer?" Frank asked, straight-faced.

"Me?" Philip asked with humorless indignation. "Look, I'm a worker like anybody else. I'm looking for a better life too. And

when your own union starts to screw you, when you see the plant
superintendent taking the union delegate out to lunch, you know
you've got to start looking out for your own interests. I sympathize with a lot of these kids today, Frank. I really do. I can't talk
as openly about it as I like . . . after all . . . you know what
I mean . . . most people think it's unpatriotic to criticize . . .
especially in this neighborhood. You should see how filthy the
bathroom is in the plant . . . but nobody does anything about it.
And they don't hire colored. There's not one in the plant. That's
supposed to be illegal, isn't it?"

"That's right," Frank said.

"But nobody does anything."

"You have to understand something, Phil. Don't you know that
today those who speak the loudest are the most ineffectual? Don't
you know that the Bill of Rights and all the other guarantors of
free speech are actually inhibitions on revolutionary progress? The
government *wants* you to speak out as loudly as you can—so they
know exactly what you're thinking and doing."

"I never thought of that," Philip said. "Christ. So that's why you
don't want to say anything."

"The real makers and shakers today are talking quietly, organ-
izing quietly . . . so that when they finally make their move they'll
have the element of surprise."

"Of course. That's right . . . that's good strategy."

"It's the only strategy," Frank said, staring impassively at his
brother-in-law.

"And that's what you're into," Philip said.

"I never said I was."

"That's right . . . of course you didn't. I didn't hear a thing.
Nevertheless, I've spoken out. You know how I feel."

"It's encouraging, knowing that the average man like yourself
feels that way."

"The average man?" Philip asked. Then he nodded to the assessment. "Yes, I suppose I am. There's nothing wrong with that.
That's where the power lies, doesn't it—with the average man?"

"In the final analysis, he's the one everyone has to court."

"That's right," Philip said, a new, stronger fiber in his voice.
"And we have our price too—just like everyone else."

"And your goals."

"Of course. Our share of the pie, things like that."

"That's right."

"Frank, I don't want to seem . . . but can you bring me in on something? Maybe this is what I need . . . to show people."

"Phil, with this sort of thing you have to commit yourself out of deep inner conviction, not to prove anything to anybody."

"I do have convictions," Philip said excitedly. "Haven't I just told you? I meant everything I said, Frank. I know what I'm talking about. The average man is the sleeping giant. I've read some books too," he said, swinging his arm out behind him and pointing to the stack of literature. "I may be a good-natured jerk, but I know what's going on."

"Of course you do."

"So think about it . . . think about me."

"I will, Phil. I promise. But one thing you've got to promise: this conversation has to have never occurred. Neither of us are ever to refer to it, until I decide otherwise. Do you read me?"

Philip nodded.

"Absolute secrecy," Frank said severely.

"That goes without saying," Philip said. He was profoundly impressed.

Later, after his brother-in-law had gone, Frank lay on the bed, his hands clasped behind his head, staring at the ceiling.

"A disciple," he said aloud, smiling with sardonic amusement. "I have a disciple. Bless his heart."

"*Comrades: The first official act of the Provisional Revolutionary Government will be to clean up the bathroom in my brother-in-law's plant.*"

ELEVEN

Once Philip Werner had called it premonition, and what satisfaction he derived from the anguish, the despair, the very insult of what he had intuitively anticipated, was the plain fact of being proved right. It was small and useless consolation, but consolation nevertheless, because in being right he believed he understood and understanding was a credit to one's perception and maganimity. Actually it was not premonition but familiarity with an almost ordained cycle of confirmed inclinations, awareness of the expectable, and finally the protracted frictions of instinct and observation (after eighteen years of marriage), ending in a helpless and despairing knowing. What he called premonition was something he was able to see coming sometimes as much as a week away (even before she herself did, he believed), see it building in her with slow, intensely concentrating concrescence, until after a day or two of quirky, lip-biting irritability, she would yield and go, with a suddenness born of deferred impulses. His resentment toward what she was doing scaled no great emotional heights nor caused any incandescent heat anywhere—it would have been totally out of character—leaving infidelity with complete freedom of movement; and anyway, even resentment could become monotonous. To a person whose life contained so few variations and diversions, being prescient even about his own afflicted days could give him a rub of satisfaction. So that when it began occurring with greater frequency and impunity, and when his regard of it evolved from premonition to expectation, it had been too long in motion on too familiar a causeway and it was too late for him to do anything (if he ever could have), because even from its inception the infidelity had never been seriously opposed or questioned, and thus unchallenged and unbridled had suppressed within itself any desire for control.

Three and sometimes four nights a week she went out, always around midnight, when the children were asleep or readying themselves for bed, and Philip himself was preparing to retire. He would be in the bedroom putting on his pajamas as she stood on the other side of the room engrossed in her own, directly opposite, routine. He would watch her, the old enchantment still clear in his eyes, as she pulled the girdle up around her remarkably taut thighs and brought it into place over her small paunch as the elastic slapped sensually against her flesh. Then she sat on the edge of the bed and drew her hosiery up along her long, beautifully curved legs. Then she stood up and admired herself in the mirror while he gazed at her full, forward-thrusting breasts and the dim mass of black pubic hair inside the folds of the bracing white girdle and the shapely swell of her buttocks: he watched with the tensions of the voyeur, removed and mute and helpless, enchanted by the unquenchable promise and mystique of the ceremony. When the dress had fallen over her head and been adjusted with pinching fingertips and groomed with smoothing hands, he would shut his eyes for a moment and swallow into his dry throat, then look down at himself in his pajamas, the baggy striped clownlike costume that covered him. He would ask: "Where are you going?" And she would smile guilelessly at him. "Just to have a beer and listen to the jukebox awhile." And she would leave and he would turn back the cover of the double bed and lie there in the dark, perplexed, and with a certain mild bitterness, not toward her but himself, because of his depleted power, his inadequacy. Sometimes he would think: *It's my fault.*

"Nature often gives us warnings, Mr. Werner," the doctor had told him. "This is what nature has just given you: a stern, painful warning; fortunately, however, not a fatal one." The doctor then went on to prescribe a sex life. Intercourse not more than twice a month. "Unless you want to die like so many foolish men say they do." Embarrassedly, he had tried to explain to the doctor about Helen, that she was a young woman, not yet thirty, and that she had "an unusually warm nature." The doctor arranged his face into an expression of patent disinterest and said, "She'll simply have to adjust." "I'll explain it to her," Philip said. When he came home and told her she looked at him and went pale. She walked to the window and stared out for fully five minutes. Then she turned around and, unexpectedly, smiled at him. "Why should we worry ourselves about a thing like that?" she said.

Philip considered himself a completely misunderstood man. In spite of everything, he thought himself lucky to have married Helen. This was a consciously arrived at and firmly adhered to belief; and what was more, worse, he let her know it, let everyone know it. To him it was a perfectly reasonable attitude, because only he knew the tribulations of his own life story. His parents had died when he was a child and his formative years had been spent being shunted from one grudging and indifferent relative to another, a financial burden, a weight on someone's conscience, sleeping on cots or sofas or doubling up with resentful cousins, recipient of offhand affection, a bothersome obligation. When he was seventeen he went out on his own, living alone in furnished rooms. No one seemed to understand the bleakness and loneliness of his early years, or was capable of measuring it against what he now had, which, in spite of a straying wife, was all he had ever dreamed of having.

He was twenty-eight when he married her, ten years her senior. For several years he had been watching her, watched her grow almost overnight from puberty through adolescence to young adult, blurring the distinctions with a street-wise swing and impudent smile, the opposite of his quiet, unobserved bachelorhood. In the beginning he talked to her in bars, and then they began dating. When she was eighteen (he had the day ringed on his calendar) he went to her house and asked her father if there were any objections to a marriage. "None at all," Ben said. "But are you sure you know what you're doing?" Philip was sure. And Helen was sure too. She was genuinely fond of him; he treated her "like a lady," she told her mother. And anyway, she had decided she wanted to get married, making the decision in the abstract, and had simply been waiting for a figure to fill the silhouette.

But he didn't get the quiet home life he wanted. They went out to the local bars almost every night, drinking and dancing—she wanted to dance to virtually every song that came out of the jukebox, and when Philip was too tired to keep going then she danced with someone else, and it disturbed him to see the other men handle her so familiarly; but nevertheless he was proud of her youth, vibrance and popularity and basked as if in reflected glory.

He thought the pace would slow after Lorana was born. But instead he found himself hiring sitters, and when none were available then he sat himself while she "stepped around to the bar for a quick drink." He really did not mind. He was cognizant of all that young energy that quickened and excited her, and he made no attempt to try and restrict her. But none of the children slowed her down. Even when she had become the mother of four, she was still "stepping out for a few drinks," and when he told her he did not think it dignified she was always able to disarm him with a mild reproach about his being an old man, saying it with her warm unassailable smile. He did not, or at least refused to, suspect her of derelictions for a long time, because frequently when she came home she wakened him and told him she wanted him, and this, to his naïveté, was infallible proof. Then he had the heart attack, one night in bed with her. When the doctor arrived, at four o'clock in the morning, he took one look at Philip and telephoned for an ambulance. Philip was hospitalized for two weeks. Soon after that he was compelled to stop ignoring the obvious as far as his wife was concerned, and learned to rationalize it, in order to live with it.

And then Lorana began complaining to him that Helen was receiving telephone calls from strange men (who asked not for Mrs. Werner but for "Helen," and some even said "Helen Dublin"). The compromise he had allowed himself for his wife, the rationale for it all, would not extend to his daughter, his oldest and favored, who had received the bulk of his secondary love and continued to receive it. So as Lorana's distress became incremental not only because of the phone calls but because of her mother's nocturnal absences as well, Philip decided he had to do something. When he finally faced up to the confrontation, he had plotted what he thought was an acceptable compromise. He told Helen he did not mind her going out occasionally, but that she must stay in the neighborhood, and insisted she put an end to the telephone calls. The first stipulation was spurious and they both knew it—she never left the neighborhood—but it enabled him to make a satisfying assertion of his authority and her to acknowledge it without inconvenience. Also, she said she had no idea who was making the calls but would try to find out and put a stop to them. So, in effect, nothing changed, since her lovers were all from Capstone anyway and those who wanted to telephone her continued doing so. When Lorana told him that the calls had not ceased he said that it was all right, that he had spoken to her mother about it and everything was going to be all right. The girl looked at him strangely and for the first time saw his helplessness on the surface and felt for him a despairing shame and compassion.

So premonition was long gone now, long ago replaced by a burdensome reality, by knowing, affirmation. And the more he knew this, the more Philip knew and understood his own fears and the burden of his futility. But still he tried not to feel sorry for himself, as he dwelled upon the human arithmetic of what he once had, once wanted, and now possessed. Even in unhappiness, he was still the gainer. Ineffectiveness was a mild sort of damnation, he felt, until it was faced with the necessity to act, at which time the proposition altered radically, dangerously. To attempt to break out of one's natural prison could lead only to deeper unhappiness at best, unforeseeable disaster at worst; for the ineffectual man always allowed time, the antiquator of antiquities, the burying-sand of oblivion, to bring settlement to his problems. No one preached passiveness in the face of challenge, but one had always to consider the practical and realistic side of the matter.

So it was that he thought about his conversation with Frank with a curious optimism and excitement. He suddenly had worthy political feelings. Frank had listened to him, taken an interest, or pretended to anyway. He tried not to be deluded, however. He knew this brother-in-law too well. What Frank was up to was a matter for guessing; but Frank always had ideas and was never afraid to take chances. *I've never taken a chance in my goddamn life. I've got to do something now. I've got to do something. Christ, just from an hour's conversation I've got the feeling that something is going to happen that can turn everything around for me.* He'll bring me in when the time comes, if it's at all possible, Philip thought, because he considers himself strong and me weak, and the strong always trust their counterparts, because what harm can a weak man do them? Yes, Frank believed he was strong. He does, Philip thought enviously. Whether he's right or wrong about it, he's got that assurance, and so he'll bring me in because he needs my weakness. *God almighty, sometimes the weak man's only strength is that he's adept at appearing helpless, achieving that way what little acceptance is available to him.* But all right, Philip thought. Let it be. At least I know myself, which puts a limit to the mistakes I can make. One adjusts.

TWELVE

No matter how strongly he believed he felt about his political opinions, through discretion Philip never discussed them with his co-workers, in or out of the plant. The prevailing political climate in Capstone was not congenial for radical activism. During the lunch break at the plant, he sat on a packing crate and ate his sandwich, on the fringe of a group of men who were presided over by one of the assistant foremen, Ed Slater. It was true that there was grumbling discontent about the union, the shop steward, and certain of the plant's practices, but none of it had anything to do with politics, with the system, the country, the world; this was simply traditional employee muttering against that benign and faceless oppressor that regulated their lives for forty hours a week and supported their modestly circumscribed dreams; and even when the grumbling went beyond immediate surroundings it was seldom more than mild commentary about the duplicity of elected officials and the alleged largess and favoritism enjoyed by blacks and other minority groups.

Ed Slater had many of the characteristics of the self-consciously patriotic man, in that more than loving his country, he opposed or despised anyone or anything that did not. While some of the criticism he leveled toward his country, its people and its institutions was occasionally more abrasive than that of the despised critics, he nevertheless considered himself sturdy and loyal without compromise as far as his country was concerned. He had fought and shed his blood in Korea, taking a shrapnel wound in the shoulder, a wound which bothered him every time it rained, he claimed; so Ed Slater's thoughts about Communism and his hatred of it were renewed as frequently (at least) as rain. Given the quality of his combat experiences, however, and the almost lifelong exposure to an environment of intransigent anti-

Communism, Slater's obsessive hatred of something he understood very little about could hardly be called irrational; in fact it
was quite reasonable, almost logical. So his hatred was pure, justi-
fied, and self-righteous, differing little from the passion he expended rooting against certain football teams and against all
Negro prize fighters.

Frequently, when a darker sullenness toward the world over-
came him, he would sit in his kitchen and rail against the radicals,
using as sounding board a wife who passed to and fro between
table and sink and cabinets nodding her head and barely listening
to him, who, if pressed, would be found to be in general agreement with her husband's politics but who thought the whole thing
boring and without interest. Because he had been shot at, and
hit, by Communists (or at least by soldiers who were called that),
Slater felt he had a more perceptive understanding of them, or
anyway was entitled to have. He understood that Communists
were behind the student riots, the massive introduction of drugs
into society, the vilification of the police, the belligerence of the
blacks, and most other social disturbances. There could be no
other explanation for it. That returning young veterans of the
war in Vietnam (even those with decorations) were less reverent
of flag and country than he and his elders had been was further
reason for distress and perplexity; and that few, if any, of these
younger veterans put on their uniforms and marched with their
predecessors in Memorial Day parades was still further cause for
resentment.

The most prominent radical in Capstone was Charlotte Breitman. Slater's brooding enmity toward her was threefold: she
was a "Communist," she was wealthy, she was a woman; and therefore he was once outraged and twice baffled, all in the same
thought. Compounding this was what he regarded as her snobbery.
He had known her for many years and yet not once did she ever
say hello to him. She moved about the neighborhood with a cool,
self-assured aloofness, cordial to many, friendly with few. And yet
he knew about her. A letter carrier reported the names of the magazines she subscribed to, while neighbors told of the "degenerate"
radicals who congregated there for meetings. And less secret, of
course (if any of it was secret), was the local electioneering she
often did for her fringe candidates who ran on tickets with such

suspect words as "Labor" and "Progressive" on their mastheads, as well as the protesting letters she wrote to the columns of the highly conservative local paper. It was bad enough for such a person to be a Communist, Slater felt, but to be so open and flagrant and unashamed of it only made it worse, less comprehensible and more unforgivable.

There were other things that disturbed Slater. While most of his friends shared his opinion of Communism, few seemed to take its menace as seriously as he. It was not that Slater was a complete fanatic on the subject—he could go for weeks without once mentioning it—but when he did begin talking about it he became more vehement and voluble than his friends would have preferred. They found the subject totally alien and extrinsic to their days and ways and not worth more than a few minutes' discussion; but no matter how skillfully they tried to steer the conversation into more comfortable areas, Slater would inevitably direct it back. And then when finally even he had exhausted the subject, and the barroom talk drifted to matters more mundane, he would sit in morose silence, sometimes nodding knowingly to himself, a terse grimace on his lips, filled with a peculiar, frustrating tension.

When the war in Southeast Asia began to expand and reach deeper and deeper into the lives and hearts of America, some of his friends, amused by Slater's obsession, asked him if he was ready to go again and fight the Communists. He sat on a bar stool, his mouth half open, staring at them with shrewd, humorless eyes. "If they call me," he said, "I'll go in a minute." The banter went no further, as normally it might have, because they all knew how seriously he felt about this, and he was a big man, with the most enormous hands any of them had ever seen, and had an almost uncountable amount of brothers and cousins and uncles living in Capstone, most of them notorious for their brawling. This was a definite loss to much Saturday night raillery—this having someone with an obsession so vulnerable to barroom humor who had to be handled with such prudence.

And then sometimes that plain, pure hatred was of itself insufficient. Simply hating, and seeing nothing changing because of it (what he wanted or expected to change, he wasn't quite sure) gave the virile hatred a sense of impotence and his self-

righteousness could become unendurable. It wasn't just Charlotte;
it could be the sight of a bearded or long-haired youth on the
streets of Capstone which was enough to set him off. "None of
them had better come in here," he said in the bar one night. "They
had just better not." It was getting to be more than Communism,
more than Charlotte Breitman—it was a whole generation and a
different world, pushing forward arrogantly and unsummoned,
with infuriating impunity; even here in Capstone which, in spite
of its being part of metropolitan New York, had always been insular and immune, nurturing its habits, its folklore, conscious of
the thin fiber of traceable history which reached back to the early
seventeenth century and Dutch farmers and Mespatche Indians;
still a community of third- and fourth-generation families, having
long ago won its battle against high-rise buildings and housing
projects and hence still smugly all white. And if Slater sometimes
felt as if his community was being assaulted from without and
eroded from within by something sinister and mysterious, then
there was still Charlotte Breitman, a tangible incarnation of the
worst of it; her physical presence in front of him, a breathing,
blood-bearing human being; living in his neighborhood like an unashamed agent of the night.

He began the telephone calls more to placate his own rage than
to harass or intimidate Charlotte.

"We're gonna get you, you fucken Communist bitch," he muttered one evening into his kitchen telephone, even as his wife and
children were sitting in front of the television set in the living
room.

"Who is this?" Charlotte demanded archly.

"The vengeance boys. The patriots."

"You sound like a psychotic."

He chuckled grimly.

"If you don't stop this," she said, "I'm going to call the police."

"They don't protect Commies," he whispered.

"But they do take care of lunatics."

"Go back to Russia," he said.

"I was never there. I was born here."

"Then act like it."

Suddenly her voice became earnest, reasonable. "If I could meet you and explain to you just exactly what . . ." she said, and then heard the phone go dead in her ear.

She was not frightened, however, and he sensed it. In fact, he soon found himself appalled by the fusillades of crisply enunciated obscenities spoken into his ear. It was language he would never have tolerated from his wife, even in jest, and which he hated to hear from any woman. He felt she was challenging him.

One Sunday afternoon Slater walked past her house and saw her just entering in the company of a man he knew slightly, Frank Dublin. Passing so close to her, unsuspected, knowing the sound of her voice intimately in his ear, gave him a feeling of smugness, as though he were an invisible power. But at the same time he felt a deep rankling, and this time it was personally rather than politically directed: He suddenly realized he hated her, as if she had somehow mocked and belittled his manhood. He realized that the telephone calls had achieved nothing, neither in intimidating her nor in palliating him.

So he returned that night, late, and from the middle of the street hurled a rock through one of the upstairs windows, listening with great satisfaction to the glass shattering on the quiet night. Then he hurried away. He went directly to a public phone and called her.

"Clear out, Commie," he said.

"Fuck you, Nazi," she said, her voice even, suppressing both her rage and her fear.

"What you got tonight was just a warning. Next time we're gonna burn you out. We don't want your kind around here," Slater whispered, lowering his voice not only to conceal it but also because he knew that a whispering voice carried much more menace over the telephone.

"Buzz off you scumbag," she said, and clamped down the receiver.

After she had told the police about the telephone calls, and about the rock (they came to the house that night and saw for themselves the rock lying so incongruously on the carpeting amid the broken glass, untouched by Charlotte, who had been afraid to go near it, as though it might detonate), and then after some strenuous efforts by her lawyers, she was able to obtain the permit for the gun. The rock, the broken window, had finally shaken her and now she felt threatened. The Dominican maid gave notice and left, and Charlotte was living alone. So she bought the revolver and every day for a week drove to the shooting range on Long Island and learned to handle the weapon. She felt very proud when the instructor walked toward her, looking at her ripped and punctured target sheet, staring at it as if reading it, and said, "Very good shooting, Miss Breitman."

THIRTEEN

Dropping in on Charlotte one afternoon, Frank was surprised to find Paul sitting with her in the living room.

"Guess who I induced in for an afternoon cocktail?" Charlotte said with obvious satisfaction.

"Paul," he said, making her feel foolish. "This calls for a celebration," he said going to the chilled martini shaker and pouring himself a drink. "It should be a festive occasion when the Dublin brothers get together under the same roof these days. My compliments to you in getting it done," he said, toasting Charlotte with a raised glass.

"I hardly have to offer *you* any inducements," she said in a mildly reproachful tone. She turned to Paul—she was sitting on a hassock in the middle of the room, he was slouched in a cavernous stuffed chair, legs crossed, holding a drink—and said, "He's here so often I'm beginning to be concerned about a scandal."

"The real scandal," Frank said, "has been my inability to create a scandal."

"I thought he was interested in your mind," Paul said.

"I think it's my money," she said, chiding on a subject that annoyed Frank. Paul glanced at him with a faint, ironic smile.

"She's got a guilty conscience about it," Frank said.

"Not a guilty conscience," she said, "only a nervous awareness —and then only when you're around, grubbing meals and depleting my wine cellar."

"Well," Paul said, "how can you hope to identify with the workers if you don't feel a little bit exploited yourself?"

"I can identify with them as a human being," she said humorlessly.

"From a safe distance, you mean," Paul said. "As Lenin said, one peasant with fire in his heart is worth a thousand wealthy sympathizers."

"Lenin said that?" Charlotte asked, frowning.

"If I say he did, he did," Paul said, gently mocking the deference she always paid to his "observations."

Frank lowered himself to the floor and sat cross-legged on the rug. It was an oppressively hot August afternoon, a day of terrific immobility, the inert blazing air drenched with humidity. The patio doors were thrown open, the room was stifling.

Frank sipped his drink and stared across at his brother, watching with keenly inquiring eyes the barely perceptible changes of expression occurring in Paul's face, feeling as though he were observing the vexed reflections of constantly shifting consciousness levels, a grappling with sudden darkening and disquiet. Paul's eyes were narrowing for a moment, as if peering into some sinister maze; then lowering, as if in displeasure with what he had seen; then rising and peering alertly around, as if trying to catch up with the conversation. Frank felt a futile, helpless compassion. Then he looked at Charlotte. She was sitting in profile to him, facing Paul, holding her drink in both hands, her legs crossed at the ankles. She was wearing a white blouse and close-fitting shorts that showed off her legs, which he now studied with a languid, incurious gaze. Good legs, he thought idly. A well-toned body. From marching in all those demonstrations. A marvelous supplement, he thought sardonically, for a lifetime of tennis and swimming and skiing and gentle nights of feathery untroubled sleep.

"What have you been up to, Frank?" Charlotte asked.

"Not one hell of a lot."

"No?" she asked, shaking her head, contriving puzzled surprise. "He's been promising to do great things," she said to Paul, a suggestion of derision in her voice. It was a tone she never affected when she was alone with Frank. But it was familiar enough; she often derided him when the three of them were together, ever since they were children; it was as if through some inverted logic she thought she could impress Paul this way.

The brothers exchanged glances.

"He probably will, some day," Paul said.

"We have his promise," Charlotte said.

Frank sipped his drink. She smiled at him.

"Stop sulking, Frank," she said.

"Why?"

"You're making the day hotter."

"Why don't you turn on the air conditioning?"

"She wants to suffer with the proletariat," Paul said.

"The proletariat have air conditioning today," Frank said.

"Then less proletariat they."

Frank turned to Charlotte. "Have you talked him into joining the Movement?" he asked.

"I haven't tried," Charlotte said. "But there *is* something we've been discussing. Maybe you have more influence with him than I."

"More than you?" Frank said with mischievous innocence.

She ignored it. "I've been trying to get him to do some writing for us," she said.

"And?"

"He won't."

"Did you offer him money?"

"Of course."

"He turned down *money?*" Frank said with exaggerated surprise. "My God, Charlotte, can it be the Revolution has begun and we don't know about it?"

"Not *everybody* is a pig about money, Frank," she said.

"What kind of writing?"

"Expositions of our programs, things like that."

"He doesn't write fiction," Frank said.

"Oh! Listen to the cynic," she said. "What is drearier than a cynic on a hot day?" She undid the top button of her blouse, then sighed. "Paul," she said, "if you come and do the work here, I'll supply all the materials, get you whatever you require. It would be child's play for you . . . just take our outlines and ideas and spin them into decent prose. Too many good ideas are lost for want of style. You don't have to commit yourself to anything, your name would never be used. Look upon it as a job."

"Like dropping napalm," Frank said.

"These are important papers," Charlotte said.

"Words," Frank said disdainfully.

"Oh yes," Charlotte said derisively. "You're the man of action. But, Frank, when? I'm becoming skeptical."

"It isn't in you, Charlotte," Paul said dryly.

She laughed, looking fondly at him.

"Look," Frank said, "if you need something written, you ought to go to someone whose heart is bleeding for the Revolution."

"Ideology and talent don't always go together," she said.

"Then that's your problem. Leave him out of it."

"Frank, I don't understand your attitude."

"Then try to understand his," he said staring at his brother, who was staring back at him with mild, contemplative interest. "He's brooding," Frank said. "He's out of things at the moment . . . detached. Can't you see he's got . . . big problems . . . an Easter Island landscape inside his head."

"Frank—" Charlotte said heatedly.

"Until he breaks out of it," Frank said, "he's no good to anyone, least of all himself. Pardon me, Paul," he said. "But I'm exercising some of the repugnant prerogatives of the older brother . . . to be arrogant and presumptuous and compassionate all at the same time. Stop staring at me like that . . . what the hell are you, a goddamn catatonic or something? You do too much of that. What do you see when you stare like that? Shit, Paul, you act as if it were your fault."

"My fault?" Paul said.

"About Janine," Frank said bluntly.

"Frank, stop it," Charlotte said.

"Janine," Frank said.

Paul's eyes remained fixed upon him, filled with cool, curious study.

"It was *her* idea to go to Scotland," Frank said. "It was *her* idea to climb. It was *her* mistake that made her fall. You wrote me all that in a letter. Don't you remember? You're walking around with a face on you as if you once taught ethics to Judas Iscariot."

"Judas Iscariot?" Paul said.

"You're carrying on as if you threw her off or something."

"Frank, that's despicable," Charlotte said angrily.

"Well," Frank said, his voice indicating regret for his impulsiveness, but unwilling to backtrack, "he's got to break out of it," he said quietly, annoyed with himself.

Paul put his unfinished drink on the table next to him, then stood up.

"I'll think about what you said, Frank," he said mildly. "Charlotte, thanks for the drink." They watched him walk out to the patio and leave.

Frank sidled a morose look at Charlotte's glaring face, then lowered his eyes. Still sitting cross-legged on the floor, he picked idly at the rug.

"Frank," she said severely, her voice poised for the beginning of a stern and angry denunciation.

"I don't want to hear it," he said.

"That was the most cruel, most detestable thing I've ever heard. How could you possibly say such a thing to him? It was heartless . . . monstrous . . . his worst *enemy* would never talk to him like that."

"I know. His worst enemy would tell him he's in fine health and let him go on as he is. Well, I think it might do him some good. Maybe a little shock therapy is what he needs."

"You're making a dangerous assumption."

"We've been pampering him too long."

"You virtually accused him of murder."

"Good," Frank said sullenly. "Let him deny it to himself. He's got to begin *some*where."

"So with all your other talents, you're a psychotherapist too," she said sarcastically.

"Damn right," he muttered.

"Damn wrong. I think you've done more harm than good. Typical of you."

He sighed.

"I can't think of a single constructive thing you've ever done in your life," she said. "Not one. I *can* think of much wonderful talk and promise. All talk and no action. Anything for the sake of making a scene, dominating a moment . . . even to the extent of lacerating your own brother."

"You think I enjoyed it?"

"I don't know what you enjoy and what you don't. I really can't begin to understand you."

She stood up now. With her foot she moved the hassock toward the chair Paul had recently occupied.

"I'm going upstairs for a shower," she said.

He watched her go. Then he got up and, carrying his drink with him, sat in Paul's chair and stretched his legs out and rested them on the hassock.

He finished his drink and threw the glass onto the sofa across the room. Then he sat still, utterly immobilized with dejection and irritation, the suspended mean-souled heat dulling him into a terrible stupefying monotony. And then he felt stirring a subtle, pernicious fear, reminiscent of a feeling he had had in California, the idea of his own futility and meagerness, a meadow of dreams bleached white by the glare of reality; a long and delusive corridor of expectations, waiting for . . . what? *If I met somebody like me, what would I think of him?* If some kindly old thaumaturge appeared and promised to materialize his, Frank's, fondest dream before his eyes, Frank would not have known what to expect. *"Your fondest dream, Frank."* Which one? *"Your dearest wish."* Let me think a moment. *"What you have always wanted."* I think I know. *"What you've been waiting for."* What I've been . . . *"The thing you've been promising yourself would happen."* Promising myself?

The heat felt like an imponderable, eternal presence, circumscribing him with an infinitely capacious, profoundly watchful stillness. He closed his eyes, found himself confronting stacks of old, time-squandering self-deluding ideas and dreams, saw his face a caricature superimposed upon the noblest portraits of history . . . saw his life as the lengthening ash of a burning stick.

Brooding, filled with a menacing self-deprecation, he got up and walked through the living room into the hallway. He stood at the foot of the stairs; he could hear the soft constant roar of the shower. He rested his arm on the edge of the banister and stared with malicious contemplation up the carpeted stairs to the arched entrance to the second floor hall. Goddamn rich bitch, he thought. Sitting in exquisite superiority, hurling a few insults, making her inane judgments, then going upstairs to wash it all away with perfumed soap *leaving me down here in my stinking perspiration like a goddamn lackey.* Going upstairs now, his hand riding lightly along the polished banister, his feet sinking silently into the yielding carpet that descended the stairs like a marcelled waterfall, his eyes fixed with that same malicious contemplation, abetted now by a murky half-smile.

Her room was at the head of the stairs. The door was open.

He paused in the doorway, gazing around with ironically amused eyes at the thick baby-pink carpeting, the huge double bed with its lush blue organdy spread reaching to the floor, the vanity with its huge oak-framed oval mirror and crowd of perfumes and atomizers and jarred creams, the long aristocratic white draperies pinioned back from the sun-bright windows, the portable television set on the night table: what a wonderful, unassailable place to dream of revolution, he thought mordantly; a veritable silken loom of fantasy.

The bathroom door was open, he heard the water storming in the stall. He walked into the bathroom. The blouse and shorts she had been wearing were on the floor. He saw her white body in the stall, blurred and distorted by the frosted door. She was singing quietly. *Furious, insulting one moment; singing the next. Probably thinks Lenin did gallopades and polkas all day in that rolling boxcar. If Paul told her she would believe it.* He lifted his sweat-stinking polo shirt and pulled it up over his head and dropped it to the floor. He kicked off his loafers as he unbuckled his trousers and let them slide down his legs. He stepped out of them and pushed them away with his stockinged foot. Then he opened the stall door. She was soaping her breasts, her back to the driving needles of water, a ludicrous flowered shower cap pulled tight over her hair and covering her ears. She saw him standing there and her eyes dilated.

"Frank!" she shrieked, incensed and shocked both: for being seen naked, for seeing him standing there in nothing but his shorts, a foolish smirk on his face. She dropped the soap and covered her small finely shaped breasts and, obeying the instincts of ancient driven modesty, clamped her knees together as if to make disappear from view her enormous tangle of black pubic hair, the abundance of which caught his eye and fixed it with such intensity she half turned from him.

"What are you doing?" she shouted, her face contorting as the swift needles of water beat against her cheek. "Go away! Close that door!"

He reached in and took hold of her arm and dragged her out, pulled her dripping body against him and forced a kiss. She struggled against his embracing arm, grimacing.

"Let go of me!" she said angrily, trying to twist away.

He backed her against the tiled wall and pressed himself upon her, forcing another kiss as he thrust his erection up against her.

"Stop it . . . stop it . . ." she said, gasping, pushing at him with all her slight strength.

"Why?" he shouted above the roar of the water.

"Have you gone crazy?" she yelled.

Suddenly he scooped her up in his arms and carried her into the bedroom and threw her onto the bed, darkening the organdy spread with splashes of water. She tried to get up, he pulled her back by the arm but she broke free again and got to her feet on the other side of the bed and stood there panting, glaring at him.

"You're slippery," he said, laughing. "That goddamned soap . . ."

"Get out!" she cried. Water was still dripping from her shower cap, running down her shoulders and across her breasts and stomach. Her body was lightly tanned, except for those narrow white patches where her bikini covered. "Get out of here, Frank," she said.

"Uh-uh," he said, shaking his head.

"What's wrong with you?"

He pulled back the top of his shorts.

"Don't you dare," she said.

He snapped the elastic band back against his stomach, watching her with a teasing grin. Then he walked around the bed toward her.

"You . . . keep away," she said sternly, crossing her wrists over her breasts. She tried to get back across the bed but he caught her arm and they wrestled over the bed, her legs kicking out helplessly as he pinned her. He brought her arms together over her head and held them down by the wrists with one hand, with his other pulling the shower cap from her head, freeing a tumble of blond hair. She glared icily at him.

"Frank," she said through gritted teeth, "get out of here. I'm warning you . . . this is . . ."

"Despicable," he said, and kissed her, flattening himself over her, freeing her arms which began struggling against him, trying to lift him off. He kissed her lips and throat and breasts, then laughed and said, "You've got soapy tits."

"Get off of me," she said. "Let me up."

"No."

"What are you going to do?"

"What do you think?"

"I don't want you to."

"Why not?"

"Do I need a goddamned reason?" she said furiously. "Get *off* of me, you stupid son of a bitch."

"Make believe it's Paul," he said.

"Frank—"

"Just a brother away."

She closed her eyes and turned her head aside.

"This is as close as you'll ever get to him," he said.

"Stop it."

"I'm his proxy."

"He would never do this."

"And so he wouldn't."

He was moving back from her now, still over her but sliding back on his knees. She thought he was going away, her eyes remained closed. She felt his hands on her knees, then around and under them, and then suddenly felt his fingers tighten and herself being lifted with a jolt, her legs being parted wide in the air, exposing her totally and gracelessly.

"Stop that!" she shouted, trying to get up but unable to, forced back by her own weight. "What are you doing? Frank . . . this is . . ."

Holding her like that, her legs up and suspended, his strong hands tightly around her knees, he lowered his head and hunched his shoulders and pushed his face forward into her mass of pubic hair, his extended tongue searching through the sharp wiry tufts for her clitoris.

"Frank . . . oh . . . oh . . ."

The water was still storming in the open stall, a loud, constant roar, rushing with mindless ferocity.

He poked his tongue around until the sudden stiffening tension of her body told him he had struck his goal. With the perspiration running in rivulets down his face, with his neck muscles aching from the taut cramped discomfort of his position, he looped and curled and flapped his tongue, poking and massaging and caressing the small hard-rubber bud of flesh that was sending electric sensations streaking through her body. She lay still, now and then emitting a gasp, her hands doubled into unmoving suspenseful fists. He had slowly brought down her legs and she was lying spread, her knees drawn up. He continued, his tongue suave and knowledgeable and indefatigable, until after a few minutes he heard her begin to moan and felt her body begin to rock as though she were attempting some huge and impossible digestion; and then she bucked so hard she bumped him back for a moment, but he pressed in again, each sweep of his tongue making her buffet and gasp. Then he pulled down his shorts and mounted her and drove himself up into her, impaling her squirming body, a flash of thought noting her surprising tightness. Within minutes he began feeling in himself the pent, building rush of release.

"Whatever possessed you," she said later, her voice slack, weary.

"The frustration of long postponement—the same kind of energy that moves mobs of people to action."

"I always looked upon you as sort of a brother." She was sitting on the edge of the bed, her head bowed in solitary introspection. He was sprawled at his ease, staring at her back.

"That was the problem," he said. "Next time it needn't present itself."

"There will be no next time." There was a firm note in her flat, drained voice.

"No?" he asked.

"No, Frank," she said, shaking her head.

"Then you'll be going through life knowing what you're missing."

The shower was still running, with tireless, imbecile fidelity, its long constancy giving it a distant, remote sound now.

"If ever you allude to this," she said quietly, "or even smirk in such a way that I know you're thinking of it, I'll never speak to you again."

"I won't tell Paul, if that's what you mean."

She turned around to him, her hair sliding off her shoulder.

"It isn't Paul," she said angrily. "It's *me*. Me."

"I don't understand that at all."

"I don't give a good goddamn what you understand or don't."

"Up the Revolution," he said wearily.

FOURTEEN

When he left Charlotte, Frank headed straight for Paul's house, though most reluctantly, impelled by an irritating sense of obligation. He was bothered on two counts: at the idea that he might have hurt his brother, and, if so, the necessity of having to explain himself.

Charlotte had remained withdrawn and reticent; there had been more melancholy and introspection than resentment. That aspect of the aftermath disturbed him more than any other—that her response had been "soft" instead of harsh, wrathful; it had been so quietly contemplative, so painfully revealing, that finally he had been embarrassed (though not at all contrite). He was persuaded from her behavior that there was very little sex in her life. With every woman he had ever known, an orgasm was pure pleasure and total abandonment; with Charlotte it had been like an influx of disconcerting information; she had borne her pleasure with an excess of tension and inhibition.

He found Paul in the living room. The house was extremely hot.

"You should buy an air conditioner," Frank said.

"The wiring won't take it," Paul said. He was standing over the desk, examining some sheets of paper. He had showered since coming home, his moist black hair carefully combed, and he had changed his clothes, wearing now a pair of khaki chinos and a tight-fitting T-shirt that showed off his trimly muscled upper torso, which had the tautness of a lightweight fighter's.

Frank stood self-consciously in the middle of the room, studying his brother's back.

"Listen, Paul . . ." he said.

Paul turned around, his frown indicating he had not fully detached himself from what he was reading; there was a tentative, intellectual "hold" in his expression.

"I want to apologize for what I said," Frank said.

"Oh, that's all right," Paul said mildly. "I understood. She was picking at you. It was directed more at her."

"It was a nasty thing to have said."

"To anyone but a brother."

Frank sat down.

"Christ," he said, "why does she bug me like that when we're all together?"

Paul lifted his hands to his face and rubbed his eyes for a moment.

"Why?" he asked, lowering his hands. "Because you seemed to take it well when we were kids. She hasn't matured to the extent that you have."

"Me matured? Thanks."

"I wasn't being facetious. A person as sensitive as you are shouldn't be too close to people with whom you've always concealed yourself. She never really understood you, and now the misjudgment becomes tiresome."

"Maybe I can change her attitude," Frank said, his mind uncovering for a moment what had occurred after Paul left.

"I doubt it. She's still in many ways very childish, and her perceptions suffer accordingly."

"She can still grow up."

"There's no compelling reason for her to," Paul said.

"Knowing that ought to give me some advantage."

"A great advantage, if you don't mind being driven to distraction. Anyway, I don't think you can talk her into anything; she's already talked herself into wanting everything she has. She's closed."

"Any woman can be talked into anything."

"Men who generalize about women ought to be equipped with shock absorbers."

Frank grinned. "My epigrammatic brother."

"She'll never marry you. You must know that."

"I'm not so sure."

"Because she was married once? You're misreading that. She wanted an unhappy marriage, to convince herself never to have a happy one."

"She would marry you."

"Do you know why?"

"Because you don't want her. Is that it? Am I catching on?"

"Frank, I think you ought to begin concentrating on what *you* want, what's right and best for you."

Frank made a despairing gesture.

"What about your revolution?" Paul asked.

"Personally or politically?" Frank asked banteringly.

"Are they separable?"

Frank shrugged.

"Christ, it's hot," he said, sighing. Then, "I don't know what the hell I want."

"That's the attitude of the true revolutionary."

"You can make fun of it; nevertheless, it's going to happen, with or without my participation or your dispensation."

Frank got up and wandered around the room. He paused at the desk and looked down at the papers lying on it.

"Since when are you writing poetry?" he asked.

Paul hestitated, then said, "It's Janine's." He turned the pages over and covered them with his hand. "I'm . . . putting together a collection."

"Is that what you're working on these days?"

"Mostly."

Paul stood absolutely still, his hand covering the pages, a peculiar tenseness in his face.

"Okay," Frank murmured, looking from his brother's face to the protective hand, then up again. "Will you be finished soon?"

"I don't know," Paul said.

FIFTEEN

He would face up to it, Frank thought the next morning. There was no question but that he was going to have to. Apologizing, superficially a direct and uncomplicated piece of business, was now drawn forward in his mind as a difficult and nettlesome necessity. While his apology would not be genuinely impelled nor sincerely proffered, still it would be more discretion than hypocrisy, because he was not really sorry for what he had done—not if sorrow was measured by regrets and the wish to undo. He did not think it had been so terribly wrong, since it had occurred spontaneously, out of exasperation, and been in some way provoked (he did not fully understand this latter explanation, but he believed it). But one thing was certain now: she would never again take him for granted; gone forever was that obstructive "brother" image, the idea that together they could plan the destruction of social systems, calculate the slaughter of millions— and not go to bed together. It would be an edifying lesson for her to realize, he thought, that powerful aggressive impulses had a real life and a real force and were not imbedded exclusively in abstract theory.

But still it put him in a rather sour whimsy that morning. He reported to his landlady at breakfast that he had burned a small hole in his pillow case. "Do you forgive me, Mrs. Van Dyke?" he asked. "Forgive you?" she asked. "Do you forgive me?" he asked again. She shrugged. "I forgive you," she said. After breakfast, sitting on the porch, he rose from the rocking chair he was occupying when one of the old men appeared. "I was in your rocker, Mr. Gray," he said. "Do you forgive me?" "It doesn't matter," Mr. Gray said. "But do you forgive me?" Frank persisted. "All right, all right," the old man said crankily, taking possession of the chair. Later, he encountered the landlady in the hall and said,

"The eggs were slightly overdone, Mrs. Van Dyke, but I forgive you." She gave him a rather dubious look. "You playing some kind of game this morning, Mr. Dublin?" "If I was, would you forgive me? And if I'm not, then I forgive you for asking." She paused to take his measure with her eyes, then said, "My late husband had a phrase." She paused again, this time for effect, then said, " 'Shove it.' "

I beg your pardon. I apologize. Do you forgive me. It was not really his style, he thought as he walked toward her house. Generally he did not reappear at the scene of his infringements. But this time there was no choice. He had to go there and apologize. Even though he knew she had enjoyed it. But I had better not even *think* that, he told himself. Walking past the old Methodist church, he glanced at it and thought, "How about you? Do *you* forgive me?"

As he approached her house he felt not diffidence but an odd, quirky self-confidence. He understood why: if he had attempted the seduction and not completed it, if she had been successful in resisting him, or in convincing him to stop it, it would be different now; he would feel like a fool. It was as if in a matter such as this a total and unremitting outrage was somehow less heinous than a partial and inept one. But he had been far from inept, and he *knew* she had been more participant than resister, even though she would never admit it, not to him, not to herself. He knew enough about women to be able to read them in those situations; they were infinitely more revealing than they thought, filled with unwitting candor. Coming right back the next morning like this was the best thing he could do, for if he stayed away it would imply embarrassment or contrition, neither of which had come close to making the slightest pressure on the furthest rim of his conscience. This morning she was ripe to be influenced by what he thought and did. Sometime yesterday, after he had gone, probably at night, alone in the dark, in sleep, in dream, the pleasure of it, the furious excitement, would have been evoked; some incontrovertible, malicious avowal of it had been made, in the honesty of solitude, with her conscience appeased somewhat by the fact of her resistance, insincere and ineffectual though it had been.

She stiffened perceptibly when she opened the door and saw him.

"I would like to talk to you," he said.

"No doubt," she said, her voice flat, dull.

"May I come in?"

She paused, staring at him with appraisal and caution. Standing in the doorway, hesitant, her attitude was telling him this: I really don't want to and I shouldn't, but if I do allow you in it means I'm placing a trust and if you violate it a second time it will be unforgivable.

She stepped aside as he entered, then closed the door after him.

He walked into the living room and stood, deliberately not sitting, as if to show he presumed nothing.

"I want to apologize," he said.

She sank into a chair, slouched, crossing her arms. She gave him a petulant look, then turned away.

"Oh, Frank, goddamn it," she said.

"I lost my head," he said. "I suppose, in a perverse way—if you want to look at it like that—it was in the shape of a compliment, though I must admit a very distorted shape. I couldn't help myself. I could say it was the heat, frustration, victimizing you out of my own despair . . . but it was more basic than that. I simply wanted you."

"Oh shit," she muttered, as though she had wanted to hear something else, something more answerable.

"After so many years . . ."

"That was never the nature of our relationship," she said.

"Which was always assumed, never defined."

"Oh shit," she muttered again, shaking her head as if experiencing insufferable woe. "Sit down," she said grudgingly.

He sat on the sofa, opposite her, but not making himself comfortable, consciously marking his prudence.

"I want to know if you accept my goddamn apology," he said.

She sighed, shutting her eyes for a moment. "Yes, I accept your goddamn apology." She sighed again, hugging herself with her crossed arms, like a person with a chill. "I had a sleepless night," she said. Her hair was uncombed, her face plain. She was wearing a free-hanging blouse, unpressed slacks.

"Well," he said, "that's behind you now."

"Is it?" she asked, giving him a look of dreary skepticism.

"We have other things to think about."

"Such as?"

"The Movement."

She threw her head back and stared at the ceiling. "The Movement," she said almost facetiously, as if putting a name to some charming, antic thing.

"My contacts haven't surfaced yet in New York. I would like you to put me in touch with some of the people you know."

"Yes, Frank," she said apathetically, still gazing at the ceiling.

"I think an exchange of information might prove useful."

"Very."

"That is, if you still want to work together."

She laughed mirthlessly. Her head came down and she studied him with an odd twist of smile. It disconcerted him.

"Which ones would you like to meet—the men or the women?"

He stared at her for a moment. Then he stood up.

"All right, Charlotte," he said. "Call me some time, when you're happy with the way the sun comes up."

He turned to leave, but, moving with a feline suddenness that startled him, she was quickly at him, stopping him with a strong, furious embrace.

"Oh, you," she said, scowling at him. "With your goddamn apology. Oh, that's a help. You fucken son of a bitch." Then, using all her strength, she threw him back down on the sofa and a moment later he felt her hair flood over his face as she pressed a tenacious, almost hateful kiss upon his mouth, then sank her teeth into his underlip until it bled. Then she thrust her hand swiftly and painfully into his groin and squeezed what she felt until with a twist of his body he freed himself.

"You knew what you were doing, you lousy bastard," she whispered bitterly. "Do you know what I thought about last night?— that you were the sweet child who once threw a stone into the wasp nest, just to stir them up, to see what would happen. Do you remember that? You were ever the one, weren't you?" she said, baring her teeth in what could have been either a grimace or a malevolent smile. Again her hand sought his groin, gently this time, probing, then massaging through his trousers with slow, circular movements. Then she undid his belt and pulled down his zipper, watching his face with a look of mischievous stealth. For the first time he responded, raising his arms and embracing her, pulling her tightly against him, kissing her with a force she tried to match, crooking his arm around her neck and locking her to him. Softly they rolled over and tumbled to the floor. Now his trousers were collapsed around his knees and with a laugh of triumphant savagery she pulled them free. He rolled away from her and when he came up his hand went to her blouse and with a single swipe divested her of it, shredding it from the throat to the waist, exposing her breasts. She leaped upon him and sank her teeth into his thigh so deeply that he had consciously to suppress an outcry of pain; then she tugged at his shorts, trying to rip them off but unable to. "Can't do it, huh?" he said, laughing. "I'll do it," she said tersely, and sat over him on her knees and with both hands took hold of the elastic band and tore the shorts from him, scowling at his bright, wide grin. Then he sent his hand up into her hair, took hold of it in his fist and roughly pulled her down against him, rolled her onto her back and straddled her with his knees. She was panting, glaring at him as though appalled by the ferment of her own frenzied pleasure. "Don't tear them," she said as his fingers fumbled with the buttons of her slacks. He didn't. He opened the buttons as she lay back, her eyes closed, her open mouth panting. She swung about to help him as he slid her slacks free. Then she said, her eyes still closed, her voice quiet, tense: "*Yesterday . . . yesterday . . .*"

But he startled her by lifting her and then dropping her roughly onto the sofa. Then, again roughly, with his strong uncompromising hands, he opened wide her legs, draping one over the back of the sofa and pushing the other to the floor until she was spread absolutely obscenely. Then he crouched and buried his face for the second time in two days in that enormous tangle of pubic growth as she began a series of soft panting moans and her hands doubled into fists and froze in mid-air and remained poised that way until it was over.

And then she bounded to her feet, with surprising alacrity, considering the terrific buffeting she had in release given herself. He swung out for her wrist but missed. With a taunting in her face, she backed away, lithe and soundless on the thick carpeting. "Come on now," he said, irascible, the perspiration glistening over him. "Don't play games," he said, still kneeling on the sofa, his heat, his anxiety bringing a meanness to his eyes. "Fuck yourself," she said with a sneer, backing away. "Really?" he said with quiet, almost cordial menace, rising from the sofa. "Really?" As he started toward her she suddenly turned and ran upstairs, looking back over her naked shoulder at him with a wild frenetic grin. Cursing, he went after her, taking the steps two at a time, watching her soft soundless white body disappear into the bedroom.

He chased after her into the bedroom and then stopped dead in his tracks with such suddenness he looked like a man prepared to wrestle, his back and shoulders rounded into a half crouch, his open hands extended. She was standing in the middle of the room, the revolver in one hand, with her other brushing the disheveled blond hair away from her eyes. Her lips were tightly clenched, as if trying to smother a grim little smile.

"You bastard," she said. "Keep away. You lousy bastard. I want to kill you . . . I want to kill myself. You don't know what's going through my mind at this moment."

He stared at the gun, then at her, a tense, uncertain half smile on his lips; then his eyes returned again to the gun; he had never before had one pointed at him, and it looked more deadly, more lethal, more frightening than he could ever have imagined: an absolutely insane and diabolic-looking thing, at once irresistible and eternally incongruous, barbarically blunt in its evocation of fear and awe, disfiguring its possessor like some ungodly additament to the human anatomy.

She spread the fingers of her free hand across her mouth and through them muttered, "Oh my God . . ." She was panting.

"What the hell do you think you're doing?" he asked.

"I want to kill myself," she said.

"Then you're pointing that thing the wrong way."

"I want to kill you too."

"Why?"

"Why?" she said, and followed with a bitter, despairing laugh.

"You're getting melodramatic now."

"You don't know how serious I am, do you?" she said. "You're wondering."

He gazed inquiringly into her eyes, and then, with less inquiry and more contemplation, at the gun, its short ugly barrel. In his time he had been cut with a knife, battered by fists, struck with a club; there were things he could imagine, anticipate, things he knew . . . but not the roar of a gun or the impact of a bullet or the swift darkening of death.

"Don't fuck around, Charlotte," he said on the intake of a short, sharp breath. "That thing is dangerous."

"Brilliant comment on the obvious," she said. She began to laugh foolishly, her shoulders shaking. "What the hell is going on here?" she asked, moving her head from side to side as if being overwhelmed by something totally incomprehensible. Then she turned away and with a petulant gesture threw the gun across the room.

So great had been his tension, that the moment the threat had been removed he sprang toward her, took hold of the hand that had held the gun and with an outpouring of relief as turbulent as any passion with his other hand slapped her sharply across the face, her head jerking aside with a flail of hair.

"Don't ever do that again!" he shouted, raising his hand again but, seeing her face still held aside, her eyes closed, her contorting features expectant of another blow, he desisted. He pushed her down on the bed. Now an expression at once glittering and defiant filled her eyes. Impulsively she thrust her hand between his legs. "Give that to me," she said.

Indiscriminate sex was considered counterrevolutionary, because it dissipated needed energies. She had read that somewhere. She remembered being impressed by the assertion, by the ascetic quality of the idea. Such willful self-denial implied a profound seriousness of purpose, of commitment. But now, challenged not intellectually but sensuously, she no longer was certain of the validity of the idea. Still, she insisted to herself, she did not believe in self-indulgence. Nevertheless, the whole question now called for sober reconsideration. Perhaps it was the shock of what had initially happened. She had been raped. Some women, supposedly, nurtured that secret desire. But she didn't want to think that of herself, she wanted to think that her reaction was more normal, natural, that something had been awakened rather than disturbed. Someone with warped and abnormal desires could hardly be trusted to be lucid and responsible in more important

matters. And there were more important matters (she was careful to remember that and lecture herself on it), things she had always believed in, had been dedicating her life to. She told herself,
too, that it was equally abnormal to abstain from sex, particularly
when there was no compelling reason to. To cramp a natural want
could be as harmful as overly indulging it. And anyway (telling
herself this sternly, emphatically) one of the things she was striving for to make a better world was this very freedom of expression,
in every way; to unshackle people from old taboos and inhibitions,
and not just economic and political and social but sexual as
well. It was all part of the same thing. And again she told herself:
It's an awakening, not a disturbance.

He had never known a woman to be as humorless about sex
as she. She made love with grim sobriety; it was as though instead
of seeking pleasure or release, she was trying to burn out her
tensions. There was always a fierce, almost bitter impersonality
about it. Even after, when they both were spent, during these
most slack and lax moments that people could share, she maintained a hard, proud imperiousness, like a vanquished person re-
fusing to acknowledge conquest.

There seemed always to be calculation behind it, hardly any
spontaneity, as though she thought of nothing else, letting it seed
constantly in her mind. "Tomorrow at my house, at noon," she
would say, then watch him to gauge his reaction, as if trying to
gain from him some insight into her own thinking about this thing
which had begun to roil obsessively back and forth through her
mind. And when he arrived at the appointed hour this might
occur: be told to twist her arm behind her and march her upstairs as though forcing her, and then follow her instructions for
undressing her: only her slacks and underpants, not her blouse,
not her shoes either. He complied; he never questioned. He knew
it was only the beginning for her, that it had just begun to mani-
fest itself, and that in one sense he was a most privileged partner.
If there was going to be tenderness, a sharing, it would have to
come in its own way, in its own time.

He never knew, when he came to her house, whether it would
be an evening of sober discussion or a long night of erotic sex in
some unexpected corner—the finished basement, a guest room,

the now unoccupied maid's room: it was as if she were out to initiate every room in the house, purge it of its pure and sterile air. He never knew if he would be leaving with teeth marks sunk savagely into his shoulder and his back raked from her fingernails, or with his head sodden from determined talk about revolution. Sometimes he found her in a mood of solitary, placid sadness, her unmoored thoughts impossible to track. And the portents of these moods were maddeningly unpredictable. One night she placed on the phonograph a stack of recordings of the wartime speeches of one of her heroes, Winston Churchill. For more than an hour they sat and listened to the strong cadences and heroic rhetoric of the indomitable leader; and then, unexpectedly, Charlotte, on the floor was languidly opening the buttons of her slacks, gesturing Frank toward her, and with the great Prime Minister almost as disembodied spectator, as auditor of the scene, they made love, long and interminably that night, with Frank being almost compelled to memorize twenty minutes of dogged and resolute exhortation to embattled Britons as the last record played over and over on the automatic changer.

"If my husband had had some of your fire," she told him one night, "I might still be married, in spite of his archaic notions." Her husband had been in bed cold, efficient, selfish. He had never treated her as a "woman." She had, she told Frank, suspected her husband of having affairs. "But it didn't really bother me," she said. "I thought I would be mature about it." She could have lived with it if only he had treated her the same way she believed he did his mistresses. "How did you know how he treated his mistresses?" Frank asked. "I knew," she said. "I could imagine it, because I knew he had his sordid side, and that was where it came out—with them. He said I was the immature one, but it was really him," she said with, he thought he detected, an inflection of callous satisfaction.

Well, he thought, at least she's begun to talk a little. That was a beginning, a good sign. But she's asking too much, he thought: to have everything while at the same time not wanting it; more than she can have and more than what's good for her. She wants to make up for lost time, wants to prove something to herself and to her husband who isn't even here any more and probably wouldn't care a damn even if he were. She had gone into it with maelstrom suddenness, blinded by the manifestation, and would probably come out the same way, not by degrees. She couldn't stop herself at this point and wouldn't even if she knew how; and anyway would not want to until she'd had enough—whatever enough was: enough in time or fulfillment or vindication or in deferment of what was really driving her, or whatever constituted that vague margin which demarcated the end of something. So far nothing significant had been accomplished between them. The sex seemed in and of itself, an outlet at once exclusive and controlled, with before and after remaining the same as always, like a tunnel with the same daylight and scenery at either end of the dark. There was no direction, unless going nowhere was considered directional; not a straight line but a circle, around and again upon the same track. He still had not spent a full night with her. Sometimes it would be as late as five o'clock in the morning that she asked him to leave, when he would pull on his clothing and walk through the empty streets of imperturbable and impervious Capstone back to his furnished room.

He understood, and accepted, that it was she and not he who was dominant in this, because it meant more, in more important ways, to her than to him; that he was being held fixed and at bay, driven back each time instead of being drawn closer; because it was more than just sex, it was an outrush of pent fury and passion, a wanton slaughtering of denial and inhibition; and that it would continue that way until whatever inner struggle she was enduring had been settled.

And then she told more, and he realized that a great part of the whole thing was the need to talk, to tell, that the frantic unbridled anomalies were needed to give release to the choked heart-locked words yearning to be spoken.

"I was never this uninhibited with my husband," she said. "Maybe it was him, maybe it was me—the way I was then. Maybe I was too young for him. Everyone said so. I didn't think so. But maybe it was true." Maybe this, maybe that, he thought sourly. Maybe it was because he wasn't me and I'm not him. "Perhaps I didn't love him," she said sadly, with dead romantic inertia. "I don't know. I really don't. And I guess I never will. The person I was then is a total stranger to me today. But he loved me. Of that I am absolutely convinced."

But if the manifestation widened it was still controlled. The talk was still monologues, abetted by his silence. He understood the function of his presence at these times: it was similiar to his role in their love-making, a necessary, mechanical service. But he thought this much: She doesn't know it yet, but it has to be me, and only me. I'm the only goddamned one. It's me or nobody.

Nevertheless, it could finally go either way, he realized. She could one day suddenly decide she wanted and needed him forever, finally mastered by her own desire; or just as suddenly she might feel he had penetrated to some unforgivable depth of vulnerability and tell him with hatred and rancor that she never wanted to see him again. More than the not knowing, he resented the fact that it would be she who decided, and that it would be final and unappealable. One night he heard the sound of that depth. After several hours of bizarre and erotic love-making in her bedroom, she suddenly sat up from an exhausted respite, raised herself to one elbow and looked accusingly at him.

"We've been indulging ourselves," she said, her voice hard, cold. "This is decadent and utterly irresponsible." He had been waiting for something, he wasn't quite sure what, except that some reaction, some upcast from the plunge was inevitable. Doubtless she felt it incumbent upon her to say this, and he listened impassively, without trying to explain how conventional and unexceptional what they were doing was, since she knew that for herself anyway and was at the moment interested only in recrimination and not rationale.

In a voice at once melodramatic and emotionless: "I know I've been undergoing a personal revolution of sorts. I know exactly what it means, why it's happening. I understand myself, and that's always the first order of business. But that doesn't justify neglecting everything else. And that's what we've been doing. It's wrong, Frank, terribly wrong." It was as if she were feeling not just the threatening implication of what she described as self-indulgence, but also the frustrating and despairing years of denial, haunted by the ruin and rot of unused time, now so brutally driven home by insatiety. But he didn't want to analyze it, because there was a thousand times more complex self-indulgence in this manner of reproach than there was in sex. Whatever was at storm in her would pass. It would be senseless and without profit to attempt to grapple with every shift of mood; nor did the moods seem to be setting themselves for challenge or rebuttal, only to be allowed their outbursts and then to be outlasted.

"When was the last time either of us did anything constructive?" she asked. "I'm corrupting you. Maybe you're corrupting me. How long ago was it—mere days—that we were talking and planning with such enthusiasm and purpose? What's happened since then? We've been naked, feasting on one another's bodies—on one another's flesh, like vultures. We have to redefine our purposes."

Those purposes were redefined (or further defined) the next day, when after the tearful and passionate parting of the night before, she called him and told him to hurry to the house. At the door she took his hand and led him to the attic where she had spread a half-dozen sofa cushions on the floor and, once again to stirring Churchillian oratory (the phonograph, the records, carried to the attic by her that morning), asked him to do—as she put it with inexplicable coyness—what he had done that first time, as if it had been unnamed and unknown since then. She would have quit after her first flush of ecstasy, but he kept her there, pinned on the cushions for hours and hours through the long hot afternoon, giving her (and himself) not only the pleasure of ecstasy over and over but also that of fighting and begging for her release, for the surcease she ostensibly struggled for but refused to categorically demand, and again his osmosed mind memorizing twenty minutes of imperial English as the last record played and played, as indefatigable as the embattled Prime Minister himself.

The one thing he waited for and never heard, or saw or felt either (wasn't it a thing for all senses?), was love. It did not seem kindred to anything. He had not really expected it, he was only aware that it was missing, and missed. She should have come around to it by now, if she was going to at all, even if only in its most spurious and debased form. He would have liked to have seen something of it, even though of the few temporary alleviations for the ills of man and mankind love was the frailest, the least dependable, the medicine man's concoction, the paralogist's tale, the beginner's fancy, the fool's extravagance, the dreamer's meditation. It was a commendable objective and a scenic way station, and at the same time a spacious dream which could empty in a moment. To search for it was a journey of conceit, exposing one to the baser mischief and malice of others, causing a vulnerability that was almost fatally sensitive.

It went on, dogged and self-contained, in a frenzied thrashing toward its own exhaustion. She was still capable of suddenly crossing the room toward him and placing her hands tensely on his face and staring with clear cold gaze into his now somewhat defensive, fatalistic eyes, simply staring until a slow smile of wise pride moved her lips and her hands slid down his face and then in a slow stimulative caress of his body and he knew she had found another reason, another resource, to continue for another day at least.

The talk continued, that slow constant draining of old turbulence which was as much a part of it as anything else, and without the sex, the crushing of barriers, she could not tell him what she felt so imperative to tell. The talk, the revelations, the confessions seemed to need this kind of ambience, as if the air had first to be steamed and debased before the constraints could be overcome, the forum of quiet and darkness established. "I was in a summer camp in the Adirondacks," she said. And she told, with great feeling and nostalgia, the tale of her seduction at seventeen by an older man; all of it, from the first contact to the end, the consummation, and the pride and the tears. And then, with even more feeling, with wistful perplexity, that for two years after she would not let a man touch her, that she had been "unnerved" by the thought of sex (and then quickly amended it, determined to utter the serrated truth: "No, revolted. I was revolted by it."). This time there was apprehension in her voice, the ambivalence of guiltful pleasure, as if she had caught a glimpse of her destination and did not like what she saw, and was suddenly fearful now of the journey back, that it would be a passage through a landscape scorched and disfigured beyond recognition, and perhaps even a hopeless transit. Impassively he listened to the despairing note in her voice, helpless to reassure or divert it, his head rolled aside on the pillow, gazing at the window, beyond which the stilled breath of summer lay in warm fecund suspension. He who had gone so roisterously through his years now felt an ineffable sadness as he listened to the parched and parsimonious spending of her youth. A dead father, an unwell mother, a dedication to ideals, business affairs to manage, an unhappy marriage: though none of it an attempt to vindicate, simply the poignant recitation of a functioning but joyless life. He wanted to tell her that she was not yet even thirty, but there was no point; she was not looking for that. He simply stared out at the ripe, yielding summer night and listened to her roam through tracts of time laid waste, a tour through an arid heartland of the soul. He listened to her current abundance permeating now that pained and mournful emptiness like so many immiscible chemicals. And then she confirmed for him the pain by reaching out in the dark and taking his hand in hers, and the evocative pain crossed the night like slow gray lightning.

It was Ed Slater who finally broke the spell, the fantasy. He had not called for more than a week, and now, at three o'clock in the morning the telephone suddenly erupted like something that had been maliciously concealed, calculating time and advantage. She released Frank's hand and picked up the receiver and said hello and then listened for several seconds, her face contorting with anger, and then began shouting a stream of profanity, her voice rising until it thinned and broke with tremulous sobbing. Frank pulled the receiver from her hand and just as he brought it to his ear heard it go dead.

"That—that—" she said, pointing to the receiver which he still held, her voice still broken, "is what we should be using our energies for . . . to fight that son of a bitch and what he represents: ignorance and prejudice and . . . and . . . fascism . . . and . . ."

She told him he had to stop (not they, he). They were draining themselves, she said, achieving nothing, while people like the caller continued rampant and unopposed in the world.

"What do you mean, 'stop'?" he asked.

"I mean a reordering of priorities."

"You said 'stop.' "

"No, Frank, I didn't mean that—not the way you think." She embraced him, resting her head on his chest, and he could feel trembling in her the myriad fears and uncertainties, the desire and the revulsion, all of it implacably melded.

"Just because some son of a bitch makes a phone call—"

"But don't you see, he represents all that's evil and corrupt."

"There's nothing evil or corrupt going on here," he said resentfully.

"No no no no no, I didn't mean that. It's that we're doing nothing to fight it. Don't you see? Here—it's come right into the bedroom and we're not doing anything about it. So I curse him, and so he hangs up—but meanwhile he's still out there, spreading his poison. Darling, don't you see—we've got to subordinate ourselves and get back to work. You're magnificent, you're wonderful—but what good is anything if we abdicate our responsibilities and leave everything to *him?*"

"Christ almighty," he said in exasperation, "don't you think he gets laid too? Does that stop him? What does getting laid have to do with it?"

"You don't understand. Damn you," she said harshly, "you don't understand. What have we accomplished since this started? You've become selfish. You don't give a damn any more. What happened to all the fire you had when you came home? It's gone. You started this and now you won't leave me alone. You've . . . taken advantage. Everything has changed and I won't allow it to happen."

"Then what does happen?" he asked.

She moved away from him, settling herself on the other side of the bed.

"Please go home, Frank," she said.

SIXTEEN

A few evenings later, at the northwest corner of Eighth Street and Fifth Avenue in Greenwich Village, a slovenly and rather obese girl with her hair braided into pigtails handed Frank a mimeographed piece of paper from the sheaf she was holding.

"Won't you please come?" she said as he accepted the paper and walked on.

He crossed the street, stepped onto the curb and paused to read what he had been handed. The leaflet urged attendance at a discussion being held that night, sponsored by an organization he had never heard of, a "Concerned Citizens" committee, featuring a panel of several academics and a writer, who were all unknown to Frank but who seemed important to the sponsors of the discussion, since the bottom of the page was covered with a hailstorm of exclamation points.

He decided he would attend. He was feeling an ennui, a bit seedy, drained, with a malaise too unfocused even to be cynical. The night before he had sat up late with his father, drinking. The old man was becoming increasingly introspective, taciturn, pallid. Occasionally he looked at Frank and smiled compassionately— or was it pityingly? Frank had drunk heavily, but Ben had gone light, as though wary of the whisky. *Doesn't want to spill anything about that money,* Frank thought moodily. *He's got a cat's instinct for what I'm thinking.*

He had wakened that morning in a state of extreme depression. There was the unabating heat, the disinterested stillness of the furnished room, the stale whisky souring his mouth, the infuriating capriciousness of Charlotte Breitman, the thought of his languishing father, and the impacting idea of his own futility and abasement. *After the summer things will get started,* he told himself, and immediately recognized the tone, the evasion, the

old ingenuous deferment, so thin and unsubstantial that it always
floated right through perception. But this time he was stung by the
attempted deception, the stalling, the emptiness. He felt a sharp
and compelling self-disgust and responded with a fullness of determination to do something, not impetuous or precipitous, not
to suppress or placate the disgust, but to resist it, eradicate it,
extirpate and abolish it altogether. Deciding only to stay away
from Charlotte for a while, he had no plan, nothing but the determined, acutely motivated passion to lash out at stagnation.

He recognized the fact that nothing would happen in Capstone.
Capstone induced a sedation of fantasy and procrastination, a eu-
phoria of momentous expectation; it was a comforting place to
do nothing and to contemplate the fulfillment of that occupation.

So he took the bus and then the subway and sat impatiently
during the long ride to West Fourth Street, then climbed from
the subway into a melting, tentative urban twilight.

The discussion was held in a small arena theater which at the
moment was housing no theatrical production. The seats were arranged on three sides of the stage, with accommodation for about
one hundred, and were nearly two-thirds filled when the doors
were shut at eight o'clock. The seating arrangement gave Frank
the opportunity to study the people around him. True to the
locale of the gathering, it was a decidedly heterogeneous assemblage, from middle-aged couples with expressions of dignified expectation, to youths whose freshly grown beards seemed to be
imposing premature solemnity upon their faces, to other youths
anxious to demonstrate their rebellion by slumping contemptuously in their chairs (whether standing or sitting, this boneless
posture seemed a prerequisite for the young radical, as though
it were an act of social decompression). There was a prominent
absence of blacks, although the Afro hair style was in evidence,
blown up over the heads of several white youths. As his eyes
roamed through the audience, Frank noted a pale youthful face
staring at him from the other side of the stage. Frank's gaze became immobilized for a moment as the youth smiled enigmatically
at him, then he continued his restive probe of the faces around
him. Each time his eyes picked out the youth he found himself
the subject of passive inquiry and once a discreet nod of the head

that was like the affirmation of a conspiracy, and Frank, annoyed, soon stopped sending his gaze in that direction.

The lighted stage was set with four chairs, and a bridge table with a water pitcher and tray of glasses on it. A few minutes after eight o'clock a muscular young bearded man wearing T-shirt and jeans and sandals stepped from the wings. He hung his thumbs in his belt and welcomed everyone to what he described as a "significant discussion of the central issues," noted that there was no air conditioning (a fact already abundantly evident) and begged everyone's sufferance, saying that the money which would have paid for that comfort was instead being channeled into "the Movement's war chest," and that if there was discomfort then they were getting "a taste of the ghetto here," and at least there were no rats. His peroration was "All power to the people," at which a man sitting behind Frank muttered, "I wish the people would go to the power and turn on the goddamn air conditioner." Many in the audience were fanning themselves with folded copies of their mimeographed invitations.

Then the four chairs were occupied by men who walked from the wings. Two were heroically wearing suits and ties, the others less formally attired. The discussion began, and fell into an instant rut of general accord. The only discernible differences among the panel on the stated theme, "The Permutation of a Corrupt Society," lay in the vehemence of attack on that society, the passion of their voices. They seemed to take the measure of one another early in the discussion and some tried to dominate with aggressiveness or belligerence, while others sought their points with understatement. There were frequent bursts of applause from the audience, while an occasional temperate or medial remark prompted a cry of "Bullshit."

Frank listened with steadily diminishing interest. The theater was becoming oppressively hot, people were leaving in ones and twos. The audience was then invited to join in the discussion and as a woman stood up to tell of her recent experience at the hands of a youthful mugger, how in retrospect her heart had filled with compassion for the "desperate ghetto child" who had stolen her purse and broken her arm, Frank got up and left. He walked out of the theater and found that even the menacing heat of August was more tolerable than the sweltering inside of the theater.

The summer night streets were a choked and knotted kaleido-
scope of so many grotesqueries that one soon stopped noticing
them. There seemed to have been an inundating immigration of
the bizarre, an endless arrival of the lost, the curious, the eccentric, the desperately singular; only the flat-roofed old tenements
gave a rendering of stability and belonging, frowning forward
upon the streets of the melting and remelting pot. More than any
part of the city, this section reflected the year of the century and
the tone of the year. It was a constant evolution of the old Bo-
hemianism which had spawned a myth long since expropriated
and debased: transitions did not smoothly blend, change was
abrupt and abrasive and forever unsynthesized; it was an unnum-
bered Dantean circle, an unsorted mélange of tourists and students and addicts and the heirs of Villon, and odd people with
odd flourishes, mobbed together in a constantly modifying atmosphere where fads were traditions and traditions inflated into
legends: the great American bazaar, a Marrakech and Casbah available to anyone with a subway token: all of it observed and guarded
and no doubt despised by the policemen posted on every corner.

After walking several blocks, Frank realized he was being followed. He had noted that the youth who had been staring at him
in the theater rose and left when he did, but Frank was unaware
of being followed until he turned to snarl back at a belligerent
panhandler and saw the youth sauntering some ten yards behind,
staring at him. Frank cursed softly under his breath and continued
walking. He had been made to feel self-conscious and he resented
it, as he resented the disjunction of thought it caused. (One of
the more lamentable defects of urban life seemed to be this very
inability to enjoy a leisurely exploration of one's mind, to con-
join ideas and speculations and conclusions, to conspire with oneself in undisturbed freedom and privacy; there was an unremitting
ambience of sound, odor, presence, interruption; an almost malevolent encroachment upon the sanctity and symmetry of intellect and sensorium.)

Frank wandered into the park, passing the chess players sitting
at their concrete tables in sculpted concentration, and followed a
path until he found an empty bench. He sat down, swung one leg
over the other and extended his arms possessively along the top of
the backrest. Frowning, with sullen curiosity, he watched the

youth come drifting toward him out of the night. The gradually
materializing wraith was wearing a blue workshirt open at the
throat, blue jeans, ankle-high leather boots. He was slender, beard-
less, short-haired, and moved with uncanny lightness. As he neared
Frank he seemed to dramatize his approach, taking very deliberate,
overly long steps, his hands so intently poised in his back pockets
he looked as though he might be preparing to draw six-guns.

Just what I need, Frank thought dismally. In a big city, where
it was easy to be lonely but virtually impossible to be alone, solitude was too often interpreted as an invitation.

The youth sat down on the edge of the bench, hunched slightly
forward and regarded Frank with a faint, impudent smile.

"Dull discussion, wasn't it?" he said.

"Uh-huh," Frank said, watching him with patent disinterest.

"I'm glad you thought so."

"What do you care what I think?"

"What you think could be important."

"To you?"

"Naturally." The faint, impudent smile widened by degrees,
became teasing, mischievous.

"I appreciate your interest," Frank said, "but I'm not interested
in your appreciation."

"That would be too bad, if it were so."

"It is precisely so."

"Which do you think is more important—thinking that your
ideas are important, or thinking that thinking they are? Someone
has said that living by the idea of an idea is . . ."

"Look," Frank said impatiently, "I don't know who the hell
you are and furthermore don't want to."

"But you already do . . . Frank."

Frank received the sound of his name from the lips of this antic
stranger with a jolt. Making no attempt to conceal his surprise, he
uncrossed his legs, brought his arms down and half turned on the
bench and gave the youth a frank, scrutinizing appraisal. The
youth laughed for a moment, then lifted one hand and covered his
face to the eyes. He knew exactly what he was doing: thus isolated, his eyes possessed a burning singularity, and in them Frank
immediately recognized the compelling intensity of Arthur Seavery,
and he was as surprised as he would have been had the eyes in a

portrait winked at him. Seeing himself recognized, Seavery brought
his hand down, uncovering at the same time a mirthless, cheek-
dimpling smile.

"Well, I'll be goddamned," Frank said softly.

"With luck, maybe," Seavery said.

"What are you doing here?"

"How are you, Frank?"

"Man, you've changed."

"Have I?"

"Your beard . . . I didn't know you at all . . . and you've
trimmed your hair." Frank laughed, as at some charming incongruity.

"Ingenious disguise, isn't it?" Seavery said. "Simply reassume
your original appearance and people no longer recognize you.
Would you care to philosophize on that? But you look the same,
Frank. A few degrees more desperate, perhaps . . ." Seavery said,
a mocking in his eyes. "But you don't know how happy I was to
see you in that theater."

"I wouldn't have known you in a hundred years."

"That's very good."

"But what are you doing in New York?" Frank asked.

"A right-up-to-date answer would be that I'm sitting on a bench
talking to you," Seavery said.

Frank had thought of him from time to time since returning
from California. Occasionally he wondered if it might not have
been better to stay on the west coast, with Seavery, until he had
become more conversant with underground radical activity; but
the thought of an ill father, a possible twenty-five thousand dollars, and the irresistible idea of announcing his political meta-
morphosis to Charlotte, had weighed in favor of his return. Sometimes, when regretting his decision, he was inclined to dismiss
Seavery as simply another vessel of empty rhetoric; but inevitably
the rationalization failed and Seavery persisted in his mind with
sinister impact and persuasion. And occasionally Frank found
himself envious of the youth's zealous and determined commitment to an idea, a doctrine; he saw in this that most paradoxical
and inexplicable, that most desirous, thing—an affirmation of purpose and meaning in one's life, the melodrama and extremism
notwithstanding.

"How long have you been in town?" Frank asked.

"Not long."

"Are you planning to stay?"

"For the time being. And what have you been doing?"

"Oh . . . nothing, yet. I'm still feeling my way into things."

"A man of action with his prudent side," Seavery said. "That's good, Frank."

Hearing himself so described pleased Frank. He felt some of the tension which had been evoked by the excitement of the chance meeting begin to abate, along with the subconscious idea that he was subordinate to Seavery.

"I've been thinking things out alone," Frank said.

"With so many fools on the premises, that's a good idea. The best people are working that way today, or else in very small groups."

"I remember your saying that."

"And what've you come up with?" Seavery asked. He was sitting back calmly, his slender arms comfortably folded, his head inclined slightly to a side, watching Frank with cool, scholarly curiosity. His total repose made Frank look indecisive.

"Nothing I want to talk about yet," Frank said, hoping to sound evasive rather than empty. Then, "But listen, why the trim?" he asked, smiling at Seavery's short, neatly combed and parted hair.

"There hasn't been an ideological conversion, Frank—if that's what you think. And anyway, there's less ideology in long hair than is generally supposed: anything that can be trimmed in a few minutes represents very little to begin with. But tell me what else you've been up to. Not preaching any more, are you? I thought not. I was wishing you'd stand up back there and inject some life into that group of brand-name revolutionaries. Radical meetings should be held in total darkness, don't you think? Just the sound of voices . . . secret . . . ominous . . . think how powerful that would be. In any event, I'm glad to see you again, Frank. I've thought about you a lot. In fact, only the other night I was telling some colleagues about you."

"You were?"

"I described you as a man of raw energy and pure dedication. Don't think there are that many, Frank. Those who subordinate their security to their convictions are rare today. The debate has become too delicious . . . the words emptily militant . . . the threats absolutely apocalyptic . . . and consequently the Movement has come to a standstill. We are so media-obsessed in this country, that too many of our people think they've attained their zenith simply by being interviewed on television or in national magazines . . . screaming their irreverence and their obscenities at a basically conservative and prudish people they know shock so easily . . . and this has become . . . satisfying, fulfilling. Our system here has the faculty of inducing its radicals to masturbate in public arenas."

"Instead of screwing it in private, eh?" Frank said.

"You see things clearly, Frank. Listen, you'd have been interested in a story that was in the papers soon after you left Los Angeles. There was a petty dispute on a bus, between the driver and three chicanos. The driver made some sort of slurring remark, and do you know what happened?—the chicanos knifed him . . . killed him . . . while the bus was running. It went roaring off the road into a used car lot, crushing a few cars . . . the chicanos got away . . . but that isn't important. Do you remember the three chicanos you pounded in the diner that night?"

"They were the same ones?" Frank asked.

"I don't know," Seavery said. "But I prefer to think so. In fact, I've convinced myself that they were, because it's important. I thought of you . . . 'Frank gets the credit for this,' I told myself."

"Credit?" Frank asked puzzledly.

"Of course," Seavery said with suave insistence, staring intently at Frank. "Didn't you show them something? What did you do when they came after us? You didn't stand there and quote Gandhi to them, did you? You simply belted them to the floor . . . you showed them the way it was . . . you put *rage* into them . . . showed them what to do when the next person humiliated them."

As though responding to an inspirational remark, Frank suddenly launched into a discourse on violence. It was man's final, emancipating answer . . . man's most positive and eloquent response to injustice. He rushed his words, like an actor too late out of the wings. Never mind an objective interpretation of a man's mind, he said; examine what he does, what he does in the world of men and not in the quiet, doubtful solitude of his mind.

Seavery listened with whimsical interest, his hands on his knees, his feet drawn back under the bench and balanced on his toes, his eyes narrowed with cool cynicism as if watching the wretched approach of an apathetic fate.

One and two at a time, a small knot of men taking casual summer night walks through the park had stopped to listen, as people were wont to do in this most abundantly informal of neighborhoods. Noting them from the corner of his eye, Frank went on with his impassioned discourse, his tongue and his yearning spirit both unleashed by the attention of strangers: only iron and fire, he said, could rescind the oppressive laws and overthrow the despotic edifices that made poverty and helplessness synonymous . . . wealth was equivalent to tyranny . . . it was the absolute sacred obligation of people to root out and gouge and destroy and rebuild in the name of their own dignity.

Seavery sat mute, watching him with a now sardonic fixity of gaze, a vague crease of smile in the corners of his mouth.

When he was through, Frank looked around at the knot of silent, staring men; their faces were thoughtful, impassive; they seemed not at all embarrassed at being found absorbing what was ostensibly a private conversation, for after all, this was Washington Square Park, in the heart of Greenwich Village, and if a man did not want to be audited, then he should go elsewhere. Frank pretended surprise at their attentiveness and lapsed into unrepentant silence. The audience drifted on, wordless from start to finish.

Watching them go, Frank felt a terrific exhilaration which he had to struggle against to keep from displaying itself.

"It's so easy to draw a crowd," Seavery murmured.

SEVENTEEN

"There is no greater satisfaction than indifference to being understood or interpreted, because those things lead to an idealization of self, to smugness, to constraints, to impotence. The most satisfying liberty lies in not being accountable. And the only meaningful use of this unlimited latitude lies in doing things that are outrageous and atrociously blunt, that are important and unforgivable and mystifying to the masses, and, most crucial of all—to wage war against injustice."

The speaker, a young man named Breenstone, sat stiffly upright on the edge of a low sofa that had cottony bulges blossoming through its burst upholstery. As he spoke, Breenstone occasionally emphasized certain words by pounding his right fist into his left palm, a device he had observed in a political science lecturer at Stanford who appeared to be stamping an imprimatur upon his own words. Now he folded his hands between his spread knees and leaned forward, a look of bright, skeptical anticipation in his face. A perceptive person just entering the room might have noted from this attentive posture and expression that here was a young man waiting to rebut an argument yet to be presented. He had wild curly blond hair, darker eyebrows that intensified the natural gravity of his gaze, thick lips that hung open over large irregular teeth when he was not speaking, and a frail specimen of blond goatee like that of a mandarin elder.

"I think you're making a serious mistake," Meyer said. He was sitting across the room, on a sheet-covered mattress, his back to the wall. He was a stocky, muscular youth, though there was a certain cultivated quality to his perfectly proportioned biceps rather than the adamant, arduous evocation of masculine power. He had thick black hair which was worn fashionably long and looked brushed, and a black drooping mustache that gave him a rather stagy Latin appearance. The abbreviated sleeves of his T-shirt were rolled to the points of his shoulders, in the manner of men vain about their arms, and his short thick thighs emerged from a pair of cut-down jeans. "If we blow up something," he said, "I think people ought to know why, and they ought to know by whom—not specifically, of course—but where we are in the political spectrum. Otherwise the action degenerates into an emptily symbolic gesture."

"Symbolic?" Breenstone asked skeptically.

"Certainly. I believe in violence—but not reasonless violence. Otherwise why don't we just go out into the street and arbitrarily machine-gun people?"

"You're missing the point entirely," Breenstone said. His long thin fingers—the sort that people always associated, wrongly, with the hands of concert pianists—groomed his delicate goatee for a moment. "Machine-gunning people in the street—and I don't advocate it by any means, though who is to say it won't come to that some day—is precisely in the *spirit* of what we ought to do. I don't *want* to be interpreted or understood; we should *not* appear to be rationally motivated. *Seemingly* senseless acts are far more effective, since what we want to demonstrate is the criminal insanity of this society. Look, we've already tried to present rational programs . . . we've tried demonstrations . . . non-violent protests . . . and accomplished nothing more than a dissipation of energy and a waste of time."

"I know that," Meyer said impatiently. "Please don't lecture me. *I'm* the one who got the explosives, goddammit. Look, for Christ's sake, I dropped out of law school in order . . ."

"Everyone has made personal sacrifices," Breenstone said curtly.

"Well, I'm as opposed to individualism as you are," Meyer said defensively. "Nevertheless, if we don't give a name to what we're doing, then someone else will. There has to be *meaning* to it."

"Dynamite is not honored by a philosophy; the force of dynamite is vitiated by a philosophy," Breenstone said calmly, his thick lips closing firmly for a moment, in pedagogic conclusion. Then he went on: "We have to create a state of terror—terror unbalances a government, making it freeze or else act impetuously. The Establishment is afraid more than anything else of losing its power—and the fact is beginning to seep into their thick heads

that they *are* losing it. The more this idea permeates them the
more paranoid and panicky and psychotic they're going to become
in their attempts to hold on to what they have. And the more
senseless the attack against them appears, the more they're going
to suspect and oppress and persecute *everybody*—from students
to housewives to clergymen to anybody who simply asks an impertinent question. The most irresistible power on earth is an
invisible, ubiquitous moral force."

Frank was sitting on a folding chair, an intent spectator, weighing the words of each man with studious impartiality. He could
not help several doubtful observations: Breenstone's call for reckless indiscriminate violence sounded ludicrous from one who
looked so harmless; while the intense, scholarly seriousness of
Meyer's New York accents seemed to dilute the poisonous course
he was advocating. The third youth, Temple, appeared closer to
the prototype, as did Seavery with his subtle suggestion of self-
regarding madness. Temple was sitting on the window sill, not taking an active, or at least not serious, role in the discussion. He was
in his early twenties, with shoulder-length black hair and a short
shaggy beard in which a manic smile occasionally showed, for no
apparent reason. His contributions to the discussion consisted
of abrupt, impatient interruptions: "Only when the theoreticians
follow the action is there any action." He was "bored unto catatonia" of all the talk of "significance . . . about whether it is preferable to be God or to be Moses." They were talking in a vacuum,
he insisted; until they could "orchestrate the sound of your verbi-
age" with some explosions, they were simply begging the question.

Frank wondered whether any of them—Seavery included—
really intended to detonate explosives. He had the impression that
they were like so many others—enslaved by the fear they had
evoked, urged on now by a consuming militant pride and even
more: the expectations of those they opposed. Their imaginations
fired by excessive attention from the media, they were inclined
to become impressed with themselves, allowing their boredom and
discontent to produce deceitful perspectives and harden into impulsive, Messianic creeds; consequently, at the same time that the
ascetic purity of their thoughts gave them absolution for whatever they did, so their freedom to think and act was severely constrained. People of little experience had no trouble anointing them-

selves and rationalizing their impetuosity, while the irony of it was that the passion of causes was the almost exclusive property of people of little experience, in pursuit of something the rest of mankind had long since abjured.

Seavery had invited Frank "home" to meet these "friends." It was a short walk from the park to the tenement, which was in a desolate industrial neighborhood on lower Broadway. The tenement, the only residential quarters for blocks around, was a narrow building that looked ensheathed in fire escapes; it was surrounded by massive piles of grime-covered brick buildings with blank sullen windows and towering rooftops roaming gigantically into the night. Several times during the ten-minute walk Seavery turned to observe the odd person afoot in the dark streets, watching with feral, almost melodramatic mistrust until satisfied the person had nothing to do with him. "You never know when they're following you," he said. "When who is following you?" Frank asked. "You know," Seavery said, passing Frank a most conspiratorial look. Then he laughed, a low giggly sound like a side-to-side rattle in his throat. "A few weeks ago," he said, "I was mugged on St. Mark's Place, at three in the morning. These two guys came sliding sideways out of a doorway and jumped me. At first I thought it might be the police; you don't know how relieved I was to find it was only a pair of junkies trying to make a living. They took my two dollars and left me there on the sidewalk, still a free man." He laughed again, pleased by a set of appealing ironies. "I wanted to tell them we were all brothers working together, but I don't think they would have been interested just then. And to have a sense of relief at being mugged, well, Frank, it shows you the tension we live under." "Are you wanted for something?" Frank asked. "Yes, but it's all right. I want them more than they want me, so it all evens out," Seavery said. "Anyway," he went on, "it's just as well. What good are you if they're not after you? Today's soldiers have their campaign ribbons in the corners of their eyes. Anybody in the Movement worth his salt is being sought. I'll tell you one thing: it sharpens your wits; it makes you much cannier and more subtle; it dispenses with the frivolities and makes you realize you're dealing with things of substance. One of our most serious problems, ironically, is that America is too lenient. I wish they would shoot their anarchists

in this country; if they did, it would create greater numbers of
dangerous and desperate people. The way it is now, people can
walk in and out of the Movement without the least sense of fear
or insecurity. I tell you, Frank, it's not easy pounding away at
something that's as soft as America; this country can take punishment, I'll say that for it. Have you ever been in a gymnasium? The
fighters don't harden their fists on pillows, do they? Those big
bags are like concrete. So the punishment America absorbs doesn't
toughen us up enough. Nothing else for us to do but toughen up
America, eh? Get it to a point of viciousness where, in trying to
savage us, it consumes itself." Seavery smiled at Frank, with a
certain capricious charm now. "It'll take a good bit of doing,"
Frank said. "I know," Seavery said. "I know. Nobody says it's
going to be easy. This country has a genius for curtailing the
rights of small numbers of people without infringing upon those
of the majority. Ah, America!" Seavery said with spurious, heavy-
handed affection. "If only thy virtues were as entrenched as thy
vices."

As they neared the tenement, Seavery paused while a car passed.
He stood resolutely still as he watched the car go slowly along
the old, cobbled streets into the night. "You just never know
who's who," he said. "The people you're going to meet upstairs,
they won't trust you right off. They're all paranoid by now. I'm
not that far gone yet; just ultra-cautious." He forced a laugh,
which for an instant was the only sound on the cloaked and
cowled streets, a terse, summary break in the massed and sinister
quiet. The street lights cast vast midnights of shadow over broken
sidewalks, loading platforms, stolid fronts of industrial bastions.
Seavery studied it all like a man contemplating a location for his
empire, like a man disdainfully proud at not feeling dwarfed by
the monstrous, his eyes picking through the bricks, the shadows,
the forbidding alleys between the buildings. Then he turned back
to Frank and they began walking again. "Ultra-cautious," he said.
"Got to be. Too many of us are gone now. In jail . . . in Canada
. . . and some are dead. The best ones are dead," he said in a
voice oddly distant and wistful. "So my friends are nicely paranoid
now. But they're all right. A little desperate maybe . . . after all,
the kind of thing we're into doesn't make for a long, happy life.

There ought to be actuarial tables on the longevity of true revolutionaries. That would blow a lot of chaff into the wind."

Frank followed him into the tenement, then up a flight of stairs, staring at Seavery's small, booted feet mount step after step. Rancid odors filled the hallway. The walls were cracked. The old, paneled doors were marked with big metal numbers.

There were three rooms in the apartment. It was furnished with old and infirm-looking furniture, the bursting sofa, bedless mattress, several unmatched and orphaned chairs, a decrepit drop-leaf table that looked bowed and docile, a few dispossessed lamps with cheap paper shades, and a seedy-looking India drugget that covered part of the otherwise bare wooden floor. The walls were decorated with several large posters depicting the latest revolutionary heroes and slogans. And as old as the building was, the apartment had an air of sullen impermanence, as if during the long years of its existence no one but transients had passed through its door, people with an almost palpable air of imminent departure about them.

No one shook hands with Frank. Breenstone nodded from his corner of the sofa; Meyer, sitting on the mattress, lifted his hand reticently; Temple, sitting on the window sill, with a background of encamped night, said hello and gave Frank the most searching inquiry of the three. Seavery introduced Frank as an old friend, a most dependable man, with whom he had worked in California, and whom, Seavery added with a caprice understood only by himself and Frank, had done much good work among the chicanos in Los Angeles. "He had a tremendous impact on some of them," Seavery could not resist adding, passing Frank a sly look.

In spite of Seavery's endorsement, Frank sensed his presence an inhibition in the room. Breenstone and Meyer fell pointedly silent, Breenstone fingering the wispy blond strands of his goatee and staring at the floor, Meyer tapping the tips of his fingers together contemplatively, with magisterial affectation. Seavery himself said little, cloaking himself in a watchful sardonic silence, as if he had just coldly familiarized himself with the content of every mind in the room; slouching in the kitchen doorway, arms crossed. It was Temple who broke the silence.

"Bomb," he said.

They all looked at him.

"We were discussing the action," he said to Seavery, showing for a moment his vague, manic smile.

"I've no doubt of that," Seavery said.

Frank thought he detected a caustic edge on the words.

"How was the debate, Arthur?" Meyer asked.

"There was general agreement among the speakers and the audience," Seavery said, "on the need to agree. There were people there who . . . will sign petitions on our behalf when we are arrested . . . who will contribute to our bail fund."

"Bomb," Temple said, his voice bland, almost affable.

"Have you selected your target?" Seavery asked.

"We haven't yet decided what the meaning of it should be," Meyer said. "We've got to nail that down first."

Seavery took little part in the ensuing discussion; in fact he evinced a total lack of interest as Breenstone and Meyer debated purpose and the purpose of non-purpose. He remained in the doorway, slouched, arms folded, eyes downcast; he had a look of insolent security, as if he had made some audacious proposition that he knew could end only in acceptance. Frank speculated about Seavery's status here, if there was any sort of hierarchy and where he was fixed in it. He could not imagine this youth subordinate to anyone, no matter the circumstances. There was a surly independence about him that suggested a dogmatic refusal of any idea or suggestion not originating with him, simply in order to assert and reassert his own stubborn, self-ordained privileges.

At a pause in the debate between Breenstone and Meyer, Temple said,

"Bomb."

"You keep saying that," Meyer said irritatedly.

"I don't want you to forget," Temple said, leaning forward for a moment from his window seat, as if to lay stress on something so obvious it ran the danger of being overlooked.

"He's right," Seavery said. He unfolded his arms, straightened his posture with a casual lift of his shoulders, and wandered into the middle of the room, slender, self-effacing, physically unprepossessing, but somehow dominant, projecting a certain enviable and elusive sense of inner security. He was a person who could never fully be known, holding forever fast to his enigmatic and unanswering riddle; and the greater the intimacy with him, the more inciting this fact would become.

They all watched him; Frank most expectantly, with a taste of *Exeunt all but Hamlet* in his mouth. Seavery stood, legs apart, fingertips poised just inside his back pockets, eyes gazing incuriously upon a poster on the wall depicting a clenched fist.

"We've all left groups and committees because there was nothing but talk," he said. "We got together and agreed voluminously on that point: more talk. We agreed that guerrilla warfare in urban areas was the most compelling option open to us: more talk. We agreed we would place our explosives and achieve marvelous things: more talk. We have established ourselves as the most vital force in the Movement: by talking about it."

"That's unfair, Arthur," Breenstone said, his thick lips pouting for a moment over his large, ill-matching teeth. "We're ready to move now. But we have to decide . . ."

"I know; I've been listening to you trying to decide on whether to decide," Seavery said caustically.

"Bomb," Temple said.

"The only talk that should be heard now," Seavery said, his eyes still fixed upon the poster—so raptly the others were compelled themselves to gaze at it from time to time, "is about the plan. Where to place the explosives, when, and how best to get away. What it all means should be left to other people . . . to talk about."

"A bank," Temple said.

"We've blown many banks," Seavery said wearily.

"And with good reason," Breenstone said.

"Just a minute," Temple said. "Is he in?" With a lift of his bearded chin he indicated Frank.

They all looked at the stranger.

Seavery turned from gazing upon the poster. "Frank?" he asked.

Frank had been enjoying his role as spectator, watching and listening as though he were invisible, weighing each word at the same time he had been trying to gauge and penetrate the thinking of the silent Arthur Seavery. Now they all were looking at him, and for the first time he felt himself the object of their curious, wondering speculation. He stared back at them without so much as moving a muscle, with perfect composure, casually slouched in his chair.

"Of course," he said agreeably. "I would have left long ago if I weren't."

"This man was in before any of you," Seavery said.

Frank wondered if this were simply generosity, or something more—another opportunity, perhaps, to demonstrate that intractable independence that seemed so integral to Seavery's every thought and decision. Frank doubted if any of the other three could have, under the circumstances, walked in here with a stranger and gained him virtually instant acceptance. The fact was, of course, discipline and security in American radical groups were almost non-existent. There was an inherent naïveté permeating these groups that made them susceptible to praise and flattery; any stranger who proclaimed fidelity to their cause was accepted at face value, and consequently there had been much official infiltration and betrayal. Measuring the caliber of the three men here, Frank thought he detected a certain softness at the core—a capillary instinct as opposed to a jugular—and wondered if they were capable of effecting their "action." The faintly contemptuous tone in Seavery's voice answered now Frank's prior question: the smallish, slender youth was leader here. In spite of their inflammatory rhetoric, the others, Frank felt, derived their strength from Seavery, and he thought again, as he had so many times, that if this Movement were to achieve its goals, leadership was going to have to be provided.

"We'll give the banks a rest for the time being," Seavery said.

"What then?" Temple asked.

"A newspaper."

"Which one?" Meyer asked.

Seavery mentioned a distinguished New York newspaper, a prideful organ of self-proclaimed independence and integrity, of international dissemination and unquestioned influence, of pardonable solemnity and self-esteem.

Seavery sat down at the table, raised his elbows on it, and rested his face between his hands and closed his eyes for several moments, looking as though he had drifted into prayer. But when his eyes opened they were filled with anything but piety; they contained an alert, cunning expression that compelled the others to watch him in silent deference. He brought his hands down, settled his arms on the table, and leaned forward on them.

"If you blow a bank," he said, "the papers will report it, dutifully and dispassionately—for a day or two. But an attack against the paper itself will be regarded in a different light altogether. The event will be treated like news of an invading army. They'll rage and splutter all over their front pages—for days. There is no indignation like journalistic indignation. They'll cry for action, and better still, they'll cry for sympathy. And in order to justify this draining of their tear ducts, they'll create in the minds of the people a conspiracy of a magnitude, complexity, and menace that will astound we five humble souls who sit in this roach-infested firetrap. They'll drive home a sense of terror to millions of people, as only a newspaper can. And a paper like this can pressure the government to act, and when this government acts, in all its myopic, bureaucratic mindlessness, and foolish flailing slugging energy—we begin to win. The loyalty of millions of disaffected people goes up for grabs."

After several moments of calculated silence, Seavery said,

"Now, anyone who doesn't think it's a good idea and would like to bow out . . ."

He was instantly cut off by a babble of protests against the insulting absurdity of such an insinuation . . .

EIGHTEEN

1

It began for Seavery in the full flush of Christmas benevolence, a few months before he left the university. He was conscious of a new experience, and it was with an acute, detached awareness that he climbed the grim and pitiless wooden staircase, each step of which had its own sullenly intoning sigh or groan, like moribund echoes of old, time-crushed, time-suppressed individuality. He had never been in a ghetto slum before, much less a black ghetto slum, and he could not resist this cool, objective curiosity, refined by a sense of interior—staring at the steps and the walls and up into the looming dimness of the second floor landing. The air of unrelieved misery gave him an increasing sense of the rectitude of his mission.

Nothing that he had ever heard or read about depressed and deteriorated neighborhoods had prepared him for the sullen, sometimes rancorous stares he had received, or the self-defensive alienation he felt. As only a well-intended person would think, he believed he had a perfect understanding of the experience, and that the compassion and indignation which were settled so genuinely in his heart were obvious and comprehended; certainly it made him feel much better, otherwise the sight of these somber buildings and incarcerating streets and entrapped people would have been intolerable. Despite the extrinsic hostility and suspicion, he believed he was totally understood and appreciated, that he, Arthur Seavery, was personally expressive of the white man's guilt and sorrow.

The idea to undertake collections in his dormitory to buy Christmas food packages for needy families in Boston's black ghetto had been proposed only a few days before, and almost everyone had enthusiastically subscribed to it. Some, like Seavery, had decided to forgo their holiday visits home and contribute that money to the fund. The university had obtained for them, from municipal sources, the names and addresses of people in need of this benevolence.

The holiday food basket he carried in his hand was filled with canned goods, fresh vegetables, soups, soft drinks, fruit, cheeses, nuts, a cake, and, most magnificently, a truffled turkey. It was all neatly and professionally packaged, covered with a taut sheet of cellophane, with a green and red ribbon tied to the basket's curving straw handle. As he mounted the stairs now with his largess, Seavery began to wonder what he ought to do after delivering it. What would be seemly conduct? The family would certainly be overwhelmed with gratitude, would surely offer him a drink, if not invite him to sit down with them and share the repast. Would it be proper to accept? Might not they feel self-conscious, devouring their charity in front of the person who had bestowed it? Would it be right for him to intrude upon such a memorable family occasion? Would a refusal be misconstrued? Wouldn't it be more gracious for the hand of charity to remain as ethereal as possible?

He reached the landing of the chill, unheated hall. At the head of the stairs he turned and looked back, as if to contemplate his ascent, give himself an elevated perspective on his new experience. The narrow stairs led to a small foyer thick with rancid odors, where two letter boxes had been torn out of the wall. The flooring just before the outside door was of white tile, and he could see part of it from the head of the stairs: everything was fixed in a dead, immutable tableau, the stolid interior soul of poverty and broken hope: and he Arthur Seavery was staring upon it from his solitary elevation, absorbing it and yet not, part of it and yet surely not, hoping to relieve at least some of it for a few hours anyway, holding his basket of food.

So preoccupied was he with the at once nearness and distance of his environment, he did not hear the two youths until they were on top of him. He turned at the last moment, in time to see the two black youthful faces coming at him, the youths striding in rubber-soled silence with an energy and a belligerence that were utterly unequivocal, so that he knew exactly what was intended, and later realized that he had known and prepared and braced for it even before he knew that he knew: knew that they were not going to utter a sound, not a threat or demand or curse: and he felt all of it, to the very end, before it had begun. One of the youths struck him in the face, knocking him back against the wall, while the other seized his arm and then wrenched the basket from his hand as the cellophane covering creaked. He tried to resist, but there was another blow in the face, then one in the ribs, another in the stomach which doubled him over and spun him around so he hung bent and gasping over the threatening staircase which seemed weirdly undulant now. He remembered a door opening, a streak of light like a suddenly illuminated lance, and then closing again as whoever had been drawn by the sound of the disturbance, having seen enough, chose to see no more. A blow behind the ear dropped him to his knees. Clutching himself around the middle with his arms he sank further, like the most abject of supplicants, then sagged against the wall, still too stunned and incredulous to be outraged or afraid. Now he saw them on the stairs. In his rapt and pain-shocked vision they looked as though they were dancing madly from side to side, several stairs apart, jiggling and leaping, the second one holding the basket with its incongruously gay ribbon. They were both wearing knee-length topcoats and black berets; in their rushing descent there was something almost vaudevillian about them, the end of some broadly played low-comedy skit.

He would not let his roommate call a doctor. He had a slight abrasion behind his ear and a dun-colored bruise on his jaw, but insisted he was all right. If his roommate had not asked about the discoloration on his face, Seavery would not have mentioned what had happened. But the inquiry incited a flow of narrative and commentary, in anger, bitterness, disillusionment. "I was trying to help somebody. Those sons of bitches. What did they think I was doing there with that basket—trying to tempt somebody?" His quiet voice was charged with morose self-righteousness. He was lying on his bed, looking at none of the appropriately solemn and sympathetic faces grouped around him (word of his experience had spread through the dormitory and friends came to see him and hear his tale); his eyes were fixed upon the ashen De-

cember sky beyond the windows, where skeletal treetops gestured
stiffly in the wind. "How can you help people like that?" he said.
"Why should we have to take our lives in our hands in order to
perform an act of charity?"

In view of his bitterness, and of the pain and danger he had
endured, and of the dun-colored smudge on his face where the
hand of a black attacker had struck, few words other than
Seavery's were spoken. Students drifted in and out, stood and sat
about the room in deferential attitudes, held by the sight and
the words of the victim, as if violence still clung to his clothing,
tangible, palpable, at once fascinating and unthreatening; the
students coming and going with both empathy and morbid
curiosity, staring at Seavery with uneasy interest as they wondered
how it had felt and what they, in a similar situation, might have
done—this experience of an experience provoking private speculations about their own capacities for tolerating pain and dealing
with assault; for most of these young men were from secure en-
vironments and pleasant circumstances where there were few
threats and sudden unexpected rage was rare.

"Tough shit."

Seavery's head rolled on the pillow and his gaze shifted with
an abrupt sideways movement and fixed upon the face of the
speaker of these jarring, unceremonious words, his eyes narrowing
at the corners with resentment.

"Why are you grinning?" Seavery demanded. "Do you think it's
so goddamned funny?"

The speaker of the jarring and unceremonious words, the lone
grinning face amid the deferential solemnity and compassion,
nodded his head up and down twice, gazing at Seavery with a
smile of sardonic mirthlessness. Appropriately, he was the person
in the dormitory whom Seavery most strongly disliked, who had
been the most brusque and least friendly to the shy, uncertain
young freshman just down from the mountains of northern Ver-
mont. Mel Easton, a Vietnam veteran, was several years older
and infinitely and tragically more experienced than his fellows in
the freshman class, whom he referred to with mild disparagement
as "my callow colleagues." He had the eyes of a cynic and the nod
of a skeptic. He was a tall, muscular, fair-complected son of the
allegedly medial Midwest, a product of benevolent blue skies,

incredibly rich heartland soil, warm yellow breezes and clean vibrant air. He had a wrestler's powerful build, thick-chested, with
heavy roundish shoulders, long free-swinging arms, leaning slightly
forward when he walked, as though advancing into a strong
wind. He wore his blond hair to his collar and had a small
trimmed beard that added age and distinction to the seemingly
inexpungible introspection of his features. The son of a wealthy
manufacturer who had made and was still making his fortune in
the allegedly medial heartland, Easton seldom spoke of his family,
and then with wry, casual disdain, referring to "the criminal
banality of their values and aspirations"; he had, in fact, totally
separated himself from them—except for the yellow business envelopes that arrived in his name every two weeks with punctilious
regularity, containing in a piece of folded blank paper a check
written in his father's oversized gregarious hand. Easton was possessed of experiences and passions and attitudes that seemed
monumental, even within the most radical circles of the university. He had spent a year of grim, soul-depleting combat with the
infantry. One night, adrift in a marijuana-induced reverie, he
stretched out on the floor of his room and to an audience of a
half dozen silent, attentive students told in a slow dreamy voice
story upon story of the throbbing, feral horror of that bitter and
embittering war. He spoke of death and mutilation and torture
and pain and atrocity, his words flowing with quiet inflectionless ease, his face distant and serene under the slow ribbons of
smoke. Easton had killed men, in the jungles and in the rice
paddies; he had seen a prisoner disemboweled with a bayonet
("Anybody here know the color of entrails?"); he had seen the
remains of infants burned as black as coal by napalm; he had seen
bawling civilians taken away and shot as suspected collaborators
("It makes it a little easier when they die in another language").
He did that only once; otherwise his combat experiences were a
silent infection he carried inside. There was another story, which
no one knew. Upon his return from Vietnam and separation from
the Army, he had gone to San Francisco and indulged in a sustained orgy of profligate living. There were times when his companions questioned his sanity, others when he seemed to them
suicidal. But it was a rite of passage, a sort of barbarous novitiate,
for one day he disappeared from San Francisco and went south, led

by some vague, undefined but nonetheless compelling purpose. An almost mystic pilgrimage of remorse and atonement brought him to the Nevada desert where he wandered, like some soul-scorched St. Anthony, under the blazing sun and across the burning dunes with glaring and intrepid fanaticism. He remained until his food and water ran out, and he remained, walking or sitting in the sun, rational, pitilessly aware, embittered by the scenes and sounds that had been sliced into his brain as by the cut of a razor, embittered by the use that had been made of his life, embittered by the remorseless haunting that he had been at once slayer and victim, witness and participant. In the end his great physical strength saved him. Fortunate to have collapsed near a road, he was noticed by a passing motorist and brought to a hospital.

It began to snow as they walked across the quadrangle. Easton looked enormous, mythically northern, in his hooded black parka, dwarfing his smaller, slimmer companion. Seavery was wearing two sweaters under his corduroy jacket. They walked silently for a time across the empty yard, heads bent to the snow's soft, windless, almost decorous descent.

"I take it," Easton said, "it's the first time you ever did anything like that."

"Yes," Seavery said.

"What got you—social conscience, Christmas spirit, boredom?"

"It was communally proposed."

"Shit on communal propositions," Easton said with a bitter laugh. "No decent idea has ever yet come out of a committee."

"Nevertheless, I expected to be treated like a human being."

"By whom—people who themselves have never been treated that way? I'll add to your catalogue of sins and omissions: you know nothing about the nature of charity."

"I don't particularly like the idea of charity," Seavery said. "The implications of it are deplorable."

"After all, you went there expecting gratitude."

Seavery thought about it. It was probably true, though not in any way invidious, he felt.

"And I don't mean," Easton said, "the gratitude of seeing oppressed people made happy. (You can only do *that* by making certain other people very *un*happy.) I refer to the gratitude of a massaged ego, a pomaded conscience. It adds up to further exploitation of these people."

They left the quadrangle and walked through the adjacent park. Nearby, a few students were hurrying under the stark, enduring trees, with the profound, self-contained privacy of people out in inclement weather, in their dark coats creating misty chiaroscuros within the veil of snow.

After several minutes of silence, Easton said,

"You're brooding, Seavery. You're still offended by what happened to you."

"Wouldn't you be?"

"No. I would have broken their heads, but at the same time still been able to understand their motives. It's possible to sympathize with your assassins, you know."

"That kind of objectivity leads to canonization," Seavery said. "And we know the saints all were mad."

"Don't underestimate madness," Easton said quietly. "It's one of the great generating powers of the world. Look, Seavery, the guys who jumped you were hungry too. Suppose they would have asked you for that food? Would you have given it to them?"

"No. But what about the people waiting upstairs for their goddamn Christmas dinner?"

"You went there to feed the hungry. You did that, and had the pleasure of having the condiment of the unexpected added to your charitable impulses. Nevertheless, you got exactly what you deserved—just like so many of the Christian missionaries who went out into the wilds to save the souls of heathen savages and wound up in the kettle. You're part of a great and ignoble tradition."

"I'll have that printed on my business card."

"You ought to make something of your experience. A person who tries to do good and gets knocked on his ass for his trouble has been given the opportunity for a rare and perceptive look into human nature."

They arrived at their destination, an off-campus coffee house. With most of the students departed for the holidays, the place was quiet, with just a scattering of people around the tables. Seavery and Easton took a corner table. Seavery removed his jacket, then pulled one of his sweaters up over his head, messing his hair which he did not bother to rearrange. Easton, however, not only kept his heavy snow-splashed parka on but also the hood up, so that now he looked, with his beard and his deep uncanny gaze, like some grim tutelary of the catacombs.

"Are you as bored as I am with all of this?" he asked.

"All of what?" Seavery asked.

"Take your pick. Whatever bores you most."

"You mean the university? Academic life?"

"Are you bored with it? Do you find it a structure within a structure, with its goddamn classes and lectures and pot-bellied shamans and mealtimes and bells and sophomoric bullshit and proctors and parietal conditions?"

"What do you mean, 'a structure within a structure'?" Seavery asked.

"It's no different from society in general, with its rules, its traditions, its conjurer's tricks, its rewards for spurious excellence. Are you doing well?"

"Quite well," Seavery said.

"That's dangerous," Easton said. "That gives you favorable prospects. You're being dressed and stuffed for societal feeding, and thence absorption by the national bloodstream."

"I don't intend to be absorbed into anything," Seavery said coolly. He was at once amused and intrigued by the massiveness of Easton's appearance before him, by the broad shoulders filling out the parka, the intent bearded face inside the cavernous monklike hood.

"Don't want to become the backbone of America, eh? Well, that's good. We have a superabundance of that kind; which accounts for all the osteopaths and chiropractors, I suppose." Easton smiled treacherously. Suddenly he whirled around to the counterman who was standing and lazily contemplating the snow. "Are you serving us or not, you lazy son of a bitch?" he demanded nastily. The counterman, a thin, balding man with the disinterested expression of an utter neutralist, stared blandly at the bizarre presence at his table, carefully considering his response. One could almost see the content of his thought: times had changed, and the students along with everything else; there was much more sloth and arrogance and presumption about the young people who walked through his door. He seemed also, be-

fore making his answer, to philosophize that times would change
again and the students with them, and that he, with a kind of
banal immortality, would be there to oversee it all.

"I'm sorry, sir," he said, more with consumed indignation than
politeness.

"Coffee, twice," Easton said, then turned back to Seavery's inquiring gaze. "It's the age of the shake-up," Easton said, not in
explanation or apology but rather as a statement of fact. "Com-
placency leaves behind nothing but wreckage. Seavery," he said
with sudden earnestness, "there is unbelievable harmony in anger
and aspiration, in violence and virtue. That's because good can
no longer with certainty be identified; there's too much of the
evil mixed in with it. The identification of good is an act of judgment, and whose judgment today is worth a damn?"

"Mine," Seavery said.

"Hubris," Easton said.

"Then I defer to you."

The conversation was suspended while the neutralist placed
two cups of coffee on the table before them. Easton's eyes remained fixed on the neutralist who in his turn maintained a mask-
like face, staring at nothing.

"Seavery," Easton said, when the man had gone, "have you
handed out your leaflets, marched in your demonstrations, hissed
your speaker, signed your petitions?"

"Some of it," Seavery said.

"And what did it do for your soul?"

"My soul?"

"Did it make you a more content man? No? Good. And what
did it do for the conditions you were protesting? I can answer
that: nothing. Things go on as ever, marching in lockstep, just
the same as if you never existed. Well, it's going to change.
They've unleashed too much electricity this time and they're not
going to be able to get it back into the bottle; the chickens that
are coming home to roost are going to be big, hungry vultures.
It's going to be the time of the oppressing oppressed and oppressed oppressors."

"There's a mouthful," Seavery said.

Easton took a long drink of steaming coffee.

"So," he said emphatically, like a preamble. "So, you went with your charity and they knocked the shit out of you. I hope it enlightened you. Their fury should be a lesson for you."

"I'm sorry I didn't kiss their hands."

"You're lucky they didn't kill you. They believe they have the right to, you know. They used to have a certain amount of faith in things, but not any more; since faith is essentially a moral act, and morality is today a thing unknown. A year ago I was in league with people like yourself. Not that I was naïve. I joined the Seaverys of the world with a sense of reality and even of honesty —I wanted it proved to me that they were failing. As you failed today with your basket of shit. All you were trying to do was feed a few people and hold them at bay for another eight hours while you went back to enjoying your expensive education. When they come storming out of those ghettos someday I want you to stand in the middle of the street and tell them you once brought them a basket of shit for Christmas, and see if you get a reduction in sentence for that. Anyway, revolutions are made by the exploited, not the oppressed, and the exploited are being kept content."

"So you need drama," Seavery said.

"And dramatists," Easton said. "That's the primary thing. Since everybody is an actor it means they're going to be their own audience, so that's no problem."

"You'll still have to please the critics."

"There won't be any. This stage will be too large. The proscenium will be arched by a rainbow." Easton drank again from his cup. He stared pensively at his huge, high-knuckled fist resting on the table. "So, I did try with the people who call themselves radicals. Let it be noted. Until I saw that the problem lay not with institutions, but with people."

"That presents quite a problem," Seavery said, "since you have no other species to deal with."

"They don't respond."

"Apathy."

"But you know the answer to that," Easton said and turned to the neutralist, who was now busily at work behind the counter washing glasses. Easton grinned maliciously. "There," he said to Seavery. "Before, he was standing still watching the snow fall. I called him a son of a bitch, got him mad, and now he's busy working away. Use him as your metaphor: violence, or the implied threat of it, gets action."

"That's how those guys got my basket of shit," Seavery said.

"Without it they might be sitting under their stolen Christmas tree in abject hunger. That's where morality has gone today—into violence."

"Everything has its logical destination," Seavery said.

"I don't know if you take me seriously or not," Easton said, scrutinizing his companion's expressionless face.

"Why give you the satisfaction, either way?"

Easton shrugged.

"You haven't touched your coffee," he said.

"I wanted tea."

"You'll drink coffee," Easton said.

To hear one's own groping, unformed, tentative dissatisfaction suddenly articulated into doctrine could be unsettling. Many of the things Easton had said had indeed been passing, with various degrees of perception, through Seavery's mind. He had not, however, been taking advantage of the many outlets for discussion afforded by a university campus. He suspected, despite the innumerable radicals of innumerable shades around him, that radical thought was as institutionalized as anything else. A monolith with certain human aspects (like the corporation, which was legally a person), the institution had tolerance for its most severe critics as long as those critics remained fixed within the structure; and what made the institution even more tolerant and unconquerable were precisely its humanizing capacities for permutation. The people in power here, as everywhere else, were in a position to make a thousand placating and conciliatory concessions without losing an inch of ground. Since his arrival in the fall, Seavery had participated in various student expressions of concern and protest, and come away from them all with a lingering dissatisfaction. He was still too immature and inexperienced to expect anything less than instant tangible results, and the failure of instant capitulation on the part of the opposition indicated they were hopelessly unreasonable. This was the most reassuring way to rationalize disenchantment with establishment and established procedures, to justify whatever tactics seemed necessary.

"Your expectations were too great to begin with," his room-mate said to him one night.

Seavery was slouched in a chair, staring out at the black, iron-souled New England winter.

"You began way too high," the roommate said. He was an ear-nest, studious, apolitical young man who was giving serious thought to medicine.

At first, the fusing of old and natural continuities had seemed the only way. But it was a well-trod way, too old and too natural, and without enough to show for long generations of effort. A freshman in college, Seavery suddenly felt he had read too many books.

"It takes time," the roommate said.

"Exactly," Seavery said quietly. "It's all so clever. They counsel patience, knowing damn well that enthusiasm wanes as you get older. Then they absorb you."

"You don't give yourself credit for maturing."

"No, no, I see things as they are," Seavery said. He believed he understood perfectly: if allowed to proceed unresisted, injustice and inequity and hypocrisy would continue to seep insidiously into the blood, until there was a congelation of despair, inertia, and ultimately acceptance. The surrender of the will impaired the clarity of the vision.

"No one sees things as they are," the roommate said with his earnest, plodding intelligence, "but as they want to see them."

"It comes out to the same thing," Seavery said.

One bright, crisp March morning, Seavery got off a bus in a run-down section near the river. A strong, bone-cutting wind was blowing in off the restive waves. He turned a corner where the wind velocity was reduced and began walking slowly along the street, studying the painted numbers on the doors above the dreary and inimical tenement stoops. Finding the one he sought, he descended several concrete steps to the basement apartment, which had an entrance under the brownstone steps. The barred windows were covered with coarse, heavy sacking. He rang the doorbell and stood and waited, while a corkscrew of entrapped wind spun the litter around his feet. Then a voice from within asked who was there, in such a wary and tentative way that

Seavery had the feeling the person had been standing behind the door debating with himself whether to query or not.

"I want to see Mel Easton," he said.

"Who are you?" the voice asked.

"Arthur Seavery."

There was silence then. Seavery waited. He became impatient. His feet were cold. He was hungry, having left the campus without eating breakfast. He adjusted his muffler around his neck and looked up at the building's old, flat, undistinguished façade.

Suddenly the door opened. Easton stood in the stone-walled entrance way, grinning through a beard which had lengthened considerably and become unkempt since Seavery had last seen him. He was wearing a plaid shirt and blue jeans.

"Arthur," he said cheerfully. Then he stepped outside into the cold and looked around. "Is it spring yet?" he asked, sniffing the air. "I've been holed up in here so long I don't know the season."

"Can I come in?" Seavery asked.

"How did you know where I was?" Easton asked, still grinning, though with a look now of wary curiosity.

"One of the guys from the dorm saw you and followed you. He knew I'd been wondering about you."

"I'm surprised I didn't notice him. That's careless. Well, come in."

"Is that an invitation or a concession?" Seavery asked, not moving.

"It's neither. It's that I can't close this door and leave you standing there."

Seavery followed him along a narrow passageway and then into a living room that was provided with stuffed chairs and a crushed-looking Victorian sofa that must once have been the prized adornment of a room furnished in execrable taste. Seavery sat down in a chair upholstered in maroon velours and immediately sank much deeper than he expected. Easton grinned at the unexpected discomfort. He remained standing, leaning against the concrete wall, his broad back covering one of the numerous revolutionary posters that decorated the damp windowless room, his powerful arms crossed.

"What the hell happened?" Seavery asked.

After six weeks of boisterous, hyperactive, nearly inseparable companionship, Easton had, without a word, without a trace, disappeared. His roommate had walked in one day and found all of Easton's belongings gone, from toothbrush to valise. Inquiries made to various university officials turned up no information, other than that Easton had requested his mail be forwarded to a post office box number.

During their weeks together their interest in academic work had rapidly deteriorated, until their attitude bordered on contempt. Books went unread, papers unwritten, classes unattended. They received several stern lectures from their proctor for mischief and disturbances in the dormitory. They joined a campus Conservative society and threw one meeting into an uproar by solemnly calling for nuclear destruction of the Soviet Union and the deportation to Africa of blacks. At radical meetings they called for militant actions which made even the most dogmatic advocates of violence blanch. Easton's days at the university were clearly numbered; twice he was called to the Dean's office for "consultation." Just before his disappearance he had risen in class to interrupt a learned disquisition of *Macbeth* to question the relevance of Shakespeare to today's world. After a lengthy exchange characterized by increasing acrimony on both sides, the lecturer, after commenting on the notice he had been taking recently of Easton's "antics," suggested the young man was making "an ill-advised assault upon all authority figures," of whom Shakespeare was one. Easton furiously accused the man of a personal attack and of "debasing" his position as fair-minded liberal intellectual. The night before his disappearance, Easton had gone out alone, not wanting to see Seavery (with whom, between pranks and mischief, he had been talking and debating endlessly), nor anyone else, feeling in himself the foul weather of old, disturbing memories rising. He sat on the freezing concrete of Harvard Square and smoked marijuana, trying to obliterate the memories, the incremental sense of bitterness, guilt, despair. Later, he wandered into a neighborhood bar where, after downing several straight whiskies, his bedimmed mind perceived ironically that he was standing in the middle of a debate on the war. Detached, sardonically amused, he listened to the fulminations of a thin, middle-aged hawk, listening to words and arguments and logic that sounded like recitations from ancient history, it was so tired, so obsolete; and realizing, too, that from his friends, the people he knew and talked to and listened to, he never heard such talk, that he had through association insulated himself from this voice, this side. And then the man, holding a dog leash in his hand, was saying, "Why, Buster here is worth a dozen of them slant-eyed bastards I'm telling you." Sullenly, Easton's eyes fell upon the small dog, a terrier pup. Later, he really did not remember how, Easton had the pup (the war hawk had gone to the men's room, leaving the dog tied outside to the doorknob) and was in the street with it. He did not remember anything after that, or maybe was not interested in remembering, carried away by the abdication of logic and coherence, and not only his own but everyone's; prey now to the infections carried by memory and the yearning to forget, to undo the fabric of his experience; prey now too to the brutal lack of compassion and understanding demonstrated by his fellow man; all of it too unbearable to contemplate; and not remembering later what happened to the dog, only that he had been holding it and then that it was gone. (Later, when the war hawk was outside looking for the dog he was attracted by the scream from the all-night laundromat, from the shocked and horrified woman who found the suffocated terrier tumbling round and round in one of the dryers.) Then he was in another bar, where his appearance had stopped or lowered all conversation while he was studied with critical and suspicious disapproval. He drank more straight whisky, standing at the bar in his parka, the hood up, looking like some awesome Carthusian wandered in from the cold. *"I'm a goddamn killer, don't you see?"* His voice, quite audible through the quiet bar, now brought all conversation to a halt. Uneasily, he was watched. Easton and the bartender confronted each other across the divide of polished mahogany. *"Do you know how many of them slant-eyed bastards I killed, actually saw drop?"* His soft, entreating eyes stared from deep in his hood at the bartender, his recurvate mind filled with ghastly scenes and chaotic noises. *"I once picked up a wounded Cong's gun and shot him with it. Just like that."* And then they were standing around him, the patrons of the quiet back-street neighborhood bar risen around him, their faces solemn and strong, admiring and compassionate. He felt a hand on his shoulder, saw a fresh drink placed before him. Bitter, incredulous, he listened to their voices: *Drink up, man. Atta way. Rough over there, eh? Good for you, man. Need more like you. Need more like him. The house is buying. In honor of.* Some took his slack, uncertain hand and shook it, and they surged around him with the vehement approbation that is exclusive to noncombatants.

The next day he disappeared.

"The time for it came, Arthur, that's all," Easton said.

"The time for what?" Seavery asked.

"To put some muscle into my ideas."

"But—"

"But what about you?" Easton asked. He smiled. "I think you were a bad influence." Easton laughed loudly at the expression on Seavery's face. "I wish I could have a picture of that. No, don't get offended. The thing is, all we did is talk and raise hell, and really, we achieved nothing. Well, now it's changed. No more pot, no more booze; just clear-headed activity and readiness."

"You're making no sense at all," Seavery said.

"A few friends of mine from the old country arrived here some time ago. Friends in a way different from what we are. Hunting companions, or 'Search and Destroy' companions—call it what you will. There are no friends like the people you've dined with after killing a few strangers. I mean, I *know* what these guys are capable of, what their sensibilities are. I don't know you in that way."

"I thought you knew me by now," Seavery said, more in pique than disappointment.

"To a certain extent I do. But not enough."

"But what are you up to, precisely? Who's here with you?"

"How are you doing in school?" Easton asked.

"School?" Seavery said irritatedly. "Who gives a damn about school? I'm planning to leave soon." It was true he had considered it, but the idea was more the product of boredom than a serious intention.

"That's a good idea," Easton said.

"Why won't you tell me what you're doing?"

"It's not a matter of trust, believe me. If it were only me, it would be different. But there are other people involved, and they don't know you, Arthur. And they're not making friends easily these days. In fact one of them back there—a guy who won the

Silver Star in the old country for unabashed heroism—is suffering right now from a gastrointestinal disorder, and not from his diet either, but from anxiety."

"You could tell them about me," Seavery said.

"What would I tell them?"

"This is pure elitist bullshit, Mel."

"That's not the way we see it."

"You can't freeze me out."

"We feel it's necessary to be exclusive."

"Tell them about me," Seavery reiterated.

"I'll try."

"Do it now."

"Now? This minute?"

"I'm here now, this minute."

"Do you know what you'll be getting into? These fellows mean business."

"Easton, you prick, whatever you do, I'm already in it. We were together so much that people will automatically assume that I'm part of anything you're involved in. Don't you think somebody at the school wasn't keeping a dossier on us? You have no right to keep me out."

Easton suggested Seavery leave for an hour or so while Easton spoke with his colleagues. Seavery decided to use the time getting himself breakfast in a luncheonette further down the street. As he walked away from the tenement he took notice of a police car cruising by and felt he had received a glance of inordinate interest from the car's occupants. He was instantly conscious of the fact that this was the first time he had ever felt wary of, or conspicuous in, the eyes of the police. It made a peculiar impression: he rather enjoyed the close, conspiratorial feeling it aroused, the sudden forceful focus it brought to his mind, the pleasingly ominous clarification of his status.

He sat at the counter of the luncheonette and ordered breakfast. He supposed he knew, in outline anyway, what Easton and his friends were up to. Easton had spoken of the inevitability of it often enough. "Everything must begin anew with violent destruction." If Easton, in his most serious moments, had a refrain, a litany, that was it. He cited the terrific stimulation of violence, the liberation of all inhibitions, and how crucial this was to the life's blood of any revolutionary movement. The fear and chaos which attended violence were absolutely essential smoke screens under which to implement strategy. When one planned for the common good, one had to be positively ruthless. The masses had no feelings, no nerve centers, were immune to pain. It was imperative this be understood, otherwise it was futile to plan for the betterment of millions.

But plan for what? What propositions, what programs, what reforms did the "betterment" consist of? There was no necessity for that, Easton insisted. "When somebody asks what you have to offer in place of what we have, you tell them nothing. Why attempt to describe a new social order while the old is still in its death throes? Why resuscitate a corrupt corpse with your own splendid and ingenious infusions?" That, Easton claimed, was where the Marxists went wrong in the thirties, in giving glowing descriptions of the new social order. They became too specific and hence vulnerable. No one had ever been a success with the public by being precise or specific about anything. One must be vague, ambiguous; one must deal in generalities. And anyway, the intelligent strategy was to attack. It was insane not to, when such fat, easy targets were available: Government. Establishment. System. Big Business. Capitalism. Technocracy. One could blame anything on them. There was nothing that could not be converted to revolutionary fuel—from the achievements of lunar exploration to the construction of a new cultural center: "Why wasn't the money better used to alleviate the sufferings of the needy?"

It was all very simple and obvious. Why deal rationally with an irrational system? Any credo put to its ultimate test failed or became modified into something different. This was as true for religion as it was for radical politics. The radical had to keep a great distance between himself and his limitations, lest he suddenly find himself circumscribed by those limitations. To accept the frailties of one's philosophy, to acknowledge its withering in the crucible of inquiry, was to love it the more deeply. It was enough to know and understand people. People were completely credulous, eager to believe, as long as they sensed some aura of mystery, exotica, or intimidation. They were much more malleable frightened or confused than informed, and this was not at all difficult to achieve, since they were always eager to give their security and their trust to those willing to assume the responsibility. "History and human nature," Easton would say in conclusion to these views, "are on our side."

Seavery looked up at the sound of the explosion. The windows of the luncheonette shook stiffly as the concussion struck them. There was a second explosion, moments later, a loud sullen roar, and again the windows vibrated. A car came to a sudden halt with the hysterical sound of brakes. Several passers-by had stopped, one man standing perfectly still, hand to mouth as if stifling a yawn; another, walking in the opposite direction, stopped in midstride, his head turned around, one shoulder pointed forward in his arrested direction.

Seavery, along with the rest of the occupants of the luncheonette, ran to the street. The moment he saw the billowing dirty smoke pouring out of the tenement he knew what it was, what had happened. Through the high, wild, pouring smoke he saw that the entire front of the building had been torn out. The street was littered with the terrific disgorging.

Alone of everyone, Seavery moved with sharp, self-conscious haste in the opposite direction, hurrying through what now seemed a flood of running people who were coming at and passed him.

The destruction was so total, so thorough, that the police could not even say for certain how many people had been in the basement apartment, where an apparent "dynamite factory" had been located. There were five apartments in the building, including the one in the basement, which had recently been occupied by an indeterminate number of "young people" (inside of the invidious quotes the phrase could be made to look rather sinister). Their comings and goings, neighbors remarked, had in retrospect seemed suspicious (whose, in retrospect, aren't? Seavery thought upon reading this). Of the other four apartments, one had recently been vacated, two had been unoccupied at the time of the explosion, while an old man had been home alone in the other. He had been killed, his body found hanging grotesquely through the ceiling of one of the blown-apart dwellings.

The interest of the police was focused on the basement lodgings, where the "young people" had been living. All indications were that it was here that the explosion had occurred. Bits and pieces of human remains were being found in the wreckage, the bodies so devastated that the police could at best estimate that at least three and perhaps as many as five people had been in the ground-level rooms at the time of the explosion. In addition, there was an unconfirmed report that another youth had been seen emerging from the building minutes before the eruption of the dynamite.

Me, Seavery thought with a dull, leaden sense of reality. He was sitting in his room reading the evening paper. It was past midnight and his roommate was asleep, enjoying that rest which, when observed by the troubled or threatened, seems so particularly sound and serene and unattainable. He was sitting in the deep leather chair, the desk lamp throwing a spotlight over his shoulder onto the newspaper which was spread across his lap. He had memorized the story by now, mesmerized by his association with an event that dominated the front page. At first he had been grimly preoccupied with the narrowness of his own escape from destruction. It had been a matter of mere minutes between his departure from the building and the occurrence of the explosion. This was more than enough to engross his thinking for a protracted amount of time concerning the horrendous stunts of chance and fortune. A later start in the morning of a few minutes, a missed bus, a wrong turn, some moment of doubt or hesitation, a slight prolongation of the conversation with Easton—the sheerness of it could turn one's mind blank. Fatalistically, he retraced his every movement of that morning, searching for the chance loss of time that could have sent him to his death, and, conversely, the providential series of movements which had timed so propitiously his appearance at and departure from the lethal basement apartment.

What had gone wrong? Easton's friends from "the old country" should have been experts with explosives. How could they have miscrossed a wire or committed some other mistake? And then Seavery's mind turned from these futile speculations to matters real and concrete. The police were doubtless looking for him. Since everyone who had been inside the dynamited premises was dead, he would be a prize catch indeed. His explanation that he was merely visiting a friend would hardly suffice. *You were in there a few minutes before it happened. Do you mean to say you didn't know what was going on?* And once Easton's remains were identified, his, Seavery's, participation in whatever was occurring in the fatal rooms would, in the eyes of the police, be confirmed. (Why, Seavery had himself told Easton that very thing during their brief conversation. Their friendship at the university had been too noisily conspicuous for any other conclusion.) The thought of police interrogation was disquieting and repugnant. They were clever and devious and irrefutable enough to contrive charges and make them stick. People with backgrounds of eccentric and unconforming behavior were decidedly unpopular today; they had already been heinously prejudged by prevailing sentiment. The conspiracy laws, for instance, were vague enough to discredit the most law-abiding citizen; and for a person who was vocal in his desire for a more responsive world, their application was absolutely tyrannical.

He studied the front-page picture of the gouged building. On the late news on the radio (he had turned the volume down and listened to the radio with his ear against it; he did not want to waken his roommate, as if even to be found *listening* to the newscast could incriminate him) he had heard that the police were sifting through the debris under the glare of floodlights. So they were there now, this moment, staked out at the site like prospectors or archaeologists, looking for remains, clues. All they needed to find of Easton was a tip of finger for them to begin their trek to this room. Seavery looked at the door for a moment and felt his insides constrict as his acutely tuned senses simulated the sudden loud impersonal sound of a fist on the door, envisioned the grim and monstrous entrance of peremptory officialdom, saw them sacking his belongings, his books, his papers, and taking him away into the night.

They would have him, there was no question of it. He had seen their faces up close, at protest rallies and demonstrations: those fixed carven faces, like so much incompetent sculpture; those cold, threatening, inimical eyes moving from face to face; those taut leashes straining under bestial instincts. Away from the public eye, what chance had an idealist in their hands? What did they know or care about principles or compassion, these upholders and defenders and yes even advocates of all that was rotten and corrupt and doomed?

Like a prisoner of war, Seavery now considered it his obligation
to escape. Easton and his friends were dead, consumed in the
premature crescendo of their efforts. Seavery closed his eyes and
lowered his head and attempted to imagine what it must have
been like. But all that came to him was the bitterness of his
friend's death, the incredible reality that Easton with his great
strength and power and vision had been torn bone from bone
and hurled like so much jelly against the walls of the crumbling
building, that Easton had disappeared as a human being with
the symbolic death rattle of the luncheonette windows. Seavery,
in his embittering descent of grief, even thought for several intense, vivid moments of Easton in some lofty Elysium, watching
him . . . until he remembered that he, Arthur Seavery, was an
atheist and that heaven did not exist, and that if Easton were anywhere, full-bodied and watchful and potent, it was in the brain of
Arthur Seavery; the truest representation of Easton, with plans
and ideals intact and unknown to anyone now living, existed
exclusively inside of Seavery, symbolized by the drama, violence
and suddenness of his leave-taking.

I shouldn't be so shaken, Seavery told himself. After all, Easton
had gone through a year of this kind of violence, had seen much
more and worse, and survived. You become immune to it, Easton
once said. But how? Seavery asked, endlessly fascinated by it all.
Oh, you do, his friend said, then added, But you know you'll never
forget it, even as it's happening; that it will come springing out at
you from the shadows for the rest of your life.—That much a soldier knew, that immunity was skin deep, that the experience of
combat is ground into grooves where thought runs deepest.

He found himself staring wonderingly at his roommate. The
potential medical student was curled up in his blankets as if he
had been kneaded by sleep. He was a totally apolitical person;
Seavery had never known anyone so detached from politics. It
was a remarkable lack of interest—considering what was going on
today. It was almost a studied, calculated evasion. Now Seavery
fixed the sleeping youth with a most penetrant stare, gazing with
somber intensity, as if at a most presumptive stranger. This fellow was lately talking of going to the medical school. A most
expensive proposition. Seavery was aware of the family's financial
situation, and medical school seemed beyond their resources. The

roommate had started talking about medical school only recently, Seavery thought, trying to pinpoint just when that talk had started. Where the hell was the money coming from? Who was this guy anyway, who evinced no interest in politics, whose avoidance of the subject was so pronounced as to be almost unnatural? What kind of impression was he trying to convey? I've told him a hell of a lot, Seavery thought. Who has he been passing it on to?

Silently, Seavery left his chair and went to the roommate's desk and began opening drawers and poking through papers and envelopes. He found letters, a laundry list, some poetry (that was unexpected), lecture notes. Then he began flipping the pages of all the books his roommate had, hoping to perhaps find there some incriminating scrap, some record of his, Seavery's, activities, conversations, ideas. But he wouldn't keep anything around, Seavery thought after finding nothing, not with the casualness of things in that room. If he was indeed informing, then he would be too shrewd to be so easily caught. They were too well trained and instructed to make such obvious mistakes. Seavery retreated to his chair, sat down and resumed his baleful, highly concentrated contemplation of his sleeping roommate, the potential doctor.

By five o'clock in the morning, after a night during which he had not even attempted to sleep, Arthur Seavery, after considering and rationalizing the danger of his situation and the rectitude of his ideals, had come to this conclusion: the police had somehow been involved in the explosion. Easton and his friends had been too expert at what they were doing to have made such a fatal mistake. Easton had indicated their expertise, had in fact been unwilling to allow an "unprofessional" such as Seavery to join them. There was no question that Seavery qualified on every other account. So it was hardly likely that such a group of men, who had survived the perilous varieties of organized death in Vietnam, would have been careless in a tenement near the Charles River. Seavery remembered quite clearly the scrutiny given him by the police. (Why had they been cruising so slowly along that particular street at that particular moment?) He believed that "they"—or some other "they"—were quite capable of causing the explosion. Was it merely coincidence that no one else had been at home in the building, except for the old man? (What was one old man, when "they" had the opportunity to exterminate a nest of "anarchists"?) It was well known that certain people were finding the courts too slow or lenient or inadequate in dealing with radicals. Movement lawyers had become adept at unmasking and overthrowing trumped-up indictments. Certain Movement leaders had already disappeared; the authorities claimed they had gone underground or left the country. It was likely some of them had been murdered, as Easton and his friends had been. *As I could be*, Seavery thought in the cold, pre-dawn grayness of his room. If "they" were indeed doing this, then no one was safe; and if "they" were spreading a network of silent, authorized assassination through the land, then the time for resistance was being rapidly depleted. And the only way to effectively resist was to place as high a premium upon one's beliefs as upon one's life.

It was all plainly clear to him now—as clear as the new day that was beginning to slip its first pale strokes through the window blinds. It was a well-known fact that informers and provocateurs had infiltrated Movement groups, instigating trouble and passing along information. Names, places, episodes began running through Seavery's mind in indisputable assertion. So many people had already been betrayed, so many plans gone astray. The brutal tactics used against blacks, which had the tacit approval of the white majorities, could not be employed against whites, no matter how radical. But since oppression could not exist without constant regeneration, some outlet had to be found for the murderous energies of the state. So a more subtle and devious tactic had to be found for the subjection of people. The silent, benign police state was now a matter of fact, proceeding quietly, with savage efficiency, allowing its façade of democracy to remain unsullied.

The composure of Seavery's thinking was never more cogent or coherent as he sat contemplating these thoughts. The absolute certitude of his conviction was buttressed by the irrefutable apparatus of names and facts he so readily conjured. The clarity and indisputability of his self-enlightenment brought a peculiar calm as he understood perfectly now what was in opposition to him, what were the threats, dangers, consequences. The congruence of suspicions and facts was overwhelming. Armed with this new, insightful and incisively correct knowledge, he felt already stronger, and better equipped for the battle for survival.

2

So he wandered, motivated by his logic and his certitude; not under threat (although the idea of threat was real enough), not from fear, but with ineffable resolve, near-messianic determination, convinced he was now buoyant upon a riptide of history. And it was as good a time as any to be on the road, since there were at the moment thousands like him scattered across the land in constant motion, and he with his fresh outcropping of beard and patchwork shabbiness was a familiar sight and definable entity in places where once he would have evoked perplexity and suspicion, and the irrational hostility he did occasionally encounter was more than offset by the general lack of interest people took in him.

With an animating spirit that was close kin to vengeance, he stared sullenly through the windows of a westward-going bus at the massive and variegated country he believed wanted his blood, whose institutions he was now dedicated to overthrowing. The cities, the towns, the astonishing breadth of farmland, the people, the rivers, lakes, fields, hills and mountains, all came under his stolid gaze, the gaze of the fugitive for his oppressor.

He learned that Americans were not an inquisitive people. He had crossed the length of the country and was in California for almost a month before anyone asked him where he was from. Like any stranger anywhere, he was self-conscious of his status and constantly expected to be questioned. When finally he was asked, by a counterman in a roadside restaurant, his answer was at once vague, mysterious, and complete: "East."

His destination was no more definite than his reticently acknowledged origins. He spent the spring and summer drifting up and down the California coast, living for a time in a commune (an experience he considered inquilinous and which he found boring and unsatisfying), making friends and discarding them with equal rapidity, visiting college campuses and involving himself with groups of militant radicals, participating in endless discussions of revolutionary goals and tactics. Finally, he splintered off with a group of determinedly committed young men. For several weeks they dedicated themselves to inciting campus disorders and confrontations with the police, and to minor acts of arson and vandalism. But the group did not remain together long. One was arrested on a drug charge, another was killed in a motorcycle accident, another simply disappeared. When Seavery convinced the group that the latter person had in all likelihood been murdered by the police or the government, and that perhaps the motorcycle accident had not been an accident, the group panicked and fragmented.

It was then that Seavery met Frank Dublin in Los Angeles. What initially attracted him to the self-propelled shepherd of the Halcyon Tabernacle was Frank's strong physical resemblance (minus the beard, of course) to Mel Easton. Each had the same kind of poised, unself-conscious muscularity, each gave a suggestion of easily summonable resources of physical strength. Seavery sensed here a raw power harnessed to a willingness to do good and change the world that was almost touching in its ingenuousness. Frank struck Seavery as a person of sincere but not totally focused commitment to the Movement, one who was capable of stepping out of character in order to make an impression upon people he admired, or on behalf of a cause he believed enhanced him. Frank had not been visibly bedeviled by the idea of committing a political murder if it were for the greater good; he had listened to and discussed the concept with apparent open-mindedness, and to Seavery's thinking this was comparable to a slight infection that could only worsen. What had impressed him most about Frank, however, was the latter's hammering fists as they laid low the three chicanos in the diner that night: and still more: the fact that Frank himself had been unimpressed by the achievement, had walked away from it and barely made mention of it later—of something that Seavery had often envisioned himself doing to tormentors real and imagined, but which he knew that with his slight strength was beyond him.

Several days after Frank's departure for New York, Seavery fell in with a bearded young man named McComb who had received, in his own words, "a psychiatric expulsion" from a midwestern university. At twenty-one, this self-proclaimed Maoist, who wore sunglasses day and night and who said he envied black people because of the purity of their revolutionary struggle, was wanted

by the Los Angeles police on various warrants from inciting to
riot, drug possession, parole violation, and assault. He was cur-
rently looking for someone to join with him in striking a blow
against the Defense Department.

"They have this computer . . ." he told Seavery one day as they
sat on the grass of a college campus. The trim, athletically built,
luxuriant-haired youth spoke with deep-voiced earnestness, slowly,
staring intently at Seavery from behind the dark glasses, as if
above all it was imperative to communicate sincerity. The computer, it seemed, was located in a small industrial plant in a Los
Angeles suburb, a plant ostensibly making parts for commercial
airlines but in reality producing pieces of highly sophisticated
sonar equipment for the Air Force, and in addition had the computer which was being used in research by the Department of
Defense. All in all, a most devious and offensive example of the
nefarious military-industrial complex. It was McComb's intention to blow up the computer. None of his "oracular, lotus-eating"
friends, however, were willing to involve themselves in such an
operation, he said bitterly. He described to Seavery a recent evening of revolutionary discussion spent with them. Did Seavery
want to know what the topic was? McComb asked with crisp, mordant enunciation. "How History Will Record Us." Certain months
had already been historically pre-empted, they pointed out: there
was the October Revolution, the February Revolution, the Decem-
brists, the 26th of July Movement. ("Serious, serious—I'm telling you all this was serious!" McComb exclaimed indignantly.)
If their great move was made in March they ran the risk of being
called Marchists, which was too phonetically similar to Marxist,
and they did not want an identity with those now discredited
revisionist dogs. May would be the most appropriate month, they
decided, giving them the proud appellation of Mayists, endear-
ingly close to Maoists. Novembrists, a strong and sturdy sound,
would be acceptable. June would be perfect, the women in the
group declared, since Juneists could also be said to derive from
Juno, and to make the ancient Roman queen of heaven and pro-
tectress of women eponymous to such a movement would be a
garland for all womankind. A late summer movement, a wit suggested, might give them the designation Augustists, or "The
Caesarean Section." (It was late in the evening by then and levity

was beginning to seep into the discussion.) But Mayists would be best. Having a specific month to work toward, the consensus was, would serve to cohere their plans and help galvanize the Movement. And thus, McComb said, another outrageous counterrevolutionary waste of time.

When Seavery, content to be a revolutionary in all and any months of the calendar, asked McComb how sound his information about the plant and its computer was, McComb cited one Walterhouse, an employee of the plant, whose brother had died in a helicopter crash in Vietnam and who consequently was an implacable foe of the war.

"He doesn't have the guts to do it himself," McComb said. "He frankly admits it. But he can tell us how to get in and just where to leave the charge."

"How reliable is he?" Seavery asked.

"I've met him from time to time. He used to come to our meetings, but got disgusted with all the talk and dropped out. He pulled me aside one night and told me about this thing. He says the sight of that computer makes him choke. The way I look at it, we can really *do* something here instead of just sitting around and bullshitting."

"How do you know he's not setting us up?"

"Man, his brother was *killed* in this war," McComb said.

Afraid of sounding like the people he had come to despise, those myopic visionaries who talked in redoubtable phrases and made magnificent, empty forecasts of things to come, Seavery decided to defer his suspicions. After all, he had traveled thousands of miles and so far had accomplished very little. He had seen the fruits of caution—protracted and self-perpetuating illusions. An action like this, moreover, would not only be valuable and satisfying but could have far-ranging salutary effects; it could be a piercing infusion for a Movement that was continually in danger of becoming stale and sluggish with inactivity and sinking into a morass of its own rhetoric. And it would also prove a stimulant for Seavery himself, who lately had been feeling bored and depressed, who was never more quickened and inspirited than when planning or participating in an undertaking that promised violent destruction.

Walterhouse supplied the dynamite, obtained, he said, from a friend who had stolen it from a construction company. They met with Walterhouse in a bar in the Los Angeles suburb where he lived and where the plant was located. He was in his early thirties, a nondescript man with vague, unfocusing eyes, with a passive, almost vacant expression, whose heavy drooping underlip suggested the skepticism of the uninformed. He gave them the package containing the dynamite, detonators, and timing device. (McComb, the self-proclaimed Maoist, was also a self-proclaimed explosives expert, having learned this revolutionists' trade, he said, while living in a "guerrilla commune" in the Sierra foothills.) Remembering the fate of Easton, Seavery was uncomfortable with the package that lay on the table; he could barely keep his eyes from it, as though if not carefully watched it might erupt under their noses.

They would gain entrance to the plant, Walterhouse told them, under the pretext of job-hunting. They would be sent to the personnel office where they would be rejected on sight by the director. ("He's prejudiced," Walterhouse said matter-of-factly.) On their way out they would stop in the public phone booth located in the corridor. There the dynamite would be placed in an open area behind the call box and the timing device activated. Walterhouse would then hang an out of order sign on the booth to insure the concealment of the explosives. Plant security, he assured them, was lax.

"Set it for exactly ten o'clock," Walterhouse said. "I live a half mile away and I want to listen for the explosion."

It was all quite neat and simple. A more experienced pair of saboteurs than Seavery and McComb would have been wary of so straightforward a plan, would have wondered at the ease with which they were able to bring dynamite into a building allegedly containing government-contracted production and research. But it went smoothly according to plan. With McComb carrying the innocuous-looking parcel, they entered the low-slung, compact plant and were directed by an incurious uniformed guard to the personnel office. There the bearded youths received a look of loathing and short shrift from the personnel director, as Walterhouse had predicted. Then they planted the dynamite in the telephone booth and left. (Walterhouse called in sick this day, not wanting to be on the premises, just in case his co-conspirators were not as expert with timing devices as they claimed.)

The operation was carried out with absolute precision, from start to finish. The secreted dynamite charge blew out the walls, blew up the ceiling, blew apart most of the machinery, including the offensive computer, and into the bargain left a lusty red fire like a Stygian landscape burning in the night. The one blemish upon an otherwise impeccable operation was that neither the factory nor its squat, chattery computer had anything to do with the Department of Defense or any other government agency. The only symbol of anything dubious or unprincipled on the premises was a young night watchman who had been conducting a comfortable and unthreatened affair with Walterhouse's wife while that brooding scheming man was at his workbench during the day. So Walterhouse had worked out his plan, with an eye for character as well as detail, and even the idle-sounding request that the timing mechanism be set for precisely ten o'clock had been functional, not to mention sadistic. For at a few minutes before ten he dialed the number of the public phone and spoke with a malice at once cold and pleasant to the young night watchman, telling him that everything was known and that he, Walterhouse, an unforgiving man, was not going to allow it to pass "unnoticed." The youth barely spoke, spending the final seconds of his life coolly listening to his remote-control murderer, wondering, in the back of his mind, how all of this was going to impinge upon his life. Walterhouse edged the one-sided conversation along until the telephone went dead in his ear, and a few moments later the sound of the blast reached him, soft, solid, and satisfying upon the sweetened suburban night. The only thing that jarred Walterhouse's pleasant savoring of his well-planned triumph was the thought, coming to him around midnight: *Holy shit, I'm unemployed now.*

Although they never learned the more intimate details of Walterhouse's involvement in the episode, Seavery and McComb heard enough to have the suspicion of deceit cross their minds. The newspapers stressed the innocuousness of the plant's operation, and from members of the suddenly unemployed work force who were interviewed in the papers came corroboration. Seavery was baffled and angry. Also, he wanted to know why Walterhouse had deliberately omitted mentioning the presence of a night watch-man (not that Seavery had any qualms about pulverizing a life or two if the cause was worthy). McComb was less curious about these things and, with understandable discretion, went elsewhere. Seavery, however, with more profound resources of commit-ment and determination, went to Walterhouse to make inquiry. He found the out-of-work plant hand busy mowing the lawn of his California-spawned bungalow.

"I don't know you and want you off my property," Walterhouse said heatedly when Seavery appeared.

"Listen," the youth said, "there are some things that don't add up."

"Get off my property you fucken Communist," Walterhouse said, glaring as if at the sight of his Doppelgänger come to haunt him. Then, in a lower but hardly less emotional voice, "You're a fucken murderer. You and your filthy-looking friend. I'd advise you to clear the hell out of here. If you don't, I'll cut your feet off." And with that he began advancing the lawn mower menacingly toward Seavery, the thing rattling with a grotesque metallic gurgle, sounding as though it were trying to digest ball bearings. Seavery had to leap out of the way to avoid the threat to his toes.

"You're crazy!" he snarled at Walterhouse.

"But I'm not a murderer," the man snarled back, reversing direction now and coming again at Seavery with the croaking grass-spitting machine. Again Seavery leaped aside. Now Walter-house paused, panting. "They're looking for you and your stupid friend," he said, his eyes glaring with malevolent satisfaction. "Take my advice and clear out. Go back to Russia." And he was about to charge again, when Seavery turned and walked away, so furious that tears of anger had started to his eyes.

That afternoon he startled a barber by walking into the shop and asking for a haircut and shave. Then he wired his father for money, and soon after that was on a bus heading back across the continent.

NINETEEN

Since the attack on the city's most august newspaper was planned for approximately six o'clock in the morning, Frank decided to go to the tenement the night before and sleep there. They all slept in the old building that night, Seavery, Temple, Breenstone and Meyer; sprawled and curled on the mattress, on a cot in the bedroom, in a chair. There was a minimum of conversation before they went to sleep, even from Breenstone and Meyer, the unabashed intellectuals, who seemed to feel that nothing was worth doing unless it first had been debated and analyzed and rationalized and made absolutely correct and indisputable: even these two sat subdued in pensive silence, perhaps intimidated by the idea that tomorrow their intellects would be subordinate to less exalted resources. One by one they retired, casting themselves gratefully into the gracious and consoling recessional of sleep, though tonight sleep was not for Frank a wholly untroubled interlude. Sometime during the night he wakened, lifting his head from the pillowless mattress, realizing that he had not been dreaming but *thinking*, calmly and rationally, about what they were going to do. His eyes opened to a strange and disturbing sight. Seavery was sitting at the table, his face sinisterly illuminated by candlelight. Seavery's expression was mysteriously and profoundly private, his eyes fixed with ironic detachment upon the burning candle, which was throwing a weaving yellow light like an exorcism over his face. Motionless in the dark, Frank watched him with a mixture of unease and curiosity, trying by force of will to obtain some insight into the person behind the unguarded, reflective, almost wistful face. But all that his inquiring perspicacity could inform him with was the idea that Seavery's raptly gazing eyes were locked in some willful and uncanny combat with the solitary point of fire that was consuming the candle.

At five o'clock Seavery wakened them (Frank suspected the youth had not slept at all during the night). Quietly, they washed, and drank from a jar of fruit juice that was in the refrigerator. There was little talk; they moved about in the predawn dimness like figures in a phantasmagory, as though each had shared the other's dream to a depth and intimacy as to render conversation superfluous. Breenstone idly fingered his wispy beard as if to reassure himself of its dignity; Meyer donned a floppy broad-brimmed felt hat that gave him the look of a pretending boule-vardier; Temple kept referring to his watch, a vague half-smile on his lips. Frank sat on a chair, watching them, absorbed into the quiet, the gravity, the nerve-edged self-consciousness that pervaded the apartment like the aftermath of an imperial rebuke. There was little talk but much touching: they seemed always, when passing one another in the dimness, to give a comradely touch on the arm or shoulder, small gestures of assurance or solidarity or perhaps even compassion. Seavery appeared from the kitchen holding a straw picnic basket. Frank stared at it, the others seemed deliberately to keep their eyes from it. The basket, held motionless in Seavery's small hand, was like a sixth presence, dominant and compelling, like some sort of fierce and leaden im-mortality, some terrible godhead beyond the range of intellectual-ity. Self-conscious about the allure of the basket, Frank looked away. Through the window he could discern now the sharp flat planes of building tops and spindly-legged water towers coming into relief against the softening sky. Then Seavery approached one of the wall posters, lifted his hand and flattened it lightly upon the face of a certain radical deity, then he turned and opened the door and went out. They followed him, going quietly in single file down the stairs.

The industrial neighborhood surrounding the tenement had not yet come awake. The deserted streets looked like a film maker's conception of a city depopulated by germ warfare—every-thing upright and undisturbed, normal to the rule, except for the magisterial collusion of emptiness, silence, and immobility. But not for very long, of course, for it was still New York City, with its majestically restive core, its ephemeral moods. A few moments after they reached the street they heard the distant, disembodied, somehow incongruous pealing of church bells (with distance lend-ing indolence to the spirituality instead of solemnity), and saw a cruising taxicab, which Seavery hailed. They got in and began heading uptown, speeding unimpeded through the rustling city. The driver, noting the basket balanced on Seavery's knee, asked if they were going on a picnic, which led into his forecast of the weather, which he insisted would prove more accurate than the radio's. And then he realized that his was the only voice running in the cab, and he sighed and desisted.

Frank wondered about the advisability of taking a taxi uptown; in fact, he wondered about the mechanics of the whole operation. It seemed to him to have been put together rather casually, though Seavery, who claimed to have experience in these matters, had planned it. Seavery stressed the importance of simplicity in these "actions," as he described them. Elaborate, precisely timed movements, he asserted, too often led to unseen complications. No one had questioned the plan, however, and little provision had been made for the unexpected, the accidental, for failure and its consequences, except that each of them had set to memory the telephone numbers of Movement lawyers. Utter belief in the absolute and unquestioned virtue of what they were doing seemed to incline them toward incaution and a sense of infallibility.

Nevertheless, despite his misgivings, Frank was firmly committed to his role in the operation, seeing it as a subsumption of a much larger proposition. And it had come along at a most propitious time as far as his relationship with Charlotte was concerned. By alluding to his participation in something imminent, dangerous and significant, he had been able to melt away some of the reserve and hostility she had shown toward him since the night of the harassing, upsetting phone call. He had spoken to her the day before and she had indicated great interest in the hints he gave her of what was being planned. His only comment about the actual details was the whimsical and ambiguous, "You'll read about it in the paper—maybe." Her titillation at the idea of violence was evident. "How dangerous is this?" she asked. "Very," he said. "How much of a risk are you personally running?" she asked. "Considerable," he said. This reticence, heavy with implication, seemed to soften the hardening of her recent attitude toward him, toward what they had been doing together. He felt she was regarding him differently now. What they had been doing these past weeks had disabused her of certain attitudes toward him, and now this "action" would knock further props out from under her misconceptions.

They got out of the taxi several blocks from their destination. Seavery, noting their tension and realizing how conspicuous they were on the streets at that hour, suggested they talk with loud congeniality and force some laughter, to dispel any suspicion that might be directed toward them. Temple initiated a discussion about baseball and elicited opinions of certain players from Breenstone and Meyer, the unabashed intellectuals, whose wide-ranging interests did not include baseball. Temple mentioned the name of a light-hitting infielder and Breenstone dutifully rhapsodized about the man's strength and power, which provoked some genuine, if nervous laughter, from the others.

So it was as a casual, laughing, chattering group that they began sauntering into the street where their target was located—the loading platform and delivery trucks of the newspaper. Seavery had already paid several visits to the site, at various hours of the day and night, studying the men and the routine. At this hour, if the normal situation prevailed, three or four sizable delivery trucks, packed with the morning edition, would be standing there, their drivers most likely inside the building having coffee, with perhaps one or two men on the platform. After warning off anyone who was there, and fire-bombing the trucks and blowing up the loading platform, the idea was to disperse in a westerly direction and head for the nearest subway. This was the plan, as conceived and proposed by Seavery and readily accepted by the others, who had immediately begun daydreaming about the success of their venture, the mere contemplation of it enhancing their self-esteem, for they well knew how word of these actions spread with inspirational swiftness and fervor across the land, coming under discussion by radical groups and being eulogized in that obstreperous and conspicuous efflorescence known by the misnomer Underground Press; and in spite of every effort to make this a depersonalized revolution, one could not help but to take pride in the dissemination of one's achievements.

The street was empty except for two derelicts asleep in a boneless heap in a doorway across from the loading platform. Several cars and a panel truck were parked near the far corner. Now the talk and the laughter ceased and the tension among them became noticeable, the sound of their footsteps inordinately loud and sinister. The actual arena of operation was much more uncertain and threatful than their idling notions had imagined it; it suddenly was starkly present, a vivid reality in all its unpredictable dimensions. They could see the huge trucks pointing out of the loading area, lined up between enormous pillars as at a starting gate. A sudden breeze swept the city's tired, vagrant night litter along the street. Every last particle of night had now turned its other face and the unmasked new day was upon them in all its crisp, unspoiled roundness. But still the street was empty, though now the quiet was no longer dominant but abeyant.

When they reached the loading area Seavery put the basket down on the sidewalk, then bent over it. Frank watched him with poised and breathless expectancy: at last the cover would be lifted from that lethal container and its contents declared. Looking about, Frank noted the terrific vulnerability of their targets —there was not a soul on the platform or in any of the big trucks. Already he was balancing himself to run, could feel the insane, irrational desire to run through the deserted streets. The anticipation of this moment had been compelling and obsessive, the taxi ride uptown through the unsuspecting city had been tense and melodramatic, like the fraught, wordless scenes run under the credits of certain movies; and now he wished it were over, that they were together back in the tenement, relieved of the burden to act, talking about it, waiting to hear and read about it, self-satisfied in what they had done, achieved, like soldiers emerged unscathed from combat, their camaraderie hammered together proudly and for all time: all of this as he waited out the single enlarging and protracting moment which seemed second by second to be consuming not only anticipation and excitement but all of the future too.

Even as Seavery bent over the basket and Frank edged forward to see what the youth would lift out, Frank noted the movement from across the street. The derelicts had come to life, were standing up now, with an erect alertness that seemed unnatural for the ostensibly hungry and homeless. And then he saw the doors of the panel truck swinging open and, incredibly, men beginning to emerge.

"It's a bust!" Breenstone suddenly yelled.

Seavery, bent over the basket like an indecisive shopper, straightened up, his face clouding with an expression of puzzled annoyance. He looked around. The ostensible derelicts were crossing the street now, coming toward them, walking not with the crushed spiritless shuffle of their kind but with a strong direct stride.

"Split," Seavery said.

They began running, in abrupt frenetic dispersal—Breenstone and Meyer in a westerly direction, in their panic running directly toward the half dozen plainclothesmen who were now out of the panel truck and moving into the street. Frank, Seavery and Temple broke in the other direction. As they ran, several men came dashing out of doorways to intercept them, shouting at them; some were uniformed, some not. Seavery, moving with feral, desperate shiftiness, avoided the lunge of one pursuer and kept going, swinging away from another pair of hands, propelling himself forward like a human missile with short blurring steps that seemed almost comical. Frank, without breaking stride, bulled flush into a uniformed policeman, knocking him brutally aside, the man landing on his back in the middle of the street, his cap askew over his stunned face.

They got clear of the street, wheeled around the corner and began racing down Broadway. Frank watched Seavery ahead of him; the youth was moving with light, weightless, incredible speed, chin up, lips expanded back over glaring teeth, elbows pumping like pistons. Frank and Temple, running abreast—the latter's shoulder-length hair streaking straight out behind him—were several strides in back of Seavery, following with pounding, stamping feet. Glancing aside for a moment, Frank was momentarily face to face with the startled eyes and open mouth of a newsdealer standing petrified inside of his shack, and then the man, the shack, the stacks of fresh newspapers, were gone and the entire city seemed to be flashing around on a tremendous circumambient screen.

Then Seavery cut to his left and ran into the street. Instinctively, Frank and Temple followed, without regard for traffic. Suddenly a horn erupted with loud importunate braying, and a moment later—as he took a mighty leaping stride and achieved the opposite curb—Frank heard a sickening thud and from the corner of his eye saw something soaring through the air. Turning his head for a moment, he saw Temple in mid-air, arms and legs flopping uselessly, long hair swirling brokenly, and the car still charging forward, the horn still blowing but with the counterpoint of screaming brakes now; and then Temple struck the ground with bone-cracking impact and rolled over convulsively several times and then was covered by the raging automobile which looked momentarily spasmodic as first a front wheel and then a rear jolted over Temple's body.

Frank was not shocked. He suddenly was beyond that, beyond shock or surprise or fright or anything else; was simply propelled by a marvelously concentrated, marvelously co-ordinated urgency and energy; was vaguely aware that he was running like a madman through the heart of the city of eight million as though it were all his to possess and trample, vaguely aware of the spectacle, the incongruity. Frozen in his mind was the sight of the car jouncing irascibly twice over Temple's hurled and fallen body, and it seemed as though—in his fixed and frozen mind—that the car and its screaming horn and blazing brakes was jerking back and forth over Temple. He did not have a thought for Breenstone and Meyer, and in another abrupt and dreamlike moment even the picture of Temple flashed out of mind as he saw Seavery running toward a car that was paused at a red light. Seavery opened the front passenger door and leaped inside. Frank followed, with a sense almost of infallibility in what was happening. By the time his broad running strides carried him to the open door he heard Seavery talking to the driver, a man with a face at once so stern and intent he looked like a scholar, staring at Seavery from behind a pair of black-rimmed glasses, his lips compressed, his hands on the steering wheel—altogether a representation of a man prepared to be reasonable if a reasonable proposition were put: and Seavery's voice was reasonable, or anyway it was not loud or shrill, albeit somewhat hurried, with an urgency and terseness that indicated he would brook neither argument nor delay, and when Frank reached the car and pulled open the rear door he saw Seavery reaching down and unsheathing a Bowie knife that had been concealed in his boot and covered by his trouser leg.

"Get moving," Seavery said, showing the knife. "Now. Fast."

The man's eyes dilated at the sight of the knife and his lips compressed even more tightly. Then he turned rigidly, as though his lower body were paralyzed, and looked at Frank: this seemed an utter imperative, to look at the second intruder who had burst into his automobile. Not until he had done this would the man obey, and then when he did it was with a celerity that was startling. Without waiting for another word, he suddenly sent the car lunging forward, turned sharply at the corner—so sharply that the rear door, which Frank had not had time to close, slammed to with a bang—and headed downtown with a pulsing, reckless speed, utterly disdainful of lights or traffic or anything else, an astonished, near-maniacal look on his face, sitting forward virtually with his chest against the wheel.

Frank looked back to see a variety of small running figures in the street. Then he heard a siren, but no car stormed into view; instead the scene behind them, which he was twisted around in the rear seat to watch, began to recede with steady, unthreatening smoothness, increased in distance, reduced in size, as if in discreet and dispassionate countermovement, and he began to feel the relief and the sanctuary of his own swift motion, his departure to peace and safety.

They got out of the car in the Chelsea district and stood on a corner and watched the driver speed off, alive and bristling with his experience, frantic with the tale. Frank looked at Seavery; the morning light was falling on the youth's face, which was set in a curiously oblivious expression.

"Listen," Frank said, still deferring to the youth, whose audacity and expertise he still trusted, was relying upon, "that guy is going to the first cop . . ."

Seavery's eyes moved sharply out of whatever reverie they had been induced into and settled upon Frank's face as though the latter were an utter stranger, eyes keenly alert now in the otherwise smooth, invincibly tranquil surface of his face.

"They were staked out," he said quietly. "Who do you think it was?"

"Who do I think who was?" Frank asked.

"One of them tipped it."

"You're probably right," Frank said disconsolately.

"Who got hit by the car?"

"Temple. I think he's dead. Or if not, then on his way to it."

"Do you think he tipped them?"

Frank looked around; suddenly he felt his nerves beginning to shatter.

"I don't know," he said irascibly, finding it difficult to control his voice. "Look, let's get the hell out of here."

They went into the subway and took the train to Brooklyn, where they got out and walked aimlessly for several hours. Then they separated, Seavery getting on a bus, Frank taking the subway back to Queens and then the bus to Capstone. Seavery's parting words were, "Next time we'll make a proper job of it."

TWENTY

Charlotte was quite subdued, dispirited by a compassion so profound it bordered on remorse. Solemn, deferential as a child, she gazed at him. Her attitude had become one of humbling self-effacement the moment he began telling her what happened. Her face reacted like an odometer to the story he told and he could see in it the distance he had traveled, symbolically and significantly, and suddenly he felt more substantially involved in that shapeless mass known as the Movement than he had when he was with Seavery and the others.

"Do you believe you were betrayed?" she asked.

"Seavery thought so," he said. "It does seem likely. Christ, they were there waiting for us."

"If there was an informer in your group, then the police could be coming for you."

"I know that," he said.

"What will you do?"

"Nothing. Be fatalistic. I'm damned if I'm going to take off and become a fugitive."

"That's very brave," she said, "and honorable."

They were sitting on lawn chairs in her garden, in the evening softness. The air was warm and placid, untroubled by wind or sound; still a man's to find even in the metropolitan boundaries of a choked and teeming city; the hushed and sweetened air which a profaned and violated nature continued to weave and scent and infuse into whatever pockets of space it could find. The death of a summer's day could still be a fragrant ceremony of muted pipes and soulful ease; its drawn shroud a womb-ritual of calm and rebirth.

"I'm proud of you, Frank," she said. "You attempted something so wonderfully idealistic . . . and now you're not afraid. The absence of fear indicates the purity of your motives."

He looked curiously at her. "I didn't say I wasn't afraid," he said sullenly.

It was ironic, he felt. When finally he was eliciting from her the kind of sentiment he had been hoping for, he was not in the least interested in turning it to his advantage—not that there was any reduction or modification in what he wanted, merely that his current frame of mind was too grim to be designing. Also, she seemed to him, for the moment, so unappealingly simple-minded in her responses to his story. Only one generation removed from a tradition of truly meaningful radical movements, she was still able to be deeply moved by the rhetoric and achievements of her ideological forebears who had risen fighting from the depths of deprivation and created a world and a life style and an environment in which she could at best feebly continue a struggle and feel guilty for not doing more, feel guilty for not having less (and unable, really, to do more, and unable, certainly, to do with less). The distinctions between one generation and the next grew faint at the line of demarcation, and sentiment and nostalgia tended to blur purpose. The new status was too abrupt to allow for moral security. The desire to reaffirm and authenticate oneself became almost overbearing; it became terribly self-conscious, inhibiting, undisciplined. Few things were more alarming and disquieting than a senseless idea of one's guilt or a ruthless questioning of one's moral worth. It was a constant state of drowning —of flailing and splashing and desperation—while one remained perfectly and safely afloat. All of this, which he believed he understood so well, made her vulnerable and gave him the opportunity of becoming a wealthy man. But for the moment he felt himself either vastly superior or else hopelessly estranged. *I had better not corrupt myself with too much morality*, he thought mordantly, staring passively at her severely uncombed hair, her *de rigueur* clothing, her slouching informality—and her tiny diamond earrings.

There was no talk or hint of sex this time; the thought had not entered his mind, and if it had roamed through her thinking then she did not show it, as if it had been subjugated by some higher authority.

"Which one informed, do you think?" she asked.

"I don't know," he said.

"It would be ironic if it was the one who was killed."

"If he was killed."

"Is it possible for them to suspect you?"

He had given that some thought, too. There was nothing he could do about it.

"So they probably caught at least two," she said, "and one is either dead or badly injured."

She knows it all by now, he thought, and yet she goes on, wanting to hear it and say it again, over and over. There was too much in the story for her not to want to lavish her attention upon it: the tenement, the predawn trek uptown, the sinister picnic basket, the august newspaper, the police, the dash to safety, the death (if it was that) of Temple, the commandeered car and the escape.

"Where is Seavery now?" she asked.

"I don't know. He said he'd get in touch."

"When?"

"Soon."

"What kind of person is he really?" she asked.

"A little bit crazy."

"But in the sanest of ways, of course," she said quickly. "How large is his group would you say?"

"His group?"

"You said he had people on the campuses."

"They're not *his*," Frank said. "They're not anybody's. They're simply waiting for the moment or the occasion to galvanize."

"But Seavery says he's going to give them that trigger . . . so in effect, they *are* his people. I think he's going about this brilliantly . . . in spite of this morning's failure . . . though if he means to rouse the students and other groups to action he's going to have to be even bolder."

"He means to be," Frank said.

"What is his plan? Do you know?"

"No."

"I'd like to meet him," she said, an excited glint in her eye, as if she were making a bold proposition.

"He won't like you," he heard himself saying, almost casually, using solely by instinct the leverage he suddenly felt he had with her.

Instead of accusing him of being arbitrary or presumptuous, she merely stared at him.

"But why?" she asked.

"He would doubt you."

"Even though I've been active all my life?"

"He prefers people who were converted this morning. He seems to doubt the staying power and long-range sincerity of what he calls 'standardized radicals.'"

"Well, you can tell him . . . that if it weren't for the long-term people . . ."

"I know," Frank said wearily, signaling with his hand.

"I shouldn't bother you, should I?" she said sympathetically. "After all you've been through. And then on top of everything else, this business with your sister . . ."

"What business with my sister?" he asked warily.

"You haven't heard? Well, that's right . . . how could you? Christ, Frank, what gives with her anyway? I know what it is, of course. But when does it stop? She's getting kind of old for this sort of thing. You'd think if not maturity or pride at last, then simple attrition . . ."

"Will you please tell me what's going on?" he said.

She was reluctant to tell him not because she found it distasteful (which she did), but because she resented the digression, preferring to talk about Arthur Seavery and the "action." She was sorry she had mentioned the notorious and deplorable Helen Dublin Werner, whose life style was not only appalling and incomprehensible but frightening too. (Paul had been there that afternoon and cursed his sister with a vehemence and bitterness Charlotte had never heard in his voice before. It was the most animated she had seen him since Janine's death.)

"Charlotte," Frank said testily.

She sighed, then looked at her watch.

"All right," she said. "We'll talk about it for five minutes, and no more."

TWENTY-ONE

The pictures had begun circulating through the neighborhood that morning, surreptitiously at first, then openly, with increasing impunity, going from hand to hand, to the accompaniment of grins and guffaws; appearing with a ubiquity that was as sudden as it was sourceless, provoking a quality of amusement indigenous to small communities. There were six different poses, taken by flashbulb in the rear of a local tavern (at four o'clock in the morning, it was said). In five of the snapshots she was stark naked, right down to the soles of her feet; in the sixth she was wearing a man's hat. In one she was lying in full figure on the bar, her insouciant face resting in her hand; in another she was sitting on a chair with her legs spread wide, holding a quart bottle of beer pointed up into her nest of pubic hair, with a coy smile for the camera; in another, a rear shot, she could be seen bent over and laughing at the camera through her legs; in another she was straddling the shuffleboard table, her lower lip hanging in slack, foolish suggestiveness; another was simply a full shot of her standing up, hands behind her back, one knee advanced, a spurious sophistication in her face; the sixth showed her wearing the hat, sitting at a table and holding bottle caps over her nipples, with a smile that was almost demure.

It wasn't just six pictures either—at least a dozen prints of each negative had been made. And because it was Helen Dublin (still called that, out of a curious fidelity and nostalgia) no one seemed terribly shocked or surprised, given their knowledge of her acquired habits and natural proclivities. Capstone was much too compact and communicative for these things to be anything less than widely known. So the men grinned and guffawed, and the women (the pictures were circulating as indiscriminately as though wind-borne) were disdainful and sourly amused, while young boys were properly impressed and enchanted by this particular glimpse into these particular mysteries. (Certain grown men were stopping youths of their acquaintance on the street and, as if to prove their sophistication, slyly palming a picture before the youth's eyes, then the two parted, each grinning back over his shoulder at the other.)

There were no problems more compelling or unfair than those that pertained to family: compelling because of the old allegiances and obligations, the mystique of blood ties—and unfair for precisely these same, irrational reasons.

Shit, Frank thought irascibly as he hurried to his father's house, taking strong angry strides—a disturbing figure upon the summer-night somnolence, watched with mild disapproval by the silent porch-sitters. Shit and goddamn, he thought over and over, irritated by this imposition upon what he considered an already overly imposed-upon life. This was ironic, ludicrous—this incredibly trivial thing suddenly encroaching upon him, at this moment. I really don't give a fuck, he thought. It's simply that I am *obligated* to give a fuck and go immediately to the head of the family and establish solidarity in the face of this new crisis which really isn't any more of a crisis than the last crisis of this nature which wasn't one either. She's been doing this, showing it, ever since—ever since she had something to show. Showing her ass to kids in the schoolyard, her tits to trembling slack-jawed pimply-faced connoisseurs in the wardrobe closets, her cunt to guys in the back seats of cars. Good Old Saturday Afternoon Gangbang Helen. All of the early promise more than fulfilled. So what's the big deal now? The only difference is now she's showing it all with greater impartiality, in photographs instead of in the flesh, for everybody and for all time, her curly-haired tunnel of love now preserved in all its amiable open-all-night splendor for the edification of chroniclers and folklorists of Capstone future. (And Charlotte speaking so disdainfully of it, as if she were any better, as if expensive perfume purified it.)

So why should I care? I don't. But I do, and precisely because I don't. I really do have bigger and better problems than this, and I really do not care if she decides to promenade down Grant Avenue tomorrow morning nude to the tips of her toes. But

Christ a'mighty, it simply is not dignified for a man who is trying
to bring progress and reform to the world to have a sister who
shows her bare ass to all comers (pun intended). Why can't that
simpleton of a husband keep her under control? Break her legs or
something. Shove a grapefruit up her snatch and plug up that
voracious salami consumer once and for all. Jesus, I'll be being
interviewed on television as the first President of the first Provisional Government, and there she'll be, sucking off everybody
behind the scenes, slowly working her way on-camera to perform
the ultimate, supreme and incomparable stunt of showing her
ass on network television. But I have to care, because they do.
Old Ben and Paul. Paul more than the old man. Paul's always
hated her, more than he knows, or cares to admit. He's been
embarrassed and ashamed and humiliated and infuriated and disgusted and outraged. Could've killed her a couple times, I remember. Maybe he's right . . . more right than I was. She was older,
so had that certain dispensation and authority . . . or so it
seemed. Can't really call him a prude, since this was more than
just letting the boys in for a feel; this was the biggest pecker
collector in a town that has never been shy about those things.
But what to do? Who was I to oppose the dissemination of so
much joy? She was relieving the tensions and lowering the
inhibitions of a generation. But Paul was the moralist. God, he'd
be furious. *Do you know what she did . . . do you know what
she's done now?* Broken her own world record, that's all. But
tears of rage in his eyes. What was he then—nine, ten, eleven
years old? A moralist even then, who saw, or thought he did, the
wanton difference between right and wrong and beset by it. Too
young to be a moralist, to be so clear and decisive about it, because if you're sensitive about it then, what happens later on
when you see how really fucked-up the world is? Cultivate thy
cynicism when young, child, and build thee a fortress in thy
breast. Otherwise. Poor old Ben. Sire to a screwing machine. Think
of the imbalance in the world—think of the parents of fags and
lezzies. Is this what's called balancing out? Nature has its own
self-perpetuating equality quotient. Created with a genius that
could come only from the Old Weaver in the sky. How to establish the logic of the median of one and a hundred being fifty without having the world die of monotony. It all adds up to propor-

tionate and equipollent percentages, but the arithmetic is a joy
to behold. But having the hundred percenter in your family can
be a hell of a burden. Poor old Ben. Fired off a Roman candle
that is yet illuminating the dimmest of firmaments. He must be
heartsick. His daughter's ass is now published. And not even copy-
righted. Public domain. Very.

When he arrived at his father's house, Frank found his niece
Lorana, his sister's eldest, sitting with the old man. The girl's
distress was evident. A bruised, wounded look filled her saddened
eyes, an empty expression of appeal muting her face.

Ben was sitting in his favored chair, a deep, padded old throne
which once his big frame had dominated but which now more
and more was engulfing his illness-shrunken body. The vividness of
his pain and despair cut to Frank's heart. The big man, the strong
one, for all of Frank's years the epitome of paterfamilias, was now
confronted with a host of vexing and insoluble problems which
had rendered him helpless. With his family in hopeless disarray
and his own doom clear and inexorable upon his own bleak horizon, the man who had always ordered and commanded and decided, who had always regarded all impinging events with an
indomitable and refractory independence, now sat in baffled impotence, not wrathful or embittered, but grieving in his drained
and reduced status, completely disarmed by the scornful and unpredictable humors of fate.

"Sit down, Frank," he said.

Subdued by the unhappiness in the room, Frank sat on the
edge of a chair, feeling, as he always did when in his father's presence these days, a curious influx of strength, of changing status,
as if what was being drained from the dying old man was permeating him with the ruthless, passionless and irreversible continuity
of life.

Lorana stared at him with a clear, disconcerting frankness.

"How are you, Uncle Frank?" she asked.

"Just adequate," he said.

Christ, he thought, what am I doing here anyway? Just because
the bare ass of the daughter, the sister, the mother is being flashed
all over town. Which one are we mourning here? The mother,

most likely. A much bigger myth than daughter or sister can ever
be.

On the front page of the evening paper, which lay on a nearby
table, Frank saw the story of that morning's adventure. His glance
informed him that Breenstone and Meyer had been caught, that
Temple was still alive. *Still alive? How? I guess it's true: they
don't make cars the way they used to.* Christ, he thought, a newspaper certainly became a live and threatening thing when you
found yourself the subject of its columns. Did the average jerk
who chased vicarious thrills through its pages realize how lucky
he was to be able to just throw it aside when the commuter special
reached its destination or when dinner was served or when the
barber called his turn? Privacy and anonymity did, occasionally,
have their delectable side.

So, he thought now, settling back in his chair amid the lengthening silence, who is it who is not discussing it in front of whom?
Them in front of me, or me and the old man in front of her? Poor
old guy, he thought, sidling a look at his father. This kid was the
last love of his life, after a lifetime's worth of disenchantment
with his politics, his ambitions (whatever that particular parental
mystery had ever consisted of), his children, the world in general.
If that kid knew how much he loved her she'd brood less and smile
more for him. But of course having the town pumper for a
mother . . . Now my mother, she caused no problems, except
those that flowed from such attitudes as believing, or pretending
to, that Helen was a virgin on her wedding night. But this kid
. . . with the town pumper and the jellyfish father *your disciple,
buddy: remember that* . . . well, in a few years she'll be old
enough to marry up and get away and begin making her own
problems . . . give the dynasty a shove down the byways of another fucked-up generation. Three generations sitting here right
now, and not a laugh in the carload.

"What have you been up to, Frank?" Ben asked, quiet, polite,
evasive, without the lightest echo of hope or optimism in his voice.

"Nothing too thrilling," Frank said, making an effort to keep
his eye from the newspaper, where the lie was recorded in what
were sometimes referred to as bold headlines. That would finish
the old man off quicker than cyanide, Frank thought *Well, I've
become involved with this left-wing group that is planning to over-*

*throw the government. This morning we tried to blow up the
. . . Say, Dad, why have you stopped breathing?*

"Let us count small mercies," Ben said.

"How is school, Lorana?" Frank asked.

"It's still summer vacation," the girl said politely.

"Frank," Ben said, "you ought to take greater interest in your
nieces and nephews."

"It's hard to keep track . . . they grow up so fast."

"That's the point. You shouldn't let them become strangers."

Well, Frank thought, even if he was interested in acquainting
himself further with the children of the town pumper and the
jellyfish, he knew, out of his own recollections, that no one in a
family became more irrelevant or of less moment than an uncle.
An uncle was of some importance until nieces and nephews
matured, whereupon he was relegated to superfluity. He remembered the jokes he and Paul used to make about their uncles, his
mother's brothers; people who came to visit and sat interminably,
telling deadweight stories about . . . about *other* uncles. Remember certain of your youthful attitudes and perceptions, Frank felt,
and you can avoid stepping into a lot of shit when you get older,
because among the young certain attitudes are eternal. Doubtless
there had been Neanderthal uncles who had heard mysterious
giggling behind their evolutive backs.

"I'd better be going, I think," Lorana said, getting up.

"Don't forget those," Ben said, pointing to several thick manila
envelopes that were piled on his desk.

Frank's idling gaze followed the old man's finger and his eyes
instantly became alert. Warily, critically, he watched the girl walk
to the desk and pick up the envelopes and hold them to her breast
with folded arm like a schoolgirl with her books. He wet his lips
for a moment, his mind speculating feverishly, then flashed a
glance at his father, searching the old man's face for some indica-
tion of triumph or irony or mischief, for something, anything.
Ben threw him a quick, sharp look, then turned away.

Son of a bitch! Frank thought. It was all he could do to keep
his body from leaving the chair like a cannon shot.

Now Ben rose slowly, his hands making a strenuous pushing
effort on the armrests, rising once more with the ceremonial dignity of a man whose risings were now painful and numbered, with

the terrible numbing pride of a man handlocked with death. He put his arm around the girl and walked her to the front door. Frank heard him whispering to her in the hall for a few moments. Then the door closed and the old man returned, sedulously avoiding (it seemed to Frank) looking at his son.

"What did you give her?" Frank asked even before the old man resumed his seat.

Ben paused before the chair.

"Mind your business," he said.

"Maybe I am. Come on—what did you give her? What's in those envelopes?"

"Frank—" Ben said wearily.

Frank got to his feet.

"I'm a son," he said heatedly. "I've got a right to know."

"You're a son and a pain in the ass," Ben said, sitting down now.

"Why do you torment me?" Frank cried, then turned and ran from the house.

He left the front door hanging open behind him as he rushed down the front steps. He ran out to the sidewalk and stopped, looking up and down the street, his lips compressed, his eyes glaring. Then he saw her, about a half block away now, walking softly under the trees. *Damn*, he thought, breaking into a trot. He ran as quietly as he could, not wanting to alarm her. As he narrowed the distance between them, he eased into a brisk striding, his eyes fixed upon the slowly walking girl.

"Lorana," he called out. He forced a smile as she stopped and turned around. So unhappily set were her thoughts that her facial expression did not change when she saw him, evincing no interest or curiosity. Uncle and niece stood under an old, time-weathered oak, next to the privet hedges of a darkened house.

"I was just wondering," Frank said. "What did he give you there?" He pointed, somewhat self-consciously, at the envelopes she was holding.

"Some things he wanted me to have," she said.

"He isn't well, you know."

"I know."

"I mean . . . it's more than that. He's very sick."

"I know," she said again, her voice quietly reverent, as if in deference to her grandfather's ill health.

"Why did he give them to you? Did he say?"

"He said in case anything happens to him . . ."

"And then . . . in case something happens . . . what then?"

"I don't know," she said.

"You mean to say he didn't give you instructions?"

She shook her head, seemed rather diffident.

Frank paused, wetting his lips. He stared at the envelopes. He had to roll his hands into fists and thrust them into his pockets to keep from reaching out and snatching the envelopes from the girl.

"Did he say what was in them?" he asked.

"Family records, some papers; things like that."

"Is that all?"

"Yes."

"Did you see them?"

"Why?" she asked, staring at him now with a shade of wary interest, unconsciously adding pressure to her grip on the envelopes.

"I want to know if you looked at them," he said.

"No. He *told* me what they were."

"Are you going to open them?"

"Why are you so interested?" Lorana asked.

"Because I have a right to be," he said. "After all, there could be documents in there that I have a right to know about."

"He didn't say that there were."

"I would like to see them."

"Uncle Frank," she said, with some distress now. "He said I wasn't to show them to anyone."

"Why not?" he said, under a terrific strain to maintain his composure. "Look, then that's all the more reason for me to see them. Look, he's sick . . . a very sick man . . . and I wonder sometimes if all the pain and medication hasn't . . . made him somewhat . . . unaccountable."

"Unaccountable?"

"You know what I mean. Unreliable."

"There's nothing wrong with his mind," she said resentfully.

"I never said there was. But he does become forgetful now and

then. I'm sure you've noticed that. It's a symptom. Believe me, I
know what I'm talking about. It's just that . . . I wouldn't want
him giving away anything that might belong to me, or to your
Uncle Paul."

"I'm sure he's thought about that." She was holding the envelopes against her with both arms now, looking as though she
were prepared to defend them.

"Why don't you give them to me?" Frank said. "Just for the
evening . . . so I can check out everything . . . just in case."

She stared inquiringly into his eyes with utter candor. He was
so agitated about what was happening that he made no effort of
guile or pretense, staring intently back at her; so fixated that it
was the fixation itself he was trying to communicate, the urgency and unpredictability of it.

"I'd have to ask him first," she said, after several moments, during which she had been groping toward a response that would be
uncompromising and still not impolite.

"All right," he said. "Until then, promise me something: keep
them in a safe place, don't open them, and for heaven's sake don't
let anyone know you have them. There could be some very personal . . . very private things there."

"I understand."

"Good."

He lingered, unwilling to end the conversation, though he
had nothing further to say. Patiently, she waited, watching him,
mistrust clearly in her eyes now.

Then, abruptly, he said good night and turned and hurried
back to his father's house. The old man was capable of it, he
thought somberly as he walked under the trees, gnawing on his
thumbnail. Ben was at the moment sufficiently disillusioned with
the world at large and his children in particular to have handed
that money over to his granddaughter. (And if so, was the girl
aware of it? Her face had been so maddeningly inscrutable, though
her manner had become perceptibly defensive, he thought.) It
was just the kind of perverse and willful thing the old man was
capable of doing, and if true, then it had been triggered by what
Helen had done, those damned pictures. Yes, Frank thought
gloomily as he approached the house. He's given her that money.
Finally dug it out of whatever gopher hole he had been hiding

it in and given it away. Today was the day for it all right. Today
was the day when all the servants of hades had their feast: beginning with the morning's fiasco, then the appearance of the
pictures: it was a natural, inevitable sequence in the evolution of
disaster for that money to have been passed to his niece before
his very eyes.

When he re-entered the house he found his father sitting in
the chair, staring balefully at him.

"Where were you?" Ben asked. "What did you do?"

"What did you give her?" Frank asked. "What's in those envelopes?"

"You think I gave her that money, don't you?"

"Maybe not the money—I don't know—but perhaps something
pertaining to it, information or something. I think you're just sore
enough at us all to have done it."

"That girl is the only human being who—"

"Bullshit," Frank said heatedly. "Look, I don't like being told—
I *resent* being told—that someone else loves my father more than
I do. So I'm not a pretty slip of a thing who gives you tender and
loving attention." Frank snorted at the image. "You'd like that,
I suppose?"

"I've no doubt that my children love me," Ben said soberly.

Frank looked at him and suddenly felt a terrible remorseful
pang. He would much rather have heard his father spiritedly tell
him to go to hell. *God*, he thought, *doesn't he have enough? What
am I doing to him?* The old man was sitting quietly but in obvious
discomfort, his arms tensely on the rests; he seemed to be sitting
in a sort of poised, tentative suspension, as if trying to appease his
pain with balance and immobility.

Frank sat down on the sofa, slumping wearily, covering his
eyes with his hand. His father stared compassionately at him.

"Maybe I should have told you the truth about that money a
long time ago," Ben said. "I guess I never really gauged the depth
of your obsession with it. But you never looked at it from my point
of view, Frank. If I had taken it, it wouldn't have been something
to be proud of." Ben's voice was quiet, contrite.

"You just let it hang," Frank said, his eyes closed now under
his hand.

"Yes," Ben murmured, nodding, "that was unfair."

"I know you took it," Frank said in a quiet inflectionless statement of fact. "Of course you took it. It was impossible for you to admit it, but always simple to deny. And you never really denied it. I won't ask you again. What's the point? I know you took it. The only question is what you've done with it."

After several moments of silence, staring pensively at his son, Ben said, "You've always attached so much importance to it, ever since you were a child." His voice had a musing quality. "But I shouldn't have been surprised at that. Paul always had something he wanted to do, some goal; and Helen had her own . . . obsessions. But you . . . were always at a loss. You made that money your goal."

"Twenty-five thousand dollars is no small amount."

"A year's salary for a middling executive nowadays."

"I'm not a middling executive. I tell you, I've worked at jobs the past few years where that is five years' salary."

"I've always felt that my performance as a parent would be patrimony enough for my children," Ben said lightly, smiling hopefully at Frank, whose eyes remained closed under his sheltering hand. "And anyway," he went on in the same vein, "how would it do for an old Socialist to leave behind so much money?"

Frank was barely listening. The long day had begun to tire and deplete him.

"Listen," Ben said, "you've heard about your sister's latest?"

Frank nodded.

"What do you think?" Ben asked.

"All it amounts to," Frank said tiredly, "is that the other half of Capstone is seeing her ass."

"She telephoned me this afternoon. Says she was drugged, that she doesn't remember it happening. She was drugged all right— by booze. She was crying though. Very upset. Philip is out looking for the photographer, to wring his neck, he says. Instead of knocking the shit out of her, once and for all. Leave it to him, to go in the other direction. 'Fart and Sin.' That's what they're called around here. Did you know that?"

Frank shook his head.

"But it isn't good, Frank. These kind of situations can deteriorate only up to a point . . . and then something happens. Your brother hit the ceiling. You should have heard him on the phone. This isn't going to help his disposition any."

"He has no disposition," Frank muttered.

"No?" Ben asked. "And Lorana . . . she was talking about running away. Can you blame her? How can she go on living in this neighborhood? God, if I had the strength I'd do the same . . . just run away from . . . everything." Ben sighed philosophically. "Ah, Frank," he said softly, "you waste too much precious life worrying about ephemera. But I know how you think . . . you look upon all these years of wondering and speculating as an investment of sorts, and now you aim to claim your dividend. Frank," Ben said, in a tone so compelling Frank brought his hand away from his eyes and looked at his father, "aren't you frightened by this obsession? I mean, to be so obsessed with something which if you had been given it three years ago would have been dissipated by now . . ."

"You said it yourself: it's the investment I have in it. Nevertheless, I refuse to believe you'd entrust a sum of that amount to a sixteen-year-old girl. So, if you've given it to her, then you've made a fool of me."

"I worry about you, Frank. Don't looked bored by that. A parent has an instinct about a child, especially a father for a son. And when one has lived long enough, one can, if he chooses to, find enough scraps and pieces from life to fit and justify any belief, philosophy or instinct that he selects. I remember a friend of mine . . . we were about twenty then. One night we went out to Coney Island and just for the hell of it stepped into the booth of a gypsy fortuneteller. We had our palms read. I forget what she told me, but she warned him to look out for someone born of the dead. We laughed it off, naturally. I told him he'd certainly got his dime's worth. But a few weeks later he was killed in a brawl in Harlem . . . knifed to death by a drunken Negro. At the trial it came out that the Negro's mother, eight months pregnant, had been killed in some accident or other, but that the baby—the future murderer—had been successfully delivered."

"What the hell is that supposed to mean?" Frank asked.

Ben shrugged. "I don't know. Nothing, if you don't pay attention. But who knows? Did the old gypsy have a premonition about my friend? Do I have a premonition about you? Or am I simply

indulging some senile whimsy after a lifetime of hard and dis-
ciplined thinking? My mind is very tired, Frank. You have to forgive me."

"You're forgiven," Frank said, and abruptly got to his feet.
"I'm going home," he said, yawning, stretching out his arms.

"Now that you think the money is gone," Ben said with a wry
smile, "will you still come to visit?"

"Twice as much," Frank said. "Just to make you feel guilty."

When he arrived at the boardinghouse, Frank was half expecting
the police to come stepping out of the shadows and arrest him.
But no one was there, and he went upstairs to his room and fell
asleep immediately.

TWENTY-TWO

At noon the next day an urgent knocking on the door wakened Frank. He opened his eyes and fixed a leaden, uncomprehending gaze, then turned in his covers, befogged and confused. The knocking went on, like a set of nervous reflexes. He sat up, making absurd faces as he parted his eyelids as far apart as he could to undo the granulation that had collected. Then he rubbed at them. The knocking continued. He stared at the door, sitting forward in his covers. There was a hypnotic, mindless quality to the sounds.

"Who's there?" he yelled, irritated by this persistence.

The knocking ceased, followed immediately by the voice, like an addendum to the knocking—it had that same urgent, tireless insistence.

"Frank. Frank."

Frank sighed, then shook his head. He threw back the covers and swung his legs to the floor. He sat for a moment, a surly expression on his face. Then he slapped his thighs and got up. He looked quizzically for a moment at the spectacular sunshine flooding through the screened window, then at the wind-up clock on the bureau, which had stopped at a dead hour of the night. He stepped into his trousers, hoisted them up and, buckling the belt, went to the door, unlocked it and opened it.

Standing there—looking exactly as Frank knew he would, with wide, stricken, self-involved eyes and pained, sinned-against features—was his brother-in-law.

"Did I wake you?" Philip asked.

"Yes."

"I'm sorry," Philip said. He looked at his watch as if to exonerate himself. "But—"

"What do you want?" Frank asked. "If it's about Helen—"

Philip entered the room and Frank closed the door.

"So you've heard about that," Philip said. He walked the length of the room, paused and stared listlessly out of the window for a moment, then turned around.

"Phil," Frank said, "I share your dismay, but she is what she is. You know it, I know it, Capstone knows it. It's not as if you're hiding some sordid secret. It's a rugged, deplorable fact; and there's nothing that can be done about it."

Philip's face was so consumed with sadness that Frank felt a twinge of guilt for having spoken so bluntly.

"Well," Frank said, softening his tone, "maybe some good will come of it. Maybe this will shock her into straightening out."

"It's too late," Philip said ruefully.

"What do you mean?" Incredulous, Frank stared at his brother-in-law, fully expecting to hear a tale of uncharacteristic rage and fury, of murder.

Rendered momentarily mute, Philip prolonged the suspenseful slippage of time, staring at Frank. When he spoke, it was in a voice edged and broken with emotion.

"Lorana's run away."

Frank's sense of relief at this less consequential piece of news was brief.

"She's *what?*" he said in a stunned and unbelieving whisper.

"Run away."

"Where? When?"

"Last night," Philip said. "She came home, packed a bag, and slipped out again. She'd been to visit your father."

"I know. I saw her there."

"You did? Did she say anything?"

"Not about running away. Listen. Jesus Christ. Are you sure? Maybe she spent the night with a friend."

"No, no, I checked. What do you think I've been doing all morning? I've checked out every conceivable place, every friend. She's gone, Frank. She'd been talking about it. She was so upset over those fucken pictures . . . Frank, what am I going to do?"

"Don't panic," Frank said, trying to control his own rising fears. "Just take it easy. We'll get nowhere by losing our heads. We've got to think calmly and rationally." He sat down on the bed and hung his head, utterly disconsolate. Last night, he was thinking. That had been his last chance. He should have grabbed those envelopes and told her to take a flyer. God almighty, he had simply let her walk off with them.

"I've notified the police," Philip said.

"The police?" Frank said looking up.

"They said they'd do what they could. Frank," Philip said, a sudden anguish in his voice, "where do you think she could have gone? She has no money . . ."

Frank looked at him with a worn, listless smile, then shook his head. I'm cursed, he thought, in those literal words, suddenly beseiged with the insane desire to laugh, feeling himself beginning to tremble with a ludicrous hysteria, with a synthesis of emotions that almost blacked out his mind: cursed, utterly and totally, beyond redemption, beyond succor, beyond pity, beyond the most elemental humane observance: by a father who had written him off completely, by a wealthy woman who did not appreciate him, by a scheming niece, and by the human doormat standing before him whose helplessness had now irrevocably sealed the disaster.

"Frank," Philip said, "she's such a timid kid . . . so unworldly . . . where would she go . . . what will she do?"

So unworldly, Frank thought ironically, that she probably opened those envelopes the first chance she had, took one long, loving look at the money, grinned appreciatively, and set sail. Where would she go?—As far as twenty-five thousand stolen old dollars could take her. To a Park Avenue hotel. To Hollywood. To Paris. To all the places and all the things she had ever dreamed about.

Now he stared philosophically at his brother-in-law. Christ, he thought with peculiar objectivity, now I know how this poor crumb has been feeling all his life, how he feels when he goes to sleep at night and when he wakes up in the morning. How does he stand it? In another moment I'm going to have to ask him for *advice* on how to survive under a constant, constantly growing pile of shit. He thought briefly of Paul. Paul would not care in the least. Paul was too quick to see the sardonic side of things and would laugh it off. And anyway, that insulated son of a bitch had already come into his share when Janine died.

"Philip," he finally said, "are you absolutely certain you've checked every possible place?"

"Believe me, I'm certain. Helen and the kids have been looking too, since seven o'clock this morning. We've turned the town upside down."

"She left last night, huh?" Frank said thoughtfully. Then, "You say she packed a bag? What did she take? Do you know?"

"Just some things, just what you'd expect."

"Maybe we ought to search through her belongings—it might give us some clue."

Philip looked blankly at him.

"What kind of clue?"

"I don't know, but I don't think we ought to overlook anything."

"I don't see—"

"Phil, do you want me to help you or not?" Frank said, unable to hide his impatience.

"Of course," Philip said placatingly. "Whatever you say."

Frank quickly washed and dressed. Then he went with Philip to the latter's house. Finding no one at home, they began going through Lorana's belongings, Philip obediently and without enthusiasm, unable to see the sense of it; Frank with frail and despairing hope. Frank soon extended his search to the whole house, going through closets and drawers and suitcases and boxes, throwing things aside with increasingly violent despair. He really did not expect to find those envelopes, and their absence only served to further shore up his certainty that one of them had contained the money.

"Gee, what a mess," Philip said later, looking around at the places where Frank had pushed and shoved and clawed and opened.

"You have no idea," Frank said, stalking from the house, Philip chasing after him.

They walked around town, each absorbed in his particular aspect of the problem, neither less gloomy than the other. Then they stepped into Jim Carson's Tavern, a run-down bar in the lower end, the Polish section, of town.

After sipping some whisky, Philip said, sighing, "I appreciate your giving me this time, Frank. I know you have other things on your mind." Philip stared meaningfully. This was the first time

he had ever alluded, however obliquely, to their "political conversation."

"Yes," Frank said.

They were sitting at a table, against a far wall, under a calendar
picture of a nude woman with a nineteen fifties hair style.

"I meant what I said that time," Philip said. "About wanting
to do something . . . active. I've been talking to some of the men
at the plant—discreetly, of course—and you'd be surprised how
much discontent there is."

"No I wouldn't," Frank said bluntly.

Even though the place was empty except for their presence,
and the bartender had disappeared into the back room, Philip
lowered his voice and leaned forward as he spoke.

"I offered my services," he said, staring intently at Frank. "Do
you have so many men that you can disregard that?"

"It isn't numbers that count," Frank said. "It's quality. You
don't seem to understand that."

"What do you mean by quality?" Philip asked, frowning.

"By quality I don't mean sweetness of disposition, nor sincerity either. Take, for example, those men who tried to blow up
the newspaper trucks yesterday. Did you read about that? All
right. There you see what I'm talking about. You may not agree
with what they were trying to do—"

"But I do," Philip said quickly.

"—but you can't deny their courage or the seriousness of their
commitment. They were risking their lives and their freedom.
Could you do that?"

"I could," Philip said.

After gazing skeptically at him for a moment, Frank went on.

"But even more than that, they were risking the possibility that
their explosives might go off and kill people who had nothing to
do with their action. Could you risk doing that?"

"Yes," Philip said without hesitation.

"What makes you so sure? What the fuck have you ever done,
what have you ever tried?"

Philip, impaled upon the unanswerable, remained leaning forward, his wide unblinking stare fixed upon Frank. Then he
blinked, and frowned.

"All right," he said. "But those men are the leadership of the

Movement. Not everybody can be a general. You need soldiers in the ranks."

"Pardon me, Philip, but that's your busted-ball psychology. Why think in those terms when so much more is available to you? Why immediately, instinctively, think of yourself as 'a soldier in the ranks'?"

"Because I don't have leadership qualities," Philip said. "I have to be honest about it. I can best serve under orders. There's no disgrace in knowing your limitations."

"That's nonsense," Frank said curtly. He was annoyed by this kind of talk, this kind of thinking.

"It is?" Philip asked, puzzled.

"You don't understand the Movement or the people in it. You're talking like a damn fool. The whole sweep of the Movement goes contrary to what you say. There is absolutely no room for your kind of timid thinking. Every link in the chain has to be strong, each man has to know without question that he can depend upon the next. In the Movement, it's an act of faith that makes a man strong. Of what earthly use is a man who comes in with your attitude?"

"You're right!" Philip said with a sudden surge of feeling so emphatic and so unexpected it startled Frank. "Of course you're right. I never saw it that way before. I know what I'm capable of, and believe me, it's more than a little. The trouble is, I've always let things get me down. I've been too quick to accept what the *world* thinks, rather than what *I know*. If a man has to ask what he can do, then it means he's capable of nothing. But you have to be patient with me, Frank. Sometimes a man needs a hint, some advice. Especially now, with my head split in so many directions, I can't concentrate my thoughts the way I would like . . . the way I'm really *able* to. You'd be surprised what I can do when I really apply myself. It's just that now it's so difficult. You understand, don't you?"

"I understand, but I can't sympathize. For the stakes that are being played for, a man has to let go of everything else."

"But how can I?"

"So why do you waste your breath with this kind of talk? What good is clarity of vision if the rest of you remains paralyzed? Don't you think that those men who attacked the newspaper yesterday had 'other things' in their lives? Of course they did, but that didn't stop them from going ahead."

"You're right," Philip said ruefully. Then, "But, Frank, I *need* to do something. It's more than just conviction—it's a matter of self-respect too. I don't care how dedicated a revolutionary is to his cause, there have to be some other grains of motivation driving him. That's the truth, no matter what you say. Believe me, I have no illusions about myself. A long time ago I took stock and realized I was a loser. That's defeatist, you might say, but it's honest, too, and there's courage in it. But *now*"—and Philip tapped the table with his finger for emphasis—"I've re-evaluated. I no longer have this morbid good humor about myself. I always thought that if you were honest with the world the world would be honest with you. All right, I've been honest. But not any more. Why should I? What has it ever gained me?"

"All well and good," Frank said. "But without that blind, almost irrational devotion to a faith, it's nothing. You can *decide* you're a great man, but it's still an illusion unless you *act* upon it. It's self-deceit to tell yourself that you can do anything you want, if only you felt like doing it. Suppose you had been asked to join these men yesterday? What would you have done?"

"I don't know," Philip said.

"I think you're somebody who likes to hear himself talk."

"But, Frank, don't you see—even for me to *say* these things is a breakthrough."

"Would you, say, incinerate yourself in the name of your beliefs?"

"Incinerate myself?"

"People have been doing that in various parts of the world you know, in protest, for what they think is right. Now *there's* a powerful act of faith, *there's* something that has impact."

"But what good is it to die?"

"Some deaths can be very inspirational. The outlines of an oppressor can be very vividly delineated by a dead man. He does to them what they can never do to him."

"Would you do that?"

"Possibly," Frank said.

"My God," Philip said thoughtfully. "To do something like that. It's a horrible death."

"But you can create a spirit that men will follow forever."

"But, Frank, the agony of it . . ." Philip said, wincing.

"Well, sometimes the gesture can be enough. I heard a story once, when I was in California, about somebody in some small African state who decided to protest that way. He doused himself with gasoline, sat down in a public square and set fire to himself. But his friends were on the spot—they'd known what he was going to do—and were able to beat out the flames before there was much harm done. Nevertheless the gesture was so powerful it provoked the consciences of so many people that the government was forced to put through reforms. And the man became a national hero."

"He did?" Philip asked.

"Naturally. He had shown a strength and courage that people were awed by. What he did was take the complexities of a situation and through use of drama reduce them to simplifications which people could understand."

"Through setting fire to himself," Philip said wonderingly.

"Could you do something like that?"

"It would wipe away a lifetime of stupidity, wouldn't it?"

"You can't personalize it, Philip. I keep telling you that."

"Frank," Philip said eagerly, "I once read about these fire dancers they have in the West Indies . . . they actually put burning torches in their mouths and on their bare skin . . . and suffer no ill effects. The trick, according to this article, is that they're burning cotton wads soaked in alcohol and the fire doesn't burn as hot . . . something like that."

"So?"

"Nothing. I was just thinking. Suppose I wanted to do something like that? Would you help me?"

"Philip . . ." Frank said impatiently.

"I mean, let's say I wanted to do it but not really . . . like maybe that fellow in Africa did. Maybe he *planned* to have his friends on the spot like that. Maybe yes, maybe no. But what's the difference? It worked, didn't it? Listen, haven't you ever seen someone put lighter fluid on his finger and set fire to it? He blows it out right away, of course, but it doesn't hurt. And he's made his effect."

"The life of the party," Frank said dryly.

"Would you help me?" Philip asked.

"How?"

"By making sure it didn't go too far."

"You're talking nonsense."

Philip sighed. He took a swallow of whisky.

"I guess so," he said in an inconsolable voice, looking emptily at his glass. He expanded his chest with a deep breath, then his shoulders collapsed in another sigh. "It's just . . . just that I don't know what to do any more," he said.

TWENTY-THREE

He had planned their lives together with an immaculacy of calculation and expectancy that amused her. "Paul," she said chidingly, laughing, "this is the twentieth century. People no longer
have the luxury of being able to plan with assurance." In this
age of the telephone, the automobile, the airplane, of predictable and unpredictable interruptions and obtrusions, one would
be fortunate to enjoy an orderly and well-planned twenty-four
hours. "And anyway," Janine said, "I'm not so sure I'd like everything so neat and consistent. The unexpected can be a marvelous
stimulus." But in order for the creative mind to function at the
top of its form, he believed, a large measure of stability and tranquillity was called for. Inspiration fed on contemplation and
contemplation on serenity. After all, they were both creative people, he with his essays and she with her poetry.

It was the poetry that brought them together. She had published a quatrain in the college paper which, in its brevity, struck
him as so exquisitely expressive he felt he must meet her. She
was pointed out to him one morning sitting on the library steps,
absorbed in a narrow-spined book which was balanced on her knee,
the sun shining brightly on its white pages. He stood at the foot
of the steps staring up at her with a mixture of astonishment and
pleasure. He had to laugh at himself: he should have known better
than to yield to the stereotype of the gifted poetess: the enchanted
Dickinson, the haunted Emily Brontë, the frail Elizabeth Barrett.
The young woman he was staring at, whose poem had provoked
so profound a sense of kinship, was more stereotypical of the
California-bred woman, radiant in tone and style and color—a per-
sonification of median America's romantic illusions. She had
long honey-blond hair, coiffured with lush sensual waves (as opposed to the more fashionable linear severity all around her);

smooth, deeply sunned cheeks; small, fine nose; lovely unpainted lips that pouted in repose; and, when they rose in discovery of his transfixed homage at the foot of the steps, meditative blue eyes that dispelled any notion of the incompatibility of great beauty and serious purpose.

Although she hardly lacked for admirers, she was pleased and flattered by his attention, by his appreciative and perceptive comments about her poem, despite her stated wariness of "literary intellectuals," this despite, again, her own pretensions toward being one herself. Lineal and collateral to old, colonially rooted, wealthy Main Line families, she was, by certain narrow standards, a rebel. Already she had returned the engagement ring of the son of one of her father's law partners. "His notion of poetry was that it's a nice hobby, good for filling the spaces between dishes and diapers," she said. "Not this poetry," he said after he had read a dozen or so of her poems in manuscript. "There's a little demon here that bites around the edges of my heart," he said. "I'm not really a critic of poetry, but . . ." "Oh," she said quickly, with a smile, "I think you're doing just brilliantly." She read some of his work and liked it. But why the essay? Wasn't it a dead form today, more or less? "Not dead," he said: "moribund. It wants a tough new approach. A bloody transfusion." "Bloody transfusion?" she asked, laughing; then said, "I like that."

He regarded himself a prudent man, nevertheless he did not consider it precipitant when he proposed two weeks later. Rather it was, he believed, sensible and inevitable; for once it had entered his mind in concept, it remained and became a fact—this kind of thinking confining and bolting in one's view of it. "My God," she said, "the son of an old Socialist rabble rouser? What would my family say?" "Disown you, probably," he said, and added, "In any event, my father has long since recanted and is probably more narrow-lined conservative than your whole family put together." "Well," she said, "I suggest we do something serious about this." They rented a car and drove to Pacific Palisades and spent four days there. They watched the sun rise out of the mountains like the blazing birth of a continent; they walked on the beach with the wind and salt spray in their faces; and under the vast warm Canaan of California night they dreamed and talked and made love, and felt their lives intertwining and interlocking, and, with all the graces of youth, felt the warming confluence of their souls and the ancientry of their hearts. *Let's not wait,* she said. *Let's not wait at all.*

All of that, the four days, the sealing of the compact, she light-heartedly referred to as "details" and "practical considerations." "Now the acid test," she said as they drove back to the university. "And what," he asked, "may that be?" "You have to meet and impress the guardian of my conscience."

He had heard of Kifner, of course, though he had never met him. The forty-eight-year-old left-wing theoretician was the most prominent man on campus. Curious about the man's reputation, Paul had read the volume of essays that was regarded as Kifner's quintessential work and, in spite of their intellectual vigor, found them turgid, muddled, even somewhat crypto-fascistic in their call for the suppression of "certain civil liberties" until other, more vital doctrines could establish their "ascendancy" and assure a "New World of the People."

Kifner was the driving, dynamic focal point of campus radical-ism. Student leaders flocked around him with unabashed, unques-tioning servility. While lionized by some, the outspoken professor had been the target of several death threats during the past few years, as well as the subject of acerbic criticism by certain factions within the board of trustees and among sectors of the alumni. He remained, however, magnificently above it all, ignoring the threats, the criticism, the grumblings. Tenured, world renowned in his field, with overflowing classrooms, he was secure. Although the call to violent revolution was clearly implicit in his writings, he was much more discreet and ambiguous on the subject in his lectures, calling for his students to "elect" for themselves the tac-tics that would most effectively bring about the "New World of the People." With an arrogance and sarcasm that flashed like light-ning bolts out of a somber firmament, he castigated fools and critics ("To call a critic a fool is a redundancy," he said), showing little tolerance for opposing points of view.

"Shouldn't he take offense at my being apolitical?" Paul asked. "Hardly," she said. "He doesn't mind being ignored, it's being challenged that he can't stand. I'm not any more political than you are. It's the man's common sense and vitality that fascinate me."

Paul was pleasantly surprised when he met the great man, whom Janine called "Stephen." From Kifner's writings, from his thinking, from all that had been told, Paul was expecting a sternly reserved, somewhat forbidding scholar. Instead, he found himself utterly charmed and overwhelmed by the most congenial of hosts, a man at once vibrant, personable, not unpretentious but not unduly self-centered either, as well as with a most unprofessorial ability to listen thoughtfully. The man seemed the most splendid, civilized sort of dichotomy, able to detach himself completely from his efforts—as Paul read them—to reduce the Bill of Rights to a shambles, and relax and disarm those around him by virtue of his great personal warmth. And in spite of a rather thick, stocky, physical unattractiveness, he somehow exuded an undeniable virility, simply by the way he slouched in a chair, spoke, stared, gestured, walked. Separated from his wife and children ("That's supposed to be a lovely scandal," Janine said with evident pleasure), Kifner lived in a stucco bungalow near the campus. In his entrance way stood a wire bookrack, of the kind seen in drug stores, which contained revolutionary pamphlets, magazines and books, from reputable publishers, obscure publishers, hand presses, mimeograph machines. The walls of his den were decorated with the now familiar posters of the world revolutionary hierarchy. At no time, however, did Kifner attempt to inculcate Paul or Janine with his political philosophy.

"Converts?" he said in his strong, exuberant baritone as they sat in the den drinking the martinis he had expertly mixed. For a time Paul's eyes could not be kept from the fire that Kifner kept going in the small fireplace in the corner; no matter the heights of temperature produced by the southern California sun, Professor Kifner's fire burned whenever he was home. When questioned about it, he merely smiled and referred with studied casualness to his "open symbol." "Who in the hell wants or needs converts to a political cause?" he said, adding, "I would much rather absorb people than convert them. The bane of any movement is an enlightened proletariat." He laughed loudly, as at some terrific absurdity; the laughter was unnaturally loud, Paul felt, and carried a certain mordancy in its tones. "They come in here all the time," Kifner said, "particularly after I've made a speech, and want to know how they can overthrow the government tomorrow morning. What am I supposed to say to them? Did Mozart go to Haydn and ask him how to write music? The number of hard-core revolutionaries at any given time is always a remarkably small one, and should be. It has to be an elitist group." " 'Men who borrow their opinions can never repay their debts,' " Paul said. "What?" Kifner said with an animated rise of his brows. "You're quoting Halifax there, the old seventeenth-century pamphleteer, aren't you? Janine—he knows Halifax; you had better marry him immediately!"

When they were married, Kifner moved in with a colleague and let the young couple use the bungalow for a week, and there they spent their honeymoon. Later, after they had taken an apartment near the campus, they were frequent guests at Kifner's perennial open house. Several times they joined him and a young female companion—from the apparently inexhaustible supply available to him—for weekend trips to San Francisco or Mexico.

Kifner told Paul that he fondly looked upon the young couple as his "diversion people," with whom he could be at his ease and pursue his other interests. "Look," he said, "a Vice-President of the United States has described my mind as 'a chamber of horrors,' a Senate Committee referred to me as a polluter of clear springs, and various colleagues of great repute have dismissed me as a mad fantast, a lunatic, a Mussolini with wit, and so on. I relish it all, but I do like a day off now and then. And believe me, this is not unflattering to you." A few weeks later, Paul saw the man truly in action for the first time, when Kifner addressed several thousand students in the gymnasium during a protest meeting. Sitting near the rostrum, Paul felt himself, quite against his will, held in thrall by Kifner, who appeared to have been transformed from the genial companion he knew so well into a titan orating to a tribunal of cloud-robed deities. Kifner's body swelled and grew, and his gesturing fist seemed to be hammering vibrations into the air, and Paul felt that voice penetrating and reverberating through his own body. The effect appalled him.

He realized now for the first time fully what a many-sided man this was. First there was the severe, formidable man of the writings, the remorseless dissenter. Then there was the living-room debater, marshaling powerful and dogmatic intellectual postures and with Teutonic-like arrogance inundating some hapless doubter: here, more than at any other time, was the absolutist visionary, preaching no limits to the means by which goals must be achieved. And there was the incomparable companion of the social occasion, with his bawdy wit, restive energy, vibrant centripetal presence, and immense capacity to relax (and there was this sense of immensity about Kifner in repose, like some giant after descending his private Olympus). And now, lastly, the public Kifner, with his evangelical fervor, his almost supernatural ability to transcend and transfigure himself and split the wind with his voice and scald the flesh of his furthest listener.

"I'm not sure I like him as much as I used to," Paul said. Janine was surprised. "Is there a real Kifner?" he asked. "Does one really exist? How can so many men live in the same body without that body being, finally, a total falsehood? What happens to all that fanatical energy when he's not using it? Is he really that agreeable a companion? Perhaps we're overestimating his greatness and thus overvaluing his leisurely side." "You're not the first to be offended by him," she said. He protested: "But I do like him. That's the thing. But what is it that I like? Am I awed by his reputation? Maybe; but yet when I read the work that has established the reputation, I find much of it either unintelligible, dangerous, or laughably naïve. I listen to him speak, saying things with which I'm in complete disagreement, and yet feel myself shaking under the power of his saying them. Look, I'm no fool. Do you think, under it all, he's a charlatan?" "No," she said. "Then what?" he asked. She seemed reluctant to answer. And then: "I could say it's simply that you've met and been exposed to your first genius. It's that, yes; but more: He has a certain biomagnetism. You can't describe it any further than that, and neither can you argue with it."

He continued to be disturbed by the image he had of Stephen Kifner, that preacher of the forbidden, whose reputation and whose convoluted rhetoric served to obscure the true contours of his ragged ensign. Social critics had long been preoccupied with the question of the American public's fascination with criminals, violence, outlawry; it seemed the sovereign mystery of the national psyche. But what of the more subtle brand of malevolence, which spoke to more rarefied levels of secrecy and contemplation? Was this where Kifner's intellectual gangsterism penetrated and titil-

lated? Was it more respectable and acceptable to preach gangsterism as long as it was in the context of social causes, movements,
historical empiricism, heroic misguided bloodstained anarchists of
the past? Was the intellectual's obsession with violence any less
base than that of the so-called common man's?

Just before he and Janine were to return East, Paul visited
Kifner. "I want to know something," Paul said. "I've noticed that
among all your friends, we were the only non-political ones. Now,
you've said you found that refreshing. But—and I think I know
you well enough to say this—I couldn't help feeling at times your
friendship had a flavor of condescension." "Untrue," Kifner said.
He was watching Paul with an attentive, curiously somber stare.
"Why then should I have felt it?" Paul asked. "Because," Kifner
said, "I'm internationally known in my field," and he shrugged as
if to disavow his interest in that, "and you have yet to achieve
anything beyond marrying the campus beauty, and so feel in-
ferior, and so try to rationalize why the great man should be your
friend." Paul's eyes moved to the small orange fire in the corner
of the den that seemed to be prowling from side to side on the
perspiring log, that maddening interminable blaze crackling and
snarling. "I want to maintain the friendship," Paul said, "and so
I want to be certain of the sincerity." "This is a very curious conversation," Kifner said. "I feel you're not saying everything you
came to say, or at least would like to." "Hasn't it annoyed you
that I stand outside of everything you hold so dear?" "No, Paul.
I told you once I wasn't interested in converts or apostles. You
choose to live in a very pure atmosphere. I don't think you can;
I think the world is going to invade you, sooner or later. It's
just as well you don't subscribe to my view of things: you would
be consumed. You're going to be consumed anyway, but this way
you won't notice." "I want to continue the relationship," Paul
said, "but I have to remain independent of you. In all matters.
That's the problem." "You have remained independent, though
not through strength of mind, but insularity. Therefore there is
no problem," Kifner said, then added, "except your passion for the
status quo."

They went East in June. They stopped briefly in Philadelphia
where Paul met Janine's parents. The family had not been happy
about the marriage, but they were relieved that Paul did not

"look" or "act" like their conception of a writer. He seemed not
in any way to be in a state of rebellion, and had no radical grudge
or design against vested interests. Their relief at his not being
blatantly objectionable was so great that, after several days, they
forgave their daughter and allowed themselves to like him.

They established themselves in a small apartment on Manhattan's Upper West Side. Using her parents' generous wedding gift
("The money they would have wasted on a big Main Line wedding," Janine said), they were able to furnish their apartment
modestly and devote themselves to their work temporarily relieved
of financial concerns. Each sat in a separate room, behind a
closed door, working at a portable typewriter. Each soon achieved
small but promising successes: Janine placing her poetry in
sparely circulated but prestigious quarterlies, Paul selling to prominent periodicals several low-keyed, well-turned essays (which the
editors, to his annoyance, referred to as "articles").

And then one morning Janine came upstairs from her pilgrimage
to the letter box—the most tense and traumatic moment of the
writer's day—and said, "He's coming to New York next week."
Intuitively, Paul knew who "he" was. The impersonal reference
perturbed him. "He" would be in town for several days, giving
lectures, and was looking forward to seeing again, as he phrased
it, his "non-disciples."

He did not for several months tell her about that terrible shard
of knowledge that was sticking in his heart, not, in fact, until they
were at Glencoe, having breakfast in the small old inn with the
crooked architecture. Holding her cup of coffee up in both hands,
her elbows resting on the table, she turned and looked through
the small-paned windows at the mountains which had outlasted
another somber Scots night, and said, "It's a beautiful day for
climbing." He was looking down at his toast, his mind idly musing, remarking again, as he had at almost every meal so far, at
what they did to food in this country, even toast. The British
genius, prevailing so admirably in the study and the drawing
room, faltered as it passed over the kitchen threshold. The surly
little shingle on his plate looked as though it had proved superior
to the toaster. It mesmerized him now. Logically, however, with
perfectly good reason. Kifner had indeed come, with great flourish

and ebullience, never a man for small talk, storming toward them
with his small suitcase and bulging briefcase which he entrusted
to Paul's hand as they headed for the cab line outside of the
terminal, the three of them talking at once, Kifner with his usual
exuberance, with great sweeps of his hand (his seatmate on the
flight had been a colleague, a classicist, "a genuine Horace's ass"),
Paul and Janine asking questions and answering questions in a
welter of unpunctuated sentences; without pause, even as they
piled into the cab and Kifner's hat was crushed against the roof as
he hunched toward his seat in the corner, and then the three of
them thrown back in their seats as the cab took off with a lurch.

They appeared at his midtown hotel the next morning and
found him pacing, irritated. He needed something typed, he
needed something researched. His "girl" in Los Angeles had quit:
pregnant, y'know. ("Oh, Stephen?" Janine asked suggestively,
amused.) Never had he seemed the absent-minded professor, but
now he paced with huge, vehement, near-comical animation. He
had left some of his notes in California. His lecture was in disarray, and this was a tough-minded political-science bunch that
he was going to talk to. Would Janine do some typing? Would
Paul rush to the library and research this and that aspect of
Bakhunin? My God, what was there about New York that drove
one to pieces the moment one landed?

If he was acting, it was brilliant. Was he? Yes, Paul thought
later, dispassionately. Absolutely. The entire performance was so
uncharacteristic, like bad comedy, like somebody's overplayed impression of a great man in agitation. Weren't his lectures the
same? His public appearances? Laced with calculated dramatics?
What made it difficult to properly assay was the fact that this was
a trait of all great men, and where did the greatness leave off and
the theatrics begin?

They had come hoping to join him for breakfast, and when he
reached the street and began heading for the library, Paul remembered that he was hungry. He stepped into a coffee shop and
ordered his breakfast. While he sat at the counter he thought of
Kifner. It had been a long time and, yes, he was glad to see him.
He had almost forgotten the range and excitement of that energy,
that unique generator; none of the small-time New York literati
who had become their friends, none of the slightly self-important

academicians, could fill a room and fire the mind like this man. *But I think I'm more amused now than impressed.* He looked down at the plate that had been placed before him, then called the waitress back. She told him he had asked for toast well done. He had not, he said; and even if he had, this was not well done, this was burned. She turned surly, with that mean-mouthed petulance that will occasionally erupt from the other side of a fast-lunch counter *and so you might say it was because of a waitress whose feet were hurting or who happened to have indigestion or who had had a battle with her lover or her husband that morning.* Normally he was not one to make a scene in a public place; perhaps it was some influx from Kifner, some contagion of that man's irascible adherence to what he believed was right. There was a sharp exchange and Paul left. Out in the street, he turned and headed back toward the hotel, where there was a coffee shop. Once there, he found himself thinking about his mission. Bakhunin was a rather complex subject; perhaps Kifner had better be more specific. So he passed the coffee shop and ducked into an elevator just as the doors were sliding shut.

"I know what happened," he suddenly said, looking up at her. She turned from her dreamy appreciative contemplation of the mountains, began to smile, then stopped as she caught some unfamiliar, unknowable levelness in his eyes. "I came back to get something clarified," he said. "It must have happened quickly. I mean your end of it. You didn't even bother to lock the door." He never let go of the doorknob. He put one foot inside and was arrested immediately by the low, gay, aborted laugh (hers), and the rest he saw reflected out of the bedroom mirror. Of one thing he was always glad—that he had not made a scene at that moment. *Frank would have torn both of them apart.* He probably wouldn't have been able to anyway; as he walked away from that room along the corridor's soft carpeting, he barely had breath in his body, appalled by the enormity of knowing that his life had been suddenly and brutally changed for all time, with an abruptness that was positively merciless. But his face never changed expression, like a person trying to brazen out some mortification. He simply allowed the elevator with its courtly parting and closing of doors to carry him away. He walked for an hour through that mind-filling tumult that was New York, grateful for once for its insane and disturbing insults and discourtesies, its vast impersonal threats and assaults that kept diverting and upholding the corners of what might otherwise have been a dangerously sinking, drowning mind. Then he called the hotel and spoke to Janine, telling her he had become ill in the library and gone home.

He wished he had not seen it, that his subliminal participation had never occurred. He wished so badly for this that at times he was able to neutralize his attitude toward it. He became capable of dominating it. Or so he thought. Because he kept thinking that he was dominating it, to the extent that he finally asked himself with wry bitterness, If I am dominating it so successfully, then why do I constantly think of it, why do I sit at my typewriter staring into space for God knows how many minutes of lost precious time?

"Is that what you've been brooding about these past months?" she asked. "Yes," he said. "Are you over it now? Have you forgiven me?" she asked. He continued to stare at her. He had not known what he wanted her to say, but that wasn't it. "You knew I'd had an affair with him in California before we were married, didn't you?" "No," he said. "Paul, do you mean to say you didn't know that?" "Who broke it off?" he asked. "You did," she said, "by marrying me." "I didn't do such a complete job of it, did I?" Speaking of it now, he felt the original pain returning, that he thought had been deadened beyond revival; that acute distressful sense of clenching inside, the original rage and anger which he had never really permitted to smoke, back again with its first sudden impact. "Was it planned that way?" he asked. "To send me off to the library like some errand boy, while—" "No," she said, "that isn't true. It simply happened. There was no plan, on my part." "On his then." "I don't know. Does it matter? God, I'd all but forgotten it." He felt the anger rising, felt it in his compressed lips; the whole thing opened again, moving through him with worse torrent than before, coming from out of that pent, brooding darkness, that idea of personal betrayal and insult and humiliation, that vivid delineation of unprovoked suffering which a man can endure stoically and interminably until he is presented with the sheer banality of it. "Why have you suddenly brought it up now?" she asked. "Why now, this time? What is the point of it all? What do you want?"

At that moment a man with a thin, slack-smiled face, wearing a tyrolean hat with a jaunty feather in it, came up to them. "Listen," he said, "you're Americans, aren't you? I knew it. I spotted you yesterday at dinner. My name's Lucas, I'm from Chicago. Say, what do you think of these Scots anyway? Not anything like you've heard, eh? Not dour at all. That was the word I heard whenever I told anybody I was going to Scotland: dour." "There are clichés for every people," Janine said to him, "which one believes at one's risk." "Well," the man said, "don't think they don't have 'em for Americans too." "Americans are loud," Paul said. "Americans are gauche and pushy," Janine said. "But—" the man said. "Americans are arrogant and vulgar," Paul said. "You've heard all that," Janine said. "But we're really very nice and sophisticated," Paul said. "Facing facts with reality," Janine said. "Less emotional than the French or Italians," Paul said. The man stared at them, trying to build his slack smile into some measure of understanding. His friendly, offhand attempt at patter had got away from him completely. When these two strangers spoke it was at one another, and then they looked at him as at an arbiter. "Americans are generous, and they're forgiving," Paul said. "That would be the greatest generosity," Janine said quietly. "But the Scots—" the man said. "The Scots carry grudges forever," Janine said. "And we're in Scotland now," Paul said.

He had thought it a good idea to spend part of the summer abroad—their first trip to Europe. They agreed it would be a working vacation, for Janine in particular, since she was preparing to embark upon her most ambitious work: a long poem about the Glencoe Massacre.

That she had chosen to write a poem about one of the most savage acts of betrayal in history, was something his brooding and susceptible mind could not ignore. That he realized his response to the irony was an exaggeration of the symbolic, that it was irrational and deliberately self-lacerating, was of little solace. They would go to this place of lonely, windy pinnacles, where the Campbells mingled for twelve days with the Macdonalds, accepted their shelter, ate their meat and their bread, extended the hand and rubbed the shoulder in friendship for twelve days before rising with the mists at five o'clock in the morning on the thirteenth day of February, 1692, to wreak a slaughter upon their hosts that to this day made grim the air and sullen the rocks of Glencoe.

"It's a beautiful day for climbing," she said.

If she once had turned around and looked at his face, she might have stopped, for he continued to be possessed by the sardonic irony that had become to him as steel-sided as the cruelest Campbell sword. Wordlessly, he followed her along the hard, lonely trails, under jutting precipices of naked stone. Silence and shadow lay over the somber storm-beaten mountainsides and valley of Glencoe where tales of ghosts and murder were told and received with the deepest gravity and most discreet skepticism. If once she had been able to detach her thoughts from the blood flow of creative wellspring as she absorbed the irreconcilable mood and melancholy of Glencoe, and turned to look at him, she might have doubted her stride and thought to history.

Because now his face was cinched with contemplation of his own abrupt and terrible unhappiness, again the indignant rage of unprovoked suffering. Because he had finally brought it into the open and she had not been shattered upon it: and even as he watched her stride ahead in her dubbined boots upon these fierce time-impacted trails where the Macdonalds had walked with their trust and the Campbells with their treachery—even as he watched her, she seemed unchanged, as if impervious to his revelation. And he began to sense that he was not going to get from her what he wanted and needed: that orderly and structured life which was essential to the pursuit and attainment of his goals. These past weeks had ravaged his mind, his time, his work. He could not go through life waiting for it to happen again, wondering each time what was the significance of a prolonged and unexplained absence. That a tension and an unpredictability of this nature should append itself to his life was intolerable.

He knew about this sort of thing, its deplorable progression, its powers of decay and erosion. He had grown up with it, borne witness to its continued and unstoppable drive. To think that he, who had for so long cursed and reviled his sister for having brought such degradation and anguish and humiliation upon him, should now suddenly discover it again a part of his life as though he had carried it with him like a plague from his home. These insidious ironies and fates and analogies mocked his desire for the life of calm and polished symmetries, tormented the illusion of sovereignty over his own destiny.

So she kept going, moving ahead with those long proud strides, insulting him further now with her remoteness from the conversation he had begun at breakfast and which had not been resumed after the interruption. Now he closed the distance between them. He could hear from somewhere near the broken rushing sounds of a mountain stream pursuing its cold unsunned channels through the rocks. He saw the hawks afloat like ragged pennants against the blue sky. Then he was close behind her, and she became aware of his nearness and began to turn, and that he would remember, vividly and forever: the partially turned face just coming into profile, turning as if on a pivot of soft honey-blond hair. And then she was falling, because he could not, would not, remember the actual physical act itself: and anyway his hands were thrust not against her back but upon the rucksack. She spun around, wholly in mid-air then, with not a foot or finger touching an inch of earth, wholly free and contained there for that split second: frowning, annoyed, perplexed, as if reacting to some careless insult; her body tilting and tipping; her hair straight out behind her in a frozen mass. And then she was gone, falling with her hands upraised in the thin rushing air (the Englishman had described it for him), toward the bone-shattering rocks below; and then as if in empathy he fell to the ground and saw the boulders above him steering colossally against the sky and felt the grim mass of Glencoe thud against him:

voices mixed murmurous in the winds carrying my cry lonely and vagrant to the dark inhospitable night the lone ghost sad and unanswering wandering in cold starlight through great bastions of time ever ever the shadow of circling hawks:

and she falls yet, through the limitless region of my soul now, will continue to fall as long as I draw breath: falling in the new boots which we bought together before I knew and so have to remember them with grudging nostalgia because we laughed at the sight of her ladylike foot sliding down into their reinforced massiveness: no I wasn't plotting murder: it simply happened, as spontaneous and unexpected as she claims it happened with him in the hotel room: and anyway who is more capable of it than the quiet introspective man? when all thoughts are crystalline some

*are susceptible to sudden and immediate breakage, the quiet man
with all his inbound ships and terrible implosions: a thousand
times more susceptible to it than my brother for instance with his
strength and impetuosity: so unlikely that no one would ever
dream of suspecting; and so deepens the tragedy even further,
beneath the unspeakably bland surface: did he know that I knew?
wasn't there a certain formal stiffness in the exchange of letters?
the news for him and the condolence for me, and that was all:
did he care about her at all? about me certainly not, but at least
for her? care she was dead smashed on rocks with a billion fragments of poems shot and scattered out of her broken bones like
inchoate galaxies: but not scattered after all: redrawn together
and strung out upon whatever mysterious wires crisscross the universe and touch nerve endings in our souls: those poems came
back from Scotland with her and slipped wily and self-preserving
out of the winding sheet and politely refused the courtesy of burial
and remain yet pulsing into coherence and maturity at which
point they find their shute, their funnel: madness, yes, supernatural, yes, and a thousand other things which I dare not contemplate: and I do not for a moment rationally believe it but it
seems not to matter in the least what I believe or do not, as I do
not believing sitting here now at midnight in this genteel and
shabby house in Capstone that falling through space she has just
touched another tripwire and a string of words like teletype is
crossing my mind.*

He started at the sound of the knocking on the door. It was a
rather timid, diffident sound; in fact, if the house had not been so
quiet he might not have heard it at all. He did not look up from
the desk, though he did stop writing, the pencil ceasing in the
midst of shaping a letter and remaining poised in his hand, its
point adhering to the page. He sat perfectly still, so that he might
have been a manikin sitting at the desk, placed there to demonstrate its utility. Then his head turned slowly, and he stared into
space, as if the sound had become an actual physical presence and
was now in the room with him and he was trying to identify its
incarnation. Then he put down the pencil, pushed his chair back
from the desk and got up.

It was probably three minutes between the time he heard the
knock and the moment he opened the door, and through those

minutes there had not been another sound, as if whoever was there was content to let their petition rest after knocking once, as if they understood—or understood that they did not understand—the mind of the man inside.

His niece stood outside on the porch in the midnight darkness, suitcase in hand, gazing at him with waning resolution, with a fortitude which seemed to be suspended on the crest of a single deeply drawn breath; whose name eluded him for the split second, which accounted for the deepening of his frown, for his momentary inarticulateness, and which in turn made her speak out impulsively more in apology than explanation.

"I had nowhere else to go."

The intensity of his expression relaxed somewhat when he remembered her name; it was enough to bring a tentative, hopeful smile to her lips.

"Come in," he said.

She walked behind him into the living room, put her suitcase quietly down on the carpet, but did not take a seat until he told her to, then sat rather formally on the sofa, fingers wrapped nervously together in her lap.

"So you've run away," he said.

"May I stay for a few days?" she asked. "All I ask for is a few days."

"You're asking for a good deal more than that," he said. "You're also asking me to remain silent about it; to say that I haven't seen you."

She stared at him.

"How old are you now?" he asked.

"Sixteen."

He remembered her as an infant. The first-born of his sister's children, his memories of her were particularly vivid. The other children blurred together in his mind almost anonymously, with interchangeable names, faces, characteristics.

"And after a few days?" he asked.

"I don't know."

"You want time to think then?"

"Yes."

He looked at her suitcase standing on the carpet. It seemed

somehow ludicrous, incongruous. She was much too young to be carrying a packed suitcase in the middle of the night.

"Where could you possibly go after you leave here?" he asked.

"I . . . haven't decided yet."

"Home perhaps?"

"I don't think so. I didn't want to run away . . . I'm frightened . . . but how can I go back there? You don't know how awful it is."

"I think I do," he said. "After all, I knew your mother long before you did."

"Why didn't someone do something about it then?"

"What did your grandfather say when you asked him that?"

"He said there was nothing anyone could do. He said it was like trying to catch water in a sieve. He said it was like a sickness . . ."

"It isn't," Paul said. "It's a sheer act of will; a contemptuous thing deliberately done."

"My father said that deep in her heart it makes her miserable."

"And him miserable, and you miserable, and all of you miserable. And it goes on."

Oddly, she felt his bitterness blunting her own resentment and unhappiness. She had been expecting some words of comfort, sympathy, hope; some quiet apologia for her mother, as she always heard from her father and grandfather. But here her unhappiness had struck a rock of more deeply ingrained emotion than her own, and now she felt some of it curling back in confusion. She stared at him sitting at his ease in a chair across the room from her, his face resting despondently in his hand, as though he were in utter desuetude; this uncle whom she hardly knew, whose own tragedy had saddened her when she had learned of it. In the peculiar, remote atmosphere of this house, she felt the burden of consoling suddenly incumbent upon her.

"I can stay then?" she asked. "I'll be very quiet. I know you have your work . . ."

Another victim, he thought. A refugee from the same storm, more or less. Come floating battered into the first available harbor. The sorrow he frequently felt for himself, for the life which had gone suddenly, unexpectedly dissilient into the winds, was abundant enough to embrace another, that sorrow which he sometimes felt was the only sane thing left to him; the ballast in his brain, preventing its total dissolution.

"You'll have to be very quiet," he said.

She might not have opened the envelopes if Frank had not chased after her as he had and, with his anxious interrogation and interest, made her curious; or at least she would not have opened them so soon. Surely, her mind was burdened with weightier considerations. When her grandfather gave them to her, she felt she was somehow indulging him in accepting them. Elderly people, particularly those terminally ill, were known to divest themselves of their valuables, out of affection, out of the desire to put a finger of influence into the emptiness of the future, or simply out of the emotion of the moment. Perhaps by showing her she was the favored in this matter, it was his way of consoling her distress, her humiliation, her bitterness, trying to divert with a kind gesture the indivertible, trying to make her feel adult and thus further removed from her shame. Ben had said nothing more about the envelopes than, "There are some things of value in here that I want you to have after I'm gone. I trust your good sense." So she had given the four bulky manila envelopes little thought, assuming they contained family memorabilia and other items of sentimental value, and in all likelihood would not have opened them when she did if Frank had not piqued her curiosity. In fact, it was only out of her affectionate regard for her grandfather that she allowed the envelopes to occupy the limited space in her suitcase when she packed that night.

The upstairs room that Paul ushered her into was furnished with only a cot and two wooden bridge chairs, illuminated by a wall lamp that cast the room in bright antiseptic whiteness. After he said good night and closed the door, she listened as he went downstairs, waiting until the sounds of his footsteps had subsided into that engulfing silence. Then she sat down on one of the chairs and stared at the blank walls. Her eyes moved along them by degrees, as if searching for some infinitesimal imperfection: some walls created a room, a home, a shelter, a repository of memories; these did little more than give a façade to silence. She looked at the lamp, at the bulb burning inside its plain white shade. There was a fine strand of gossamer stretched from the rim of the shade to the area below the switch. The cot was in the middle of the room, stretched in white sheets, white pillow, white blanket; it looked as though a dead body might recently have been lifted from it. The closet door was open, the interior empty except for a pair of wire hangers suspended triangularly from a wooden rack. The other bridge chair was at the blind-drawn window, looking uncannily empty for its position there.

From downstairs there was not a sound. Writing was such a quiet business, she thought. What possessed a man to sit alone in soundlessness tracing his thoughts across a page with a pencil? She stared at the floor as she thought of him. She had never read anything he had written, though her father, with that eager, almost impulsive, enthusiasm he had for certain things, said Paul was extremely talented and seemed quite proud of him. She wondered whether her father had ever read any of the work; he took so much on faith, particularly those things he wanted to believe were true.

She got up, lifted her suitcase, and placed it on the cot. She undid the hasps and raised the lid. She stared down at her belongings, the things she had so hastily and surreptitiously put in there while her father dozed in front of the running television set, and her sister and brothers slept, and her mother was not there at all. Her skirts, blouses, slacks, sweaters, shoes looked so forlorn; their appearance in so narrowly contained and transient a place as a suitcase heightened her loneliness and deepened her despairing resentment for having been forced to leave her home.

As she rummaged through her belongings her hand touched the envelopes, and now she remembered Frank's anxiety about them. She wondered if she ought to tell her other uncle about them, out of some vague sense of obligation. She decided against it, though not from guile, but simply because she did not think he would be interested, and she did not want to say or do anything beyond maintaining a minimal, unobtrusive presence.

There were four of them, 9 by 12 manila envelopes, their metal clips closed, their flaps sealed with brown paper. Each had a certain loose bulkiness. She tore open the first one—not quickly, but slowly, self-consciously diminishing the force of what she felt was an unseemly curiosity. She lifted out a handful of old family photographs, recognizing her grandfather as a young man, saw her grandmother, her uncles as children, her mother (upon whose youthful, coquettish face she gazed with sullen, lingering interest). There were also some yellowed newspaper clippings, with stories and occasional pictures of her grandfather, dealing with one aspect or another of his public political activities. One picture showed him addressing an assemblage in Union Square, standing upon what looked like a wooden packing crate, leaning toward his listeners, one fist clenched in the air, his face thrust aggressively forward, his mouth wide, and belligerent. With the image fresh in her mind of the moribund, poignant old man sitting in his chair in the reconciled near completion of his life, the teeming person in the old photograph was an utter, anomalous stranger. And then she came to the final clipping. Trimmed from an old newspaper now long defunct, with the quaint bloodless look of near antiquity, was the story of twenty-five thousand dollars in campaign contributions and other moneys stolen from the headquarters of an "extreme left-wing group." The police were "investigating."

That last clipping was laid aside and she opened the next envelope, and then the other two, and then in stark, incredulous amazement sat sorting it out in denominations on the cot as if engaged in some bizarre game of solitaire, the sight of the old, plundered money making her heart race.

Later, after she had put the money into a single envelope and buried it under her clothing in the suitcase, she sat in a darkened room on the chair by the window staring out at the bland stillness of the Capstone night. *Why did he give it to me? Why so much? What am I going to do now? Did he steal it? Is it the same money?* Now she was frightened and intimidated, who in her life had never had more than twenty-five dollars to call her own, who like any young person had her dreams, her aspirations, but which— those dreams, aspirations—had never been particularly dependent upon great sums of money for their fulfillment. She felt the force of change that had come steaming out of those envelopes. She felt as if that option of walking back to her home, which had been so readily available to her, no longer existed, or at least not with its former ease and simplicity. The money was like a flood and a whirlwind blocking the way back. Not greed or exultation dominated her mind, but bewilderment. Altered by the pressure of the money, everything was changed, and without clarity or discernible purpose.

Sitting in the dark room, in the quiet house, staring out at a vast, mysterious night, she felt more lonely and unaccompanied than ever.

But if I didn't sleep, how could I dream that I didn't sleep?

There was a line about a tree. Yes, he seemed to recall that, sometime during the night. Catatonia is a landscape of my mind. Or is it was it simply Caledonia? When was my last lucid, coherent thought? As the insinuating transgressor began darkening the borders of his mind once more. I think she does sleep, she must, even falling through space; but even then, am I immune from her dreams, her subconscious spasms? Too many things long since gone vagrant in his mind, nomadic memories recurring from time to time with diminished vividness, fading among the increase and the fostering of what had supplanted and what was superseding. There was a line about a tree. But did I think it, did she think it, or did I dream it? Now, I do have my own thoughts occasionally. Of course. The problem is: Which are mine and which hers, and which are dreams? And to whom do the dreams belong? I don't mind her thoughts in mine, but mine in hers, no. Because mine in hers will come back to me as hers and then what is mine? The first thing he knew about the new day was that he was sitting on a chair on the porch, watching the beckoning sky brighten and thinking of the rustling primordial opening of the Ninth. The blacktopped road that ran past the house was more or less untraveled at this hour, except for the milk delivery trucks that came monstrously out of the dawn from the nearby dairies. He was wearing a white sport shirt and slacks, but no shoes, no socks. What does that mean? Did I sleep? It's important to know. In order to legitimize the authentically mysterious. There was a line about a tree. And the soul-weary unkempt amerced amanuensis had missed it. He had seen her, sometime during the night, falling. No, she wasn't falling: she was simply suspended in mid-air, arms raised, legs hanging, head hung to a side, eyes shut, hair afloat; not falling, but the universe behind her was rising at astronomical speed: galaxies and planets upshooting into the darkness. So I must have been sleeping, because that never happens when I am awake and walking or reading or buying the groceries. She does let me sleep occasionally. She had better, if she would like me to have any mind at all to write them down. In fact, as it is, I can't seem to remember them all. There were a few sometime during the night that came so lightly they left neither echo nor imprint; or maybe she wasn't sure about them and all I got were her musings. She could be such a perfectionist. Didn't I occasionally take a phrase she had rejected? There was a line about a tree, with strength and beauty of limb and bough perpetually undiminished, fecundity eternal, autumn leaves windborn a thousand miles: and the poem was that it was rooted in parched and arid earth and was therefore some sort of miracle tree. Was that it?

He got up and walked through the house, silent in his bare feet. He stepped out through the rear door and stared at the back yard, where the dawn light was beginning to reach and where soon the roof of the house would appear on the ground like a waterline: another full day of it. He looked back over his shoulder; the silence had an undertone of insidious persistence, as if the precursors of a new order were heaving at the doors and windows. That line about the tree. But he wished it would leave him be for the moment. He was tired. He might or might not have slept. You could be tired from not sleeping or tired from sleeping, and at the moment he felt it was important to know which it was with him. As it was important to know certain things, with solid, unquestioning, unimpeachable knowing. If I have written an essay how do I know she hadn't decided to write an essay? And so who wrote it? Who wrote the essay? How far how deep do the incursions go? Am I totally public to her ghost? Whose eyes open in the morning, who rises, eats, walks, thinks, returns to sleep? The poems, yes, because I don't write poetry, or at least never that well: But what happens when finally they do go to the publisher? After all, from my hand, even though her voice. Do I really believe that? Absolutely irrational to—admitted. But how else to account for them? They do exist. I do see them. Frank said since when am I writing poetry. He saw them. But suppose I cease to believe and they cease to be? Then what happens to her? We knew each other's mind so well that it is not impos—. But how well did I know hers, considering; and, considering her back to me the whole time along that trail, how well did she know mine? I do not by any means exclude the perfectly normal and natural possibility of a perfectly normal and natural and prosaic everyday guilty conscience. Why then this curious sometimes thought: Was she dead before she hit the rocks? Black out during the fall so as not to feel pain? Do you concern yourself with the idea of pain for the person you hate so much you want to kill? But did I hate her? I told myself yes, which was absolutely imperative to the moment but not necessarily a permanent state of affairs, for what am I to do with the hatred later—send it back to its deadly crouch to await its next summons? I hated, yes but no; not her but the abstraction, the representation, the threat, the fear of the worsening thing.

He walked back into the house and through it with nervous haste, looking over his shoulder again as if being pursued. He stood on the front porch, a quiet, emergent figure confronting the shy discretions of the new day. *There was a line about a tree. But maybe she rubbed it out. The perfectionist. Revising right inside my head. One wall of my skull a blackboard. Why don't I just have my nervous breakdown and get it over with?* He looked up at the sky: white clouds, like furnishing moving into the new day. *Ah, how you could indulge yourself with such nonsense when you were a poet, and even more when you were only the conveyor: as quiet as a death in a rented room—gratitude ends with fulfillment—lonely as an echo—all Gods belong to all men, all men to one God—a single triumph is the end work of many failures— winter's momentum has overrun the hour of spring—who seeks a sty in the eye of the diamond—the wind leaps nimbly over the grave—blasts of laughter for the fool—it is chilling and exciting to watch the suffering giant—what chance has logic before wit?—how do you recognize the prayer that has been answered?—the strength of the current determines the thrust of the oar—beauty, the self-corrupter—not defeat but the struggle's end destroyed him— happiness the slayer of time—the doer and the done for—cynical of their own cynicism—make the moralist define his law—a fault so subtle as to elude even conscience—hot marigolds in yellow sunshine—when immorality becomes habit the immoral becomes respectable—the living spare no blood when the dead cry vengeance—do not reverence by fear your tormentor—contentment begins when desire is whipped—Nature created Man, Man created God, God created Nature—the piled snows surrounding the*

*shuttered heart—you dreamed long ago the evil you claim now you
see—the bloodstains of religion—cohesion is established through
the creation of an enemy. All of this we are so enviously privy to
and privileged to utter and put on paper and describe as our
philosophy profundity discernment erudition wit shrewdness: the
care and vigilance of our sacred holy thoughts, carrying banality
to mediocrities, pronouncing solemnly the world round and the
sky blue: saying look listen we commune with the dead, are the
transmitters of immortality. Isn't it all so grand, this gnomic and
inextinguishable wisdom of the ages, by the sages, for the pages,
and all so neatly packaged—that if you are so attuned you can hear
even the dead, their tiny voices speaking through our pores? We
turn even the straw of murder into the gold of art, weaving endlessly for your edification upon our ethereal looms, orchestrating
celestial visitations as infallibly as the wind plays the harp, and
where is your homage and where for us is graceful termination?*

He walked back inside, restive, weary, hungry, too, now, that
simple nudging reminder that he was human, that even those who
communicate with the dead are human. And so like any other
human being, he made himself breakfast. He heard his niece walking about upstairs. Up early, he thought. But what is early, when
you never sleep. The sun was inside now, flooding the house. For
some people it meant go, it meant hope, promise, the abiding
structure of another day. But he might have been some cold remote Arctic person, for all the significance the round yellow sun
and its black demarcations had for him, or for Janine, who falls
through space with unsunned velocity and aloneness and what will
happen to me when she hits those rocks?

He ate, he walked through the house, to the yard, the porch, he
stared morosely at the pencil and white sheet of paper lying
treacherously and implacably on his desk, insatiable absorbers of
his soul. He was standing on the porch, still barefoot, still weary,
still in his tumultuous loneliness, when the car appeared in front
of the house, coming slowly to a halt, as with some enormous
gravity. The driver sat there looking at him. They stared at one
another, Paul from across that insuperable divide which separated
him from other people. He recognized the face: Harry Desser, his
father's maudlin old remembrancer, that fallen-to-earth remex
from out of gray diminished skies long since dropped to the hori-

zon, his bereft face gazing with its acolyte's softness. They sent
me round to get you, he said. Then he slid across the seat and his
face filled the passenger window and he spoke his message. Paul
listened, nodded, then lowered his eyes. My father is dead, he
thought, and I'm not even wearing shoes.

TWENTY-FOUR

There was an expression, at once bemused and poignant, that could cross only the faces of brothers upon meeting after their father's death.

Frank rose when Paul walked in. The brothers stared at one another, Paul suddenly uncertain and ill at ease. Frank went to him and took him gently by the arm. They went together into the kitchen, where they were alone.

"When?" Paul asked.

"Sometime between midnight and dawn," Frank said. "When else? Those are the hours when everybody seems to get born, so . . . Christ," Frank whispered, an unnerved incredulity in his voice. "I still can't believe it."

Paul stared tenderly at his brother's tears. Frank smiled self-consciously, shrugged philosophically, then wiped his eyes with the back of his hand.

"He was in great pain," Frank said. "I mean really terrific pain. I saw him the other night. He looked like he was being fractured by it. Even the look on his face was a deep concession; you know how he was, old blood and guts. But it became just too much. I understand completely. It's no disgrace. A man has a right to it, I think. Anyway, he wasn't a religious man, as far as that part of it goes."

"You mean—"

"Didn't he tell you?" Frank asked, gesturing with his thumb toward the living room.

Paul shook his head.

"Oh," Frank said softly. He thought he might be spared that part of it at least. "Hanratty found him this morning," he said. "She has a key and she let herself in. He was on the bathroom floor. He'd opened a vein. She's very graphic with the details, if you're interested."

"He was alone?"

"Of course," Frank said.

Paul looked vaguely around the kitchen, as though waking from a sleep. "Of course," he said abstractedly. He looked down at his feet; he hadn't remembered putting on his shoes and socks.

"Are you going to be all right?" Frank asked.

Paul nodded, looking at his brother with a nervous, quirky smile.

"There's nothing anyone could have done," Frank said.

"No."

"So . . ."

"Did you know this was coming?" Paul asked.

"No."

"We should have."

"And done what?"

Paul stared out of the kitchen window, into the sunshine. "I can tell you one thing," he said. "We're going to feel guilty as hell."

"About what?"

"Everything. We're the sons," Paul said with a peculiar, unhappy logic. And then his face took on a perfectly vacant expression, evoked by the stark sequential realities of life, of the frailty of man in his kingdom; evoked as well by the sudden stillness and emptiness of the life-giver, the bulwark against the ghosts of generations past, that wall which had always stood to resist and turn aside the threat of those dead catenated forebears who did not drift further away with elapsed time but came always closer, menacing strangers hovering near to reclaim their blood. Quietly, Paul asked, "Where is he now?"

"In the bedroom. There's a cop in there, and a doctor."

"A doctor?" Paul asked, turning around suddenly.

"Paul, he's dead," Frank said bluntly.

They returned to the living room, to a most wordless gathering. Philip and Helen were there; and Mrs. Hanratty, the stern-faced housekeeper (who had frowned disdainfully at Paul's entrance, as if to say *I told you he was sick*); and Harry Desser, the faithful, tolerated friend, still faithful, still tolerated, with his look of gray, self-conscious anonymity, looking as though he were apologetic for not being a full-fledged shareholder in the grief.

Helen was sitting on the sofa, sobbing, her face bent forward into a handkerchief. Frank sat down next to her and put his arm

around her shoulders. Paul ignored her, ignored everyone, standing aloof and unapproachable in the middle of the room, his face
fixed in an ironic expression now, as if gradually absorbing the fact
that the last of life had left the house in which he had grown up.
For all its godlike stillness, death was an incredibly reverberant
and conspicuous entrant, mutely and vehemently demanding. He
could feel it upon his mind like some wild and ravaged thing
shorn of its reason, chased into an intolerable eternity.

Charlotte appeared then, walking through the open door. She
went directly to Paul and threw her arms around him and kissed
him lightly on the cheek. He nodded and murmured to her whispered consolations. Then she went to Frank and took his hand
in hers.

"I'm so sorry, Frank," she said.

He stared down at his enfolded hand.

"Thank you," he said.

"He must have suffered terribly."

"Yes," Frank said, withdrawing his hand.

Charlotte took a chair next to Mrs. Hanratty, who had been
sitting with proud, redoubtable dignity.

"I found him," Mrs. Hanratty whispered leaning toward her.
"It was ghastly."

The woman exuded an odor of rancid cheese. Charlotte wanted
to change her seat. The woman was staring intently at her from a
distance of ten inches, eyes glowing with the malevolent need to
tell her tale.

"It was ghastly," Mrs. Hanratty confided.

"I'm sure," Charlotte said, trying as discreetly as possible to
draw back.

"Do you know who I called first?" the woman whispered. "Mr.
Desser," she said, shaping the name with her lips, her voice barely
a breath. "Not the sons." Now the woman withdrew her face, an
expression of knowing satisfaction etched into it. Staring at Charlotte, she nodded once, with emphatic righteousness. Then her
eyes swept the room, coming to rest with contemptuous detachment upon the sobbing Helen. "Look at that one," she said with
cold skepticism.

Frank, moving restlessly around the room, through the soft tension of grief, suddenly felt his arm touched by his brother-in-law, and then was confronted with Philip's mournful face.

"Frank," Philip said, "is there anything I can do?"

The man's face contained a sorrow so profound as to border on the lugubrious, to the extent that Frank was momentarily distracted by it.

"Listen," Frank said quietly, "have you heard from Lorana?"

"I don't want to bother you now with my troubles."

"We're all one family, Philip."

"Thank you, Frank," Philip said solemnly. He took Frank's hand and shook it, solemnly and appreciatively. "If there's anything I—"

"You haven't heard from her then?"

"No."

"Any ideas? Any leads whatsoever?"

"No; but if she hears about . . . this," Philip said delicately, "I would imagine she'd get in touch. She was very fond of him you know, and he of her. She was his favorite."

"I know," Frank said moodily.

He left the group in the living room and went upstairs. The upper floor was eerily silent and empty. He paused in the doorway of his old room. Almost as if in resentment of its long desuetude, the room threw off a cold air of hostility. He stared at the bed, the chair, the bureau, the oval mirror tipped slightly forward from the wall, the desk where he had sat and written innocuous letters to Presidents and governors and senators in order to receive their form replies with those august return addresses which he left lying around to impress whoever came into the room. Frank rubbed his chin thoughtfully. Given the old man's sardonic humors, he might well have stuffed the mattress with it. Hoping that someday I would come home and sleep on it even as I dreamed about it.

He continued on up to the attic. It was a small room, under a gabled roof, with a narrow dusty dormer window that suggested a view of a wild landscape covered with wintry flowers. He put on the light and looked around at an assemblage convoked by ghosts: cardboard cartons and wooden boxes and suitcases and a steamer trunk and oddments of furniture; all of the unassigned and unrenounced residuum of a lifetime; the preservations of spent time, vague hopes, slumbering years, left as an undeliverable consignment to the future.

He was unprepared for the assault of memories, the potency of reality as still life, and was immediately vulnerable to the decaying nostalgia that lay around him. He began, however, on the crest of his stubborn hopes, searching with a glaring fixation, a ruthlessness; but these swiftly eroded and diminished as recognition and remembrance slowed him, stopped him, until he was sitting cross-legged on the floor surrounded and transported by toys and games he had long ago forgotten, which were drenched with his past, his childhood, the innocence which had long since foundered on harsher rocks. He stared into his mother's old rococo mirror that stood on the floor against the wall, as he held slack in his fingers the snow hat she had knitted for him when he was six years old and which, to his distress, he remembered. There were toy soldiers and books, and, worst of all, photo albums which showed a family so young and gathered and content as to be almost preposterous, strangers who had slept in those bodies long ago. He remembered now walking home late one night several weeks ago and seeing the light burning in the attic, and wondering what the old man was doing up there. Going through this stuff? he asked himself now. Trying to sedate his pain with better times? He closed the photo album that lay across his lap, hiding the faces pasted onto the heavy black pages, and lowered his head and shut his eyes and let the tears slip through the lids, shedding with his control his years and his experiences and disappointments and everything he knew, as he surrendered himself to the vigilant ghosts of his youth which came sliding from the shadows to possess him in soft hypnotic thralldom, his mind afloat with sweet, fleeing arabesques from the past, like tunes raised with the lid of an old, old music box.

Then he looked up and opened his eyes with pained incredulity. *What the hell am I doing?* He threw the photo album skidding across the floor so that it traced a broken trail through the dust. Then he stood up. *You stupid morbid son of a bitch. Gone is gone.* Angrily, he aimed a kick into the side of a bulging cardboard carton. The old man knew exactly what he was doing. It was not an impulsive thing. He was too intellectually conditioned not to savor thoughts of his own death. And so he would never have left money behind in a mausoleum like this where it was liable to be thrown out or found by some unprincipled scavenger . . . *like me*, Frank thought bitterly. Yes, I loved him and am heartbroken and will miss him, but goddammit I still can be pissed off at him. If I never was able to fool him, then he seldom fooled me either. I knew exactly how he felt about me. He simply didn't think I could do myself any good with that money, and so gave it to her. And since I understand that—what am I doing here? Now he looked around at all the old, dead, unburied remnants of the past. If I am what I am today, he thought, then none of this could have done me any good, and should mean nothing to me. If I am what I am today, then it's due partially to this pile of shit and everything in it that ever deluded or misdirected me, and instead of weeping over it I ought to set fire to the whole lot of it.

As he came back downstairs, Frank saw the policeman leaving with the doctor. He paused on the stairs until they were gone. Being under the same roof with the law had given him an uneasy feeling, not to mention having to sit through a dispassionate bureaucratic interrogation about his father, during which he was expecting the officer at any moment to suddenly look up at him with a squint of recognition, as if every policeman in New York had set to memory a description of Frank Dublin.

He went into the kitchen, where he found Paul with Harry Desser.

"Ah, Frank," Desser said. "I'm glad you're here. I was just telling Paul . . . I have something I always wanted to tell your father, but never could."

"You don't have to tell us anything you don't want to, Harry," Frank said.

"But I do want to," the man said. "That's just it—I want to."

Paul, who apparently had been led in here reluctantly, was leaning against the sink, arms crossed. Now he uncrossed his arms and put his hands into his pockets and shifted his weight. Obviously he was not interested.

"It's not something I'm particularly proud of," Desser said. "Nevertheless, it should be said." He seemed to have an aching anxiety to tell whatever it was that had arched his conscience. There were some people who could not abide the report of their failures or mistakes from any but their own lips, who displayed this peculiar alacrity to tell on themselves, as if confession mitigated or nullified a weakness, were some pale imprimatur that imbued with an aura of nobility. "Listen," Harry Desser said, plunging into his tale, "you know how he and I used to argue about the old days." He looked at Paul, found an averted look of uninterest, then turned back to Frank. "He used to needle me about having gone to Spain to fight. Well, I've never regretted it for a moment, and he respected me for it. After all, it was a cause we all believed in. And I continued to believe in it. Remember, some years ago, when I went to Europe with my wife? I had vowed never to set foot in Spain again until things had changed there. Remember, I told everyone we went to France and Italy? Well, now I'll tell you the truth. I was going to tell your father someday. My wife and I did go to Spain. We stayed in good hotels in Madrid and Barcelona and ate like pigs and spent three years' savings in an orgy of luxury living. It was the only place we could afford, after the air fare. And do you know something, Frank—I didn't have a single conscience pang. *That* was what ate me up."

Abruptly, impatiently, Paul walked out of the kitchen. Desser watched him go, then his eyes shifted back to Frank.

"You understand, don't you, Frank?" he asked.

"Sure."

"I always meant to tell your father."

"He would have understood, Harry."

"Do you think so?"

"He was a very understanding man."

"But I didn't even visit the old battlefields . . . where I got shot. My wife didn't want to."

"Can't blame her too much for that."

Desser shook his head. "Sometimes I think that maybe your father was right to throw it all over. After all, was it worth it? Was it all so important? I left college to go there to fight. Sure, when I came back I was a hero. I even made a couple of speeches. But maybe I should have finished college. Others did, and today they're successful. Guys I thought were fascists in those days now have houses in the country and vote more or less the same way I do today. Sometimes I have to think hard to remember what the issues were . . ."

"Well . . ." Frank said.

"And now he's gone," Desser said. "My best friend. I was going to tell him, Frank."

"Tell him what?" Frank asked.

"That I visited Spain," Desser whispered excitedly.

Frank put his hand on the man's shoulder. "Harry," he said, but didn't have the heart to go on.

"Severith said there was virtually nothing there," Paul said. Severith was Ben's lawyer, to whom he had sent a parcel of papers a few days before, marked TO BE OPENED UPON MY DEATH. "Just a lapsed insurance policy, some recently paid bills, and the cemetery deed."

"Nothing else?" Frank asked.

"Nothing."

"No will?"

"He had nothing to leave. There will be an estate of sorts. There's the house, of course," Paul said. "He made no provision, so it goes to the three of us, eventually."

"I'm not interested," Frank said. "Let Helen have it. I wouldn't want to live here. Would you?"

They were sitting in the living room some hours after their father's body had been carried out on a stretcher under a buckled-down canvas cover, negotiated through the living room and hall and down the front steps by two white-clad attendants who seemed to have a genius for not looking at people.

"No," Paul said.

Frank was slouched in gloomy introspection, his mind filled with vague, undefined thoughts about his father, trying to shape them into some kind of evaluation, conclusion.

"You know what annoys me, and always annoyed me?" Frank said. He straightened up and sat on the edge of his chair. "He was a man of such ability, such dynamism. Did you see the faces on those people streaming through here all day? They just didn't seem able to believe he was dead. You know, looking back now, I realize I was always waiting for something to happen—a call from the goddamn President or something. I think he could have been or done anything he wanted. But he let it all slide; he just exiled himself here and let it all slide."

"You wanted your father to be a great man?" Paul asked.

"Is it so childish? I wanted it because I knew it *could* be, that he had it in him. What the hell did he allow himself to be—a goddamned carpenter, a Mr. Fixit who walked around town smoking a cigar and carrying a toolbox. You know what he had in him —you know that everyone held him in the greatest respect, some even in awe."

"Like Harry Desser."

"Paul, the world is *made up* of Harry Dessers."

"What good are the accolades of fools?"

"Who else gives them?"

"Then that should tell you they're worthless. He knew that. He was disillusioned, Frank, not embittered."

"I maintain he ignored his potential, and at the same time his responsibilities. If the world is indeed made up of fools, then his obligation was even greater. How many men like him have you met?"

"Few," Paul said.

"If he had a failing, it was this lack of ambition. He had the talent and the capacity to lead, but he did nothing. God, I waited for him, I waited . . . but nothing happened. You see what the tragedy is: there are so few leaders available, not one should be wasted. That's the tragedy. Otherwise we end up following and honoring mediocrities."

"Frank," Paul said, "the fools who do not put their trust in the great man . . ."

"Yes?" Frank asked.

"Are not fools."

Frank did not go directly home after parting from Paul in front of the dark, now empty house. After watching his brother go alone into the night, he went off in the opposite direction, walking with his own brooding preoccupations, in the capacious isolation of the bereaved. He thought first of going to Charlotte at her invitation, but then realized there would be little for him there other than maudlin reminiscing, tales of her own dead father (she was vulnerable to these occasions, he felt, was one of those people who used bereavement to depart upon philosophical explorations of man and the cosmos), and none of it held much appeal for him at the moment.

Where am I going now anyway? he asked himself. He was not in the mood to go to his furnished room, would not go to Charlotte, had not been invited by Paul. So he headed for the Hamlet Tavern, with the idea that he would get perhaps two-thirds drunk and see what that would bring. With luck the two-thirds would obliterate his grief and leave the rest of his mind to function with reasonable cogency about the missing money and the whereabouts and future plans of Arthur Seavery. Thoughts of Seavery had been coming to him in sudden, unstructured flashes all day long, darting through and around the gloom of his father's death. At times he found himself adamant about not wanting ever to see or hear from Seavery again, and at other times was beset with curiosity about the enigmatic young revolutionary, wondering what he was doing, thinking. With the twenty-five thousand dollars now apparently irrevocably gone, it seemed that whatever odd shapes the future might assume, Seavery somehow remained their architect. This was a most bizarre way to look ahead, Frank conceded, but at the moment he had no other, for included in the tangled briers of the future was a path he hoped might yet irreversibly lead him to Charlotte Breitman.

When he entered the back-street tavern he was surprised to see his sister sitting at the bar with a man. With contrite and dolorous eyes, Helen watched him walk toward her.

"You ought to be home tonight," Frank said.

"I was," she said.

"She was," her companion said.

Frank knew him. If Frank's dreams and fantasies went upright toward the sky like obelisks and as far afield as the wind, then the other's remained bound and chased by what Capstone could afford. Schemes and deceptions flowed from Joe Geeb like water, and with as much stability. He had attempted through the years bookmaking, usury, pandering, and other irregular attempts at success, each failure inherent with a tawdry new beginning. In his mid-thirties now, chronically unemployed, he lived on the melancholy charity of his elderly parents and by what few dollars his schemes netted him. His long and unvaried calendar of disappointments had etched into his face a perpetually lachrymose expression, as if his ears were filled always with gothic threnodies and lamentations. There was, however, a certain wild alertness in his eyes, as though he had been forewarned that his greatest opportunity would occur with subliminal swiftness. At the present moment he was sitting close to Helen on adjoining wooden bar stools, his eyes studying her crossed legs.

"Hello, Joe," Frank said.

"I was sorry to hear about . . ." Geeb said, looking up at him.

"Thanks," Frank said. He was standing with his hands on his hips, staring at his sister.

"I feel so miserable," Helen said, looking at Frank, one hand holding a glass of beer on the bar. There was sad, wounded confusion in her eyes. Her skirt was short and her crossed legs revealed a mound of white thigh. Her breasts were pushing forward against her navy blue sweater, their tips delineated by the snugness of the fit. She lifted her free hand and pushed several strands of hair back from her face. Frank noted her ringless fingers; they seemed so much older than the rest of her.

"Don't you think you ought to go home?" he said.

"I was," she said. "But Philip was picking at me."

"He was picking at her," Geeb said.

"What am I going to do, Frank?" she asked, her voice and face aged with despair. "He blames me about Lorana."

"Have you heard from her?"

She shook her head.

"She could be a thousand miles away by now," Geeb said.

"I've never seen Philip like that," Helen said.

"Everything happens at once," Geeb said.

"Shut up, Joe," Frank said.

Joe Geeb hung his head, gazed contemplatively upon Helen's thigh.

"I'm worried about her, Frank," Helen said. "She's just a child. And I know why she ran away," she added, nodding her head ruefully.

"You ought to go home."

"I will, in a little while."

"Staying here can't do any good."

"I'll just have a few drinks . . ." she said.

The half-dozen drinkers scattered along the bar were silent. The bartender was standing in a corner, staring at the floor, his arms folded across his white shirt.

"You want me to walk you home?" Frank asked.

"No . . . I'll wait awhile," she said. "I'll wait till he goes to sleep.

If he does. He hasn't slept in two days. He hasn't gone to work or eaten or anything. All he does is go around asking people if they've seen her. He doesn't realize I'm just as upset as he is . . . and now, what happened today." She shook her head. "I just don't know what to do," she said sadly.

"Frank, can I buy you a drink?" Geeb asked, looking up.

"No," Frank said.

Then his sister fixed him with a most appealing and plaintive gaze. "By rights we should all be together tonight. Frank," she said, "tell Paul . . . I'm sorry."

He nodded, then turned and left.

TWENTY-FIVE

Frank was nearly at the entrance of the boardinghouse when he saw the rear door of the car parked in front of it open and swing slowly out. He eased and shortened his strides, becoming keenly alert, moving his eyes to a side and fixing their gaze upon the car. He thought it curious that no dome light had flashed inside with the opening of the door. He watched the tall man step leisurely free of the car, take two steps, then wait for him.

"Mr. Dublin," the man said.

Frank stopped. The man was wearing a dark suit, white shirt, tie. His blond hair was neatly parted. He appeared to be in his early thirties, with a look of decaying innocence. He was taller than Frank, standing with tall, relaxed confidence. He gave the impression of a man who might be graceful and proficient at track or basketball—he had that athlete's look of being at ease with his body. The man allowed himself now a pinched, rather parsimonious smile at the corners of his mouth (or perhaps not a smile but some reflex of self-satisfaction); otherwise his smooth-surfaced, coolly intelligent face was totally without suggestion.

Since the utterance of his name had come as a statement of fact, as passionless as the reading of a deposition, and not shaped as a question, Frank felt not alarm or wariness but a curious interest. He believed he knew exactly who they were (there were two other men in the car) and why they were there; and with this in mind, his primary response was to wonder where it was going to lead. His curiosity was so strong it was almost objective, as though he were watching the encounter being played out on a motion picture screen.

"Would you mind coming with us?" the tall man with the utterly professional face said, his tone closer to civility than politeness.

Frank looked at the black, four-door automobile. Its polished roof caught the glare of the nearby street light with a sharp, silvery glint. Inside, two men were sitting in absolute stillness, almost as if they were witnesses rather than participants.

The eyes of the tall man gazed at him with such steady, dispassionate intensity that Frank began to feel inside of himself the fumbling clumsiness of lies preparing themselves for the telling.

"We won't detain you for very long," he was told.

"What is it about?" Frank asked.

But he knew that they knew; there was suddenly that terrifying and debilitating awareness that everything he had ever said or done was known to these bloodless automatons who had appeared from out of the night with their air of cordial menace, who similarly did not care, who only knew: that was the strength hewn into the dispassionate gaze now confronting him, that insensate expression of tireless skepticism and mistrust—the unbreakable conviction that the world was divided into good and evil, friends and enemies, and all that mattered was that some hand had moved the pawn which was Frank Dublin into the shade.

"Mr. Dublin," said a voice from inside the car, from the man in the rear seat. The voice was at once conciliatory and impatient.

Bending slightly at the waist, Frank peered into the car. The man was sitting in the far corner with his legs crossed, engulfed in shadows. He had a most comfortable look, as of a man accustomed to being chauffeured. He was dressed the same as the tall one, except that he was wearing a hat.

"It's just for a chat," he said from his corner of shadows. "We're not arresting you or any such thing. If you say you don't feel like a chat, why, we'll simply go away and leave you to your curiosity. We may come back tomorrow, or next week, or maybe even never."

"Who are you?" Frank asked.

"People who simply want to have a chat with you. Look now," the man in the shadows said, "you're into something and what we want to say could be to your advantage. Do we look like the sort of people who go around wasting someone's time? We know about the other morning and want to talk to you about it."

"The other morning?" Frank said, feeling uncomfortable with what he knew was a feeble pretense of ignorance.

"With Seavery and the others."

Instead of fear or alarm, Frank instead felt foolish, as if the covering over some childish secret had been rubbed away. He said nothing, resolved not to demean himself with futile and hollow protestations.

The man in the back seat remained absolutely still, as did the tall one on the sidewalk; while the driver never even turned his head. The patient, united silence of the three was like a suggestion that they had said all they were going to and knew precisely what they must hear in response and that anything less would not do; that within their assigned limitations they were eminently reasonable men, trying not to worsen for Frank a situation which was already pulsing with threat and uncertainty. Their cool, detached demeanor deepened Frank's dilemma and illuminated his isolation. Quite consciously, however, he resisted the temptation to break the silence, knowing there was little he could say to men who could not speak for themselves.

Finally the one in the shadows spoke.

"I promise you," he said, "you'll feel much better about things."

Frank sat in the back, between the tall one and the other. The car headed along Grant Avenue, entered the Manhattan-bound lanes of the Long Island Expressway and cruised smoothly through light traffic toward the Queens-Midtown Tunnel. In an assertion of something, he was not quite sure what—a spurious show of unconcernedness, or perverseness—Frank did not utter a word during the twenty-five-minute ride. He sat back with his arms folded and his legs crossed, meditating in the silent car. The men around him seemed bored. The tall one stared out of the window, the one with the hat sat with his chin slightly raised, his eyes narrowed, as though contemplating prosaic details of his personal life. The driver's eyes, which Frank occasionally glanced at in the mirror, never left the incoming road ahead.

They entered the long, brightly lit tunnel and drove under the river into Manhattan. Emerging on the other side, they turned downtown at Second Avenue and headed toward lower Manhattan. They stopped finally amid a grim empire of municipal buildings whose ponderous architecture seemed designed to crush the humble petitioner to servility.

They got out of the car. Hemmed in on all sides by the god-sized buildings with their titanic façades, the streets in the late-night silence had a withdrawn and watchful air. Here and there in some window thrown high against the dark was a lone and mysterious light.

The driver remained in the car, and Frank and the other two walked up the low, broad, innumerable steps of one of the buildings. A warm, city-bred wind blew dead leaves around them. When they reached the top of the steps Frank saw a guard standing behind thick glass doors staring out. An elderly man, the guard was wearing a tieless blue workshirt and black trousers supported by wide white suspenders. His round, tough Irish face was wrinkled with implacable suspicion. A holstered pistol rested on his hip. He raised his hand and with a snap unlocked the door.

Walking between his two escorts, Frank went along an empty, high-ceilinged corridor. Rows of closed doors bordered on either side. Being virtually alone in a building of this magnitude gave Frank a sense of importance which he realized was false and ingenuous but which was irresistible.

They stopped at the end of the corridor, before an unmarked wood paneled door.

"Go on in, Frank," the one with the hat said turning the knob and pushing the door slightly open.

Frank entered alone. He turned around when he heard the door close behind him. When he turned again he found himself alone with a man sitting behind a desk.

The room was approximately twelve by fifteen, with terrazzo floor. It was windowless. The lighting was from above, from one of three fluorescent pipe-bulbs, and had a subdued though not dimmed quality. There were two low-backed wooden chairs, a row of filing cabinets against one wall, and a bridge table heaped with papers and folders so disorderly and unorganized as to confirm the cynical citizen's most dire suspicions of bureaucratic efficiency.

The man behind the desk had short, neatly combed white hair, though he looked no more than forty. His smoothly shaven cheeks had a florid look from numerous burst capillaries. His eyes were small, set in rather narrow sockets, and contained a level, scrutinizing gaze that suggested a certain quality of wry self-amusement, which suggestion extended to the slight curl of his lips, which were so finely shaped as to make one expect nothing less than the most impeccably enunciated syllables to fall from them. He was wearing an expensive lightweight blue suit, powder blue shirt, and a red tie clasped with a gold pin embossed with fraternity lettering. His elbows were up on the desk's surface, his chin resting lightly on the fingers of his clasped hands.

Frank, determined to appear casual and in control in the face of this cool and immobile composure, allowed himself to be contemplated by the blandly staring man. He soon absorbed the impression that this man disliked him, had disliked him—because of breeding, schooling, opinions, life style—even before Frank had walked in, would dislike him under any circumstances and not merely because they had come together as antagonists in this room in the middle of the night. This subtle, tacit antagonism soon was in the air and Frank felt it somehow clarifying the situation, that through undisguised disapprobation the man behind the desk was establishing a sense of mutual understanding, as if some bothersome and time-consuming formalities had been dispensed with and that nothing was more professional than to be able to communicate civilly with someone whom one intuitively disliked. The man behind the desk finally relaxed the detached persistence of his stare, brought his hands down flat on the edge of the desk, leaned back in his swivel chair and smiled. It was a pleasant smile, given the circumstances.

"I'm glad you came, Frank," he said.

"Who are you?" Frank asked.

"Mr. Bennett."

"I don't mean your name—I mean officially."

"Just a cog in the machine, Frank." Bennett smiled again, self-deprecatingly. "No more important in my machine, say, than you are in yours. Subject to orders, to impositions, with an occasional word of praise, an occasional moment of satisfaction. You know how it is—you wake up one day, realize you're suddenly a certain age and have fallen into your permanent niche, and you might as well be realistic about it." Bennett lifted his expensively tailored shoulders in a philosophical shrug. Now he made a gesture as if to shake hands, but was actually showing Frank to a chair. Frank pulled one of the wooden chairs across the floor and sat down directly in front of the desk, so near to it that when he crossed his legs the tip of his shoe touched the edge of the desk.

In front of him on the desk Bennett had a container of coffee and a narrow carton of plain butter cookies. Now he sipped some coffee, then opened the carton of cookies, removed one, then carefully closed the lid, folding it precisely shut. He put the cookie into his mouth and chewed slowly, making a mumble of crumbs between his teeth. He raised the container to his lips again, sipped for a moment, then put it down. The only other object on the desk was a manila folder which lay at his elbow.

"Have you heard from Arthur Seavery since your fiasco of the other morning?" Bennett asked.

"No," Frank said.

Bennett smiled thinly, the rims of his upper teeth showing for a moment.

"You don't deny knowing him then?" he said. "I think that bodes well, Frank, quite well. Yes. No games of cat and mouse, eh? This pleases me more than you can know. I find nothing more refreshing than candor. I'm sure you'll agree that few things are as frustrating and unproductive as a conversation in which one of the parties is trying to be coy. And I'll tell you something out of my experience, Frank: when a man is trying to be coy he often gives away more information than he would otherwise, without ever being aware of it. Ah," Bennett said wearily, smiling with his lips, "sometimes this job of mine deteriorates into . . ."

"What job precisely is it that you have?"

Bennett's face settled once more into gazing repose, as if Frank had just put the most abstruse and unexpected question.

"I have the job of talking to you," he said after a moment, the distaste implicit in the very flatness of his voice.

Bennett rolled his chair away from the desk and swung slowly about until he was sitting in profile to Frank. He looked much stronger in profile, Frank thought, with strength in his forehead, nose, jawline. As if aware of this, Bennett remained in this manner for several moments, staring reflectively at the file cabinets.

So this was Bennett's moment to swing around and stare at the file cabinets, Frank thought, watching the man with great curiosity. So much of it had to be contrivance, a device, carefully planned and designed to disarm and divert, to disturb the poise and clarity of one's thinking; there was no telling which among the sighs, shrugs, gestures, inflections were genuine, which attempted subversions. The man was at once advancing and retreating; was by turns jaded and acute and detached and affable and sympathetic and hostile and banal and shrewd, edging upon one's fears and doubts with subtle pincer movements.

"You were very lucky the other morning," Bennett said. "If we hadn't stopped you, you might have killed people. In that case, we wouldn't be here talking so *politely*. I suppose, if you wanted to, you could logically explain to me what you hoped to gain by blowing up those delivery trucks."

"I could," Frank said.

"Would you like to?"

"Are you open to conversion?"

Bennett smiled; in profile the smile seemed bitter. He swung slowly back to face Frank.

"I would like to call a lawyer," Frank said.

"You're not being charged with anything," Bennett said. "You came here voluntarily and you're free to get up from that chair and walk out any time you want to."

Frank remained wary. It was almost as if Bennett were deliberately implying a sense of importance and invulnerability, in order to throw him off his guard. He knows I'm intrigued, the son of a bitch, Frank thought. What good was the option to come and go freely once your curiosity has been stimulated? In fact, he had to suppress that curiosity now and keep himself from becoming trusting and voluble. He wished he could engage this man under other circumstances; he found himself increasingly fascinated by his interrogator, who had summoned him in the middle of the night to this nearly deserted building; this man who, apparently, had the power (and the grounds) to effortlessly arrest him, but was not doing so. Frank felt an anxious desire to talk to Bennett about the latter's work, to confide and receive confidences, to talk as equals playing a lonely and devious game. It was as though old hopes and aspirations, long reduced to dead romance and mere passing dreams, were seeking to regain their oldtime authority. But be careful, Frank kept reiterating to himself. If they did not have their purposes he would not now be there. They bring you in the middle of the night to these august places in order to impress and intimidate you with their power and your insignificance, in the same insidious way that the monu-

mentality of ancient cathedrals was designed to crush the minds
and spirits of the superstitious.

Bennett opened the carton again and withdrew a single cookie,
then carefully folded the lid shut. He fed the cookie into his mouth
and washed it down with a sip of coffee.

"You're an honest man, Frank," he said. "At heart, an honest
man. You came home. I put very little credence in psychological
theories, but if I did I would say the fact that you didn't go into
hiding might be an indicator of your true feelings in the matter."

"That I was hoping to be caught because I really don't believe
in what I did?"

Bennett smiled and shrugged. "Psychological theories. For what
they're worth. Nevertheless, you did come home. Which is more
than we can say for your friend Seavery."

Frank was pleased and relieved to hear, officially (for whatever
it was worth—he realized he could not place one iota of reliance
on anything this man said), that Seavery had not been picked up.

Bennett lifted the corner of the folder between thumb and forefinger, stared for a moment at a yellow lined page within, then
lowered the folder.

"I take it," he said, "you're no longer in the service of the Lord?"
Frank was puzzled.

"As you were in Los Angeles," Bennett said with a certain innocence, as if apologizing for the information.

"Oh, that," Frank said.

"We know about it."

"I'm flattered. If I'd known you were spying on me, I would
have preached better sermons."

Bennett laughed pleasantly. "No doubt," he said. "No doubt a
lot of people would become better citizens if they knew they
were being watched. But, frankly, I'm not at all surprised you
got duped into this business. Men of the cloth can sometimes be
remarkably naïve."

"Look, I was not a bona fide minister and you know it."

Bennett laughed again, as though caught in some small embarrassment. "Yes, you're right, Frank. We know it. Nevertheless,
it was because of your position there that you got involved. And
apparently it was more than just missionary zeal. Frankly, one
of the reasons you're here now is because we want to help keep you

out of trouble. We could arrest you, of course, but what good would that do? There are some people who want to do that, but reason has, so far, prevailed. I must warn you, however, that the situation could turn around without warning; you could be arrested at any time. You understand that, don't you? I mean, according to the rules of the game, you should be put in jail, shouldn't you?"

"You've made your point," Frank said.

"The days when a person could simply vanish into thin air are gone forever, I'm sorry to say," Bennett said. He was sitting back now, his arms stretched before him, his hands resting on the desk. "Just think of the way society is structured now: computers, sophisticated criminology, instant communications. How long can a person go before he's caught? Our modern society with all its crowds and chaos, instead of providing a perfect camouflage for the fugitive, is conditioned to regurgitate him. And in your case, the egos of some of your colleagues make it additionally difficult for you. My God, they can't do anything without issuing manifestos or writing letters to the editor or calling up the police. We would have to be deaf, dumb and blind *not* to notice you."

"You ought to be grateful to us," Frank said. "We've gained you more public support than you've ever had in your lives. Because of us the police are now more popular with certain segments of this country than ever before."

"And becoming more so every day. We know that. We're hardly insensitive to it. You see the way it works: when the most repellent people in the country attack us, it can only gain us sympathy with the masses—the very people whose allegiance *you've* got to have."

"You plant agitators, don't you?"

"Would you blame us if we did? We have our dirty-minded strategists too. The difference between us is, we know the minds of the masses so much better than you do."

"That's bullshit," Frank said. "The world is changing and you ought to get with it."

"No," Bennett said, shaking his head slowly. "You're wrong. Parts of the world are changing, without question. But that has nothing to do with us. Some societies are simply immune to the catalysts of others. You can't pre-pack solutions in vacuum-sealed jars and transport them around the world and expect to solve problems wherever you drop them. In this society the revolutionary can't win; he can only bring a disastrous counterrevolutionary holocaust upon all our heads. There won't be any surprises either. This country has been issuing its warnings for two hundred years. I tell you, Frank, the masses in this country have always known instinctively who their enemies are; they've been so conditioned to mistrust and repudiate a certain type of person, a certain type of thinking, a certain type of life style, that all we have to do is keep the pot boiling, so to speak—as long as we're able to hold the lid in our hands. You know as well as I, that in this sort of combat it's the untruths and exaggerations that stick. Your people use the same device."

"So above all else, you have to discredit us, even when we might be speaking the truth."

"Especially, some people feel, when you *are* telling the truth, since you generally use truth as a convenience to paste over with lies. So what up until now were for us tactics, have now become moral imperatives. Frank, would you like me to tell you what's happening in the country, from our point of view?"

"Do," Frank said with cool politeness.

Bennett launched into a monologue during which his face remained stern and his voice earnest, though he spoke with few emphases, as if his purpose was to enlighten rather than convert.

"Society has always turned its police work over to a certain kind of mentality," he began. "This is work that a certain other type of person would never soil his hands with, but always feel quite competent to criticize. Now, if more of the allegedly high-minded people went into police work they might be able to raise it to the standards they seek—which they think they seek and which they think are possible, and desirable. But these standards are neither possible nor desirable. And the criticism goes on. And now it's getting worse. Some people think it's a good idea to weaken the police, as well as society's entire chain of authority. They see this as an opportunity today because the conflicts have come down to grassroots levels. But instead of being weakened, the police have been *changed*. They're no longer what they were originally intended to be—impartial and objective protectors of life and overseers of society.

"The nature of the job has always conditioned the nature of the man, all throughout history; and now, in the case of the police, so has the nature of the abuse. The police have become united in their work as never before. They've begun to act and think like a single unit against a single *other* unit and are most vulnerable to becoming politicized. You might think this is what we want. It isn't. The more this trend continues the more detached the police will become from government, the more they will pander to repressive prejudices, the more they will become the arm and implementation of a single style of thinking; and after that, there is only one direction in which things can go. They'll become the arbiters and organizers of society, leaving little room for dissent of any kind. And inevitably the government will follow the same course, on the grander scale, because the government has to support the police. So you can see how it begins and where it ends. This is not what is desirable. A lot of us in police work recognize the drift and even though we may sympathize, it isn't what we want, because in a police state not even the police are secure."

"What is it you want?" Frank asked. "I mean with me?"

"Your help, obviously."

"What can I do?"

"It's most valuable to have someone on the inside."

"What makes you think you can trust me?"

Bennett spread his arms and shrugged.

"A guess," he said, smiling. "We can only guess and hope we're good judges. We haven't, for instance, put this to the two we picked up the other morning, Breenstone and Meyer. We think they're hopeless. We think their minds are dead."

"I'm not very flattered by your proposition," Frank said.

"If you think about it, you'll see that you ought to be. I mean, *think* about it. Forget your indignation for a moment. Frank, everyone feels they have some qualities that are either ill-used, unappreciated, or misunderstood, and this can lead to illusions, which leads to being misled, carried away by the enthusiasms of the moment. They stand to lose everything, and for—nothing. The man who can resist the fanatics and the fashions and take the long, hard view is the man who knows his own mind. There are many injustices in this country, but you people want to burn down the house to get rid of the termites."

"You want me to go into meetings and stir up trouble so the police can come in . . . you want me to befriend people and then betray them . . ."

"Are you insulted?"

Frank did not answer. He watched Bennett again open the carton of cookies, lift one out, neatly fold the carton closed and begin nibbling. *You'd think he'd offer me one, the son of a bitch,* Frank thought, feeling hunger pangs.

"Remember this about our society, Frank: social problems are like magnets—eventually they draw to them their proper solutions."

"You had someone in our group, didn't you?" Frank asked.

Bennett nodded, feeding the last rim of the cookie into his mouth. Then he sipped some coffee.

"Who was it?" Frank asked.

"Temple," Bennett said putting the container down. "In fact it was he who told us you might be just the man for us. He said you seemed to have good common sense."

"But wasn't I deluded into going into a crazy plan with a bunch of lunatics? Where was my common sense then?"

"He suspected you had your doubts, that somehow you'd got into something you couldn't get out of."

Almost morbidly, Frank thought what an opportunity it was for him to say Yes, Yes, that's just what happened; what a marvelous chance it was to leap free of the serious charges they could lodge against him. He gazed with lifeless, ironic eyes at the floor for a moment. If he made that leap and joined forces with the man behind the desk, he would become a "cog," be in fact less than Bennett; with Seavery there was still the chance of something greater—perhaps the only chance he would ever have. If he had doubts about the viability of that opportunity, then Bennett with his expressed concern about what was happening across the land had shored them up somewhat. Perhaps their sole intention in all this was to get Seavery—a possibility Frank could not overlook and which impressed him.

"What happened to Temple?" he asked, the thought sudden to him.

"He died," Bennett said.

"So you lost a good man."

"Very good. He may have saved your life, Frank."

Frank grunted.

"We have lots of good men scattered about," Bennett said. "So even if you go back to what you've been doing, you'll never know who you're confiding in, who's leading you into what."

"Just how frightened are you?" Frank asked bluntly.

"We're never frightened, Frank," Bennett said quietly, suddenly with a force at his back that Frank envied. "There are simply different levels of concern."

"And you want me to enlist with you."

"As I said," Bennett said casually, "it's a guess. A risk. We can never really be sure of a man. We prefer people who are passionate and who will do this out of conviction. We're always uncomfortable with someone who's in it just for the money, though that sort has done very nicely for us. Money can be a passion too, I suppose," Bennett added with a curious tone of regret.

"It's a dirty business," Frank muttered.

Bennett stared sympathetically.

"And if I say go to hell?" Frank asked.

Bennett smiled enigmatically.

"You have those two golems waiting outside to arrest me, don't you?" Frank said.

Bennett shrugged.

"It's blackmail, isn't it?" Frank asked.

"No. This is a reality situation. And anyway, you haven't been threatened, have you?"

"Not directly."

"And indirectly would be your inference."

"I'll need time to think this over."

"We can give some," Bennett said quietly. He was sitting back now, running his finger along his underlip, staring intently at Frank.

"My father died today," Frank said. "It's really a . . . confusing time for me."

"Yes, we know about that. You have my condolences," Bennett said without irony.

"You knew about it? You knew what happened this morning . . . and then bring me here tonight?" Frank asked heatedly, and then for the first time suddenly felt genuine fright as he found himself looking at a pair of absolutely glazed, almost lifeless eyes.

As Frank sat quietly trying to contemplate what seemed an ever-growing array of problems, Bennett pushed a scrap of paper across the desk toward him.

"There's a phone number written on that," Bennett said. "Any time you want to reach me, call it. Twenty-four hours a day."

Frank stared cynically at the scrap of paper for several moments, then reached forward and picked it up and held it in his hand.

"Christ," he said softly, as if to himself, "I feel like just running away."

Bennett opened his hands and raised his palms into the air.

"Where to?" he asked, his face and voice conveying both innocence and sympathy.

TWENTY-SIX

Who could you even tell about such a thing as this? Frank asked himself as he rode home in the subway. The mere fact of being *asked* to be an informer was stigmatizing. Breenstone and Meyer had not even been approached—their minds were "dead," Bennett said. What did that really mean?—that their minds were too imbedded in dogma to be receptive to Bennett's reasoning, or too determinedly alive and independent for subversion? What makes them think I'm susceptible to it? he wondered sullenly. A guess, Bennett had said. Was he being charitable? It was almost diabolically clever—planting something so lethal in him, knowing full well it was not a thing he could discuss, knowing it was a proposition he could reject at his peril. They had fed a little of everything into his mind, from flattery to patriotic appeal to threat, hoping something would take root. It was all so indiscriminate as to make him wonder whether they knew everything about human nature or nothing at all.

They were much more devious than he had thought. (Curiously, even though he was seeing the face and hearing the voice of Bennett, Frank was consciously thinking in terms of "they" without realizing it.) They could arrest him, or ignore him, or play upon his nerves until he broke. There were no limits to what they could do. He was nothing to them, was less than a human being. But they were frightened—in spite of what Bennett said. Of course they were—why else haul him down there like that in the middle of the night? This was no casual meeting. Bennett obviously was an important man. They knew me from California, Frank thought as he sat in the subway with his arms folded. Temple had surely reported the high esteem in which Seavery held Frank. (That pleased him, even though a corner of his mind told him there doubtless were dossiers on everyone in the Movement.) There was no question but that they were concerned. Maybe more was going on than Frank was aware of. After all, he had never really penetrated the inner circles of the Movement. Or had he? Was Seavery more important than Frank thought? (After all, hadn't Seavery commanded the unquestioning allegiance of men like Breenstone and Meyer, who were willing to go to jail rather than co-operate with Bennett, who apparently were tougher and more dedicated men than Frank had thought.) Seavery had hinted at some master plan in California, something more significant than the mere planting of bombs. Were "they" aware of this? Frank suspected they were. And perhaps their informers had so far not succeeded in learning exactly what was being planned. Temple had been their man in the group, but he was dead now. Perhaps Seavery had confided to Temple, as he had to Frank, hints of the master plan that was being formulated within the Movement (though Frank knew that Seavery was extremely cautious and mistrustful). Temple had died before getting the details. So now they need me, Frank thought. A man utters the name of his successor, then dies. He supposed he ought to be grateful to Temple, Frank thought morosely; if not for Temple's assessment of him, Frank would no doubt be in jail now.

The object of all this was to get Seavery. Frank was beginning to believe that now. But who knew if Seavery would ever be in touch again, in spite of his promise to do so? This was the sort of person who wrapped himself in the wind and went off with it. And at the same time he represented some hope for Frank, a way out of the mess. Bennett's fear, Seavery's guarded intimations— were they totally without significance? Maybe something was about to happen that would topple things, bring about the crucial rent in the social fabric and with it the chaos and upheaval that Seavery insisted would be the signal for the downtrodden and the alienated and the oppressed to rise: a grim, determined outpouring of violent insurrection advancing from the campuses, the factories, the ghettos, from every corner of the land. But soon, Frank thought. If it is to be, then let it be soon. What good would it be if it happened after his time had run out?—time that was now being measured between the thumb and forefinger of Bennett.

He left the subway at Grant Avenue and instead of waiting

for the bus, began walking. It was a pleasant mile's walk, along a main thoroughfare that actually had some trees standing along the way. It was late enough now for some of the bars to be closed, and the gentle, settled Capstone night was soothing.

Bennett was right about one thing, Frank grudgingly noted: he, Frank, could not run away. Not only would it be difficult and futile and impractical, but the very idea of it was appalling. And even if he tried it, there really was no place for him to go. A person like Seavery could find sanctuary in any number of places and hide out indefinitely. And anyway, Frank told himself, he didn't have any money (in fact, he made a mental note to visit Paul in a day or so to borrow some). Now if that twenty-five thousand had come into his hands, as rightfully it should have. . . . Or if Charlotte would suddenly see him in a different light . . . (She would love to hear tonight's tale, Frank knew. The deeper he got in, the more appealing she seemed to find him. The day of his execution, he thought bitterly, would doubtless be featured by expressions of eternal love from her.)

He thought vaguely of Temple, recalling the latter's quiet urging: *Bomb. Bomb.* At the time Frank suspected the man might be psychotic. But that was the job. Instigate. Edge things along. Get people into a situation where they were vulnerable. Cause the same fear and mistrust within the Movement as the Movement was trying to cause in society. How was it possible for a human being to find the motivation for such a thing? How did one cope with conscience and memory and the threat to sleep? If ever there was a soul-killer, it was this foul and despicable business of betrayal, a thing of short and rancid glory. From what grim and arid place in the soul did it rise? And yet—what a game it was. A veritable labyrinth of plot and counterplot. Bennett would never fully trust him, nor he Bennett. And yet they would be partners. Somehow, this manner of thing seemed natural to Bennett. But Frank—how could he, he thought, turn around and intrigue against people he might genuinely like, in a sordid back-alley game? Why didn't they just arrest me instead of giving me decisions to make? Frank suddenly asked himself miserably. Had they picked on him because they thought he was strong, or because they thought he was weak? What shape did this Darwinian selection assume? What did that son of a bitch Temple see in a few hours acquaintance that made him presume to judge? What gave him the right to suggest the bequeathment of his shadow to anyone? Resentfully, Frank became momentarily resolute as he strode through the night. Literature was stocked and history abundant with examples of men who had valued honor above all. Better to sit in jail than to barter his soul.

Or was it?

As he walked slowly through the surrounding, watchful night, he rubbed thoughtfully at the back of his neck. How deeply did he really believe in "revolution"? Had he ever been truly candid with himself in this matter? He had been listening to the logic and the reasoning of both sides. Which was right? Both? Neither? Each, partially? If each was partially right, then it was up to him to decide where the moral weight lay heaviest. It was also up to him to decide whether Bennett was telling the truth about the danger of a police state, or whether that earnest speech had been cynically contrived to influence Frank. *I will not be manipulated I will not be deceived.* Why should Bennett fear the expansion of police power? Who was ever opposed to the increment of his own power and authority? There never yet was a man who did not think he could control the beast.

Frank watched a police car cruise by. It looked sinister to him now. What were they thinking in there, those two men riding through the quiet unoffending night? To what dimensions were their resentments expanding, which of their appetites were being fed? Frank felt his head beginning to ache. It was so easy to make decisions and come to conclusions when nothing was at stake. But now the problems were freighted with genuine consequences, the answers were intricate and hard to find. It was all so grandiose: everyone was maneuvering to save the country, or so they claimed; each with his own solution, each with his own poisoned vial of sincerity. And where in all this was the entrance of principle? Was it possible for this unambiguous quality to exist in such a climate? And how did a man know if it existed for him—when it lay within the tangled embrace of survival?

I could ennoble myself through all this, he thought mordantly. Nothing was more readily available than a sense of martyrdom, that elder brother of paranoia. There can be no victory without profound moral suffering, no worthwhile endeavor without profound moral purpose. Oh, that sounded so lovely, Frank thought derisively. Who is not an enchanted beholder of his own pure, suffering soul?

As he approached the turn-off to the boardinghouse, Frank saw a group of five or six men standing outside of a tavern, laughing. Their relaxed conviviality heightened his own sense of damning isolation and self-pity and made him envious.

For the second time that evening he walked toward the boardinghouse. This time there was no black automobile parked outside, no tall bloodless professional rising from the dark to utter his name. But then Frank stopped himself as he was mounting the wooden steps of the front porch. Passing idly through his mind had been the idea that he would like at last to unburden himself to that infallible repository of common sense—his father. The realization, the stunning impact of a known fact—that his father was dead—suddenly struck him. He leaned with one arm against a porch pillar and stared blankly at the empty rocking chairs lined along the porch. When was it? Yes, this morning. Harry Desser had come by to tell him. It isn't so remarkable that I'm not used to it, he thought . . . what was remarkable . . . was that one's father should be dead. *Whom do I talk to?* He felt an emptiness spreading through him, vast areas of himself lying mute and permanently vacant. *Damn him! I need him now. Selfish old bastard!*

He walked inside and began going upstairs. A nightlight illuminated the hall and staircase. He went to his room, key in hand. When he opened the door and turned on the light he saw the piece of paper lying where it had been slipped under the door. He picked it up and read it. The message was scrawled in the landlady's quavery handwriting, with one misspelling and one mishearing:

Mr. Seebree called. Will call tomorow A.M.

TWENTY-SEVEN

Frank's problems were of such magnitude, were throbbing in his consciousness with such compelling and unrelenting urgency, that probably even if he had known why those men were standing in the street at that hour of the night in so bouyant a group, he might still have ignored them, under the reasoning that a mind which accepted the entrance of every problem found the resolution for none.

The idea had begun evolving in Joe Geeb's mind soon after Frank's departure from the Hamlet Tavern. As Helen's grief and self-pity deepened and darkened, she began confiding her unhappiness to Geeb, who never regarded himself as unscrupulous or opportunistic, but rather as one who was, in his own words, "creatively alert." Speaking from out of her bleak, sodden sadness, Helen told the sympathizing Geeb things that he knew: her father was dead, her daughter had run away, she herself was a victim of her own uncontrollable urges. To the litany she now added something fresh to the ears of Joe Geeb: she would reform. She had to, she said tearfully, shaking her head. She had brought nothing but pain and disgrace to her family. One daughter already was gone, the other children were pathetically bewildered, her husband seemed to be going mad, one brother hated her. It was a depressing, self-lacerating accounting. Joe Geeb, with tactful compassion, began buying whisky chasers for her beer. She put her hand on his arm and told him he was "a loving person who understands."

"Joe, what am I going to do?" she asked.

"As you say, you've got to reform," he said.

"But how? You know me . . . how many years?"

"We grew up together," Geeb said, making solemn reference to his impeccable accreditation. (In fact it was because of Helen Dublin Werner that Joe Geeb and many other young men of Capstone had grown up as quickly as they had.)

"Help me, Joe," she said. "Jesus Christ, you went to college."

"What you've got is a sickness," Joe said. "A recognized medical sickness. Nymphomania."

She nodded resignedly. "I know," she said.

"A lot of good-looking sexy women have it."

"Joe, what do they do about it?"

"It's abnormal and uncontrollable sexual desire," he whispered.

"But what do they *do* about it?" she asked irascibly.

"There's a cure, but it's drastic," Joe said. Then he said, "Do you know how they cure extreme cases of alcoholism?" For the idea had now fully evolved in his head and it was merely the details he was trying to work out. There was a tavern on the avenue, Godfrey's Place, where the night bartender was a personal friend of Joe Geeb's. Downstairs from that tavern was a basement room where until recently a middle-aged slattern named Clara Murphy had lived, paying her keep by "servicing" some of the customers, who were therefore induced to patronize the place. One night a few months before, one of the favored customers had primed himself with several whiskies, winked at Godfrey, and slipped downstairs. Several minutes later he was back, steaming with indignation. "You son of a bitch," he said to Godfrey. "She's dead."

So the room, equipped with cot, chair and table, was empty. It was damp, windowless, roach-infested—Geeb described it to Helen in the most base terms available. There Clara Murphy had perished of her sins and her soul gone to hell. The mere sight of the place should be sufficient to redirect any wayward female who had "the wrong ideas." If a person was able to sample beforehand the ultimate degradation which threatened them, Joe said, it could, if that person had any sense at all, save them from their fate.

Godfrey's basement was the perfect place then, Joe maintained, to purge oneself of nymphomania. If the cure for extreme alcoholism was to pour vast quantities of whisky into the patient until he became deathly sick and never wanted to taste the stuff again, then logic followed that if one, in Joe Geeb's words, "screwed exhaustively and indiscriminately for one night," until one could "no longer bear the thought of another pecker," and do it in such a place as Godfrey's basement, from where Clara Murphy had been dispatched for her sins, one might be freed forever from the curse of nymphomania and returned to a normal life.

"Oh, my God," Helen said miserably, staring dimly at her reflection in the back-bar mirror.

"You asked my advice," Joe said.

"Will it help? Are you sure? It seems . . ."

"You'll never want to see another piece of salami as long as you live."

"I don't want to turn into a goddamn nun."

"No no no no; what I mean is, your desires will become normal."

"Normal?" she asked dazedly, gazing at him with barely focusing, barely perceiving eyes. "I'll be normal." Normal, she thought. The word had a healing, euphoric sound to it. *Normal? You mean I won't want any more to bang priests and astronauts and basketball players . . . basketball players, God, they must have the biggest . . . no, I won't think about that any more.*

"I want to be normal, Joe," she said wearily.

"Your friends will help you."

"How many do you think? About how many?"

As many as I can line up, Joe thought. At that hour of the night, at least twenty. But it would have to be done with discretion. Nobody wants to be twentieth, or even nineteenth.

A telephone call to the night bartender at Godfrey's established the availability of the basement room. After Helen was brought to the tavern (by car—by now she could hardly walk), Geeb hurried around town rounding up his customers. Generally, the response was heartwarming. From several, however, he heard the same thing:

"That son of a bitch. Since when is she charging ten dollars?"

TWENTY-EIGHT

Arrogantly, or perversely, or perhaps simply out of some illusion of immunity, Seavery walked the streets of New York continuously following the aborted attempt on the newspaper. He stared defiantly at policemen, believing he knew how their minds worked: *They think we all look alike,* he thought contemptuously—so even if they did have his description fixed in their minds, what good was it? He had been sought before and never found. He was wanted, he believed, in Boston and Los Angeles, and now New York. And still he walked the streets with impunity.

He walked from Greenwich Village a hundred city blocks north to the Columbia University campus, which was rustling now with the beginning of the fall semester. He felt a certain scorn for the students, they seemed so callow. He walked along the East River, a stolid, solitary figure, brooding over the moving waters. He passed the United Nations building, where his father had once brought him when he was ten years old, and he recalled cynically now the sober lecture on the design and aspiration of that institution which his father had given him. Tireless, tense, infatuated with the content of his own mind, he roamed the city streets, a slight, obscure, nondescript youth who nevertheless stared at other people with a curious sense of superiority because he knew he was contemplating the making of history. The days were long and sunny, the night air soft and secretive. He slept one night on a loading platform near the West Side waterfront, another on the grass in Tompkins Square, where a group of youths sat all night chanting passages from the Koran. Rationing his few dollars with great care, he went into supermarkets and bought bread and stole packaged cheese and meats, and these were his meals, washed down with containers of coffee.

He went daily to the Central Post Office, hoping to find in his

box there a check from his family. Each time the box was empty.
Finally, in a rage, he called home. With great eagerness in her
voice, his mother took the collect call.

"Where is my check?" he demanded angrily, standing in a door-
less outdoor phone booth, shouting so that whoever passed
turned to listen.

"Your father wants you to come home," his mother said. "He
wants to discuss things with you."

"I'll come home when I'm ready, he shouted. "Where is the
check?"

"What are you doing?" his mother asked. "Why don't you come
home for at least a little while? We want to see you. Arthur?"

Standing on piles of wind-blown paper, he covered the mouthpiece in exasperation and looked away for a moment, cursing
bitterly, muttering through stiffly set lips. Then he uncovered the
mouthpiece and shouted into it,

"Send the check! Send the goddamn check!" And he hung up
the phone with vehemence.

He returned to the Village, where he felt more at home than
anywhere else in the city. But even here he found himself staring
malevolently at people. He reserved his most embittered feelings
for those whose appearance most closely approximated his own.
In his mind he accused them of being frivolous, romantic revolutionaries who thought that by conforming to a certain style
of dress and attitude they could bring down the government. They
were to be most loathed, because they were dissipating advantages, because they were being guided by ceremonial rites as
precise and as rigid as those they pretended to abhor, instead of
being motivated and driven by urgency and conviction. They
were leading lives of diminished responsibility, content to be cheer-
leaders for those who were taking the risks, who were creating
the ambience in which these poseurs strutted and reveled.

He sat on the grass at a protest meeting in Central Park, dully
listening to the stale and tattered phrases that had become sub-
stitutes for action. Imperialism. Knee-jerk liberals. Democratic
socialism. Liberation. Racism. Genocide. System. Establishment.
Capitalism. Sexism. Military-industrial complex. He stared at those
around him with sullen incredulity. People were actually listening, applauding, cheering. When did it stop? He hung his head

and gazed somberly at the grass. These were soft and gentle people, who absorbed frustration and disillusionment without resistance, unaware of their impotence, their failure, making their revolution with petitions and speeches and harmless, carefully observed activities. Didn't they realize that enthusiasm was doomed to exhaustion, while action was tireless and decisive? How many of the cheering revolutionaries around him were fugitives from the law; how many had ever put their convictions and their vaunted freedom to the test of a smoking crucible? They were all content to lie abed at night while history roamed vulnerable in the shadows.

But you're not going to get away with it, brothers and sisters, he thought bitterly. You're not going to turn it into one long, never-ending social function. We know how to snap you out of it and turn your energies blood-red. You're not going to wallow with your spurious determination in the achievements of others. There is much more to it than writing SCREW THE ESTABLISHMENT on a subway wall.

TWENTY-NINE

Frank had taken the most ingeniously deceptive and circuitous route he could imagine to get to Seavery. The idea that he might be being followed became an obsession the moment he stepped out of the house, and remained with him as he got on and off of buses, changed subways, took a short cab ride. He stretched what was normally a forty-minute trip into Manhattan to almost two hours. And then, once he emerged from the subway, more time was spent walking warily toward his destination, looking over his shoulder, pausing before store windows and peering in for telltale reflections, feeling all the more conspicuous for trying to appear innocuous.

At first he thought what an annoying and frustrating way this was to live, how intolerable such a situation could become. (Doubtless Bennett was counting on him to react in a certain way; if only Frank could know what was expected of him he would be able to resist it.) But then he realized that today these extraordinary precautions were necessary, since he had no intention—at the moment—of co-operating, willingly or otherwise, with Bennett. The idea of appearing one day as a government witness at a conspiracy trial he found totally repugnant.

After reading the landlady's message the night before, he had resolved not to take Seavery's call in the morning, determined not to get any further into this thing. Cursing his own treacherous curiosity, however, he had taken the call, then found himself unable to resist the youth's intense and earnest voice that flowed with such intrepid assurance over the house telephone. When he had hung up the phone, Frank thought, *Well, there's no harm in going to hear what he has to say.* He had two separate and distinct reactions to what he had heard. Seavery had made oblique reference to a climactic effort on the part of the Movement, something that "the finest minds in America" had worked out, and which, the youth said, was out of the planning stage now and into the area of "imminence." This had great appeal to Frank's curiosity. Also, he realized to his despair, he had no choice but to go. Seavery was his only real contact inside the Movement, and if he ever decided as a last resort to avail himself of the option offered by Bennett he had to maintain that contact or face the possibility of having his tenuous hold on his freedom evaporate at any moment.

I'm boxed in, he thought irascibly as he headed through the industrial grimness of the lower West Side streets toward the river. He had to laugh sardonically at his predicament—either Seavery and his friends brought the country to instant revolution or Frank was ticketed for five years in jail. (The third possibility, turning informer, came reluctantly to mind with nagging force, like an uninvited guest.)

Thoughts concerning his own security were becoming more intrusive now, with sobering effect. The question most central to his thinking as he got closer to Seavery was whether to tell the youth about Bennett. The more he thought about it the more colossal the problem grew in his mind. There was no way to gauge Seavery's response to such information. The group had already suffered from the infiltration of one informer, and for all Frank knew he himself was under suspicion of having been that person. The fact that he had even been approached and offered such a proposition could be enough to frighten Seavery away. Thinking objectively, Frank, to his dismay, could not conceive of Seavery ever having such a meeting with Bennett. One look into the eyes of Arthur Seavery, Frank thought miserably, would be enough to convince Bennett.

Suddenly he stopped in his tracks and turned around. He could be leading them to Seavery right now. He reacted to the idea with angry resentment. He did not want to be so callously and unscrupulously used. Bennett could have filled his head with that nonsense last night with this very hope in mind: that Frank would go immediately to Seavery and warn him of the danger. But then Frank's self-esteem reacted against this possibility. Bennett would not be so foolish as to think he could get by with such a trick. Frank was too shrewd for that. They were trying to induce him to work for them because they knew he was capable of greater things and would not waste such a man simply for the sake of a single arrest. Frank turned and continued walking.

The appointed place was a pier that extended out into the Hudson River alongside an abandoned warehouse that was being dismantled by time and weather and looked as if it were longing to sigh away into the water. As Frank crossed under the shadows of the West Side Highway, he saw a lone figure sitting on the pier in the bright afternoon sunshine, looking solitary and wistful, as people so often did when staring into great bodies of water. He realized this was the second time he had seen this enigmatic youth off his guard (the other was the night Frank had slept at the tenement and covertly watched Seavery sitting by candlelight), and each time there was an aura of isolation and melancholy about him. Deliberately, Frank slowed his pace as he walked toward the pier, taking full advantage of what suddenly felt like a rare luxury —watching Arthur Seavery without being seen.

Staring mistrustfully down at the planks of the pier, Frank walked toward the end of it, where Seavery was sitting on a wooden box. Another box was beside him, and Frank wondered whether this was the youth's thoughtfulness or merely coincidence. Seavery's far-off staring was so intent that Frank looked into the distance, but there was nothing on the water and nothing of distraction happening on the Jersey side of the river.

Seavery did not move until Frank was a few feet away; then he lifted his head slightly and swung it around, pensive contemplation fading from his eyes as he began a slow smile.

"I think I know your footstep, Frank," he said. "It has an honest ring. Do you know there's a certain sound to a police footstep?"

"I know," Frank said. "Flat."

After their first meeting of eyes, both looked out to the river for several moments, as if in some ritual of homage, Seavery sitting on his wooden box, his slim shoulders pulled forward in an unwashed short-sleeved white shirt, a windbreaker folded neatly across his narrow thighs; Frank gazing at the swells of the soiled Hudson waves on their way to sea in completion of a journey begun far away in shaded, rock-bedded Adirondack streams. At the mouth of the harbor stood the poised, startlingly familiar figure of the Statue of Liberty.

Seavery turned, raised his hand and swatted the wooden box next to him.

"Sit down, Frank," he said.

"Isn't this risky?" Frank asked, easing himself onto the box. "I mean, sitting out in the open like this?"

"No. People who have something to fear don't sit out in the open." Seavery seemed amused. "You're edgy, Frank," he said, passing his companion a sidelong look.

"You act as if nothing happened the other morning."

"Nothing did, if you recall."

"Except that one man was killed and two arrested."

"In war you mourn your casualties quietly; it gives them dignity."

"But it gives the survivors something to think about."

"If a man doesn't learn from survival," Seavery said, "he has no business surviving."

"He can learn, and he can learn," Frank said philosophically.

Seavery shrugged. He brooded for several moments, then quietly said, "Frank, the other morning was a disgrace, I don't mind telling you."

"You don't have to tell me; I was there."

"But it doesn't change anything."

"I think one of your friends was an informer," Frank said, could not help saying, given the pressures of his mind. Merely speaking the insidious and threatening word *informer* made him feel positively conspiratorial.

"I know," Seavery said. "There had to be."

"Who do you think it was?"

"Temple."

"Why him?" Frank asked after letting his surprise register for a moment.

"Have you been giving it thought?"

"Well, yes."

"You don't think it was Temple?"

"I can't decide. I hardly knew any of them."

Seavery chuckled. "Breenstone and Meyer, in their jail cells, are no doubt thinking it was you."

"Me?"

"Because you were the last man in. But I think it was Temple. The man lacked passion. Didn't you notice that?"

"I suppose."

"But then again, if either Breenstone or Meyer come out of jail in a few months, we'll know it was one of them."

"What would happen to them?" Frank asked with more than idle interest.

"You never can tell," Seavery said disinterestedly. "But I still think it was Temple." There was a mildness in his voice.

"He paid a heavy price."

"Well, *c'est la guerre*. Do you know French?"

"No. You can speak freely," Frank said sarcastically.

"I used to live up near the Canadian border . . . French Canada, that is. The language sort of drifts across. I never studied it, just picked it up by listening. You can pick up a lot of things just by paying attention. Frank, are you a student of the Movement?"

"What do you mean, 'student'?"

"Are you sensitive to its moods, its ups and downs?"

"I like to think I am."

"It's down now, isn't it?"

"Our end of it, anyway."

"No, there you're wrong. Dead wrong. Our end of it is one of the few places still containing life. There are always ups and downs in any endeavor involving large numbers of people. The danger is that it can go so far down it doesn't come up again. Too many dilettantes and self-indulgers have come in. It's become fashionable, a romance. These people are like sand in an engine. They're impairing the running of the thing. They're slowing down everybody else's reflexes. It's in danger of dying, Frank."

"You've told me there are thousands of people across the country waiting to go into action," Frank said, after sitting for a moment with the dismal thought that if the Movement died it took him with it, no matter which course he chose.

"There still are," Seavery said. "Still waiting."

"And for how long must they hold their breath?"

"Not for long, I can tell you. Frank, this is a Movement that relies on youth. And when you're young, then even a year can be crucial. Even a year can change every idea in your head and make you a different person. I'll tell you precisely for how long they have to wait: until someone defines their purposes for them by action. Look, I know what's going on on the campuses; the electricity is there, waiting to be plugged in and released. There are thousands and thousands of students and underground people and those who are simply disaffected. Give them the proper motivation and a rising will be instantaneous and violent."

"You're giving me a stump speech," Frank said bluntly.

"I know, I know, and I hate that," Seavery said, lifting for a moment a placating hand. He fell silent for several moments, staring with a curious smile at the water. "I hate a lot of things," he said in an oddly detached way. "Live in this society . . . and hatred and disgust are the signs of a healthy and realistic mind. When you begin to loathe yourself for your helplessness, you know the time has come for action. And, Frank," he said turning to him with a face so filled with controlled fury Frank seriously thought for a fleeting moment that the youth had suddenly gone mad, "when you reach that moment no action, no matter its severity, can be called irrational."

"Seavery, for God's sake, tell me what it is you're talking about," Frank said in exasperation.

Quickly, excitedly, the moment Frank had finished speaking, Seavery said, "What act more than any other will light a fire across this land that no thunderstorm could ever extinguish? Listen, Frank, the Establishment is waiting for us to lose our cool and become obsessed, because they know an obsessed person is vulgar and a fool and will exaggerate reality to such a degree that it becomes distortion. So why should we attempt reason? The only way to get through to people is with violence, because violence has a terrible effect on those who witness it or hear about it."

"But . . ."

"No, let me finish," Seavery said fervently. "Don't ever try to reason with the masses. It can't be done. There is no median mind. Don't you see? But a mob . . . you can't reason with a mob either . . . but you can *control* it. In a mob man is a beast, Frank. Believe me."

"Shit," Frank said, "set the mobs loose and we'll be the first ones they tear apart. What the hell are you talking about?"

"I'll grant you, the majority of the population is against us right now. But for God's sake, do you expect it to be otherwise? We're the only ones who've been honest with them. Of course they loathe us. The people most admired by the masses are those who give bland promises of idyllic sterility. But think of it, Frank: simply because we're scorned and hated, for these very reasons we can win the masses, because it will be discovered that we're not as evil as we've been painted. What will then rush forth from the masses will be more than their affection; it will be their relief and gratitude and worship because they'll see we've been fighting for their interests all along."

"It seems to me you've taken a long jump," Frank said, after having kept his guard up against Seavery's impassioned rhetoric. "Now you have the masses worshiping you. There's a piece missing from the scenario."

Seavery smiled slyly. "How do we get to the altar, eh?" he said. He had been speaking with great excitement and animation, and now he let several moments pass. When he spoke again it was calmly, staring at the water.

"Do you recall a conversation we had in California?" he asked quietly. "You ought to. It was about murder."

Frank felt a chill run through his body. Instinctively, he half turned to make sure no one had stolen up on them. Then he looked at Seavery with such piercing scrutiny it was as if he were trying to see behind the youth's eyes.

"Do you remember?" Seavery asked.

"You spoke about killing someone and throwing the blame on a particular group in order to incite a mass reaction."

"Yes. I don't suppose you forget such a conversation," Seavery muttered. "In any event, that's the idea."

"The idea?"

"Frank," Seavery said impatiently, "I don't want to hear any talk of morality or anything like that. We're going to discuss something now and it has to be on high, impersonal levels; cold-blooded, if you like."

"Don't prejudge me," Frank said resentfully.

"I've already prejudged you," Seavery said savagely, looking at him with a candor and intimation of perception that frightened Frank. "If I hadn't, you wouldn't be here now. How many human beings do you think this can be discussed with?"

"You have your thousands across the country—so you say,"

Frank said heatedly, stung into defensiveness by Seavery's abrupt shift in mood.

"Yes, and they're out there and we're here. They're waiting for us to act. They're ready to do their share. Each is prepared to draw together his pocket of responsibility, ready to stretch out to the next, until we're one solid band across the continent. Leaders will appear to bring it all together. And there will be leaders of the leaders. And you can be President, or Czar, or Emperor . . . whatever you choose. That's all you want out of it anyway, isn't it?" Seavery said contemptuously.

Frank said nothing, swallowing his indignation.

"A death is needed," Seavery said, his manner again suddenly changed. Now he was speaking quietly, his voice earnest and reasonable, emotionally detached from what he was saying. "A human sacrifice. A martyr. Call it what you will. The Movement needs blood, Frank," he said with the raptness of total self-conviction.

Frank held his tongue. He was now extremely wary of and sensitive to not only Seavery's words but also to the youth's smooth, almost entreating manner; listening to the purposefully understated and reasonably proposed scheme. He's flattered me by telling me he can discuss it with me, Frank thought; he's forbidden talk of morality, he's impugned my reasons for being in this. Cynically, on his guard, Frank listened, his hands clasped tightly between his knees, his eyes cast down upon the old, sun-bleached timbers of the pier. Below, the soiled Hudson waves slapped around the pilings.

"Just the right man," Seavery said. "It has to be the perfect victim, one who appeals most passionately to the most passionate people. Think about it: How many men are there whose deaths would enrage a large segment of the population? Most men in public life are bland and uninspirational—which is why they're there in the first place. We must have someone whose death will do more than provoke speeches and a day of national mourning."

Sound and logical, Frank thought derisively. Perfectly acceptable strategy, impeccable and pragmatic. Who could argue with such cogent thought? It was a pleasure indeed to sit there in this sunny, pleasant place on the water and discuss murder. They should have packed a lunch.

"Frank," Seavery said. "Do you know who will be in New York on Saturday night to deliver a lecture? Kifner."

Now Frank turned and looked aghast at him. His shocked reaction illuminated Seavery's subdued conceit as the youth's lips expanded in a slow, pleasantly malevolent smile.

"Kifner?" Frank asked. "But he's . . ."

"I know very well who he is. One of us. And a great man, too," Seavery said soberly. "Professor Kifner is a very great man. Nothing less will do, for what we have in mind."

Who is that 'we'? Frank thought, shaken.

"Have you ever seen him speak, Frank?"

"Yes."

"Then you know what he can do. I've seen him turn an audience of thousands into a foaming mob. Frank, this man has reached into the heart's blood of every man and woman in the Movement. He's a revered spiritual and intellectual leader. His death will send thousands into paroxysms of rage the likes of which will leave you breathless. It will revitalize the Movement, give to it a momentum it can never lose. Frank, for God's sake," Seavery said, raising his voice as he took note of Frank's noncommittal gaze, "it will send students into the streets by the tens of thousands . . . it will provoke state authorities into bringing out the National Guard . . . there will be riots, burning, destruction . . . probably shooting and killing. Millions upon millions of uncommitted people will be revulsed and outraged by the government's brutality. The tide will turn against the government, and then they're going to have to deal with us; finally, at long last, they'll have the people against them, and they're going to have to deal with us as the only organized spokesmen for the people."

"I'm sure Kifner will be delighted," Frank said dryly.

"This man has never proscribed the necessary use of violence. If you've read his writings you'd know that."

Frank grunted. "Poetic, isn't it?" he said. "But listen, what a man says in his study and what he says on the field of battle are apt to be two different things."

"If he doesn't believe the things he's written, then he's a hypocrite and deserves to die," Seavery said coldly. "Anyway, he's not going to have anything to say about it. His death will be blamed on those who would like to see him dead. It's a matter of record that his life has been threatened a number of times. This will teach those people a lesson."

"So you've got it all worked out," Frank said.

"There's your metaphor," Seavery said, pointing out to the river. "There's your America flowing past. By land, by sea, and by air, they've polluted and corrupted this country almost beyond redemption."

Frank stared indifferently at the water, his big hands tightly clasped.

Seavery suddenly laughed; it was a most unnatural sound to Frank's ears.

"I was just thinking," the youth said. "Someday there might well be a plaque right here, where we're sitting. 'On this spot Arthur Seavery and Frank Dublin sat and planned the decisive act instrumental in bringing about a new and better America.'"

Hearing his place in history thus predicated did not at all cheer Frank. It unnerved him to think that the idea of murder could rest so lightly upon the mind of someone, to the extent that history was already seen vindicating and memorializing the fact. He wondered from out of what festering abscess of the mind such thoughts could rise, from what irreducible kernel of unreality. Seavery raised his head and smiled inscrutably out to the passing waters. *Through what wild centuries of dream and nightmare does he roam, subscriber to the contentions of zealots, seeing visions of injustice on the air before him?* Seavery turned to him. They stared searchingly into each other's eyes for a long moment.

"You're a fool," Frank said.

Seavery's lips remained parted in soundless mirth, but his eyes gazed coldly back into Frank's.

"Why, Frank?" he asked politely.

"It should be obvious."

"Frank, do you know what any revolution is founded upon? What lies at its heart and soul?" Seavery's voice was gentle, and in his eyes lay an expression near to wounded innocence. "Love," he said. "That's what this is all about. That's what we have to get back to. Not only in America, but all over the world. Look how far we've strayed from it, if we have to use murder as a way back."

"Love," Frank said skeptically.

"Do you believe it's dead?"

:5:5:5:5:55555

"Don't ask me these goddamn abstract questions," Frank said irritatedly, turning away.

"There are plateaus along the way where men do fall out," Seavery said suavely, as if he were the soul of understanding and forgiveness. "At the last moment I myself might falter. A person never knows what's inside of him. The challenge is never easy. Only the strongest make it to the top, and only the strongest of the strong stay there."

Frank gazed upriver at the smoking industry on the Jersey shore.

"I had to ask you, Frank," Seavery said, almost apologetically now. "There was no other way to find out. Believe me, I won't hold it against you. You've done fine work for the Movement, and I know it."

Frank suddenly got to his feet, startling Seavery, whose eyes stared with uncertainty up from out of a frowning face.

"For Christ's sake," Frank cried, "you're one hell of an insolent bastard, you know that? You've been thinking about this scheme for months . . . then you just spring it on me . . . and expect me to jump in. Think what you're asking a man to do. I've got to . . . got to . . . give it some thought."

"If you think about it you'll say no."

"So what's wrong with that, once I've thought about it?"

"Nothing . . . once you've thought about it," Seavery said sarcastically.

"Stop patronizing me you little son of a bitch or I'll throw you into the river."

Seavery shrugged. "Frank, I can only speak *to* your conscience, not for it."

Seething, Frank walked some twenty feet back along the pier, then stopped. He turned around and glared at Seavery.

"This is *murder* you're talking about!" he shouted. Then he extended his arm and raised it to eye level and shot one finger from out of his clenched fist and pointed it at Seavery, who was half turned on the wooden box, watching him calmly. "Cold-blooded, premeditated murder!" Frank cried. "Of a man you profess to admire, no less. To trick a whole raft of other people you profess to admire." Frank lowered his arm and stood glaring at the calmly staring youth. Panting with anger, he waited for his composure to return, then began walking slowly back to Seavery.

"Don't feel bad about it, Frank," Seavery said. "I know, come Saturday night, you'll be wishing me well . . . wherever you are."

Frank leveled a sharp, steady gaze upon him.

"I said I wanted to think about it," he muttered.

Seavery shrugged. He scratched idly for a moment at his calf, and Frank caught a glimpse under the raised trouser leg of the sheathed Bowie knife tucked into the youth's desert boot.

"I want to think about it," Frank said, his voice barely audible. Seavery's ineffable calm was beginning to rattle him.

"There's a telephone booth across the street there," Seavery said, indicating with a lift of his head. "When you walk by it, memorize the number. I'll be standing outside of it on Saturday afternoon between three and three-thirty. If you want to join me that evening, call. If I don't hear from you . . ." Seavery's voice trailed off and he shrugged again. Then he turned to gaze at the river.

Frank watched him for several moments.

"I'll think about it," he said, then turned and walked away.

Seavery listened to the footsteps go back along the pier. Then he turned around. He grinned when he saw Frank enter the phone booth and remain in it for several seconds. When Frank stepped out of the booth he looked across the street at Seavery sitting at the edge of the pier, then turned abruptly and walked away. Seavery shifted around on his wooden box and resumed his staring upon the placid Hudson waves.

THIRTY

When Frank returned home and began mounting the steps of the boardinghouse, he suddenly had a transported feeling of almost giddy elation, as if some miracle were occurring. Ironically, the transmitter of the apparent miracle was the unlikely person of his brother-in-law, who rose from one of the porch rockers the moment he saw Frank coming up the steps.

Frank's grasp for even the slimmest and most incongruous reed of hope was easily understandable: he had come away from Seavery embittered and depressed. The conversation had left him numb, in some unfeeling limbo between fear and confusion. He felt as if he had stepped out of the realm of normal human experience into something so lunatic and decadent as to defy comprehension. Obviously Seavery had not been talking idly that night in California; he had been walking around all this time with a devilishly conceived murder plot germinating in his head, with Frank one of the few "privileged" to know about it. The piece of information was deadly. The depraved, like the contaminated, were only too generous in their sharing. Frank's resentment was toned by a righteous bruise, as if his trust had been abused—he had regarded the conversation in California as little more than an interesting hypothesis.

So when he saw Philip rising from the rocking chair, Frank's first thought was that some tireless subconscious prayer had been answered, that Philip was there to report the return of Lorana and the restoration of the money; and in that fleeting, burden-lifting moment of exhilarating, almost maniacal relief, Frank envisioned his immediate future so vividly he was nearly stunned by its reality: he had gained possession of the money and was in flight out of the country, to Canada or Europe or South America, relieved of all his sins and mistakes, reprieved from all threats and maledictions, given a blessed second chance.

All of this was in his mind for perhaps five seconds, until he saw the usual look of despair in his brother-in-law's face, darker this time, more rock-bottom and end-of-the-world than ever, and Frank suddenly felt for him a keener, more irrational hatred than he had ever before felt for anyone, as for one who had embodied the miracle and then become its slayer.

"Frank," Philip said as they met at the head of the stairs. Off to the side the rocking chair he had just vacated was nodding drowzily in slowly diminishing gestures.

"You haven't heard from Lorana?" Frank asked despairingly.

"No, no, nothing; not a word. Listen, can I talk to you? I've got to talk to you."

"No, not now," Frank said. "I have some . . . some thinking to do."

Philip stared at him with such stark, piercing intensity that Frank became resentful. He did not like being stared at in such a manner, particularly by this brother-in-law of his.

"Another time," Frank said morosely, bowing his head and going inside.

Nevertheless, Philip followed him into the house and up the stairs. Frank was so preoccupied with his thoughts that even though he knew his brother-in-law was following him, there wasn't room in his mind to think about it. At his door, however, Frank finally turned to him.

"Philip . . ." he said.

"I've got to talk to you."

"I'm busy now."

"Frank, it's important."

"How important can it be?" Frank said irascibly.

"I've got to see you now," Philip said. There was a certain uncharacteristic insistence in his voice, a certain fixed and stubborn determination in the way he was standing.

Frank surrendered to the thought that the sooner they talked the sooner he would be rid of him.

"Phil," Frank said idly as they entered the room, "do you have any money to lend me?"

"If I did, Frank, you know you could have it," Philip said as he closed the door. "But look, there's something I want to talk about. Something happened with Helen last night . . ."

"Shit, I'm tired of hearing about Helen," Frank said disgustedly. "I'm sick and tired of listening to you whine about her."

"I agree, I agree," Philip said hurriedly. "Anyway, that's not what it's about."

Frank walked to the window, pulled aside the curtain and looked out. There was the vague thought the house might be being watched. He listened to the word *paranoid* mute itself upon his mind, and did not resist it. Did paranoia define the truth, or did truth blur all definitions? In any event, he had inside his head such a superabundance of grotesque truths as to be able to be selective and settle realistically into any kind of justifiable neurosis; he could make the shift between reality and fantasy without the least friction, without the least sacrifice of logic or rationality.

"Remember the things we talked about in the bar?" Philip was saying. "Do you remember . . . what a man can do . . . one man alone?"

Frank nodded, barely listening. He walked away from the window, suddenly feeling claustrophobic in the confines of his room. Already they had waited outside for him; it was conceivable that one day he would open the door and they would be sitting here, staring at him with their cold, detached, professional faces. Was it possible the telephone was being tapped? Had they listened to the conversation with Seavery? He had seen in the movies men sitting in the basement of a house, wearing earphones, listening to and recording telephone conversations. He suddenly had the mad impulse to run downstairs and look in the basement.

"I've been giving it thought . . . a lot of thought," Philip said watching his restlessly pacing brother-in-law. Frank raised his hand to his mouth for a moment, gnawing his thumb knuckle. Then, for some reason, he opened the closet and looked at the few articles of clothing that were his: jacket, topcoat, trousers, second pair of shoes on the floor. He closed the door. I don't even have a wardrobe, he thought in reasonless frustration.

"A man suddenly reaches some peak of despair . . . or maybe it's a pit of despair . . . whatever . . . and realizes he can't just go on the same way," Philip said, his eyes riveted to his pacing, inattentive brother-in-law. "He realizes he has to do something . . . something . . . not just to change things, but wipe away everything his life has been . . . and maybe at the same time . . . in some crazy way . . . help other people. Frank, you don't bring about change simply by standing still and being a nice guy and hoping. You don't help yourself or anyone else by saying, 'Yes, this is the way it is and always must be.' Well, just because it is doesn't mean it has to be."

Frank stopped pacing and looked at him as if Philip had just materialized on the spot.

"What the hell are you talking about?" he asked.

"Do you remember our conversation . . ."

"Yes, yes," Frank said impatiently.

"About how a man can take hold of his life and . . . do something?"

"How the hell can he do that? And why should he, when it's all decided for him anyway?"

"But you said it can be done."

"Then do it and don't talk about it," Frank said angrily. God almighty, he said to himself, what does he want from me?

Philip paused, staring inquiringly at him.

"A man must have dignity," he said quietly, resentfully.

"He does, huh?" Frank muttered.

"Frank, I know what I have inside of me. I know what I'm capable of."

"Then share it with the world!" Frank suddenly cried in almost comic exasperation, throwing up his arms. Then, subdued, "For Christ's sake, Phil, other people have problems too . . . but they don't go around mewling about them."

"Yes, yes, I know," Philip said. "That's the trouble; there's too much talk . . . too much standing back and watching things just spin themselves out."

"Philip, leave me alone." Frank's voice was quietly imploring. "I've got things I have to think about."

"All right, Frank. All right." Philip was quite calm now. He smiled, an expression of quiet resolve in his face. Unexpectedly, he offered Frank his hand. Wearily, Frank shook it. Then Philip turned and left, closing the door behind him without a sound.

An hour later Frank walked into his brother's house. He found Paul wandering through the hall holding a cup of coffee. When

he saw Frank, Paul extended the cup toward him. Frank shook
his head.

"I need more than that," he said.

"Do you need money again?"

"As a starter."

"And what as a finisher?"

Frank laughed bitterly. "That I'll have to find God knows
where."

"Do you at least know what it looks like?"

"Not even that."

As they talked they strolled through the downstairs part of the
house, through the hall to the kitchen, then back again and
through to the living room, bedroom, back into the hall. Paul kept
sipping coffee as they walked.

"Can you spare two hundred?" Frank asked.

"I'll write you a check."

"You never ask what I'm doing, do you?"

"I don't have to; you generally tell me."

"Well, there are certain things that I can't tell. I've been talking to a lot of . . . strange people lately. Getting stories and view-
points and facts and fears and so many things . . . my head feels
like it's in a vise. I wish I could tell you all of it. Really, I wish
I could confide. But I can't. Do you understand?"

"I understand," Paul said.

"I mean, things are coming to a head now. I'm going to have to
make some ball-busting decisions."

"This pertains to your revolution, I take it."

"Yes." It sounded positively ludicrous to Frank: *My revolution.*

"Then I'm sure you have colleagues to talk to, who will help you
decide things."

"Oh yes," Frank said quickly, feeling for some reason the urgent
need to lie. "Top people, all of them. Fine minds, Paul, really
fine minds. You would find them a challenge. But sometimes
. . . an outside perspective is needed. Sometimes you get too close
to the thing. Like you . . . aren't there times when you feel the
absolute need to have someone read your work and give you an
objective opinion?"

"No," Paul said.

"No?"

"Why let other people muddy your mind? There's no one really qualified to give advice anyway, particularly when they're approached in a crisis. For instance, there are some things, some problems of my own I'd love to be able to discuss with you. Your view of the world is so different from mine; it might help."

"I know there's been something pressing at you," Frank said.

"Yes," Paul said with a short, ironical laugh.

"Then what good are brothers, if they can't talk when there's something burning them up?"

Paul shook his head. "I don't know. Maybe it's enough to say, 'Brother, I have a God-awful problem but I can't talk about it.'"

"You can say that to anyone."

"No you can't," Paul said quickly.

"You can trust me," Frank said sullenly.

"Frank, there are a lot of people we can trust; it's ourselves . . ." Then, abruptly shifting the conversation, Paul said, "We went around to your place this morning, but you weren't there."

"Who went around?"

"Severith and me. We made the arrangements this morning."

"The arrangements? Hell. Listen," Frank said, "I should have been there, or at least contacted you. It's unforgivable. But I had to go into the city this morning. It was imperative. There really shouldn't have been anything else on my mind, but . . ."

"It's all right. I'm just glad I didn't go alone. You need somebody along, especially somebody who's not a member of the immediate family, who can be detached and look at it as purely a business transaction. Which is what it is, I suppose."

"So it's when?" Frank asked.

"Tomorrow morning. Do you have a suit?"

"Yes, in a pawnshop in Los Angeles. Can you lend me one?"

"Yes, though it'll be small on you."

"And speaking of loans . . ."

"Money."

"I know I've been hitting you a lot . . . but it isn't as bad as it seems; it's just that I keep coming around for small sums, so it seems more than it is."

"Frank, you can have whatever you want. I'll give it all to you. It means nothing to me."

Frank smiled and shook his head.

"Brother of mine," he said, "don't do that, or I'll go so far it'll take seven daredevil astronauts with telescopes to find me."

They sat down now at the kitchen table. Paul finished his coffee and sat toying idly with the empty cup. Frank, sitting quietly, suddenly looked up at the ceiling.

"Did I hear someone up there?" he asked.

"No," Paul said.

"Well, if I'm hearing things, I'm not surprised."

"It seems the Revolution has taken a turn for the worse."

"Fuck you," Frank said glumly.

"Frank, you're a synthesis of contradictions. And therefore impossible to define. Sometimes that makes you interesting, sometimes it makes you a pain in the ass."

"There's nothing complicated about it."

"Nothing coherent either."

"I can assure you of one thing—your money is not going to any radical causes; it's strictly for my support."

"I don't care if you feed it to radical causes," Paul said. "I don't give a damn what you do with it. Go ahead and buy rose-colored glasses for your theorists; use it any way you want."

"There are no longer theorists, I'm afraid; only activists."

Paul reflected for several moments, then said, "I sometimes think a revolution is possible. I think there exists a kind of politicized second law of thermodynamics—continued social disorganization and deterioration will eventually create an effective external counterforce. Like sin and conscience," Paul said with an uncomfortable laugh. He smiled reticently at the empty cup in his fingers. "Yes," he said, "by all means, damn the theorists. Their hypotheses are too exciting and glamorous to risk rational invalidation by action. Sunbursts of . . . of fustian rhetoric and infantile intellection are much too precious to be challenged. It's all the art of . . . selecting and declaiming."

"Well, anything is," Frank said.

"It's dangerous, that's the point. Especially in this country, where so many dreams and visions have come true. You can be deluded by the legend into trying to smash the tradition that built the legend. Why, that's asking an entire nation to step out of character. There are certain fundamental, inflexible, *American* facts, and anybody who tries to circumvent or ignore them, or adds supplementary dimensions to his illusions is either a fraud or a fool."

Paul put down the cup and leaned back and stretched out his arms and yawned.

"Ah, but communal issues are sometimes attractive," he said, bringing his arms down. "A silken quicksand. It's certainly in the air these days. I met Philip on the street this morning and you'll never guess what he wanted from me. I tell you, Frank, I think he's going off the deep end."

"What did he want?"

"He asked me to write a creed for him. 'A statement of creed,' was how he put it."

"What was he talking about?"

"I don't know, and believe me, I didn't stand there and discuss it with him."

"A statement of creed?" Frank said puzzledly.

Now they got up and walked along the hall to the living room.

"I spoke to Philip a little while ago," Frank said. "He was in a bad way; I mean in *really* a bad way. He was incoherent, almost." A shadow of thought, derelict, tantalizing, indefinable, passed over his mind, giving him pause for a moment. "He said some crazy things," Frank said thoughtfully.

"About what?"

"I don't know. Frankly, I wasn't paying that much attention."

"He has his burdens too, I suppose," Paul said philosophically.

"Listen," Frank said, "about the money . . ."

Paul went to the desk and wrote him a check. Then they walked out to the porch.

"I'll pick up the suit tomorrow morning," Frank said.

"Be here early. There's going to be a limousine."

"Style," Frank said abstractedly. He looked around at the scattering of old houses, the tall patriarchal trees. A fluttering wheel of homing pigeons turned and banked against the late afternoon sky. He could hear the beat of their feathers.

"What will you do tonight?" Paul asked.

"I think I'll go home, sit in a chair, concentrate, become ten years old, look into the future . . ."

"And?" Paul asked with an amused smile.

"Choke on it," Frank said.

THIRTY-ONE

Lorana saw her uncle only twice during the two days she was in the house; that is, she spoke to him only twice, and then merely to inquire about food. Each time he answered her politely but perfunctorily, letting her know she was free to do as she pleased. Which was not entirely true and she knew it. It was never explicitly stated but was there by implication: he preferred she remain quiet and out of sight. And to the best of her ability she obeyed, even though never in her life had she greater need to talk to someone than she did that first night. But she knew that not even telling about the money would be sufficient to elicit interest or comment from her uncle. Perhaps the act of running away (even though she had gone barely over a quarter of a mile) had sharpened her sensibilities to a most delicate edge, or perhaps it was simply the aura of intense self-involvement that her uncle projected, which she knew would resist any approach or attempt at contact. In any event, she did not, or could not, talk to him.

She did not try sleeping that first night until almost four in the morning. All night there were lights burning downstairs and she could hear him stirring about. She slept only a few hours and when she wakened heard him walking back and forth through the house as methodically as though pacing off distances. When her hunger grew into a cramping pain she realized she was going to have to go below and get something to eat. Uneasy about facing him, she sat still for hour after hour, trying not to think about food. Several times she slipped out of the room and went to the upstairs bathroom and drank water. Unable to appease the hunger any longer, she went downstairs sometime past the noon hour, careful to make herself heard, so as not to startle him.

He was in the living room, putting his shoes on. He paused to look up at her. "Are you all right?" he asked. She nodded. "There's food in the refrigerator," he said, anticipating her. "Help yourself." He finished putting on his shoes and stood up. He stared into space for several moments, lost in thought. Once, his eyes shifted to her, briefly seemed to consider something, then looked away again. "I'll be out all day," he said. "Until very late probably." "May I stay?" she asked. "If you like," he said indifferently, then added, pointing to his desk, "Please don't disturb any of those papers." "I won't, I swear," she said. He stood very still for several moments, deep in contemplation. Deferring to him, his mood, she did not move. Then he said, quietly, "It seems your grandfather died last night." Her eyes widened a fraction, her lips parted. "But I just saw him," she said softly, ingenuously, as if trying to disprove what she had just heard. "It was . . . sudden," Paul said.

After he had gone she went upstairs. She took out the envelopes again and, ignoring the money, stared at the old photographs, saddened, vaguely disbelieving. Death was still the most unmanageable of abstractions, and the fact that she had been talking to her grandfather just the day before made it even more bewildering. With great tenderness she stared at the pictures of Ben Dublin as a young man, and somehow she was better able to relate to them; now that he was dead there was more comprehension. The old man's life was done, complete, and for some odd and obscure reason the fact that once he had been young and strong and vigorous was easier to grapple with. Now she was able to connect the old man with the young, the young with the old, knowing that neither, anymore, existed.

Her sorrow did not have the penetrating quality a child might feel for a parent, but was rather the melancholy grieving reserved for a grandparent, for one who had been gentle and unoffending, not a stirrer of emotions but instead some pleasant dividend, a warm but somewhat remote extension of life. She mourned him softly, crying herself to sleep on the upstairs cot, the pictures strewn around her. The money, that remorseless self-driving, self-renewing life force was, for the time being, given little thought.

She slept away most of the afternoon. When she wakened she saw the pictures and remembered. She wondered what she ought to do. Death cast its obligations and she considered going home, except that running away had been, among other things, a desperate, despairing act of protest, and to walk in now and not be at the center of the situation would be to have her gesture end in emptiness.

Again she wondered why her grandfather had given her so much money, and what she was supposed to do with it. Perhaps he had been expecting her to return today to receive the explanation, the instructions. Perhaps he had given it to her mistakenly. Now, the money was an inhibition. When she had decided to run away, the idea of being without resources had frightened her, though her determination had overcome that. Now, with so much money, she was differently frightened. She did not dare wander around carrying such a sum. The fact that her grandfather trusted her with it, while she herself did not, left her in total indecision.

As the hours lengthened, the one night she had slept away from home seemed like months. Lying upstairs on her cot, she wondered what was happening outside, as if because she was hiding from the world it was a signal for cataclysmic events to occur.

Paul returned just before midnight. She waited for him to come upstairs and tell her what was happening. Gradually she realized that he wasn't going to. She opened her door partially and stood there listening. She heard him in the kitchen, heard the refrigerator open and close, the sound of something being unwrapped, the light metallic tinkle of silverware. When he had finished eating, he walked into the living room, where his desk was and where he spent so much of his time in that interminable, almost vigilant silence she could not understand. He seemed never to go to his bedroom, but remain, awake or asleep, in the living room, near his desk, near the pile of papers she had been asked not to disturb (and which she had not gone near, out of both propriety and incuriosity). After about an hour she realized that she had been fascinated and intrigued at listening to nothing, at listening to the silence evoked by someone who might or might not have been awake. Finally, she eased shut the door and lay down on the cot again.

She appeared downstairs early the next morning and again their conversation was limited to food, and again he was aloof, barely paying her any notice at all. This time he did not tell her that he was going out and she was surprised when, later in the morning, she heard the door close. She ran downstairs and from a window watched him get into a waiting automobile and drive away. She went back upstairs. The silence, the emptiness, was growing upon her now. She realized that not only was it a house without voices, but it had no radio, no television set, no telephone. The absence of these things—things to her normal, natural, essential to a house —gave her a lost feeling, as if this house was some shelter hidden within the remains of time spent, unnoticed by decade after drowned and fallen decade.

A few hours later he returned. This time she did not bother to stir from the cot when she heard the door close. Some time later in the day, as she was dozing off, she heard the front door close again, but this time it was someone else entering and, when a moment later she heard voices, she sprang to her feet and stood at her partly open door, listening. She recognized the voice of her other uncle.

At first she was puzzled at the way their voices came and went, until she realized they were walking around downstairs as they talked. Then they sat in the kitchen, and for a time the conversation was lost to her. Once, she walked across the room to the window, glanced out at the late afternoon sunshine, then returned to her post at the door. Soon the conversation from below became distinct again. She heard them in the hall and then in the living room. They were talking about her father now.

After Frank had gone, Lorana remained standing by the door. She was thinking about her father. He had seldom been so vividly focused in her mind as he was now, to the extent that she was suddenly seeing him with a clarity that astonished her. It wasn't simply that he was in some sort of trouble (even these uncles, whom she knew had little use for him, seemed sympathetic), but that it was a trouble she had been unaware of. He had always seemed sadly encumbered, and this she was accustomed to associating with the familiar problem, so long enduring it had come to seem part of him, as natural as the color of his eyes or the sad slump of his shoulders. But now she believed she had discovered something, and like any child in possession of a new, disturbing revelation about a parent, she felt suddenly impelled by a terrible maturity. That her father should be so concerned about money as to "be in a bad way," and saying "crazy things"—left her nearly incredulous. Perhaps this had always been the problem, the irritant that had shaped her mother's way of life. Unexpectedly, it all became explainable and humanized; and not only that, but solvable, too.

She was almost dizzy with the possibilities at hand. Perhaps her grandfather had given her the money for the express purpose . . . it wasn't entirely clear, but nevertheless . . . She believed she understood it now. It had melded in her mind beyond contradiction: her father's distress, the mention of money, the envelopes lying in her suitcase (added to it was the awful fact of her grandfather handing her the money hours before he died, so that it was almost a benefaction from the grave). With the money they could leave Capstone, go somewhere else, where they knew no one and no one knew them, and at least escape that bane of so many trouble-ridden people—familiarity.

A pleased, mischievous smile lit her face as she fell to her knees and lifted the lid of the suitcase and removed the money. Then, with the envelope in her hand, she ran downstairs, making all at once more noise in the house than she had in all her hours there put together.

"I'm going home," she blurted to Paul in the living room.

"All right, Lorana," he said.

"Everything's going to be all right now."

"I hope so."

"I'll be back for my bag," she said. "It's just that I'm in a hurry. I won't tell anyone where I've been . . . I won't put you in any trouble."

"Thank you," he said, smiling.

Then she hurried from the house.

THIRTY-TWO

Early that morning Philip had renewed his tireless rounds of the neighborhood in search of information about his missing daughter. He kept returning to houses he had already visited, asking for a second and third time whether anyone had seen or heard anything of his daughter. Tense, sleepless, all he kept hearing were words of sympathy and reassurance: it would be all right, young people did those things, she would turn up in a day or so. In some houses, where there were adolescents of restive notions and inclinations, he was greeted as the carrier of a plague, one who by association might infect the susceptible innocents; and at these places he received speeches of sympathy from a parent who stood guard at the front door. Irritated, weighted with a lifetime's worth of pity and self-pity, he was weary of hearing these things, weary of being the embodiment of doom and futility. Nevertheless, he maintained his characteristic polite and stoic façade, murmuring his thanks for the sentiments and encouragement.

At a one-family house across the street from the school he was received with a startled expression by a man named Gustin, whose teen-aged daughter was a friend of Lorana. Gustin looked at Philip, threw a nervous glance back over his shoulder, then stepped out onto the porch and closed the door behind him.

"Listen," he said, "I had nothing to do with it. On my honor. They invited me in, but I told them I wanted nothing to do with it. I want you to know that."

Confused, his mind momentarily untracked by this, Philip gazed at the man.

"You've got to believe me, Phil," Gustin said. Fresh out of bed, wearing coffee-stained T-shirt and unbelted slacks, sockless feet in bedroom slippers, his reddened eyes looking bathed in some ineffable sorrow, Gustin was whispering in a voice heated with sincerity. "I think it was a lousy trick. After all, she was drunk . . . you've got to remember that."

"She was drunk?" Philip asked in disbelief.

After taking a moment to wonder at the man's naïveté, Gustin went on.

"She didn't know what she was doing. It was all Geeb's idea, not that I told you anything."

"Geeb? Joe Geeb?"

"That low son of a bitch. She was drunk I tell you. So far gone . . . she didn't know night from day."

"She was *drunk?*" Philip asked incredulously, his mind fixed to the one thing.

"For Christ's sake, Phil, Helen does take a drink now and then," Gustin said, annoyed. "I told Geeb, for Christ's sake I said, Helen is Helen, but you can't go pimping off a . . ."

"Joe Geeb was pimping off Helen?" Philip asked.

Now Gustin saw it dawning, realized it. He lifted his head warily, his mouth opening slowly.

"You didn't know?" he asked.

"I came to inquire about Lorana," Philip said quietly, with that strange, inscrutable dignity which was so mocked and derided in Capstone, and yet which so mystified all who came within its range.

Philip turned and walked away as Gustin yelled after him from the porch:

"Listen, you didn't get it from me, you hear?"

The dignity, or whatever it was—strength, defiance, pride, anything but weakness or passivity now—sustained him, kept him walking along that street without change of expression, his shoulders back, his face set with a peculiar transcending resolution and invulnerability. At the corner he stopped and stood alone, contemplating the morning shoppers on the avenue, the traffic. Never was he more aware of the content of his mind, never was he more sure of it, never was he in possession of such calm and certitude. The lone emotion he allowed to intrude, and even this was integral to the rest, was a soul-drenching compassion, and this not for himself but for his missing daughter.

Later, he saw his brother-in-law. Paul was walking toward a parked car.

"Will you do me a favor?" Philip asked, approaching him. It was an impromptu thought and a rare moment of pretense and self-consciousness, spurred by the sight of his writing brother-in-law. After making his request, he received Paul's puzzled reaction and abrupt dismissal without any reaction of his own. Perhaps it was exactly what he had expected. In any event he did not let it bother him. He watched Paul drive off with a man Philip recognized as Sam Severith, old Ben Dublin's lawyer. He understood perfectly: they had things to do.

So he went to Frank, who had given him the idea in the first place. Not finding his other brother-in-law at home, he sat on one of the porch rockers and waited, sitting immobile in the chair, staring at the trees across the street with a calm and poignance that gave him a look near to wisdom.

But Frank, too, was diverted by concerns of his own. Some great tremors seemed in commotion inside this brother-in-law, and Philip was not surprised or depressed, since Frank had never been one to hide his feelings. Why should Frank, in the throes of his own involvements, pause to pay attention? Frank had said, recklessly, uncaringly: *Do it.* But did he know what? Doesn't know, doesn't care, Philip thought, and that was the very point of it; because all I did was stand there and talk, and that I've done before (*God, have I*), making myself heard instead of felt, and that was all he expected.

The trembling excitement he felt while talking to Frank vanished the moment he left the house, replaced by the conviction that it had not been necessary for him to have gone there. Talking about it had only troubled him, brought further, unnecessary distress; whereas thinking about it brought great repose to his mind.

He went home then. His children were out, his wife was sleeping on the couch. He stood over her, gazing down upon her, feeling now all the pain and hurt he had so effortlessly suppressed since speaking to Gustin; but instead of being demoralizing and debilitating, as it had always been, this time the pain and the hurt had a soft, wistful quality. For once he did not curse his palliative feelings: again, it was not passivity, not this time; it was empathy and compassion, and he was pleased by what he felt. He did not think it particularly ennobling; rather he felt defined, secure in profound self-understanding.

He survived the epiphany without smugness.

He allowed himself a drink of whisky and sat at the kitchen table for a while, his thoughts threading abstractedly through the ironies of his life and the injustices of the world, about all of which he now felt so knowledgeable. Not once did he so much as sigh. Then he got up, took his raincoat from the closet and went out.

He had gone but two blocks when he saw Lorana running toward him. Where before he would have been overcome with a tearful and joyous relief and excitement, now he felt only a deepening of the calm, a sense almost of sanction and mysterious intercession; a reward for the man who had asked for nothing.

She ran up to him and he warmly embraced her, closing his eyes for a moment and burying his face in her hair.

"Are you all right?" he asked.

"Yes," she said.

"You're sure you're all right?"

"Yes," she said, laughing, pulling back from him. There were tears in her eyes.

"Where have you been? We've been looking all over."

"I'm all right," she insisted.

He ran his hand gently back across her cheek, staring affectionately at her.

"My sweet darling," he murmured. "You needn't have done that. But everything's going to be all right now. You'll see."

"I know," she said, handing him the envelope.

"What is it?"

"You'll see, you'll see," she said, laughing with mischievous gaiety.

"It's for me?"

"It's for all of us."

Not taking his eyes from her for a moment, he placed the bulky envelope into the capacious drop pocket inside his coat.

"Aren't you going to look at it?" she asked, disappointed.

"Later."

"Where are you going?"

"I have something to attend to."

"Don't you want to come home with me?"

He paused. "I do," he said. "With all my heart. I want to, very much. But first I have something to attend to. I think . . . you're going to be proud of me yet."

"I'm proud of you now," she said quietly, stubbornly.

He touched her cheek lightly with his fingertips.

"I know," he said.

"When will you be back?" she asked.

"I don't know."

"You're not running away, are you?" she asked, half seriously.

"One runaway in the family is enough, don't you think?"

Embarrassed, she forced a laugh.

"Let me go now," he said. He put his hand gently on the back of her head and bent and kissed her forehead. Then he began walking away. He stopped for a moment to turn and say—she was standing there watching him, an uncertain expression in her face—"Don't make any noise when you go in. Your mother's asleep."

He walked quickly for about a half mile and when he saw the big round trade sign looming over the service station began walking even more quickly, as if to demonstrate to someone—himself perhaps—the vitality of his resolve (knowing subconsciously, however, that if he stopped or paused even for an instant he might go no further, that he was operating under the momentum of decision rather than anticipation). With a sobriety approaching self-importance he went past the rows of pumps and entered the station's glass-walled office. A middle-aged man wearing a peaked cap and a blue denim workshirt sat behind the desk; he had the set imperturbable features of a man who had spent a lifetime dealing with transients, strangers, people in a hurry, people in trouble, people wanting directions.

"I need some gasoline," Philip said.

"Break down?" the man asked out of that set, unchanging face. He had a toothpick in the corner of his mouth.

"What?" Philip asked.

"Where's your car?"

"I don't own a car," Philip said.

The man waited, his eyes fixed not expectantly or even interestedly upon Philip, but simply with an interminable patience that was the product either of character or vocation: he was through asking, he was going to have to be told.

"It's for my brother's car," Philip finally said, his mind finding at last the practicalities of the situation.

"How much gas you want?"

"How much?" Philip stared blankly at the man, the uninterested man who wasn't going to ask any more than he absolutely had to. "I'm not sure," Philip said. He wet his lips, unnerved at being stared at with such unfaltering patience. Then he saw an empty pint-sized milk container lying in a metal trash barrel. "That much," he said, pointing to the container.

The man's eyes moved, took note of the container, gazing upon it for an instant longer than he really wanted to, then moved his eyes back to Philip.

"High-test or regular?" he asked.

He had selected the union hall as the site after some thoughtful consideration and what he believed to be very pertinent reasons: it was an official building, he had a status there, and, most importantly, he wanted his gesture to be made amid the very men he felt it crucial he reach—the supposedly impervious and unknowable Working Man, that traditionally misled and misjudged band of brothers in whom Philip was convinced lay great untapped reservoirs of fairness and compassion. So he believed that the stage would complement the act, add to it meaningful and symbolic weight. They would have to ask why a loyal, steady, paid-up member did such a thing in the corridors of his own local. Why indeed. Let them think about that, examine it carefully. It was critically important that they know he was one of them and not some radical or unbalanced outsider. It would be impossible to either ignore or misunderstand him then, and if he achieved his purpose then millions of people would find their consciences and become moved and inspired by what he had done; and perhaps there might even be dividends beyond his most extravagant expectations—his gesture being the long-awaited, mobilizing act of sanity, pulling taut the lax fibers of justice and equality, and his name becoming the rallying cry and spear point in the drive toward a better and more responsive world. He could not resist contemplating the heroic role. It remained quite possible for him to step into that exalted frame. Despite the dismal road he had walked all his life, he was not defeated, had never been; because he had always felt keenly the stings of pain and humiliation, and he never believed that the struggle for dignity and a modest share of happiness was either vain or inexplicable. The most admired and memorable men were the unlikely ones, the nameless and little noted who after a lifetime of lulling the gods into soporific inattention suddenly hurl an illumination into the firmament for all time, with the immortality of a named comet or galaxy.

As he walked along the side street where the union hall was located, holding the gas-filled milk carton steady and upright in his hand, he seemed to have taken on a completely different appearance. Subtly and peculiarly he now had an oddly ascetic aspect; his eyes held the profoundly wary look of careworn intelligence, his face was sallow, his mouth thinned with suffering determination. He was not quite sure now what he was feeling—a numbness that precluded all sensation, or a serenity that transcended it.

He did not break stride until he had mounted the steps outside of the building and reached out his hand to open the door. Then a very definite feeling—a welter of feelings—swept over him in a swarm of doubts and fears and sharp incoherent questions; there was recessive fortitude and a sense of aloneness as acute as gnawing hunger. He remained indecisively at his Rubicon for these several moments, one hand extended forward like a man groping in the dark for a light switch; and there was no telling how long he might have remained like that, what he might have decided, what direction he might have chosen, had not another man come up the steps behind him. Flustered, caught in his indecision and feeling it like a stroke of guilt, Philip looked around, and then quickly and with an embarrassment understandable only to himself pulled the door open, held it while the other man entered the building, and then followed him.

Sitting behind the reception desk in the lobby was a man wearing a checked vest and an expression of mistrust rather than reception. Off to one side a knot of men were standing, engaged in loud crosscurrents of conversation. Philip's eyes shifted to an-

other man bent over a drinking fountain in a corner, and still
another studying the postings on a bulletin board, hands on hips
in what looked like an attitude of morose skepticism. Behind the
reception desk stretched a corridor where an attractive middle-
aged woman holding a sheaf of papers was in earnest conversation
with a short balding man whose lips were pursed. The ringing of
a telephone startled Philip and his eyes dilated as he watched the
receptionist uncradle the phone on his desk with a resentful
gesture and close his eyes for a moment in a jaded manner while
he said hello. Two more men entered the building and walked
past Philip into the corridor, each with a laborer's muscular
swinging freedom.

Clutching his milk carton, Philip sidled away from the desk
toward the bulletin board where he stood next to the skeptic and
contrived to stare with great interest at the postings, though not
seeing a thing as his mind began swimming in panic at the
thought that he might not be able to do what he had come to do,
that something other than failure of nerve or resolve would
thwart him. The thought seized him that if he were prevented
from doing it then he would certainly be adjudged mad, whereas
if he was able to go ahead with it he would have to be reckoned
with. "It's all bullshit," the man next to him muttered and strode
away. "What?" Philip asked, wheeling around. "What did you
say?" The man, however, was gone through the doors without
another word. With an expression almost tragic now, Philip
turned back to the bulletin board and glared at it, still too intensely self-involved to be able to read. Then he walked to the
public phone in the corner and lifted the receiver and held it to
his ear. He stood like that for several minutes, staring at the milk
carton in his hand, trying to contemplate the task before him.
"You using the phone, buddy?" a voice asked. He turned slowly
around and was confronted by a short man with an unlit cigar
thrusting out between leering teeth, with an expression of
sullen pugnacity, as though he had just suffered through some act
of bureaucratic impertinence. "No, no," Philip said, and quickly
hung up the receiver. "I gotta call my doctor," the man said, posi-
tioning himself at the telephone. "Why?" Philip asked. "Why?"
the man said with sudden indignation. "What do you care?" With
an agitated shake of his head Philip walked away. He wandered

through the lobby with the sharp, perturbing anxiety of a man dissipating his privileges, reducing his advantages. He was certain now that his intentions were transparent to any casual observer, to the extent that he half turned to stare warily after whoever passed him in the corridor, lest they make an attempt to double back and seize him.

He saw the door marked "Men" and impulsively, gratefully, headed for it and entered. A man inside was just drying his hands on a paper towel; he passed Philip a casual glance before going out. Alone in the lavatory, Philip stood in vexing, solitudinous indecision. A look into the mirror astonished him, for there he saw graphic evidence of his complex inner turmoil—his perplexed and frightened face, his slumped shoulders, his entire cringing and irresolute appearance; and what he saw was a sharp insult to his pride. *I'm not that man,* he thought. He turned away from the mirror, angry and self-reproachful, stung by the glimpse into his own wandering desolation. Another man entering startled him and put him terribly ill at ease. He removed his coat and stepped into the lone stall and locked the door. He remained standing there in utter immobility, the coat over his arm, the container in his hand, his eyes fixed in a gaze of several inches upon the stall door as if he had been ordered to memorize something written on it. He listened to the quiet trickling at the urinal, then the metallic hiss of a rising zipper, then the closing of the door, and the ineffable silence that comes hard upon that sound. He slid back the bolt of the stall door and stepped out. His eyes moved to their corners and took note again of his reflection in the mirror, this time with a cool detachment; then he became aware of the weight in his hand and his gaze rested upon the milk carton, which he lifted chest-high and somberly contemplated. A train of thought had begun, a resolute chain-link progression. Smoothly and assertively it moved across the undulant landscape of his mind, thrusting aside the debilitating fears and doubts, contemptuously bypassing the pusillanimous shadows of wavering resolve. With his perceptions sharpening and becoming more attentive, as though experiencing some spiritual enlightenment, he draped the coat over the wash basin, then opened the milk carton and brought it to his nose, sniffing at the gasoline. This time a study of himself in the mirror was like an affirmation of purpose, a signal of alliance from a comrade. He pinched the carton's spout shut to the point where its opening was a mere slit. Then he began shaking it toward himself in annointing gestures, watching the leaping jets of gasoline splash his shirt. As he did this the spout unexpectedly widened under the pressure of the oscillating liquid and he was aghast when several large splashes struck him and stained his shirt and trousers. It made him pause for a moment, stare dubiously down at himself. Then he gathered a slow, deep breath and closed his eyes, released the breath and opened his eyes and again studied himself in the mirror, curiously, searchingly, as if hoping to gain some further approbation or promise of support there. He nodded mysteriously to himself, then pinched the spout almost closed again and continued with his curious baptism, splashing his shirt and trousers with methodical steadiness, stopping finally when he felt it was enough. He put the carton down on the edge of the basin and stood motionless for several moments, waiting for—and this was defined only in the deepest recesses of his subconscious —waiting for some emotionally heightening sensation, some corroboration from destiny that it was aware of his imminent approach. If he succeeded now—found the final sustaining thread of courage—it would mean his life had been a success, for the triumph would wield its impact from the very fact of lifelong insignificance, of reticence, of modest pride; it would be an inspiring climax to long years not of abysmal failure and ineptness but virtuous forebearance and humility. And then with an uncommon surge of fortitude, he picked up his coat, opened the door, stepped aside to let a man enter, and went back out into the corridor.

He straightened his back and lifted his chin, pervaded by an enabling pride, realizing the crucial thing—that he was in process of elevating himself to plateaus that were rarefied and magnificent, that they were strange to him simply because he had never dared them before, and never dared because it had always seemed so meanly improbable. His face was calm, gentle, as though viewing the most idyllic vista, and he had an ennobling sensation of time parting like some cosmic Red Sea to allow his entry into it before sweeping shut again to fix and establish forever his indentation upon history. He walked several steps,

reached into his pocket, and came to an abrupt halt. He did not
have a match. With wild panic flashing into his eyes he swung
around with such suddenness that a woman approaching from
the far end of the corridor stopped for a moment to watch him.
His face seemed to be crying out for the deepest consolations.
The woman came forward now, passing him warily, with a sidled
glance, wrinkling her nose at the strange odor. Then a man came
toward him from the other direction.

"Give me a match," Philip said.

Annoyed by the unceremoniousness of the request—it was
actually almost a demand—the man paused, then showed a pained
look, suggesting that it was not the brusque incivility of people
but the idea of becoming accustomed to it that he resented,
fumbled in his pocket and came out with a book of matches
containing four sticks. "Keep it," he said, expressing his largesse
with as much sarcasm as he could.

"It's for all of us," Philip suddenly, unaccountably blurted. "The
betterment of all—blacks, whites, rich, poor . . ."

"Yeah?" the man asked, staring curiously at the matches, as if
wondering what magical elixir he had just relinquished.

"But it's a cool, sane, rational thing," Philip said drawing back
from the man. Then he realized he had better not say any more.
He did not want anyone saying later he had been talking irra-
tionally, did not want to run the risk of being dismissed as a
madman (that was one of the ironies—the one who tried most sincerely and most desperately to help always had his sanity questioned, his motives disregarded). "Okay," Philip said, forcing a
smile that lingered hopefully, grotesquely, around his mouth. The
man stared back, advanced his lower lip for a moment, then
shrugged and walked on.

Philip walked to the center of the corridor and, hardly aware
that he was doing it, let his coat fall to the floor. There was something he wanted to shout out, he remembered planning to say
something, remembered thinking it was necessary and important;
a statement about his purposes, about better working conditions
and fair play and peace and justice and a more equitable world:
but it was impossible to recall any of that now *Frank will tell
them, he'll know why I did it and he'll tell them*: now he was
beginning to feel his mind clouding, causing a departure or obliter-

ation or sheltering of things—fear and doubt and resolve and purpose and courage were being driven out, replaced by a certain inviolate purity, a blurred but unyielding instinct, a steadfast and vestigial iron nub of primordial soul, passed up from the nebulous brain through tens of thousands of generations, survivor of all the Ages of Man, a sinister and tainted chemical inheritance, the sleeping iron nub burning in the soul with brooding incandescence. He lifted the book of matches and ripped one free and even as he was striking it against the rough paper he heard a voice from behind saying, "Hey, Mac, you left your milk in the bathroom." But it was too late to say anything to that, to respond to it, explain that he did not drink milk in the bathroom, that it was not milk: because with a spasmodic movement of his fingers he had already thrown the burning match against his shirt. The eruption of fire, of heat, of pain, of maddening hysteria were simultaneous. He threw his head up and his eyes bulged toward the ceiling for a moment as a croaking babble of sounds swarmed into his throat. He ran against the wall as if in an attempt to smother the flames, then whirled around, twisting and flailing as he saw people crisscrossing in blurring streaks and heard screams and yells and saw one man with a face so astonished it looked like a party mask, holding a milk container. His mind became a fixed concentration of pain as he sank to his knees, tried to embrace his blazing chest, glared in horror at flames eating at the hair on the back of his hand, then fell forward with a terrible rumbling groan like a dying animal and rolled over several times, trying to fight the flames, the pain with motion and fury; and then suddenly there was a flashing red explosion whooshing from his legs and a searing bone-twisting agony as he saw what appeared to be a milk carton bouncing against them. He was alone, horribly and dreadfully alone, without breath to yell, rolling and scrabbling over the floor in a furious hellbent attempt to escape what was clinging to him, feeling his body being consumed by hot storming gusts, his eyes filled with molten tears. He rose halfway to his feet for a moment, looking as though he were throbbing with savage red spears, and ran headlong into the wall as if trying to waken himself from this relentless nightmare, banging maniacally into the wall and knocking himself scuttling backward, a tumbling blazing monstrosity, falling with his fiery legs kicking into the air, then rolling over and over as if hurtling down some brutally angled declivity, a wild discord of noise filling his ears, fighting back now with nothing more than an indomitable will to survive, feeling prodigious reserves of inner strength rising with almost strangulating fury, hurling himself over the floor like some puny man-figure resisting with his illusions of immortality the cracking of the earth and the plunge of the heavens, resisting the exhaustion of mercy and the glacial detachment of God. He was being sucked into a steamy tunnel, pounded on fire-edged rocks; his fingers entered the heat and tried to wrestle the flames, the inescapable cage of fire. Again he got to his feet and again he ran against the wall, swinging one shoulder against it, battering himself several times and then finding the breath to scream out and twisting around and falling face forward and rolling over and over with kicking feet and helpless pounding fists. And then he was aware of men standing far above him, on the tipped edges of clouds perhaps, and there was furious but soft beating being done upon him, a rising and falling of dark limber things; they came after him as in his palpitating frenzy he could not remain still; they continued their soft furious flailing at him, from all sides, the darkness lifting and falling as the beating of so many triumphant black wings against the sun; and he began to shriek, *"My wife! My wife!"* Swift and formidable, like the descent of giant wrath, the relentless beating continued until his mind swooned into nothingness, diving away from the raging pain, the tortuous heat, leaving behind a multitude of savagely pursuing flashes.

THIRTY-THREE

Cynic or not, Ben Dublin probably would not have liked being upstaged at his own funeral. As the small group of mourners stood around the rim of the grave waiting for the minister to bind the soul of the deceased in prayer and hope and send it heavenward through the September sunshine, hardly a thought was turned upon the old man who had taken his own life. While all eyes might have been upon the coffin, all thoughts were fixed upon the missing mourner, who had set fire to himself the day before.

Even Paul, who of the three primary mourners was most selective about where he placed his thoughts, found images of his brother-in-law intruding upon his mind; though even now what most interested him was what seemed the answer to something about which he had been mildly curious: Why had Philip wanted "a statement of creed" written? And what sort of creed? Perhaps there had not been anything passionate or philosophical about it; perhaps he had wanted some statement to leave behind simply to give significance to a suicidal act (those things were supposed to be contagious, weren't they?). Philip's reasons for suicide would be so tawdry and degrading that it was possible even for him to reject them as disgraceful, hence the desire for "a statement of creed." And even if it had been written, what would he have done with it—mailed it to the newspapers? Who would have taken notice?

Occasionally Paul raised his eyes from the appallingly patient and impartial opening in the ground to glance distastefully at his sister who was standing across from him supported in her congested sorrows by her eldest daughter, his recent house guest. Overnight Helen seemed to have shed the last of her youth, her spark of wanton irresponsibility. It had taken near tragedy for her to spend a full night with her husband, at his hospital bedside.

Philip would survive, though now the scars of his frustration and humiliation would be public.

The minister kept intoning. It was a mild, bright, windless day, and his resonant pulpit voice carried far across the stones and seraphs. The rituals of his incantation, however, seemed hollow, as if even he realized he was addressing the wrong tragedy, that his words were water upon water, that the minds of the mourners were otherwise occupied.

Frank, in his ill-fitting borrowed suit, did not have enough vents for his emotions. By turns he was swept with grief and regret and bitterness and despair. In addition he was weary. He had spent most of the night in the hospital with Helen and Lorana. (Paul, although notified of what had happened, had chosen not to join their vigil.) It was there, from the police, that they received the details of the episode. And they were introduced to one of the men (his badly burned hands swathed in white bandages) who had helped save Philip's life.

"We smothered it with our coats," the man said.

"I know." Helen murmured.

"I hardly knew what I was doing," the man said, in his voice an oblique hint of self-reproach.

"Do you know why your husband did such a thing?" the policeman asked Helen. "Does anyone have any idea?"

"I know why he did it," she said. "Nobody has to wonder. I know why."

"Can you tell us?"

"I know why," she reiterated spiritlessly. "That's enough."

Frank kept watching Lorana, and she, self-conscious, avoided his gaze. She would not leave her mother's side, as much to provide comfort as to give her uncle no opportunity for interrogation. The girl's thoughts, however, merely brushed against the question of the money, were more concerned with the condition of her father who lay nearby wrapped up like a mummy, whose kiss and embrace she had accepted even as his thoughts were fixed upon self-immolation. Sensing the frozen content of her uncle's mind, and resenting it, she was almost consciously rejecting any concern for the money: it seemed of very slight consequence now.

That was one o'clock in the morning; now, at the graveside, his primary obsession had not by a degree moved. He was still holding out some vague hope of getting his hands on those dollars, stubborn in his fanatic's desire, belief, that because it had not yet positively appeared it yet might, thrown up somehow by his father's death, as concussions are supposed to make drowned objects surface. So now, if anyone at the graveside was thinking of the deceased, it was he, gazing somberly at the coffin, trying to penetrate the mind of his dead father to either damn him or else ask him: *Where?* his head teeming with all that might yet be done —searching the house room by room, board by board if necessary, ripping out and tearing apart every possible hiding place; digging in the back yard; and even, in a heated moment, having the thought that perhaps the old man would for some perverse reason arrange to have the money buried with him like some superstitious Pharaoh.

And then he found himself compelled to reject all of that. It was all impetuous, futile. Committing suicide, knowing he was going to die, the old man would not have left so substantial an amount of money to chance. He would have made his disposition, his arrangement . . . and given it to the one person he claimed loved him more than any other. A pinwheel of outraged resentment spun through him, directed by turns at himself, his father, his niece as he realized he might indeed have had the money literally within grasp the night he had faced Lorana on the street. All he had to do at that moment was reach out and take it, and then damn her and damn his father and damn Bennett and damn Seavery and damn even Charlotte Breitman whose expensively tailored figure his brooding eyes now speculatively sought out among the mourners. What made it all so insufferable for his overreaching imagination was that in spite of its fevered sprinting and scheming there was not a chance in the world that the girl would, if she did indeed have it, part with any of those dollars now, with her father lying where he was, as he was.

Moving his eyes from Charlotte, he set them stonily upon his niece. He felt the calm, unheated desire to wring her neck and pitch her down after his father. And then some wisp of prayer from the minister's tireless lips caught his ear and he bowed his head and wondered which of his thorns was provoking the tears.

THIRTY-FOUR

What good were powers of perception when you could not celebrate their acuity?

With painfully objective retrospection, Paul granted that he had suspected his father was contemplating suicide. There had been nuances, gestures, intimations, that brooding sense of concession and relinquishment. *I could not have stopped him, of course, but I should not have ignored it when probably all he wanted was a hand on his shoulder for a moment. But did I believe he would actually do it? I refuse to accept the idea that I saw it and was indifferent. After all, not every thought I have is my own. But what was his reading of the situation, if indeed he was trying to convey something and I was ignoring or not noticing it?* He was disturbed now. There could be deep and harrowing reverberations from such an idea—that his father had killed himself not from pain alone but in the bitter solitude of abandonment, in fierce and climactic renunciation; with a loneliness at the end so towering he was reaching out to death even as it was coming toward him. Paul wondered: Am I so subservient to my visions; and if so, am I allowing them to romanticize my life and engender, continually engender, old and self-perpetuating tortures of the soul; polluting a fountainhead and creating a potential dynasty of savored miseries? The problem was, guilt so privately and jealously nurtured inevitably infringed upon the lives of others.

So, what did you think of him?

He's sweet, Janine said. *He's just what you said he was.*

But what was it I said? A bitter, disillusioned old man? I can't remember what I told her, but it wasn't that. No, she hadn't liked him, nor had he liked her. Main Line money, education, *breeding,* sitting there on the reinforced furniture in the run-down old house (he had never noticed how run-down until he caught her

glancing at the cracks in the ceiling, and he had squirmed), talking to the spent, cynical, soul-withered old Socialist who was not
even reformed or reconstructed but simply a person of voids and
departures. It had been too terribly polite. She had been put off
by his intelligence, by the occasional blunt comment with its
barbed phrasing (what was expected of old men in her world?),
and by the fact that the sharp old man had perceived and acknowledged her dislike and responded with amused tolerance (no, it
was politeness; after all, this was my wife) and the wise look in his
eye. *And I said later, He's not feeling well these days. And probably he wasn't, though I didn't know that then; I was ashamed,
trying to explain the cracks in the ceiling and the old man father
who was not what he should have been. Frank at least had said it:
the old man had let us down. But don't worry, we paid him back
for it. Each in our own separate and distinct way. Nevertheless
I do believe he manfully accepted the parent's traditional burden
and loved us all to the end, and forgave us our sins and omissions.
A parent and the wise father, too, of course. The good planter
knows his harvest. So we didn't really disappoint him, didn't take
him by surprise; we simply fulfilled his nonexpectations. But one
should never be thoughtless and inconsiderate with a parent,
unless one expects to predecease. But, dammit, would it have
changed anything if I had said to him: You're in pain aren't you?*

He was sitting, as was his custom, on the easy chair in the living
room, legs stretched before him, hands folded over his belt buckle,
eyes lightly shut; looking as though he had just ingested a kingly
meal. He had not moved since returning from the funeral. Daylight had faded from the windows and it was that moment now
when dusk seems in subtle motion, an imperceptible transitional
gray swirl in the air.

The pamphlet containing that fall's list of guest speakers at the
midtown auditorium had come in the mail about ten days ago,
was lying on the table next to him. He had not looked into it
again since first reading it and had no intention of attending any
of the lectures; but there it was nevertheless, like some perversely
enduring and resistant thing. He knew exactly why he had not
thrown it out, and the reason disturbed him. Keeping a piece of
literature simply because it contained, among others, Kifner's picture, was almost a self-flagellant act.

He must always have looked upon me with disdain, Paul thought; not as Janine's husband but as a holding company for his ex-mistress. Though perhaps not even that. He probably thought of me—if he thought about me at all—as simply another satellite in his orbit. The great man believed he possessed all who fell into his magnetic field. I'm sure he never thinks of me at all today, nor of Janine. We existed simply to burn a little of his energy and in the process be ourselves consumed.

Now he picked up the pamphlet and opened it to the picture. Staring at the stern, strong face gave him a feeling of unease. The fixed unchanging eyes in the photograph seemed to be staring directly and humanly into him. Kifner's familiar expression, Paul thought. Mocking him with casual contempt. Now the unease became restive, creating a friction of fervent resentment. *But you didn't murder her, did you?*

He put the pamphlet down and got up and walked through the house to the back yard, where he stood in the darkness. The moment he had seen that pamphlet and knew Kifner was going to be in the same city with him, he got sick. If Kifner were to come walking through the darkness toward him now, what would there be to say. It would be easy, he thought bitterly. All righteousness would be on my side. How I could posture and hurl my accusations, my condemnation. And perhaps make even him feel a pang of remorse. The guilty shout loudest and with most fervor. (And why not, for aren't they—given a conscience—the longest sufferers?) Surely they do, for listen to that silken trickle of words out of the dark, possessing my brain in a hangman's noose. If only she would raise her voice; perhaps some scream, some mind-rending outraged commotion from her would solve it for me, give me something either to resist or collapse totally under.

No, Kifner did not push her to her death. That was my hand alone. Blame who then? If there are no culprits, and if ghost-poems in the night are neither solace nor solution, what then? Come, come, he chided himself, you know the answer. Think of your masters: Anything that involves intolerable pain and humiliation can't be all bad. And anyway, what is worse than this? For how long, how often, and in how many ways can you justify a thing? Ghost-poems in the night or the murmurous blackness of your own conscience? And even if the poems are true, and you are conversant with the dead, it's hardly a solace or a penitence, but rather a dealing with the handmaiden of insanity. Or will you try to tell yourself that only the uncommonly sane can understand insanity and therefore all thought of it is rational and unthreatening? But if you convince yourself that a constant unilateral dialogue is the epitome of sophisticated self-understanding . . . then how do you know? In what chamber of the mind and under what circumstances was it debated?

He covered his face with his hands for a moment, feeling a dull, yearning, tireless pressure on his brain; not really pain, more like the pulsating heat of too many voices, too many things. Then he lowered his hands and raised his eyes to the sky and scowled at it, like a man first realizing his insignificance before the cosmos.

He went back into the house, to the living room, where he stared for several moments at the neatly arranged stack of poems. Then he sat down, as a thought came to him which he found particularly astounding: as Philip was to him, so, no doubt, had he been to Kifner. For several moments the idea froze him with astonishment. As much as it hurt and mortified him, still he could not entirely dispel it. *Is this, suddenly, the new honesty, the new awareness? After all, with my stoutly professed political indifference, my stress on the quiet life of creative endeavor, my desire to withdraw or at least not participate in a world which Kifner was striving to reshape, was I anything but a foolish and negligible dreamer to him?* "It devolves upon some to work to preserve the social conditions within which it is possible for revolutionary change to occur." *Yes, I said that. Christ, how he must have laughed at me. The arrogant son of a bitch. My telling him that I wanted to be independent of him was probably what set him off. He didn't like that. I could tell he resented it. No friend of his could be allowed such independence. That was his message to me. And to this moment it persists and holds true. Or so he thinks.*

I have something to tell you, Professor Kifner. (I won't call him Stephen; under the circumstances I'll renounce that privilege.) Something of a rather bizarre nature. You may be bored by it, but I think you'll understand. We both know something of the psychology of guilt, the need to confess. I want to tell you I know what you did, and now you must hear what I did. You don't have to speak a single word, you don't even have to pretend you're interested. You simply have to be.

He heard footsteps on the porch, then a knock at the door. (He ought to reconnect the bell, he thought; these rappings on the door had a sinister quality.) He rose, put on a light, and went to see who it was. When he opened the door the hall light fell into the eyes of his sister, staring somberly up at him from out of a taut, tight-lipped face. Not only was the last of youth and mindless coquetry washed from her, but in its place the years of dissipation had risen, as if overnight, delineated by deep lines flaring from the center of her face to the corners of her mouth, by soft puffy flesh under her eyes. The expression in her eyes was a stark mixture of pain and entreaty. It seemed impossible for her bright and coquettish smile ever to light that face again as it once had. That smile, under those eyes, would be grotesque.

"What do you want?" he asked.

"I want to talk to you," she said.

"Now?"

"Do I need an appointment?"

The tone of that reply—his sister had always been extremely circumspect around him—gave rise to curiosity.

"You've never been here before," he said.

"I never felt I was welcome."

"That's nonsense."

"Really?" she said, giving him a skeptical glance as she slipped past him and went inside.

He closed the door and followed her through the hall into the living room. She stared curiously at the room, her hands in the pockets of her belted topcoat, standing legs apart, balanced on her high heels.

"What do you do here?" she asked.

"Work," he said, watching her from the doorway.

She glanced at the pile of papers on his desk; they were so neatly arranged that if looked at from above they would have seemed a single sheet.

"Everything just so," she murmured.

"What do you want, Helen?"

She shrugged.

"May I sit down?" she asked.

"Of course."

Again she passed him a somewhat doubting glance, unbelting her coat and taking a seat on the sofa. She crossed her legs and he glanced moodily at her white thighs which seemed to him blatantly sensual under their short skirt.

"Do you want something to drink?" he asked.

"I've had enough," she said with a wan smile.

"Do you mean today, or all your yesterdays?"

"My sweet brother," she said with a soft-edged rancor. "You know damn well what I mean."

"Don't tell me there's been a reformation?"

"What do I have to reform from?" she asked challengingly. "Have I done something I shouldn't?"

"Helen, I've never given you credit before for a sense of humor," he said with a mocking smile.

"Have I done something I shouldn't?" she asked again.

"I'm sure there are people who are much better informed on that subject than I am."

"I'd much rather hear it from you . . . from the point of view of one who is so pure."

"I'm not so pure."

"For twenty years you've been the purest person I've known," she said, a melancholy flatness in her sarcasm.

He came into the room now and took a seat across from her. Sitting up straight, her hands in the pockets of her coat, she was disconcertingly resolute, surer of herself than he was accustomed to her being.

"Helen," he said, "if you've come here to tell me that you've got regrets for having done for twenty years exactly what you wanted, then I'm not sure I want to hear it."

"Doesn't twenty years sound like rather a long time for any person to have been doing exactly what they wanted?"

"Twenty years is pretty close to it."

"And you feel I've enjoyed every moment of it."

"Haven't you?"

"Absolutely—to the point where the people I love most can't stand me any more."

"Who would that include—your husband?"

"Yes, my husband," she said angrily. "My husband most of

all. You have no right to say that." His bland, disinterested staring angered her still further. "Of course I love him, and believe it or not, he loves me." She was resentful that a contrary opinion should even be assumed. "If you weren't so intelligent," she said sarcastically, "you would see it was really a very simple fact and not complicated at all. Maybe you didn't have enough time to find things like that out for yourself."

The very idea that Janine could be brought into the conversation, as analogy or otherwise, however obliquely, irritated him, made him feel suddenly defensive. His sister, obsessed with her own emotions, did not notice the guarded expression in his eyes now.

"I cried for you when she died, Paul," Helen said. "But never to your face. I knew what you would think of my tears. I had sense enough to know that when a person is in grief they don't want to see someone who . . ."

"Someone who what?" he asked quickly. "Look," he added, "I don't want to talk about her," he said coldly.

"I'm sorry," she said, shutting her eyes for a moment and shaking her head. "I barely knew her . . . I liked her. God knows what she thought of me."

"I could tell you."

"Yes, I suppose you could," she said pensively.

"So stick to your Philip and leave me to my . . . Janine," he said, pronouncing the name with great reluctance.

"Yes, I'll stick to my Philip," she said. "My poor husband," she said with soft despair. "You know so little about him. Why do you think he did what he did? Love him? You know so little," she said with what sounded like compassion, shaking her head. "Who else would have put up with it . . . looked for reasons to understand? After all, Paul, he was *living* with it. That poor son of a bitch. I always hurt him . . . took advantage . . . but never from malice. And he knew that. If it hadn't been for him, then God help me, and God help those children. One almost slipped away as it was . . . but she came back . . . because of him, not me. And now look what I've done to him. You're supposed to be so goddamned bright and educated. Don't you know anything about women?"

"Enough," he said tersely.

"The hell you do. You don't know a thing," she said, as tears started to her eyes. "Don't you know I'm helpless? Don't you know there isn't a damn thing I can do for myself? Can't you understand that?"

"Anyway, you don't want for self-pity," he said.

"Is that what you think it is? Do you think it's out of self-pity that I came here to talk to *you*? I know what you think . . . I know what you've *always* thought. Self-pity? My God!"

"Self-hatred then," he said casually, his mind shifting with utterly effortless, weightless thought.

"This is all my fault," she said abstractedly, covering her eyes for a moment.

He remained curiously uninvolved, staring passively at her, as if the conversation was yet to begin, feeling little more than a waning indulgence.

"I don't know why you've come here," he said.

"I've come here for a lot of reasons, Paul. One of them is because I know you're as unhappy as I am. All our lives you've barely confided a thing to me. I know what you think of me. For God's sake, at least you were honest about it. I don't know . . . maybe it's just that I'm more sensitive to you because I know what you think of me."

"And because of this beautiful relationship you've come to help me with my problems," he said with a tight, hostile smile.

"I've come to *talk* to you. Paul, just a few hours ago we buried our father. If we can't talk now . . ."

"This is absurd," he said, turning away, a vexed and impatient expression on his face now. "Look, Helen, I don't know what you're talking about. If you're here because of a guilty conscience, then that's a good thing for you to have. It's a good beginning, if you'll listen to it."

"I want to listen to you," she said, adding, "it seems you've been my conscience all my life."

"I'm no one's conscience," he said irritably. "Look, you have no right to come bursting in here like this."

"Yes, how unlike your sister to come bursting in on you," she said. "I should think you'd want to listen."

"You were the one I always counted on to leave me alone," he said with a bitter laugh.

She responded with the same bitter laugh, as if the same mordant humor appealed to her.

"But I'm not leaving you alone," she said quietly. "Because, God help me, you're the only one I want to talk to."

She spoke that with such quiet fervor and determination that he paused to give her a long, searching stare. Of all the things he least expected, least wanted, was this. For this sister to suddenly appear before him repentant and with guilty conscience, he thought, after a lifetime of such mindless and unbridled debauchery, called for a convocation of saints.

"Paul," she said softly, her voice calm and patient in explanation, "I can't feel sorry for myself. I know myself too well. I would be a hypocrite if I felt sorry for myself. Self-hatred. Is that what you said? Yes, that would be closer. I never thought of it that way before. It isn't easy . . . to think such a thing. How do you explain it to yourself?"

The tears were running down her face now and her eyes were shining with a curious strength, a kind of wretched, dredged-up but nevertheless sustaining pride.

"Isn't it enough?" she asked. "Do I have to have your hatred too?"

"I don't hate you, Helen," he said blandly.

"No?" she asked skeptically. "But you have every reason to. I've given you every reason, all our lives. Are you such a holy person that you can overlook all of it? I know goddamn well you hate me and that you always have and probably always will. I just wanted to tell you, Paul, that I couldn't help myself, that I . . . just had to do what I did. What good this does, God knows."

Curiously, with one finger pressed to his lips, he stared at her, feeling something in his mind loosening from its moorings. Then he thought: No, Janine could never have been reduced to this, to the crying, the emotion, the self-laceration, the passionate confessional. Janine hate herself? A woman of her self-esteem? The idea provoked a nasty laugh.

And then, as if deliberately entering his carefully modulated, carefully balanced thoughts and breaking them apart, she said, "People are weak, Paul. Sometimes they make one or two mistakes, sometimes their whole lives are mistakes . . . and if they mean a damn to you then you don't condemn them but try to help. Goddamn it, don't you see that sometimes you get the lousy goddamn responsibility of having to help someone? Who wants it? Who needs it? But if it falls on your head you had damn well better accept it. It can make you a better person . . . if you try to understand someone and help them."

She wasn't defending herself, but her husband; tearing herself apart in front of him to make him understand her husband. He resented it. It was an unwarranted aspersion. She was saying that Philip, that most inept and ineffectual person, was the better man. She was saying that Philip endured not from weakness but strength. *Who is she to speak for Janine? Where is that voice coming from?*

They had no right, these women, to expect so much from a man, to make such demands, he thought. Life, a relationship . . . should be something else. They had absolutely no conception of their capacity to hurt, to undermine.

He lowered his eyes for a moment, feeling a pressure at the back of his head. It was almost as if someone had slipped past his vigilance to have a dialogue with all the imprisoned and forbidden things deep inside him. The discomfort caused by this bitter, unexpected, unwanted encroachment was acute. Unable to answer, to state his side of it to anyone, ever, he was like a captive. The difference here, of course, was that Janine had felt no remorse, no self-reproach. What was it she'd said?—She had all but forgotten it. Could she have, really, when it was the thing uppermost in his mind for so long? *Perhaps it was her way of telling me that it had been a single slip, unimportant, self-forgiven, that it truly had meant nothing, and that this was as close to explanation or apology as she was going to get, or felt it necessary to get . . . while I in my wounded masculine pride said nothing but let it build and worsen and fester inside of me as if searching for justification then and redemption later, relishing the retaliation as though I had been looking forward to the insult: even to the extent of thinking she was being deliberately ironical and contemptuous when she chose to go to Glencoe, when in truth even to link the symbols made me the devious one. God almighty, the conclusions we come to out of all the choices available.*

"I used to think," Helen said, "and ask myself why he didn't do something to stop it. Why doesn't he *try?* I asked myself. I remember one man saying to me that if I were his wife he'd kill me. I thought, 'Why isn't my husband that sort of man?' But now I know he's more than that."

"That isn't fair," Paul said impulsively.

"Why isn't it fair?" she asked, absently wiping her fingers across her tear-stained cheek. "Jesus Christ, don't you understand what I'm talking about? Don't you give a damn? Why are you looking at me like that? What are you thinking? Not fair? Of course it isn't. I knew him perfectly. What was he going to do? Beat me? How many times?"

No, he was thinking. Such an imputation was definitely unfair. He had had his reasons, his very good and substantial reasons . . . if only he could explain them. No one could begin to understand the experience-pocked soul of another; that was the trouble. On the surface people all looked alike and sounded alike, but every man's interior was a different, unknowable, inaccessible universe, where apparent simplicities became lost in tortuous labyrinths. God only knew how many other times Janine had been unfaithful, or what lay ahead. That was the thing: what lay ahead. That was what he did not want to face. That was the impossible thing to explain—that you feared something which lay ahead. It was for that, for evoking the fear and bringing such turbulence and uncertainty to his mind . . . that was what made him do it, so impulsively. Except that he did not believe in the impulsive act; the impulsive act was the crowning conclusion to long, careful, subconscious decision making; the irrational vengeful thrust against . . .

She gave him a scornful smile.

"You're not even listening to me," she said. "What is it you want to hear? What will make you listen? All right, then I'll tell you what you want to hear: I've had a hell of a time, I don't give a damn about Philip or anybody else. I'm not sorry . . . I'm not. I knew he wouldn't beat me and I knew he wouldn't leave me because I knew goddamn well how much he loved me. So I did what I wanted and will go on doing it, with no regrets. Is that what you want to hear?"

"No . . . that's not right," he said, protested.

"Do you want me to tell you that I don't think I'm a slut and a tramp and that I'm proud and who the hell are you to sit in judgment? Or do you want me to tell you that I'm the goddamn town whore and a drunk and garbage and not worth . . ."

"No . . . that isn't true!" he said excitedly.

She stood up, her tears streaming, and went toward him, her hand reaching out.

"Don't touch me!" he cried, leaping to his feet and moving away from her, trembling.

Startled, she stood in the middle of the room, her hand reaching forward in mute and yearning supplication.

"Paul, I want you to *help* me," she said.

He brought his hand to his face and rubbed it hard across his mouth as if to wipe away a stain, at once frightened and astonished by what he had felt.

"I'm *afraid*," she said, sobbing. "I want to help myself. You're the only one . . . don't you realize what it's cost me to come here?"

"I think I do," he said quietly. Drained, exhausted, he wished he could have time to think, to sort through everything which had all at once overtaken him. He felt the pain of a terrible incision, as if some sudden, emotional surgery had been performed on him. And he felt, too, at the same time, both the impulse to get away from her and the desire to stay and talk and finish this as best he could.

"You never knew it," Helen said, "but I felt closer to you after it happened."

"After what happened?" he asked, the effort of trying to understand and respond making him frown.

"When Janine died. I knew how much you loved her."

"Goddamn you," he said savagely. "What makes you say that? What gives you the right?"

She gazed puzzledly at him.

"I didn't love Janine," he said.

"What are you saying? Have you lost your mind?"

A weak, insensible smile crossed his lips.

"Sister, don't ask dangerous questions," he said.

"Don't ask questions—when you say something as shocking as that?"

"I could shock you even more," he said in a dull inflectionless tone that frightened her. "You're not the only one in the family with a 'history.' Your sins are . . . are *nothing*." He laughed bit-terly. "You said I was so pure. Oh, I am. Absolutely. And I thank you for mentioning it." He laughed again. "Your twenty years of . . . of self-indulgence can't hold a candle to what I've done. What are you staring at? You don't think it's possible? The differ-ence between us is that you've been out in the daylight all your life . . . you've been either stupid, uncaring, or ingenuously honest. I've done better. Not only am I still 'pure' but I also have the world's sympathy."

"What are you talking about?" she asked warily.

He sat on the sofa, rubbing his hand back and forth across his yellow polo shirt for a moment. She sat next to him, watching him with deep concern. He contemplated her for several moments, a shrewd, searching look in his eyes. Then his lips moved with a cool, remote smile.

"Do you know how she died?"

"She fell."

"I pushed her."

"You're lying," she said. "You're making it up, just to . . ."

But she stopped when he began shaking his head from side to side, firmly and insistently and interminably, that cool, remote smile on his lips; until she said,

"But why?"

"She was like you," he whispered.

"Like me?"

"I caught her with a man."

Now it was her turn to contemplate him, first with disbelief, then skepticism, then—as she gauged and perceived his pained and profound seriousness—with a cool, calculating superiority; her entire demeanor in transformation before his eyes.

"You pushed her off the mountain," she said as if to confirm beyond any question this fact.

"Yes," he said.

"For that."

"What do you mean, 'for that'?" he said, frowning.

"I meant . . ."

"You think it's nothing, don't you?" he said irately. "To you it's an everyday occurrence, isn't it?"

"No no no no," she said, putting her hand on his arm as he made a move to get up.

"Not everyone looks at these things the same way," he said, his voice heavy with emotion.

"Of course not."

"I'm not Philip," he said churlishly.

"I know who you are, Paul," she said softly, compassionately, her hand at rest on his arm. "But I didn't know what was in your mind. And I was concerned. I've always been concerned for you. My God, you've been carrying this terrible secret, all this time. And there was no one you could turn to for help."

"No one," he said sullenly.

"You could have told me."

"Why? What could you have done?"

"I could have shared it with you. At least that . . . made it easier for you. You were so . . . alone. If only you would have told me. I always tried to be a good sister, Paul. You only saw . . . what you saw; you never knew what was in my heart. I was good to you. I looked after you, I cared about you, even though I knew what you thought."

"What did I think?"

"You were ashamed. I always felt that . . . how ashamed you were. You were the last one I ever wanted to hurt. You were always the good one."

"You see I'm not such an angel," he said with caustic irony, suddenly resentful of the world's evaluation of him.

"But that's how everyone thinks of you: a suffering angel."

He smiled wryly.

"She was your only girl?" she asked. "The only one you ever had?"

"More or less."

She tilted her head slightly to a side and studied him with shrewdly scrutinizing and compassionate eyes. Then, barely perceptibly, she moved her head back and forth several times. "And since?" she asked, her voice just audible.

He sat silently, staring at her, and she felt as if he had imparted the most dreadful thing.

"You must be so . . . unhappy," she said.

She took his hand in hers, moved her face closer toward his,

remained poised for a moment, tentative, then moved still closer
and kissed him lightly on the cheek. He gazed at her with wide,
curious, suspenseful eyes. His face moved toward hers, a fraction
of an inch—almost like an involuntary reflex—then stopped, his
eyes continuing to study her, their expression altering subtly to
wondering disbelief as he felt a wayward persuasion moving
against him, causing a steady melting somewhere that was feeding
into a slowly gathering desire, not impulsive or overwhelming or
even ardent, but simply a slow and excruciating concrescence,
tenderly permissive and indulgent, gathering through dark and
nameless collusion. He felt an old and forbidding bondage yielding under the new, powerful, long-struggling dispensation,
muffling outcry and echo alike, the first life of it beginning to
palpitate in his fingertips as their special paralyzing inhibitions
disappeared as the yearning to reach forward and touch and hold
became consent granted, stifling the lifelong strictures of the un-
thinkable, the forbidden.

Now she lifted her hand and touched his face, gazing at him
with a look of tender inquiry, with an intimation of strength and
understanding, as if trying to soothe and reassure what she believed she saw. This brother had never conceded to her so much
as an unguarded word or gesture; and now, suddenly this, all at
once, broken forward and risen to the surface, intense and unmistakable. Any doubts or hesitations she might have felt were
unequal to the task of overriding what she wanted to do, what
she felt it incumbent upon her to do, as desire and glib rationale
swung piously together, yielding to a nagging sense of inevitability. Above all she felt the need to be strong, decisive, and not let
this brother who had finally stumbled in his wounds and loneliness get away from her, this brother who had finally allowed
himself to be seen, known.

"I know what you're thinking," she said. "You want to, don't
you? It's all right, darling," she said, her hand still lightly upon
his face. "I don't want you to worry about it." He remained still
as she withdrew her hand, his lips parted, drawing soft deep
breaths that were accelerating and becoming more audible, almost
a panting. "There's nothing dirty about it," she said quietly. "It
can be as beautiful as . . . anything else. If we want it to be.
That's all that matters, isn't it? If it's beautiful . . . then it doesn't

matter, does it? You do want to, don't you, Paul? You've always wanted to, haven't you? I know. I understand. There's nothing wrong . . . if we believe in what we feel. Will it help you? I want more than anything else to help you."

She removed her coat, letting it slide back from her shoulders, then took a deep breath and held it for a moment and sat in all her pride and self-esteem, pleased with the softening yearning response in his eyes. Then she released the breath and came forward and kissed him on the mouth with sensual, lingering lips. He closed his eyes and bowed his head. She ran her hand slowly along his thigh as he leaned back into the sofa, his eyes half opening, watching her with deep languor, allowing her hand to move caressingly over him.

"There, darling, easy . . . I want you to relax," she said, moving closer to him. "Do you like that? Do you remember when you were a little boy and I used to give you your baths . . . and how you used to laugh when I washed you there? You don't remember, do you? You were my little man . . . my own little man. I'll bet you don't remember. Here, you can touch them. You always wanted to, didn't you? I knew it. I could always tell. I saw how you stared. Sometimes I let you see them . . . didn't I? I knew you wanted to but were afraid to ask. You don't remember, do you? Here . . . put your hand here. Gently, darling, gently. Yes. Oh, yes, I knew you were watching. A little boy with big eyes. Little Paulie. But I never minded. Some older sisters mind . . . but I enjoyed it as much as you. Women like to be admired. You understood that, didn't you? But you were shy. There . . . now you have it . . . after so long. Ah, you're not shy any longer. My own little man . . . is grown up now. We'll help each other now, won't we, Paul . . . my little man . . . my little lover. There . . . sit back . . . let me do this . . . let me do it . . . let me do everything . . ."

THIRTY-FIVE

Never in his life had Frank felt so alone. The impersonality of his furnished room and the quietness of the boardinghouse only deepened his sense of isolation. He felt as if he had been the victim of every conceivable kind of malice, from petty unkindness to monumental betrayal; with a self-pity almost ingenuous, he was like a child discovering that this world of brilliant promise was in reality a place of slowly dissolving masks and worthless affirmations. Nothing ever turned out to be what it had first seemed or professed. Not, at least, for him. As his vexed and brooding mind traced through the events of recent days he began to feel as if he were actually diminishing in physical size. Standing at his window, hands in pockets, staring moodily into the night, he consciously straightened his posture. I should have stayed in California, he thought; then corrected himself: I shouldn't have gone to California. He should never have left Capstone, but stayed right here, playing up to the old man the way Lorana had. All his father had wanted was a little companionship, to feel that there was still for him in this world a modicum of affection. Again, as he did every time he thought of the money, he winced and shook his head.

And then he saw someone walking jauntily under the trees across the street, emerging from the shadows into the light. Watching the whistling, side-to-side swaggering figure move through the night, Frank's eyes narrowed, his mouth drew back into a firm line, his hands came up from his pockets and doubled into fists. He watched for another moment, then turned and hurried from the room.

When he ran down the front steps of the boardinghouse he could see his quarry a half-block away now, continuing on in that maddeningly nonchalant stride.

"Geeb!" Frank roared.

Joe Geeb stopped, turned, had one look, then took off in a sprint.

"Geeb, you son of a bitch!" Frank cried in a voice that felt as though it were going through his body like a hurricane. Then he began running.

Running along the sidewalk, under the low sweeping boughs, past the privet hedges, Frank felt an exhilarating surge of anger, like a raucous cleansing force. Wheeling at the corner, he saw Geeb going at top speed, running the same way he walked, with a ludicrous side-to-side oscillation as if performing some fanatical ritual. Frank's fury was incited further. Geeb ran across Grant Avenue, startling the few nighttime strollers, and then along the school block, his untucked shirttail flapping behind him. Closing the gap, Frank ran past the broad, deserted schoolyard, his eyes fixed upon the man ahead of him. Geeb suddenly cut across the street and with two terrific leaps bounded up the brick stoop of his house and disappeared inside.

Undeterred, Frank went after him, running up the brick steps. He paused at the front door for a moment to compose his heavy breathing, then went inside.

He stepped into a tiny foyer, went along a hallway, then turned and found himself standing in the Geeb living room, face to face with Joe's mother.

"Why!" the old woman said, looking up at him from her chair in front of the television set, her face at once pleased and surprised. "Bobby!" she called out. "Bobby, come look who's here."

Then, with some effort, the tiny old woman pushed herself up from the chair, politely turned off the television set and came forward to give Frank a kiss on the cheek, which he had to bend far down to receive.

"We're so sorry about your father, Frank," she said, her doleful face nodding solemnly, her underlip bunching. She clasped her hands and gazed up at him, her small clear eyes filled with sympathy.

Bobby Geeb appeared from the kitchen at that moment. He, too, was quite short, standing barely more than five feet tall in his slippers, made even shorter by his stooped, rounded shoulders. He was wearing an oversized black woolen sweater that swung around him as he came tottering forward with his old man's rickety, graceless step, waggling the fingers of one hand in greeting. Having procreated unusually late in life, the Geebs were each nearly forty years older than their son, who was their only child, and even at that, some people were inclined to think, one too many.

"Frank, Frank," Bobby Geeb said, his dentures bursting forth in a grin so youthful it gave the rest of his face an appearance of senility. He offered his small, bony hand, which Frank shook gently, feeling its knuckly protuberances.

"I'm sorry we couldn't make it to pay our respects," the old man said, shaking Frank's hand until the latter felt obliged to disengage. "I knew your father God knows how many years. It doesn't seem like he's gone, does it? Here, take a chair."

Speechless, looking around, Frank obeyed.

"Can we offer you a beverage, Frank?" Mrs. Geeb asked.

"Don't offer—get," Bobby Geeb said crankily.

"No thanks," Frank said, suddenly finding his tongue. "I just came by to see Joe."

"Joe?" the old man said with what sounded like a croak. "Joe's not home."

"But I thought . . ." Frank said, then let it drop.

"We're so sorry about your father," Mrs. Geeb said, pressing her hands to her tiny chest.

"So Big Ben is gone," Bobby Geeb said shaking his head.

"He built our kitchen cabinets," Mrs. Geeb said with a kindly smile. "Would you like to see them?"

"A-1 carpenter," Bobby Geeb said, giving Frank a fraternal wink.

Frank nodded. He looked down, saw two pairs of bleached white ankles in two pairs of worn and crushed carpet slippers. What the hell am I doing here? he asked himself. He got to his feet so suddenly he startled the old couple.

"I'd better be going," he said.

"You didn't have your drink," Bobby Geeb shouted, his good and simple nature perverted by the high, excitable thinness of his old man's voice.

"Another time," Frank said, retreating toward the door.

"We'll come soon and pay proper respects," Mrs. Geeb said.

"Yes, yes, thank you," Frank said, heading out.

He walked into the hall, then into the foyer. He opened and closed the outside door, and remained in the small, unlighted foyer, his mouth drawn back into a tight angry line again. Some ten or fifteen seconds passed as he stood absolutely still, listening to the Geebs mumbling in fragmented sentences, listening to the slow slide and scrape of their slippers on the carpet. And then the door of the hall closet began to slowly edge out, furtive and cautious, as if to outwit the creak of an ancient hinge.

Bastard, Frank said to himself, moving toward it. When the door had been pushed halfway open, he saw Joe's face appear, led by its jutting hook nose. Frank put his hand on the doorknob and suddenly jerked it back, then stepped around and with his other hand took Joe by the shirtfront and pulled him forward and glared into his widened and astonished eyes.

"You cocksucker," Frank whispered as noise from the reinstated television set began to rise from the living room.

Without another word, Frank pulled the unresisting Geeb from the house and down the outside steps with such rough abruptness that Joe ended on his knees on the sidewalk.

"You filthy-looking son of a bitch," Frank said.

"What are you talking about?" Joe asked.

"What am I talking about?" Frank said furiously, his big, gripping fist shaking Joe. Then he pulled the frightened man upright. "How much did you make on her?" Frank demanded. "I'm asking you, you goddamn degenerate."

"N-nothing, Frank, I swear."

"Nothing?" Frank asked coldly, unbelievingly, threateningly.

Joe read it in Frank's eyes, read with perfect clarity the message relayed from Frank's free hand, and before that other hand, fist, could come sweeping up with its devastating power, Joe said, as quickly as he could,

"Two hundred."

"Two hundred?" Frank asked in astonishment.

"That's all, Frank, I swear."

"Where is it?"

"I spent it."

"You? Spent it? You, you tight-assed prick, you don't spend two hundred in six months. Where is it?" This time the other hand, the fist, had risen chest-high, poised mere inches under Joe's face.

Joe closed his eyes for a moment and sighed.

"In the bank," he said.

"You put it in the bank?" Frank asked.

Joe nodded, an embarrassed look on his face, as if having put the money in the bank was the most incongruous thing.

"I need that money," Frank said.

"All right," Joe said. "All right. But I can't get it to you until Monday. Tomorrow's Saturday, the bank's closed."

"Naturally," Frank said with a bitterness Joe could not understand.

Now Frank let him go, pushing him away.

"You in trouble?" Joe asked.

Frank nodded abstractedly.

"And two hundred would bail you out?"

Frank glared murderously at him.

"What the fuck do you care?"

"I was only asking as a friend."

"Don't 'friend' me," Frank said.

"I'll get it for you Monday."

"Stick it up your ass Monday."

"I wish I could buy my way free for two hundred," Joe said wistfully. "It'd be a bargain."

Frank looked at him resentfully. Suddenly he became annoyed with himself. What was he doing here talking to Joe Geeb? The very fact of his trying to squeeze two hundred dollars out of this repugnant, failure-hobbled person was further symbol of his futility. Suddenly he hated the somber-faced man standing next to him not because Geeb had basely used his drunken sister but because Geeb symbolized further descent, further self-abasement.

Abruptly, Frank turned and strode away.

When he reached Charlotte's house Frank had dismissed Joe Geeb from his thoughts entirely and was concentrating on a new idea, one which had come sweeping into his head like a comet, full-born the moment it struck his mind. It was as if desperation had finally shattered under pressure and instead of bringing total collapse set free a soaring, daring ingenuity. The idea was not entirely new, but until now it had always existed in some vague mist of speculation, far from the margins of realistic aspiration. Now, however, by the very nature of its old endurance, it had a force and vigor that bordered on the inspirational.

She was duly solemn and subdued when she welcomed him in. She had changed from her funeral attire back into her jeans, a man's free-hanging shirt, and sandals. Her hair, which had been decorously pinned, flowed loosely again. She led him into the den, where they sat on maroon leather easy chairs which gave comfortable and affluent creaks when first sat upon.

"I thought the minister spoke beautifully," Charlotte said.

Caught off guard by the comment, Frank had to pause a moment before he caught up with its relevance. Then he nodded.

"Would your father have objected to a religious service?"

"Only if asked."

"I'm going to have it stipulated in my will that I be cremated," she said, thoughts of death begetting thoughts of death. "I know someone who's done that, with the added request that a book of his favorite political writings be put in with him."

"What book, 'Of Mice and Mensheviks'?" Frank asked moodily.

"You're incorrigible," she said mildly, shaking her head. "How is your brother-in-law?"

"He'll live."

"Why did he do it? Do you know?"

"No."

"Did you know he was going to do it?"

"Of course not. What kind of question is that?"

"Where could he have got such an idea?"

Frank looked at her warily. "From the newspapers," he said. "That sort of thing has been happening here and there in the world."

"I suppose," she said thoughtfully. "Do you think it was a political act, or was he deranged?"

"I don't know. I don't want to talk about it."

"I understand," she said. "After all, you buried your father today. God, what a sequence of events for your family. Beginning with what's-her-name going off that mountain . . ."

"Janine, her name was Janine," Frank said testily. He closed his eyes for a moment, remembering why he was there, what he had come to accomplish.

"How is Paul doing?" she asked.

"Fine."

"I ought to visit him."

"You ought to leave him alone, if you can't even remember his wife's name. Listen," he said, changing his tone to indicate a shift in the conversation, emphasizing it further by sitting forward in the chair, "people die and get buried, but certain things go on. We have to be absolutely callous about that. Everything personal has to be subordinated."

"What are you talking about?"

"I'm talking about the Movement. Things are at the point of no return, right now, right at this moment."

She watched him with great interest.

"Confidentially now," he said, "I'm involved in some pretty hot things. Important things, with the top people. Charlotte, this country could go up like a tinderbox at any moment. Do you realize that? The bomb business, the other morning, is child's play compared to what's being planned. And let me tell you, the finest minds in America are planning it. Do you know what it includes?"

She shook her head, staring intently at him.

"Can't you guess?" he asked.

"No," she said.

He held the moment, protracting it for fullest effect, then said, in a voice deliberately casual, "Murder."

Her eyes dilated a fraction. "Frank . . ." she said softly.

"I'm nervous, I can tell you," he said.

"Of course."

"Nevertheless . . ."

"But have you . . . has everyone . . . thought this through in utter detail? I'm not just talking about the act itself and your personal security, but about motive and expectation."

"You don't undertake something like this frivolously. It's been worked out . . . for months. And anyway, I'm sure you'll agree that every alternative has been exhausted. The only alternative left is to talk ourselves to death. Don't you agree?"

"I don't know what to say."

"I shouldn't have told you."

"Oh no," she said firmly, "you had to. After all, I'm part of it . . . intellectually and spiritually."

He shook his head. "Sometimes I look back and wonder how I got in so deep."

"Don't do that," she said. "Don't ever look back. You know in your heart what's at stake."

"Of course I know," he said angrily. "But do you know? I don't seem to be getting much understanding here, do I? Look, I could be dead in a couple of days and all you say is, don't look back. No, I certainly won't look back, not when I'm lying in the street riddled with bullets."

"No, please, Frank . . . you're misunderstanding. I feel this with all my heart. It's just that . . . I'm overwhelmed. Your safety means as much to me as my own. Whatever it is you're doing, I know it's dangerous, but it's right. No matter how drastic this thing is . . . what I'm saying is I have complete trust in the Movement people."

"All the same, you toss murder off pretty lightly," he said indignantly. "If it was Paul sitting here telling you what I just did, you wouldn't like it very much, would you? You'd try to talk him out of it, wouldn't you?"

"How can you say such a thing?"

"Listen, if you want to know the truth, what's being planned is absolutely insane and suicidal. It's motivated by the highest ideals, of course, but . . ."

"What is it? Can you tell me?"

"No, certainly not . . . for your own protection. I've told you too much already. Hundreds of lives are at stake. You don't seem to realize the seriousness of this. To you murder is an abstraction, a word, something you see on television or read about in the newspaper. How do you like the idea of ramming a knife into somebody's gut and hearing him scream? A *real* scream, with *real* pain, with *real* blood. What do you think of that? Let's hear your opinion. What do you think of it? For or against?"

"Frank, this is unfair. You tell me a fragment of something, then ask me to decide. Why? Why are you doing this?"

"Because I think you're frivolous about the whole thing."

"That's insulting," she said.

"Do you know what will happen if a revolution occurs . . . how much blood will be spilled . . . how many people will die?"

"Of course I do."

"And you still want it?"

"You're trying to test me, aren't you?"

"And what do you think will happen to you if it comes . . . to this big house and all your money and your goddamn property?"

"Under the proper circumstances, I would be proud to divest myself of everything I own, and have no more or no less than anyone else. You know that."

"There might not be time for you to be noble . . . to make grand gestures. The rich can survive only in prosperity, they can't stand the shock of deprivation; while the poor can endure anything—that was proved during the Depression; it was the rich who went diving out of windows, not the poor."

"Why are you saying this? You're trying to frighten me, aren't you? You're not being rational, Frank. But I understand. Your father's death was a great shock. A parent's death . . . suicide . . . those are horrible things. Are you going into a state, like Paul? Frank, you've got to take hold of yourself . . . be strong."

"I've never been stronger or more cogent in my life," he said. "Stop trying to evade the issue and listen to me. You believe that a revolution is coming?"

"I think it's inevitable."

"And you'd welcome it?"

"With all my heart."

"All right then," he said emphatically, slapping the arm of his chair. "Then do something about it. And I don't mean your pamphlets and petitions and fifty-dollar contributions to bail funds. I mean come out in the field with me and work. Get your hands dirty. Charlotte, I'm offering you an opportunity to put all your principles and ideals into action. And I mean *real* action, out where the smoke and the sweat is. Goddammit, together we can do anything."

"What are you proposing?" she asked bewilderedly.

"Marriage," he said bluntly.

"What kind of marriage?" she asked, still bewildered.

"Legal, bona fide. A real marriage . . . with a minister and a ring."

"Frank . . ." she said.

"Let me tell you something. Why do you think they're planning a murder? I told you, it's a suicidal act. They're desperate.

Charlotte, I'll tell you bluntly: a revolution is not going to occur
in America. Not until it occurs elsewhere first. I'm asking you to
come to Europe with me. Do you know what's going on in Europe?
Do you know how far ahead of us they are? Their revolutionary
traditions are centuries old. I say we have got to go there and
work with those groups. It's the best chance . . . the only chance."

"Marry you? Go to Europe?" she asked, shaking her head in
amazement.

"Why not?" he asked defiantly, as if no logical reason could
possibly exist. "I tell you, you'll be a sack of bones before your
precious revolution comes here. But if we go there, work with
other groups, we can make it happen. Charlotte, I've been talking to people . . . Frenchmen . . . Germans . . . Italians. You
have no idea what's fermenting there. I say it's our chance to be
part of it. There is no chance here."

"You're wrong," she said excitedly. "It has to happen here.
What happens in Europe doesn't count, what happens anywhere
doesn't count. There's only one country in the world where anything matters, and that's right here. You're underestimating
America, Frank; you're underestimating the people and the pride
and the strength. Underestimating America is a mistake a lot of
people have made, to their lasting regret. This country is the
world's leader . . . everyone looks to it. The work has to be done
here; nowhere else matters."

He gazed incredulously at her for several moments, then said,
"My God, that's the most patriotic speech I've ever heard."

"Frank, you're wrong, you're wrong, you're wrong. Believe me."

"You're speaking from the outside," he said sullenly.

She paused, letting her excitement subside. Then she smiled
at him in a very patient, almost flattering way.

"I think we can work together, after a fashion," she said. "Listen
to me, Frank. Forget Europe. We can do more right here. I can
show you a better way. I agree with you that the work has to be
done in the field, at the very roots."

With tense expectation he listened, watching her.

"Will you do something for me?" she asked quietly.

"Anything," he said.

"Something true and meaningful?"

"Of course. You know how I feel about you. Listen, I said some intemperate things. Before we go an inch further, say you forgive me."

She smiled again. "That isn't necessary. You've always been such an undisciplined volcano of strength and enthusiasm. I always felt, if only it could be harnessed . . ."

"Charlotte . . ." he said, ready to swear himself to her.

"I want you to do something for me," she said. "Wait, I'll show you."

She got up and left the room. He sat absolutely still, filled with almost unbearable tension. Then he touched his forehead lightly and the perspiration he saw on his fingertips he looked upon, for some reason, as a favorable sign.

When she returned she was holding a multicolored woolen blanket.

"Here," she said, holding it up by the corners. "Do you know what this is? It's a blanket, woven by a Navaho. Do you know the time and the skill that went into the making of this? Do you know how much I paid for it . . . and how little the Indian was paid? That's what we're fighting against here . . . the exploitation of people. Our own people. That's why I say we have to work here, that this is where we're needed, that this is where we can make things happen. Frank, listen to me. You have courage and spirit and brains. You're needed here. Forget about Europe. Go out into the field here . . . go to the Navahos and work with them."

"The Navahos?" he asked, stupefied.

"Work with our own people . . . our own indigenous Americans . . . where you're most needed. Go out to the reservations and bring hope to people who are being starved and exploited."

"This is insane," he muttered incredulously.

"No it isn't," she said. "Look at this blanket."

Perplexed, amazed, he glared as if hypnotized at the blanket.

"Frank, I'll give you a thousand dollars," she said. "Take it, get out of this crazy murder scheme, and go to the reservations."

"I *can't* get out of the scheme!" he cried. "Don't you understand? If you have any principles you'll come to Europe with me."

"Don't you see," she said patiently, shaking her head, "Europe is unimportant."

"I'm asking you to marry me," he said, an excruciating calm in his voice.

"Frank, you said it yourself: all personal considerations have to be subordinated. Marriage is a pleasant idea, and to indulge pleasant ideas in times such as these is decadent. I say there are important things to be done. I say . . ."

"You say, you say," he said with building rage. "Do you know what you're saying? Do you know what you're talking about? You're telling me you don't care if I live or die. If they find me riddled with bullets tomorrow, what are you going to do—wrap me in that goddamned blanket and ship me out to the Navahos?"

"You don't understand."

"No, no, I don't," he said as he got to his feet. Furiously, he pulled the blanket from her hands and shredded it, then flung the pieces to the carpet.

"Frank . . ." she said.

"You're crazy," he said bitterly. "You're absolutely crazy . . . and you'll see . . . the whole world is going to come down around your ears."

With that he hurried out.

THIRTY-SIX

"You seem very tense," Seavery said.

"Well for God's sake—" Frank said.

"But tension is actually a good thing, sort of emotional iso-
metrics. I have a theory about that."

"Spare me."

Seavery gazed at him for a moment with wryly amused eyes,
then suddenly gave a short, skeptical laugh that sounded curiously
false.

They were sitting in a midtown Manhattan coffee shop, at a
small table near the window. Neither had touched his coffee. The
table was so small that when they happened to lean forward
simultaneously, Frank could feel Seavery's breath on his face. The
coffee shop, around the corner from the auditorium they would
soon be going to, was crowded, filled with murmurous voices
abruptly punctuated by bursts of laughter, close with cigarette
smoke.

"Everybody going to hear the great man," Seavery said, studying the people around him, a flat, thoughtful expression in his
eyes. "What good would it be otherwise?" he added. He leaned
toward Frank, whispering. "Tonight these people are spectators;
tomorrow they become troops." He smiled. He had begun the
growth of another beard and his smallish, sensitive face had an
untidy-looking outcropping of soft dark hairs, giving his thin
mirthless smile a satanical look. "God bless these people," he said,
still whispering. "Our intellectuals. Intellectual Robin Hoods: pil-
laging affluent minds and distributing their loot as largesse to
other minds less endowed. But bless them nevertheless, Frank.
They're willing to die for a cause the rankest patriot doesn't know
exists. They have these magnificent centers of energy, but so
thickly insulated it takes a genius to get through. And I'll tell you

something else: They don't understand Kifner. Nobody understands Kifner."

"No?" Frank asked, moodily wary of this youth.

"Do you?" Seavery asked. Frank made no answer. "I'll tell you
why nobody understands him," Seavery went on. "Because they
think he's addressing their minds, when it's really their instincts
and their guts he's after, and which he hits. All those hits he makes
in their guts and which their instincts respond to they think are
intellectual revelations; but the truth is he's bypassing their minds
and trying to move them to irrationality, which generates the
only pure and true action. Not many intellectuals get through to
their peer groups that way. He's prepared them for his own death
more than they know. But he would understand." Seavery had
appended this last without a trace of humor. Then he leaned
against the backrest of his chair and crossed his arms over his un-
zipped windbreaker and white shirt.

Outside, the night pulsed with the sounds and colors of a balmy
Saturday evening in New York, an entertainment situation which,
when one was aloof from it, was like a cruel and gaudy Roman
circus, mindless and ephemeral in a frenzy of self-consumption.
A prostitute sauntered along the smoky window, wearing a leather
jacket with the collar turned up, her youthful face pale and stark
under a swirling pile of platinum-blond wig; her dead glittering
eyes focused on Frank for a moment and her lips parted. He
returned her frozen gaze with simple uncomplicated candor; and
then, unaccountably, he moved his head twice from side to side,
and she walked on, away from the smoky window back to the
night. *Even she is happier than I,* he thought, feeling a surly
tension.

"Well, so be it," Seavery said abstractedly, looking into his untouched coffee. "Does anybody know what Columbus said when
he set sail, or what Hannibal said when he had his first look at
the Alps? Frank, 'the world will little note nor long remember'
what we say here tonight . . ."

Frank smiled privately, affectionately, for some reason moved
by the sane, warm, old familiarity of the words.

"What made you change your mind?" Seavery asked. He would
do that, ask those unexpected questions, and when he did his
voice sounded like it was coming from a different direction, taking
one by surprise.

"What do you mean, change my mind?"

"When you walked away the other day you were definitely negative. Poor Frank, I thought; he would have come down to the dock with his duffel bag just as the *Nina,* the *Pinta* and the *Santa Maria* had sailed; he would have missed the Crucifixion because there was something more interesting happening around the corner; he would have been abed with a whore at Hastings, wondering what that racket was outside."

"I didn't change my mind," Frank said evenly, suppressing his annoyance. "I simply hadn't decided anything at that moment."

"Then what made you decide yes?"

Frank shook his head to express his impatience with the question. Seavery shrugged. He put his finger into his coffee and brought it up to his lips and licked it.

Actually, Frank was still uncertain about whether he had decided anything. Even though he was sitting there with Seavery, there was nothing firm or decisive about the reason. He did not view his presence as a commitment. All night long his mind had been a turmoil of decisions, conclusions, rationalizations, contradictions, to the extent that he had finally lost track of his thoughts, affirmation and negation blurring into one and the same. His rage at what he considered Charlotte's puerile, muddled behavior had kept him awake half the night and had barely subsided when he wakened this morning. At that point he found himself accepting with full faith propositions which the night before he had dismissed as dangerous and irrational, since they suddenly had become motivated by an intense desire for personal revenge. He accepted Seavery's claim that Kifner's death would trigger "great and cataclysmic events," leading to the rising of the masses, the coming of the revolution, the destruction of established government, the triumph of the proletariat, and—the ultimate goal—the sacking of the rich. He had to laugh sardonically when recalling her insistence that she would welcome this "under the proper circumstances." In thinking this, he subscribed to Seavery's analysis of the consequences of the murder, that a violent and transforming uprising would ensue, a wave of insurrection so sudden and so unexpected in intensity that no one would be able to deal with it—all for the express purpose (he conceded he was personalizing an earthquake but reveled in it nonetheless) of having booted revolutionaries stamping through

Charlotte's elegant house spitting through their beards onto the Persian rugs. To support this apocalyptic vision, he recalled Bennett's concern about the potentialities of civil unrest. Perhaps it was closer than was realized, the situation far more combustible, and that Seavery knew exactly what he was doing. And then—with his every thought intertwined with another, each with its teeth in the other—he considered the possibility of the whole thing being a ruse, some devious scheme of Seavery's to test him. (In fact, Seavery had appeared so surprised when Frank met him that Frank actually believed for a time this was possible, that at any moment the youth would turn to him and say, "All right, you've proven yourself. Now I'll tell you what's really being planned." And at that point Frank would tell him about Bennett, about the threat to himself and the danger they were both in, confident Seavery would know how to get them out of it.) And then there was the nagging realization that his choices were few, coupled with an irresistible curiosity to see how far it, and he, would go. After all, he told himself, as indecision trailed off into dilemma, he was not signing a contract, the option was his to step out at any moment he chose.

As Seavery's self-amused eyes roved over the crowded coffee shop, Frank studied his face, as ever, trying to penetrate the thinking of the strangely elusive youth. From the expression on Seavery's face, Frank believed he knew what the youth was thinking—what a shock he was going to throw into the people around him, that tomorrow morning they all would be discussing what he, Arthur Seavery, had done, and because of it would be springing to action; as if they all were in his power, unsuspecting even as they sat near him, the poised but inconspicuous and unsuspected *Kapellmeister*. The look of private pleasure on Seavery's face was too cunning and mischievous to suggest anything else.

Frank suddenly had the urge to reach out and slap him—not from any sense of affront, but simply from curiosity, to see what this youth would do, how he would react. I could call him a fool and a madman and a murderer, Frank thought, and he would only smile. But the idea of hitting Seavery—more than a slap now, taking him outside and knocking him to the sidewalk—possessed so fascinating a concept of experiment that he was tempted to do it. The youth would either curse him or come up fighting or seek an explanation—or, simply, disintegrate before his very eyes without a trace of flesh or moisture, like the end of a science fiction film.

"What are you thinking, Frank?" Seavery suddenly asked, again with that voice coming from an unexpected direction.

"I was thinking of punching you in the mouth," Frank said.

"There's your circumscribed mind again, Frank. Socrates drank hemlock, Christ accepted Crucifixion, Alexander conquered the known world, Lincoln freed the slaves. Why do you allow your deepest perceptions to lie in your knuckles?" And then, uncharacteristically, the youth winked at him. "Save your violence," he said. "You're going to need it."

You son of a bitch, Frank thought irascibly.

It was all done, Seavery said, except for the final "thing." He had spoken to Kifner on the telephone earlier in the day, requesting a meeting with the professor after the lecture, citing "important personal business pertaining to the Movement." Secrecy and urgency were stressed. Kifner agreed, though the amused indulgence Seavery thought he detected in the man's voice piqued the youth. (He had reached Kifner at the latter's hotel through the sponsors of the lecture, representing himself as a former student of the professor's.) Kifner had agreed to see Seavery and the latter's friend, but for only a short time.

When it was over, Seavery told Frank, a telephone call would be made to the newspapers in the name of a certain right-wing organization, announcing the murder, appending some appropriate slogan and then hanging up. The telephone conversation would be quickly picked up by other papers and spread across the country, propagating itself with a fierce and irresistible momentum, and no matter what evidence to the contrary was eventually adduced, the name of the right-wing organization, through first association, would be indelibly upon the event. No information that followed in succeeding days, Seavery believed, would be potent enough to rub away that initial impression. The people who were so fanatical as to believe and continue to believe a lie, were precisely the ones Seavery was after.

So many tickets had been sold for the lecture that folding chairs

were set up at the rear of the auditorium and along the side walls,
surrounding the military symmetry of the permanent, bolted seats
which ranged back from the stage and its lone prop, a wide-based,
narrow-stemmed lectern which dominated the stage with a certain
severe authority. In contrast to the last time Frank had heard
Kifner speak, on the campus of the California university, the audience here was a mixture of young and old, though with youth still
in the majority. Enthusiasm for the speaker, however, was fervently in evidence on the part of both generations. Kifner's entrance from the wings was greeted by a unanimous standing
ovation, which he acknowledged with a long, cool stare, and then
a slow nod of his head. And none was more spirited, ardent, or
prolonged in his applause than Arthur Seavery; while Frank's
demonstration was precisely the opposite, dispirited and perfunctory. As he stood pounding his big hands listlessly together, he
noted Seavery's almost boistrous display with puzzled incredulity.
When they were seated (they had folding chairs at the rear of the
auditorium), and there was general throat-clearing in anticipation
of Kifner's first words, Seavery whispered excitedly to Frank, "See?
I told you, they're crazy about him." Seavery grinned as if in
vindication, as Frank nodded dumbly, like a man who has only
fragments of the language. The expression on his face was one
of frank and explicit disbelief, to the extent that he could feel its
distortion in his facial muscles; and his sense of the situation became even more perplexed when he realized Seavery had stared
directly into his face and not discerned what was there.

Of the hundreds of people in the auditorium, Frank alone was
inattentive, Kifner's voice skirting the fringes of his consciousness
like sea sounds to a daydreamer. He sat with his arms crossed and
his head down, occasionally startled into looking up as the audience responded with applause and approving shouts as Kifner
electrified them with some particularly dynamic thrust of rhetoric,
and then throwing a wild glance to the man at the lectern who
was standing there erect and indomitable with a clenched fist
his lone histrionic. "Listen to them, listen to them," Seavery whispered, squirming about in his chair, and then, with the rest of
the audience, getting to his feet, raising his hands to face level
and slamming them together with vehement enthusiasm. Frank
suddenly leaped to his feet and stared with terrible awe at the

stage where Kifner stood at the lectern, the man somehow larger
and more dominant now, framed into the proscenium arch and
gazing stonily at the audience he had brought to its feet, aloof,
dispassionate, maybe even contemptuous in his stillness, his even-
ness, his tolerant gazing; the unmoved mover, the impassive shaker,
like some unpitying and unreachable titan in his pride. And then
Frank looked at Seavery—the applauding youth seemed transported, his mouth was open, his lips expanded in an exultant grin,
his bared teeth moist and incredibly white, a senseless affirmative
chant bursting out of him like some primitive incantation. The
applause went on in a rackety roar as Frank alone of the hundreds stood with idle hands, glaring around him with eyes that
from sheer fright seemed unable to focus. And then there was a
murmurous shuffling of feet as the audience resumed their seats.

Kifner went on, that strong, shrewd, manipulative voice building toward its next peak, its next entrapment, preparing its
next assault upon the expectant, vulnerable sensibilities assembled
before him. Frank, sitting with his fists clenched tightly upon
his thighs, looked down at Seavery's trouser leg, to where the
cuffless edge rested at ankle length against the youth's desert boot,
beneath which that knife surely was sheathed. He suddenly found
himself gasping for breath. *What the hell am I doing here?* he
asked himself in consternation. *This is insane.* Now there was a
burst of ironical laughter from the audience and it shot terror
into Frank. He looked at Kifner; the man's head was lowered
almost demurely, as if to emphasize the mischief of his caustic
humor. Next to him he heard Seavery laughing in short, breathless bursts, and again he had to gasp for breath, feeling a heaviness in his chest. He knew that in the next moment he was going
to get up and walk out. There was absolutely no question of that;
he had gone his limit. *I'm just going to get up and walk out and
not come back. I'm going to get up and walk out.* He glanced at
Seavery's eager, attentive face as if daring the youth to stop
him; but Seavery was transfixed, his eyes riveted upon Kifner, his
lips firmed against his teeth. I'm going to get up and walk out, he
told himself again, as if performing some stunt of clairvoyance for
his own benefit. And do what? he asked himself. Go where? Well,
it didn't matter, really, and he shouldn't think about it; as long as
he got away from here, away from this deliriously fixated crowd

of adulators whose cheers were like dirt burying the mortal soul of Stephen Kifner, away from the man himself, the fatted calf, whose death was already being celebrated in the demonic mind of the youth sitting in the next chair.

"I'll be right back," he whispered to Seavery, and without waiting for a response rose and walked to the double door at the rear of the auditorium and quietly let himself out.

Outside, in the lobby, the air seemed saner, easier to breathe. He took a deep, gratifying breath, like a man rising from under water, and began walking across the marble floor toward the front door. But he stopped at the glass doors and looked out at the street. *And do what, go where?* He did not know even in which direction he would turn when he stepped outside. From behind him, muffled by the door, came another approving roar for the words of Stephen Kifner. Again his isolation fell upon him, more harrowing, more menacing than before; and even worse: it was as if by some unholy choosing he had been singled out for torment, he alone of the world's billions. He stood still, a lost, martyred expression on his face. People were passing outside in the street, automobile horns brayed in the anguish of crosstown traffic, lights flashed with meaningless monotonous regularity, as the great city built and structured with massive and relentless delicacy its millions of Saturday night crescendos, with the dreadful black sky awaiting in its urban starlessness the lost and faltering echoes, poised to unmask with merciless dawn, leaving the sobs for daylight, and life was a short time in the sun. I can't go out there, he thought, not with alarm or despair but with helplessness. The city of bruising life and raucous laughter and barbarous brusqueness did not exist for him; he would walk its teeming pavements as through a wasteland; there was no haven here for the lost, the bewildered, for those impaled upon the insoluble. No matter how energetic his desperation, how swift his mobility, he would be as stationary as a pillar; no matter what he did, no matter where he went, he would be waiting. It was no longer the dream, it was not even the nightmare: it was the crude and implacable reality.

Slowly, he turned around and walked to the public phone booth in the lobby. He stepped inside, closed the door and sat down. He lifted the receiver and rang a coin into the box, then began dialing the number which some stubborn corner of his mind had refused to forget, suggesting that certain areas of the mind were never closed to the most improbable, inconceivable of actions. He heard a telephone ring twice, and then a connection was established, but some moments passed before he heard a voice.

"Hello?" Frank said, repeating it again, and again.

"Yes?" a male voice said guardedly.

"Mr. Bennett?"

"Who is this?"

"I have to speak to Mr. Bennett. It's urgent. He told me to call him."

"Who is this?"

Frank felt himself gagging again and covered the mouthpiece as he coughed several times.

"Who is this?" the voice asked into his ear, pat, repetitive, but not insistent, not hostile, not even inquisitive, not anything; simply a tireless, exemplary sound with the implication of interminable dispassionate patience.

"Frank Dublin," Frank said finally, with the wearying sense of confessing a crime.

"What can we do for you?"

"I have to speak to Mr. Bennett."

"Mr. Bennett is not here at the moment."

"It's you . . . I recognize your voice," Frank said excitedly.

"Mr. Bennett is not here at the moment."

God almighty, what am I talking to? he thought, covering his eyes with his hand for a moment.

"Is he available?" he asked now, calmly.

"He is available, but what do you want?"

"I've got to get a message to him. It's urgent . . . there isn't much time. Look, he told me to call him."

"What is the message?"

Frank paused, looking quickly out at the lobby as if his name had been called. Then he brought his free hand up and curled it around the mouthpiece in so obvious an attempt at secrecy that he would have been conspicuous had anyone noticed him.

"Listen carefully," he said, dropping his voice. "Tonight, at about ten o'clock, in his room at the Hotel Claymore, an attempt is going to be made to murder Stephen Kifner. Professor Stephen Kifner. It's all a crazy insane scheme . . . it's his own people

. . . they think they can start a revolution by this. Have you got that?"

"Yes."

"At about ten o'clock," Frank said.

"I read you."

"You read me? What am I, a book? Listen, why can't I talk to Mr. Bennett?"

"Your message will be relayed."

"Will you contact him immediately? You can see the urgency. Can you reach him?"

"Yes."

"Are you certain?"

"Yes."

"Tell him this is from Frank Dublin. He knows me. I'm one of his . . . people. Look, I'm going to be there. Will you tell him all this?"

"Yes."

"Are you absolutely certain you can reach him?"

"Yes."

"A murder is being planned."

"I understand."

Frank paused, waiting for the voice to say something, to give some advice or instruction, make some contribution. He could hear the man's breath in his ear, soft, rhythmic, interminable.

"To whom am I talking?" Frank asked.

"Is there anything else?"

Frank sighed. He shook his head in response, then realized this wasn't being communicated.

"No," he said resignedly.

"Good enough," the voice said.

The phone went dead in Frank's ear.

Son of a bitch, Frank thought. You'd think I'd called to order lunch. He remained in the booth for several moments, rubbing his hand across his chin, staring at the telephone. Then, with great reluctance, he left the phone booth and returned to the auditorium, walking into a thunderous ovation.

THIRTY-SEVEN

Standing with proud and steadfast indestructibility on a side street in the midtown area, the Hotel Claymore, architecturally nondescript from the outside, was actually a warm and comfortable place, reflecting in tone and ambience the immutable stability and virtues supposedly characteristic of the middle-aged heartland America prototypes who generally filled its rooms. Never elegant, never pretentious, it was today what it had always been, with defiant potted palms and enduring high-backed easy chairs and plump sofas in its restive and murmurous lobby whose quarried floor was covered by large, fringed rugs: one of those durable places cornered in a big city, possessing its veiled secret of dignified survival as it outlasts most of its more lavish, celebrated and preposterous neighbors.

Frank and Seavery came through the revolving door and headed for the self-service elevators, Seavery walking one step ahead and moving rather rapidly. They stepped aside as the arriving elevator discharged a flow of passengers, and then entered. Alone in the rising elevator, each stood with his eyes raised to the inexorable ascent of illuminated floor numbers. When their number flashed and the elevator had slowed to floor level, Seavery turned to Frank and with exaggerated solemnity made the sign of the cross, then grinned almost lewdly.

"We spoke on the phone earlier," Seavery said when Kifner opened the door.

"So we did," Kifner said dryly. "Come right in."

Seavery first and then Frank walked into the room as Kifner closed the door behind them. The room was rather large and more attractive than might have been expected from looking at the hotel's dreary outer façade with its protrusion of fire escapes. There was a double bed neatly covered with a satin spread, modestly decorative furniture, a television set, carpeting, inviting chairs, a small sofa. A broad sweep of drapery hid the windows— an arrangement which Frank immediately took note of, thinking that perhaps Bennett and his men were standing behind the drapes now, a prospect that filled him with such scintillant excitement that he immediately became convinced they were there, brilliantly and strategically positioned—otherwise why should the drapes have been drawn? (His mind, on the hunt for significant things only, did not even consider the possibility of Kifner's wanting privacy.) Next he looked at the bathroom door, which was slightly ajar, and realized they could be in there, too, waiting for their moment. And the certainty, or at least strong assumption, that Bennett and his men were near at hand gave at last some surcease to the restive guilt and doubt which had been plaguing him since the phone call; and within a few moments the sense of relief turned into a brightening and purifying surge of justification which relieved his mind of its last lingering uncertainty, and as if in righteous denunciation of all that had given him pause, he thought this: he had made the call not because it was the only thing to do, but because it was the right thing.

"Now, who is who?" Kifner asked.

"I'm Lee," Seavery said. "This is Wilk."

There was an exchange of handshakes. Kifner's hand was strong and at the same time stiff and formal; the man was not offering friendship with the gesture.

"I heard you speak once in California," Frank said.

Kifner smiled politely with his lips. He was shorter than Frank, but built strongly, broad through the chest and shoulders. His face was coarse, unhandsome, yet with certain compelling qualities of strength and tension, suggesting an ego that placed little emphasis upon the importance of physical attractiveness. He had shed his jacket, though not his tie. He took a seat now, in a chair in front of the drapes, which further reinforced Frank's conviction that Bennett and his men must be concealed there, in perfect position to protect the intended victim when Seavery tried to strike. Frank and Seavery remained standing; in fact, for the length of their stay in the room they were on their feet, Seavery engaging the professor in conversation while Frank hovered in the background, tuning in and out of the exchanges as his growing anticipation diverted his attention.

One other thing Frank noticed upon entering the room was
how uncomfortably warm it was. It felt as though the heat
was turned on, and with the drapes covering the windows there
was no air circulation and the room was stifling. Kifner, however,
seemed to take not the slightest notice of the discomfort.

"I heard you once in California too," Seavery said to the professor. "Your speech ended in a riot."

"You mean a riot began after my speech ended," Kifner said.
"I remember that. It was provoked by the police."

"Some people thought it was provoked by the speech. I know
I did."

"No, the chemistry was there even before I said a word. I sensed
it the moment I looked at them. Too often a speech is characterized by the response rather than the content."

"Nevertheless, they were set off by what you said. Did it please
you?"

"The riot? Of course not."

"But why?" Seavery asked. "To think that your words can
stimulate people like that. It's a gift, and you have it whether you
like it or not."

Kifner shrugged. He was sitting with his legs crossed, the fingers
of one hand drumming idly on the chair's armrest. His face wore
a look of moderate interest, as if he was prepared to commit only
limited resources to this conversation.

"We heard you speak tonight," Seavery said. "Frankly, I was
disappointed."

Now Kifner's features shifted slightly with the merest rising of
amused interest. He was accustomed by now, wearily so, to hear
in his debates and discussions with young people the blunt, the
discourteous, the peevishly rude. Their capacity to shock or surprise, in which they seemed to place such pride, had become, for
him, vastly reduced.

"I was hoping you would come down on what has been the
primary theme of your writings," Seavery said.

"Which is what?"

"Violence."

"My dear friend," Kifner said with a tolerant grin that creased
his face and reached his eyes, "that is hardly the theme of my
work."

"That's the one which has reached the most people."

"I thought tonight's talk much more pertinent. After all, I was talking about reality, in its most personal application."

"But you've written that the only true reality is violence, that violence makes action a reality and that justice therefore becomes inevitable."

"Well, you've muddled it a bit," Kifner said indulgently.

"You've said that because of its openness and simplicity, violence is basically a moral act."

"You're taking things out of context and mixing them together. You're interchanging the word 'force' with the word 'violence.' They're two different concepts altogether, and shouldn't be misused or misinterpreted. A worker going out on strike is using force, an act of civil disobedience predicated upon conscience and principle is force. That's what I was talking about tonight—the obligation of every man to use force, the fate of a few to employ violence. But there's a danger today of even *force* being subverted by the system, for the sake of confrontation. That will lead to violence, but on their terms, not yours, and when the opposition chooses the time, the place, and the weapons, you stand very little chance. If you're going to use violence effectively and in the name of justice, you have to know precisely when, where and how. But more important, you have to know *why*, because it doesn't, or it shouldn't, come in small doses."

"But why should it come as a last resort?" Seavery asked resentfully. "Anything done as a last resort is being done out of weakness and desperation, after a dissipation of energy, and can only be disorganized and chaotic—which generally means it's too late."

"I didn't say violence should be a last resort," Kifner said, raising one finger for a moment. "I've never said that. What I'm saying is it should be thoroughly understood before it's put to use, since you seldom get more than a single crack at it."

"But now you're complicating the nature of it. First you say it's simple and now you say it has to have a structure, some kind of basic design. It seems to me you're hedging, beginning to resist an idea that's suddenly begun to materialize."

"No," Kifner said patiently, shaking his head. "No. Not at all. Look, my friend. There are all kinds of violence. There is physical violence and there is the act of doing violence to a man's image of himself. This latter has to come first, otherwise the physical violence will be meaningless, something for the balladeers instead of the lawmakers. Think of reality. Of human beings and their will and their aspirations and the yearning for creativity in their lives. Think of each man's simple dream of personal fulfillment. This is reality—and it's being concealed from man. And now, what I was saying tonight, if you were paying attention," Kifner added with subtle sarcasm, "is that learning and knowledge have become, through distortion and corruption, the enemies of reality. Your shrewd men at the top—some of whom, if you remember your history, were unhappy with the invention of that great intellectual equilizer, the printing press—they know that great scientific and technological achievements have always dazzled people; it tends to subjugate them the way religion has been known to. And today more than ever. A man today hears all about atoms and electrons and energy masses and a thousand things he doesn't understand but which awe him because they make his television set work and his astronauts fly, and he thinks what a fine and wonderful world it is he's living in and how lucky he is to be here, part of this miraculous age. But what, actually, do these things have to do with his intrinsic life? His life as a unique, creative human being who is deserving of such simple things as justice and equality? What good is it to be told that you live as part of a universe which has billions of mysteries in it, if that information only intimidates and inhibits you, and your only function in that universe is simply to be a computerized, compartmentalized, well-oiled and, sometimes, well-fed slave? Instead of it being drilled into a man's head that he is the only thinking, creative creature in all of that known universe, that colossal emptiness is made instead to make him feel small and insignificant. Man is greater than nature, if he will only believe it. And if he is greater than nature then he is greater than the man-made strictures that bind him. To do violence to man's image of himself—to de-educate, uplift, and re-educate him—that's the essential part of the program. You can make your revolution, certainly, but if man's image of himself hasn't changed then it's only a matter of time before he and his society slip back to what they were before."

"But when does the talking stop?" Seavery demanded after having waited with impatient skepticism for Kifner's monologue to end.

"Never," Kifner said, "if you're equating it with thinking. If and when physical violence comes, it, too, should have a structure, as you put it, a fiercely defined goal. It should, ideally, be a natural flow, out of man's reasoning, his self-enlightenment, not his fury and despair. *Then* it becomes a moral act."

"Since when have reasoning and enlightenment lit fuses?" Seavery asked. Contending with Kifner, a man he had so long admired, was beginning to fill him with a heady exhilaration.

"They had better, and soon," Kifner said with a harsh laugh, then sat forward and coughed several times, clearing his throat.

Frank was moving nervously back and forth behind the conversation. (Occasionally Kifner passed a glance at his muscular second visitor, noting his nervousness, attributing it to embarrassment at what he, Kifner, considered Seavery's impertinence.) Once Frank edged near to the bathroom and contrived to glance in, but the door was only partially open and the interior was dark and he could not tell if anyone was within. And then he fixed his eyes on the drapes again, trying to detect some movement there. His apprehension was growing; the possibility that Bennett and his men were not in the room was beginning to dawn on him. It seemed inconceivable. A sense of panic began building in him. He suddenly felt trapped in an expanding situation not of his making, one which could consume him without warning; it was as though he and not Kifner were the intended victim in this room. Perspiring now from the mugginess of the overheated room as well as from his own mounting tension, he began to wonder if his message had been relayed. *Of course it was,* he told himself. *It had to be. I made it absolutely clear what was at stake.* It was possible they were standing outside the door. But what good was that? How quickly could they move? After all, Seavery was standing but two or three strides from Kifner; it would take him mere seconds to strike. Maybe there had not been enough time since the phone call for Bennett to make his arrangements and get there. But even so, surely Kifner would have been warned. No one, least of all the intended victim, would be taking unnecessary chances in so dangerous a situation. *I should have called earlier . . . given them more time.* Then he had a maddening thought: What should he do if he saw Seavery preparing to strike, before Bennett had a chance to intervene? No, that couldn't happen. He was convinced it would not come to that. And anyway, what had it to do with him? He had notified them and thereby discharged all responsibility. The fault would lie with them. But the heat of the room. He ran his hand across his moist forehead, amazed that Kifner should be sitting so comfortably in his white shirt and tie and buttoned collar. Kifner was sitting so comfortably, so confidently—perhaps there was good reason for it. He must know about it, Frank thought, and he knows he's got the upper hand. He's playing a game with Seavery. *Did I say it would be a knife? No, I don't think I said that. How do they know he doesn't have a gun?* He felt himself getting dizzy, paying not the slightest attention to the conversation.

"We have to rise to the level of events," Seavery was saying.

Kifner laughed. "But whose events?" he asked. "Yours, or the system's? If it's theirs, then you have to drop below the level; if the events are yours, then you have to rise far, far above. You see, though violence is of itself a simple thing, that which precipitates it is most complex. It has to be handled correctly, otherwise it will go on and on, and each outburst will consume yesterday's victors. A successful revolution is that in which the sword and the soul are in harmony."

"But if you put such stress on the ordinary man being the generator of the violence, how can it ever come about, if he is advised to move through such complexities? I can tell by your expression that you think I'm splitting hairs. But I'm not . . . this is important . . . crucial. You're saying we should make a rational revolution or not at all; and I say that by definition revolution has to be irrational."

"You're underestimating the ordinary man," Kifner said. "There's one of the problems with you young Turks today. You're a bunch of snobs who look down on the workers. Well, let me tell you, the ordinary man has a mind and emotions and a will, and given the chance he can use them as superbly as any self-proclaimed intellectual. What you're saying is that violence is an elitist act beyond the capacity of the ordinary man."

"I didn't mean that," Seavery said, protesting. "I didn't say that. Look, you're an experienced debater and you're playing tricks on me. Don't play tricks on me. What I'm saying is you're preaching procrastination."

"Look, my young friend," Kifner said in a placating tone, "if you've studied the history of revolutionary movements then you know the energy they discharge. It's wild and violent and indiscriminate. We're both in favor of revolution. The difference is, I want mine to succeed absolutely, while you're willing to take your chances. All right, so you may take over and throw out the oppressive elitists. But the problem which concerns me is, what force prevents *you* from becoming in your time an oppressive elitist?"

"That attitude is cynical and defeatist," Seavery said with heat. "With that view, history should have stopped at the mouth of the cave. Even if I do in time become the oppressor, at least society will have made some progress in that time."

"But you'd resist being thrown out?"

"Perhaps," Seavery said sullenly.

"In any event," Kifner said, glancing at his watch, "you said you wanted to discuss something concerning that amorphous pillar of strength known as the Movement."

"Why do you mock it?"

"I don't mock anything; I'm a respecter of nothing."

"Not even of your own ideas, apparently," Seavery said with soft malevolence. "Men have died for the Movement. Some of my friends . . ." Seavery said abstractedly, his voice trailing off as Kifner watched him curiously.

Now Frank had the impulse to open the door, to tell Bennett (for he was convinced the man was outside in the hall) to come in, that time was running out. How could they possibly play so lightly with such danger? Then he stared at the drapes again. Was it possible for men to stand still for so long? But how long was it, really? He was not sure of the time. Perhaps they had got there before ten, perhaps it wasn't even ten yet. He wished he was wearing a watch. The heat in the room felt as if it were baking his brain. What good could Bennett do in the hall, or even in the bathroom, or even behind the drapes, if Seavery suddenly struck? But maybe there was some sort of plan; after all, Bennett was experienced in these matters and should be trusted. Perhaps it had to be done exactly this way. Maybe Kifner was wearing some protective shield under his shirt, and that was why he had his collar buttoned to the neck in this stifling heat. But suppose Seavery stabbed him in the eye? Frank brought his hand up to his own eye as he tried to dismiss the lunatic thought from his mind.

Was it possible that Kifner, who doubtless hated all official authority, had rejected Bennett's offer to help, saying he would handle the situation himself? After all, the man had had death threats before. But to invite his would-be assassin into the room. He's been told about me, Frank thought now. He knows I'm not in on it; he's expecting me to help him. But they had no right to expect that. *I've done all I can.*

He heard a police siren in the street below, and the sound gave him a jolting sense of hope. He was certain the siren, which soon droned off, had wailed to silence below, at the entrance to the hotel. Now he stared at Seavery and came to the strange, nagging conclusion that Seavery would not, could not, do it as long as Kifner was seated, that the youth did not have the stomach to simply step forward and make a frontal assault, that he needed a standing target. *That's why he needed me,* Frank thought. *He's waiting for me to move in and help him.* A man with a knife, with concealed motives, should need no one.

Frank edged forward now, listening to them, while at the same time keeping his head slightly turned, hoping to hear the arrival of Bennett.

"Do you feel the Movement has lost its momentum?" Seavery asked.

"There's no question of it," Kifner said.

One is committing murder with his questions, the other suicide with his answers, Frank thought, feeling now a deadly, helpless fascination as he gazed past the poised, slender body of Arthur Seavery at Stephen Kifner sitting in the chair looking up at the youth. The two were a tableau of tentative immobility, like a frame of action film momentarily frozen. Frank's eyes roved from Kifner's intent face to the cuff of Seavery's right trouser leg where, if it was anywhere, that Bowie knife was sheathed waiting for its unforeseen unexpected entry, the tempest of the last act.

"I agree," Seavery said eagerly. "But it shouldn't, should it? It's got to keep going, hasn't it? It's the hope, isn't it?"

"A political movement that dies, deserves to die," Kifner said curtly. "A healthy movement is its own momentum. You might think you're the physician, when in truth you could very well be the disease."

"But even with a healthy movement, one that's running under its own momentum, the very fact that it *is* continuing means that something is being done to keep it alive. And you will agree, I'm sure, that the movement is more important than any individual."

"How can you say that, when a movement is people?"

"What I'm saying is that if . . . say . . . the death of one person . . . let us say . . . can thrust the movement ahead by light-years, isn't it worth it?"

"The world is becoming too sophisticated to accept martyrs, if that's what you're talking about."

"If a movement is dedicated to the betterment of people, to the overthrow . . . the lasting overthrow . . . the permanent dispossession of tyranny and oppression," Seavery said excitedly, "then people should be willing to die in its name, shouldn't they?"

"In the abstract, perhaps. But it's a dangerous hypothesis to posit. I certainly haven't met anyone who's willing to do that. Have you?"

"Yes," Seavery said. "I am."

"You are?" Kifner asked skeptically.

"Yes . . . yes . . . and if I am, then doesn't that give me the right to take someone else's life . . . if it will help the Movement?"

"That's fanatical thinking. It doesn't do any good. You'll wind up with a cult, not a movement. I repeat: I haven't met anyone who even remotely advocates the things you say."

"These decisions would have to be made by others."

"By what authority?"

"Authority?" Seavery cried. "There isn't any more authority. It's gone into disgrace and disrepute. There is only the authority of history."

"And who speaks for history?"

"Those who have the courage to make it," Seavery said, with such savagery that a look of concern entered Kifner's eyes.

"When you talk of making history," Kifner said, speaking with extraordinary care now, guardedly, watching Seavery as if (Frank thought this) he was trying to read the youth's mind, "you are talking of a craft that requires long years of apprenticeship. And anyway, there is a theory," Kifner said, his eyes looking as if they were peering into Seavery, his voice quiet, his words slow, almost as if being uttered by some vocal reflex, detached from a mind that was in concentration elsewhere, "a theory that men do not make history, that it is quite the other way around."

"I don't believe it," Seavery answered quickly, petulantly. "I

believe that the fully committed man can make history. And
there is no other way for a revolution to come except through
men who are fully committed."

"As you are," Kifner said quietly, ironically.

"I want to know if you justify violence in the name of a people's
revolution," Seavery said as if posing a formal question, the challenge bluntly in his voice, cold, unmistakable.

"If there is no other alternative, if it is for the greater good . . ."
Kifner said, warily eyeing Seavery as if to judge the impact of
each word.

And then, watching Seavery, curiosity began gaining increasing
mastery over Frank. He became dreadfully transfixed, wondering
what the youth was going to do, when he was going to do it, how,
what would come of it. These questions, pressing one upon the
other, felt as though they were sealing off his mind, leaving him
vulnerable to this single moment and all its unforeseeable consequences. He began to realize the horrible absurdity of his situation. He longed to turn and run from the room—there still was
time for it; not much time, minutes, seconds perhaps: mere particles of elapsing time in which to make so crucial a decision and
act upon it. But he felt consciously, maddeningly, his inability
to do it, to save himself; he did not think he could even have uttered a sound had he been asked a question, he was mute, paralyzed; it was as if he had expended his last resources of decisive
energy upon the telephone call, and was capable now only of a
horrible helpless curiosity.

At that moment Kifner brought his hand to his mouth and
coughed several times, his face making that expression of querulous
seriousness so often summoned by a cough.

"Excuse me," he said, rising.

With all the mysterious unsubstantiality of a manipulated
shadow, Seavery drew aside as Kifner walked past him, past Frank,
to the bathroom. Seavery had a strange, churlish grin on his lips
as he watched Kifner, then turned to Frank with a look at once
of smug and sinister delight. They both stood absolutely still and
listened to Kifner coughing several more times and then make a
gutteral sweep of his throat and expectorate. And then Frank
was aware of the shadow that was Arthur Seavery dipping surreptitiously and dropping one hand to the cuff of his right trouser
leg; his eye caught the momentary ruffling of the cuff and when

Seavery straightened up the Bowie knife was in his hand, concealed against his thigh. The youth was not looking at Frank now but at the bathroom doorway, his tongue touching his upper lip for a moment, the expression on his face changed to one of bland innocence, like a child trying to disguise the commission of some minor infraction.

Kifner emerged from the bathroom, emitting a light cough. He looked at Frank.

"Those damned speeches are a strain," Kifner said.

Frank, rooted in his unshakable and paralyzing curiosity, could do no more than barely nod his head, staring with morbid fascination at the man as if Kifner were deliberately inviting his own destruction or else defying or ignoring the very real possibility of it. Kifner passed him and walked back toward the chair as Seavery turned slightly to a side, hiding the hand that was holding the knife. Frank continued to stare, disbelievingly now, at the man's back, solid and broad-shouldered in the white shirt, like the heart of a painted target. Unconsciously he pressed thumb and forefinger together and brought them pensively to his lips as he anticipated Seavery's move, as he waited for that sudden irrevocable thrust to occur which was now beyond prevention, watching that broad inviting back moving toward the chair in front of the spread of drapes, Kifner abreast now of the intently staring Seavery who was himself absolutely immobile, as if poised at the crest of a deeply drawn and tensely suspended breath; Kifner still moving toward that chair but seemingly making no progress, as if this was an interminable journey foredoomed to interception, the chair before him looking as distantly placed and unattainable as a Judgment throne, standing in front of the drapes, the robes, with grim and ruthless emptiness, as inconsolably empty as the favored chair of one just dead, Kifner in his seeming immobility as if gazing longingly at it, faceless and wistful. And then the word *Don't!* flashed through Frank's mind even as he was unsure as to who or what the unuttered cry was intended: for Kifner not to turn his back or for Seavery not to strike. And then he saw the light glint off of the blade as Seavery moved the knife out from his body and suddenly raised it high above his head and hold that maniacal pose for an instant as if enacting some barbaric ritual, then advance his left foot and jerk his body down and forward to give weight and impact to the descending blow as the knife began its downward arc, an expression of frantic hateful exertion contorting his face.

The blow—ill-aimed—struck Kifner in the shoulder and the man cried out and spun around, his mouth open, his face stunned with ghastly surprise. He stumbled back, his arms rising. And then, incredibly, he dove at Seavery, and for several moments Frank stood back, still the paralyzed spectator, thumb and forefinger still pensively at his lips, as though keyed by suspenseful curiosity and nothing more, watching the grotesque struggle, barely aware of the knife falling to the floor in a savagely independent motion of its own. He watched Seavery fall back and Kifner lunge after him with extended fingers reaching for the youth's throat as though making the gesture of a mad stalking hypnotist, and then the two colliding again, twisting around, bouncing against the wall and then wrenching violently to the floor.

"Frank!" Seavery gasped.

Stung by the sound of his name, Frank moved forward, not quickly but tentatively, poised but uncertain, seeing the blood running from Kifner's fingers now as the entire white sleeve beneath the wounded shoulder began raising a color like bottled claret. And then he was looking almost point-blank into Kifner's raised, wildly storming eyes that fixed him for just that instant with bloated fear and pain and most of all a terrific animal fury.

"Frank," Seavery gasped again as Kifner's fingers worked into his throat, the youth kicking and squirming.

Like some heroic thing out of the ancientry of heraldic combat, the knife presented itself to his eye, ancient and teeming with armipotent grandeur. He crouched and picked it up as if reclaiming the prize of his forebears, and it was as if the knife had seized his hand and clenched his fingers upon it. He extended his free hand toward Kifner as if making some last vague gesture of warning, of appeal, wanting Kifner to see it, to make him withdraw and desist before the moment became totally irretrievable. But the man was gripped by his own blinding and uncontrollable furies now, the lustful fanaticism of survival blasting one climactic crescendo after another, his body rocking and thrusting over Seavery's. And then as Kifner suddenly raised a bloody fist into the air and poised it like a hammer over Seavery's face, Frank's hand followed the sharp plunging descent of the knife and drove it into Kifner's back, falling to one knee as he completed the blow, the soft unresistant sinking of the blade, and then to his astonishment accepting Kifner's slowly twisting body in his arms, the imbedded knife jutting out like a lever. Kifner's eyes gaped up at him, moist and bemused, still not fully comprehending the shock, the pain, the reality, his eyes beginning now to quest and search in Frank's face, a noise peculiarly like self-relief passing through his slack lips.

Gently Frank placed the body face down, then stood up and suddenly felt his stomach constrict and throw a sickening wave through him. Gripping himself as if just struck a terrific blow in the abdomen, he gagged, then whirled and ran for the bathroom. He shouldered aside the partially closed door and plunged into the darkened bathroom and leaned over the bathtub and began retching violently, his body bucking and being sucked in and blown out by his coughing and choking, the vomitus splattering into the tub, tears streaming down his cheeks. For a moment he thought he was blacking out. Then Seavery appeared in the doorway, a frantic, nagging figure.

"Frank!" he cried. "What the hell are you doing? Come on, move your ass! Move, move, move!"

Frank straightened up, raising his head, gasping.

"*Come on!*"

When he emerged from the bathroom Frank saw Kifner lying face down on the carpet, an enormous splash of blood under the imbedded knife, the thick sumptuous flow continuing unabated, creating a brilliant efflorescence in the white shirt. And then he noted something else and stared at it as though it were of the greatest significance: one of Kifner's socks was a shade different in color from the other.

"Pull it out," Seavery said.

"What?" Frank asked dazedly.

"Pull it out," Seavery repeated, insistently.

"Do it yourself," Frank said, with not the least inflection or assertion, his voice flat, dull.

Seavery stared dubiously at the knife, then muttered, "It isn't important."

Frank turned away, breathing deeply, trying to compose himself.

"He tried to kill me," Seavery said. "Crazy bastard." And then he added, with a sickly laugh, "He believed in violence all right."

"What do we do now?" Frank asked.

Seavery looked at him contemptuously.

"Call room service," the youth said caustically, "and ask them to send somebody to clean up the mess."

Frank gave him an almost pitying look and then asked, as he turned back to the body, "Is he dead?"

Reluctantly, Seavery glanced at their victim.

"He's dead," he said, and added after a pause, "he would have betrayed us in the end, Frank."

But Frank barely heard this last whispered petulant remark as he gazed upon the fallen man and the flat sightless eyes which did not look so much dead yet as they did shocked and disbelieving, as if what had happened had been an incongruity more than anything else; upon the incredible indignity of a proud man betrayed and brought low; upon Stephen Kifner sprawled on the floor of this hotel room with one cheek flat on the rug, with the blood still pulsing and dispersing through the wound that had been stabbed into his body, the knife imbedded in his back as emphatically as an explorer's pike claiming a wilderness for his monarch. Frank drew back, at once sensitized and toughened by the idea of his own ghastly role in this thing; stunned but not so stunned he did not know that something had been so deeply incised upon his mind that the heart of his every thought would forevermore bear its imprint.

Seavery opened the door and peered out into the corridor, then turned and nodded to Frank.

They walked along the empty corridor to the elevator, where Seavery pressed the button. Then they stood apart from each other as though they had been strangers. Frank kept sidling furtive glances at Seavery, who was standing stiffly, eyes raised suspensefully to the dial indicator above the elevator door. Then Frank looked up and down the corridor; it seemed unnaturally quiet, almost as if the violent death which had just occurred was spreading an uncanny reverence through the air. His stomach had begun to settle but his throat felt dry and raw, as if it had been scraped.

In spite of their complexity, magnitude, and awfulness, Frank's

thoughts about what had just happened drifted listlessly through
his mind, as if they could find no hospitable plain upon which
to settle. He had been taken by surprise. He realized now that,
naïvely, he had doubted Seavery. And what had happened to
Bennett, he could not begin to guess. They have my name, he
thought dully. They know I was there. The idea of that, however,
seemed unable to achieve any responsive depths. He exchanged
glances with Seavery. The youth's face was expressionless,
though there was an odd, faraway softness in his eyes; it was as if
he had by some incalculable act of will removed himself from
where he was, from what he had done, or else not let the act
penetrate that tense inner core where his innermost feelings were
lodged.

A light fell at their feet and a moment later the self-service
elevator opened. They stepped inside as the only passengers and
began their descent to the lobby. To Frank it felt funereal, as if
they were being lowered into the earth. When the door opened
again he was startled by the people in the lobby, the lights, the
noise, the prim ringing of the desk bell, all of the mundane, self-
concerned activity. It seemed to him strange that there should not
be excitement, consternation, as if the silent dead man would
have by now somehow communicated his outrage to everyone in
the building.

Frank followed Seavery out of the elevator, shouldering past
an elderly couple who were waiting to get on. As they walked
through the busy lobby, Frank kept shifting his eyes from one
person to another. It seemed to him as if people were deliberately
avoiding looking at him; and instead of feeling like a flagrant and
conspicuous presence, as he had when he stepped out of the elevator, he now felt a curious sense of ostracism, ignored and
unnoticed. And then, with surprising lack of concern and involvement, he was watching Seavery's stiff, self-conscious figure moving
away from him at a quickening pace; and he came to a standstill
in the middle of the lobby and allowed it to happen, wanting it
to happen: watched the slim, harried-looking youth aim remorse-
lessly for the revolving doors, spin a half circle through them and
disappear into the night, without once looking back.

THIRTY-EIGHT

Upon leaving the hotel Frank got into a taxi and directed the driver to Capstone, heading for Charlotte's house. He sat through most of the twenty-minute ride with his fingertips touching his lips, looking like a man contemplating some crucial lapse of memory. He seemed to understand that it was going to take time before he would be able to comprehend what had happened, what he had done. There was no attempt to escape from or to modify reality, but simply the overwhelming realization that something so monstrous and unexpected had happened that he felt as if he was going to have to wait for its determination and disposition of him to occur rather than his of it. As the taxi crossed the Queensborough Bridge he looked back once, through the girders and cables and across the black shimmering East River at Manhattan massed in the night with its burning lights, its disdainful and invincible indifference; and for the first time the city appeared menacingly personalized, as if he had relinquished to it all his secrets and by definition his hopes and his security, because somewhere in all that incurable hugeness, behind one of those lights, was a body and a knife which sooner or later the city was going to regurgitate with a sharp bloody spasm.

When she opened the door and looked at him he realized from her expression of sudden apprehensive tension what his own face must look like. He hurried inside and paced around with great agitation, announcing the need of a drink. She handed him a shot of straight whisky which he downed with a single gulp and then continued pacing while she watched him with increasing disquiet. He paused for a moment to mutter with savage self-mockery, "I should have gone to the goddamn Navahos." Then he continued his striding back and forth across the living room, releasing the flood of nervous energy that had been so pent during the taxi ride. Suddenly he stopped and stared at her.

"Can I trust you?" he asked in a sharp, demanding, inordinately loud voice.

When she did not immediately answer, but only stared at him in wonderment, he said, "I have to know."

"Of course you can trust me," she said.

"Something happened tonight," he said, pacing again, passing back and forth before her eyes. "It was supposed to and yet it wasn't. Maybe you thought it was all foolish melodrama, the things I told you last night." He laughed bitterly, walking back and forth, rubbing his hands together. "I got the feeling you didn't take it seriously—or at least not seriously enough. Well, maybe it'll be an eye-opener for you, let you know there's a real world out there and that if you want to play in it . . ."

"Frank, I don't know what you're talking about," she said, at once apologetically and emphatically.

"You know what I'm talking about," he said. "But you don't want to believe it, you want to draw back at the last moment and enjoy the spectacle from the grandstand; that's the way amateurs play it, leaving the professionals way out on the limb. These lessons . . . all that we do . . . are aimed at people like you . . . to put a little steel up your asses and get you mobilized . . ."

"Tell me what happened," she said. "For God's sake, stop that pacing and sit down."

He stopped pacing, though he did not sit down.

"I do have your trust?" he asked.

"Of course," she said impatiently. "Why must you even ask that?"

"Because this is something quite extraordinary." He smiled faintly, studying her. No, she had not forgotten what he had told her was going to happen, nor had she disbelieved him; it had simply been stricken from her mind—it had been unpleasant and nettlesome and so she had decided to ignore it, which was a marvelous faculty to possess, as long as one had the life style to sustain it.

"Everything you do is quite extraordinary," she said in a somewhat arched tone which, under the circumstances, he did not like—it was like the first faint drawing in the sand of a line she was preparing to retreat behind.

"This more than anything else," he said.

For one fleeting moment he had the thought that perhaps he ought not tell her after all, wondering whether it was necessary or was merely romance on his part, as for an instant what he had done flashed across his mind with a stark unembellished vividness like an icy glare illuminating for a moment a shattered landscape. But the thought vanished as quickly as it had come and he went on, urged by his own immitigable fear.

"I was very serious when I said that a murder was being planned," he said. "Did you believe me? I hope you believed me. It would be a hell of a thing to declare something like that and not be believed, wouldn't it? I can't think of anything worse or more insulting . . . at the moment."

She watched him intently, her hands slowly rising, her fingers falling together over her breast.

"Except that it didn't quite happen as planned," he said. "It sort of got out of hand. Things got . . . twisted about. You plan these things with utmost care and precision and then hope they go right. To a certain extent it did go right, I suppose . . . though not exactly right. It isn't easy to murder a man. I don't mean from the point of view of what's inside of you, but from what's inside of him. That's what makes it difficult . . . and unpredictable. You can bring yourself to it, if it's absolutely necessary . . . but it's what *he* feels that seems to determine the *nature* of the thing. *He* decides how it's going to happen, the son of a bitch," he said bitterly, resentfully. "You can never really prepare for that. That's the unexpected element, and you can only be as ready as you can."

"Are you telling me . . ." she said, her voice trailing off.

"Am I telling you what?" he asked. "What do you think it is I'm telling you?"

"That something happened and the police are after you."

"The police? I'm not sure about that. That's the great unknown at the moment. We weren't seen, if that's what you mean. That part of it at least went according to plan. But the situation itself got out of hand. I still don't know how it happened. Can you believe that—that I actually do not know how it happened the way it did? In some ways that's the most extraordinary thing of all, that your mind can suddenly black out on you like that, in such a situation. But these things happen so quickly . . . and I guess there's something in your head that moves faster than reason. Anyway, it ended up, it got so turned around, that I was the one who had to do it. That was never part of the plan . . . I insisted . . . I stipulated . . ."

"I'm not quite sure I know what you mean," she said.

He scrutinized her, a pale, malicious smile straying across his lips. "Aren't you?" he asked, a faintly amused skepticism evident in his voice.

"You killed someone?" she asked quietly.

He spread his hands as if to describe a certain helpless innocence.

"The way things got twisted around," he said, "it became almost self-defense, because of him . . . the victim."

"But who was it, and why?"

He would not tell her; it would entail too long and complicated an explanation, and maybe not even a convincing one. (After all, it was Seavery's theory, Seavery's lunatic plan, idea, and he did not know how persuasively he could explain it at the moment. When things were calmer, more settled, less pressured, then he would try.)

"Just . . . someone," he said. "I don't want to go into it now."

She sat down, almost collapsed, a slack, bewildered figure, trying to put it all together in her mind. She was frightened, of so many things she could barely sort them out.

"I wish you hadn't told me," she murmured.

He smiled at that.

"Well," he said with a taste of irony, "after all, we're compatriots, all of us."

She raised her eyes dubiously to him. Compatriots with whom? she wondered. She had no idea with whom he was involved, what kind of people (though she was beginning to have some idea). She felt unfairly implicated, threatened. She had had nothing to do with this (had, in fact, tried to talk him out of it), and now found herself part of it, through some insane and inexplicable sequence of events. God knew what he had told his "compatriots" about her, what was expected of her, what sort of danger she might have been thrust into. She had the disturbing sensation of strangers knowing all about her, strangers having a hand in her life now, could feel that control slipping away from her. Everything was suddenly terrifically and hopelessly amiss.

"We have no choice now but to get out," he said.

"Get out?"

"Obviously we have to get away, at least for a while."

"Where?" she asked reluctantly, feeling herself making unwilling concessions, saying things she did not want to, being drawn inexorably into a sinister and storming vortex.

"Canada, for a start. A lot of our people are there. I can assure you, we won't come as either strangers or outcasts."

"Just pick up and go?" she asked.

"Tonight."

With an expression of bewilderment and disbelief she looked around the room, trying to assimilate the incredible idea that she was being asked to suddenly leave it, leave her home, her life. He's doing this deliberately, she thought. She had become simultaneously implicated and subjugated the moment he told her about the murder; she could feel the wretched weight of that information hanging over her like an iron pall.

"How much cash do you have on hand?" he asked.

"I have . . . enough."

"Where?"

"In the den."

"How much?"

"Enough . . . I don't know." Her mind was reeling. Suddenly, hysterically, she cried, "Why do I have to go? I don't want to go anywhere . . . I haven't done anything."

"You think not?" he said heatedly. "You think you can step in and out as you please. You're as much a part of that murder as anyone else. Jesus Christ, Charlotte, what kind of dream world do you live in? All your life you've been working to drive people toward certain goals, been steaming them up to go out and rip things apart. Don't you realize what you're committing yourself to when you do that? Do you have any conception of the minds you might be reaching, the kinds of energies you might be releasing? Do you think your responsibility ends somewhere along the line at your convenience? Or maybe you're just some sort of eccentric dilettante radical looking for kicks."

"That's not true, it's not fair. You keep accusing me of that."

"I want to know if you really believe in everything that you claim you do."

"Of course I do . . . it's just that I'm . . . confused."

"You can't avoid your responsibilities, whether you like it or not."

"I'm not trying to avoid anything," she said, shaking her head, feeling all the symptoms of crying without actually shedding any tears. "It's just that . . . it's happened so quickly." She felt intimidated by the urgency and desperation that was fairly throbbing out of him, by what he had done and by what he had brought with him into this house; she was unable to resist this hurricane of demands and decisions, unable to marshal her senses and find the rationale; it was all so tempestuously sudden and unexpected.

"God God God," she said in a voice burdened with emotion, "nothing has been right since that time."

"What time?" he asked.

"You know," she said, bowing her head, as if in shame or contrition.

"I don't know."

"When you pulled me out of the shower," she said, raising her voice for a moment, though not heatedly or resentfully, but as if this was the only way she could get these words spoken. Then, in a normal voice again, "Up until then everything was orderly and productive."

"Are you trying to tell me you didn't know what was going on, that you weren't enjoying it? What were you—some goddamned automaton, being programmed against your will?"

She moved her head sadly from side to side. "I don't know," she whispered.

He went to her and took her hands in his.

"This can be the most wonderful thing for us," he said. "We can work together, really work together as we never could here. You'll find excitement and opportunities that you never dreamed possible."

She nodded vacantly and in an ironic voice said, "Running away in the night."

"Every revolutionist worth his salt has run away in the night at one time or another."

She felt a pain and a helplessness that were on the verge of flushing tears from her. She withdrew her hands from him.

"I want to see Paul," she said.

"Why?" he asked warily.

"I'm not going anywhere without seeing Paul first."

"But you can't tell him about this. The fewer people who know the better."

"You told me," she said resentfully.

"I told you because you're part of it, you've always been part of it."

"I'm not leaving until I see Paul."

"He'll want to know why we're going and where."

"We don't have to tell him everything."

"It's late; he's probably asleep."

"He never sleeps."

He did not like the idea. He was afraid that if they went to Paul something might occur to change things. The situation at hand was so tenuous, so delicate and lethal, that the least external shadow or pressure could throw it off course. But he realized how resolved she was, and rather than be detained arguing the point, he yielded.

"All right," he said. "We'll go and come right back."

THIRTY-NINE

He continued to be nagged by misgivings as he walked with her the short distance to Paul's house. Walking around like this was extremely risky for him. She didn't seem to realize just how serious all of this was for him, how dangerous and uncertain. So many of the more somber episodes of life were for her merely theatrics, a vivid but heatless entertainment, with always a safe exit for her at the end. But not until the obligatory grand scene had been played. He knew, he supposed, in a vague disinterested way, why she wanted to see Paul—and all of that seemed now so intolerably trivial. This was a wanton waste of time—with such a pressure and intricacy of plans to be made and myriad of details looked to.

When they reached the lonely, stand-offish house, Frank said, "Look, only a few minutes now. Tell him and then let's get moving."

"Suppose he wants to come with us?" she asked.

"He won't," he said, trying to suppress his impatience.

"But if he does?"

"We'll see, we'll see," he said, taking her by the elbow and urging her toward the house.

They went onto the porch and Charlotte knocked several times on the door.

"He can come with us if he wants," she said, a petulant firmness in her voice.

"Yes, yes," he muttered. "We can all go climbing in Scotland."

"That's a horrible thing to say," she said in a whisper which sounded stormy for its suppressed anger. "Why do you say such horrible things?"

"Charlotte, there isn't much time."

Again she struck her fist on the door, insistently, as if offended by the lack of response.

"He doesn't seem to be home," Frank said.

"There are lights on."

"He often goes out and leaves them on."

"Sometimes he doesn't answer," she said, knocking again, her impatience beginning to turn to anxiety.

"Then leave him alone," he said.

"No," she said, hitting the door again as if striking blows at some antagonistic thing. "I've got to see him . . . I . . . I won't go till I've seen him." Then, impulsively, she tried the doorknob and as she turned it, much to her surprise, the door swung back. She gave Frank a puzzled look, then entered.

With the prudent, tentative hesitation of the uninvited, they went forward into the house. Lights were burning in all of the downstairs rooms. A yellow polo shirt lay on the living room floor and she picked it up and held it in her hand, draped over her fingers, staring at it momentarily as if upon some dreadful symbol. Then she looked up.

"Paul?" she asked, in a quiet, somewhat inhibited voice.

"He isn't home," Frank said.

"But the door was unlocked."

"He does that. It's not the first time."

"But where is he then?"

"I don't know . . . it doesn't matter. Come on, let's get out of here. We have a million things to do."

"I don't want to leave without seeing him," she said, not with resolve now but with the rueful softness of waning hope.

"You can call him in a few days."

"He doesn't have a telephone."

"Then send him a goddamn telegram," he said. It was getting to him now, this unreasonable, dangerous standing still: again she could not distinguish between the conflicting worlds of reality, where time clipped by with constant and remorseless precision, and fantasy, where time was forever malleable and unspent.

She looked forlornly at the polo shirt in her hand. She wanted to wait, did not want to leave without seeing him; but she was afraid to say it, she was suddenly terribly afraid, possessed by a congestion of fears and threats. For the first time in her life she found herself unable to say or do what she wanted.

"Come on," he said.

"Wait," she said.

He watched her go into the kitchen, and a moment later heard her gasp like a person being sick, and then scream his name. He raced along the corridor and wheeled into the kitchen just as the polo shirt was falling in mid-air from her hand to the floor. He came to an immediate, frozen halt, standing behind her, wincing as he stared over her shoulder to where Paul was sitting on the linoleum-covered floor, cater-cornered against the wall and the stove. He was wrapped in a khaki blanket, his bare legs folded under him, a wide, blank, starkly unknowing gazing in his eyes. Wrapped in his blanket, his hair disheveled, an overnight stubble on a face that was a mask of inarticulate helplessness, he looked like a man suffering wild weather in the wilderness. As he adjusted the blanket around him a flash of white thigh implied he was coldly naked under it.

"Frank," Charlotte whispered, "what is this?"

Moving her aside, Frank went slowly toward him. At his brother's advance Paul's eyes filled with pitiful entreaty and he began to tremble.

"What's the matter?" Frank asked gently, crouching before him. "Why are you sitting here like this?"

Paul drew back, pulling the blanket more securely around him, his eyes suddenly filling with a shining unfathomable fear as his head began shaking agitatedly from side to side.

"What's wrong, Paul?" Frank asked.

"He's sick," Charlotte said.

"Jesus Christ," Frank muttered.

Paul's pained, terrified gaze remained fixed, directed insistently at Frank, with somewhere deep in its profundity a soft, lost plea.

"Paul," Charlotte said.

"He can't hear you," Frank said. When he reached out to touch his brother, Paul recoiled, hunching his trembling shoulders under the blanket, lifting his head and pressing it back as far as it would go against the oven door, a posture which evidently made swallowing extremely difficult—he grimaced as a mouthful of saliva worked through his tautly pulling throat. Frank became acutely and painfully aware of the total mystification each had for the other at this moment. Paul was sitting there before him, and yet not, was brokenly adrift in the soul's deep regress, prey to the manic twists and lunges of a billion particles of ripped-up experiences and sea-swarms of clotted and chaotic memories; Frank's face was to him probably no more than a ship's light at the final surge of horizon. Only the faintest hint of intelligence and comprehension remained in Paul's face, and these recognizable only through the old conformations of lines and muscles, like some last reflex of pride; except for the eyes, of course, which were lost in abysmal child-terror, child-appeal. What Frank saw before him was not a complete surprise, however; whatever had finally worked its way into the machinery and seized control with the tidal fury that follows unheeded warnings, whatever had done this, had been casting its shade, pushing its signs and omens.

Frank had been studying his brother with such haunted candor that he suddenly felt self-conscious and was compelled to look away.

"We ought to call a doctor," he said.

"No," Charlotte said. "I'll take care of him."

"You?" Frank asked, turning around to look up at her.

"Yes . . . yes," she said, Paul's mute, terror-wracked face filling her with a sublime tenderness.

"How can you take care of him?" Frank asked, at once incredulous and resentful.

"Lift him up," she said. "Get him into bed."

"Charlotte—"

"We can't just leave him sitting there," she cried.

"I have no intention of leaving him sitting here," he said, angry and frustrated at his own irresolution.

"Put him in bed . . . in bed," she cried again.

Frank turned back to Paul, held fast in heart-riven despair, reluctant to touch his brother, whose catatonic immobility was punctuated now by a slight shuddering of the shoulders.

"Lift him up," Charlotte commanded. "If you don't, I will."

"Goddammit . . ." Frank said, and rose, then bent and lifted Paul in his arms. Paul did not resist, allowing himself to be gathered in his blanket and hauled up from the floor; but the terror in his eyes turned panicky for a moment as Frank wheeled with him, marched past Charlotte to the bedroom. Gently he lay Paul on the bed, withdrew the blanket from him and eased him under the covers.

"We've got to call somebody," Frank said. "A doctor, or an ambulance."

"I said I would take care of him," Charlotte said, moving past him to the bed. With her hand she tenderly brushed Paul's hair back from his forehead, then arranged his pillow more comfortably—while his face remained unalterably remote, his lips hanging softly open as if passing some wild, muted outcry.

"Charlotte," Frank said, "how the hell can you?"

"How can I not?" she said, turning savagely on him, her long hair whirling across her shoulders.

"But we can't stay. You know that."

"He'll die here if he's left alone."

"I have no intention of leaving him here alone. We'll get him to a hospital."

"No!" she cried. "I won't do that. He needs me."

"And what am I supposed to do?"

"For God's sake, Frank, this is your brother."

He glared murderously at her.

"You don't give a damn what happens to me, do you?" he asked. "You want me to stand still until they catch me, don't you?"

"Leave me alone," she said, turning back to Paul.

"*I can't stay here!*" he cried.

"Then go away," she said in a mild, indifferent voice.

"Charlotte—" he said, then saw she was not paying him the least attention. He was not just being ignored, he had been totally removed from the situation, insulted and abandoned. "You selfish son of a bitch," he said bitterly, then left the room and stalked from the house.

Peevishly, she looked around to where he had been standing, tossed a most perfunctory glance at the now empty spot, and then with an expression of compassion almost noble in its sublimity resumed her attention upon Paul. "Just rest now, darling," she said, smiling wanly. "There'll be no more distractions. I want you to rest, and not worry about anything. I know what you've gone through; I understand completely. I'm going to take care of you. Tomorrow you're coming to my house, and you're going to stay there. Everything's going to be different from now on. The world is going to come back together again for you . . . for both of us. Oh, God, I don't even know if he can hear me," she said,

her voice suddenly plaintive, studying his face, which was in absolute, impervious repose now, and even though his eyes were
fixed upon her she nevertheless had the distinct sense of being
unobserved. "But no matter," she said abstractedly, sitting on the
edge of the bed. She touched his face lightly with the tips of her
fingers—that mask of senselessness under her fingers as close to
tangible emotion as they would ever come. "I'll call a private
ambulance tomorrow and have you brought to my house. You'll
get well there, and no matter how long it takes I'll never leave you
for a moment. It'll be just the two of us, darling. You'll see how
right that is, how happy we'll be." She smiled sadly, as tears over-
ran her eyes and trailed slowly down her face. She withdrew her
hand from him to brush them away. "Shall I make you something
to drink? Will you drink tea if I bring it?" His eyes never left her
face, gazing up from his partially turned head, their incomprehensible mystery unchanging. It began to disconcert her and she
turned away.

She got up and went into the kitchen and opened several
cabinets. A coffee can was empty, there was no tea, no milk. She
found some orange juice in the refrigerator and filled a cup with
it and returned to him. She found him asleep, or at least with his
eyes closed, his head to one side. When she spoke his name there
was no response; his eyes remained shut, his breathing deep, slow,
exhausted, almost like sighs. She put the juice down and watched
him for several minutes. He would most likely sleep through the
night, be all right until morning.

She began to think ahead. Already in her mind she knew which
room he would occupy—upstairs, across from her bedroom—and
which would be his study. She would redecorate both, with soft
colors and contemporary furniture for his bedroom, and a lot of
wood and leather, with warm colors, for the study—she believed this appropriate for a writer's workroom—with perhaps a
selection of eighteenth-century English landscapes for the walls, or
perhaps woodcuts might better complement the desired ambience, something that would reflect his own quiet gentility. She
would provide him with whatever he needed, even soundproof
the study, if he needed that kind of privacy. And he would have
complete freedom—that would be most emphatically impressed
upon him, that he need not feel the least constrained or obli-

gated. All she wanted was to have him near and have him content
—that was all she wanted and all she had ever wanted and never
stopped hoping for, through the slack and loveless years of her
own marriage and her silent partnership in his, and this was why
she had accepted (and perhaps even encouraged) the deterioration of her marriage with equanimity and the tragic termination
of his with a cold and selfish detachment. It was as if the separate
journeys of convergent couples were destined always to be complex and mysterious, as if an ardently desired conjunction must
first be put to severe testing; this was almost akin to the laws of
commerce, whereby nothing precious was obtainable without
great cost and labor and of course journey, be that journey one
of time or distance. Her joy at this new state of affairs was so
transcending that it virtually obliterated any speculation about
what might have been responsible for it—what tragedy or despair
or emotional breakage had suddenly become so tumultuous or
subjugating to have reduced him to so shattered and helpless a
state of dependence—for no matter what it was it had drawn
them together, made them shareholders now in one another's
lives, and nothing else could be nearly as important as that.

She went into the living room and paused there, looking about
with narrowed, almost possessive eyes. There was a veiled, secretive atmosphere here. She felt it most palpably when she studied
his desk, where several pages of manuscript lay, a pencil lying
alongside like a fallen sentinel. For just an instant she had a feeling of deepest disquiet and alienation, as if there were eyes in
this room too preoccupied to take notice of her. She felt a
morbidity here, a residue of old unrelinquishing passion. This was
no place for him to be, no place for an artist to work. He would
be much better off—any sensitive creative person would—in
bright, comfortable, congenial surroundings, with nothing to
worry about except the task at hand. The room's terrific silence
began to unnerve her—it was as if the very air had been drained
and stilled by the obsessively seeking artist alone here night after
night with his inward bells and thunder. She went to the desk and
looked incuriously at the topmost page of manuscript. That was
strange, she thought idly: Since when was he writing poetry? But
that of course was his concern and his alone. He could write whatever he wanted, as long as he did it under her roof. And again her

imagination became enraptured by this so perfect turn of affairs, and she smiled for a moment, transported, nurturing the thought of Paul there with her, mornings and afternoons and nights (he could sleep with her if he wanted, and if he didn't, then that was all right too), in the garden again in the sunshine, as when they were children and the world had no thorns, a serene and onward togetherness of smiles and tranquility, a lovely and unflawed binding of heart and soul, with no clamor or tension, with nothing sordid or abrupt: simply two people reaping the sweet harvest of long pursuit.

She returned to the bedroom for a parting look. He was still asleep, breathing easier, but frowning now, as though this sleep was tense and baffling. And then for several moments she gazed upon him with great curiosity, for the first time wondering what had happened, what shock or fear or memory had so run amok inside his head, and undone his knot of reason. She soon dismissed these speculations, however, and quietly went out, leaving the lights on, lest he waken in darkness.

It wasn't until she was outside that her fright returned, with knife-stroke suddenness, startling her. Where was Frank? What had happened to him? Where had he gone? All of the night lay around her, immensely silent, its cover penetrated by the scattering of street lights, which made it the more sinister. Her so recent feelings of tenderness and excitement receded now before the swift onrush of fear. She walked through the empty streets with deep, uncertain mistrust, as if every shadow were treacherously possessed, tensely anticipating Frank's appearance from behind a tree or hedge, or him simply to materialize before her eyes as though he had been disembodied into so many floating atoms. Her long blonde hair fell forward over one shoulder and she brought her hand up and unconsciously clutched and held onto a fistful of lank strands. Despite the fear which had come with that knife-stroke suddenness and was permeating her now like high temperature, she was walking slowly, as if to demonstrate her innocence, her amity. She was so certain that he was somewhere about that his name was all but uttered upon her lips. Once she stopped and listened for him, sensing his nearness—the silence was too full, too pressing. She was momentarily diverted by the sight of a ring of keys lying in the street, its small, strange presence glittering in the street light. For several moments her eyes remained fascinatedly upon the several keys that lay spread one from the other. Then she looked ahead once more to the night and began walking again, hurrying now, still clutching her hair.

Grudgingly, she allowed that she might have been somewhat tactless, swerving her attention from him too abruptly. But he should have understood that—after all, he was not a stranger. Couldn't he see that her whole life had just changed? And then she realized that was exactly what he had seen, why he had stalked out, with his seething baggage of problems. Bitterly she damned him for having put such terrible information into her possession. She was a passive, accidental, unwilling participant in all of this, her only involvement being that she knew what he had done. If only by some miracle he would disappear, be swallowed by this soundless and gargantuan night and never seen again—for now he was the looming threat to the perfect, idyllic happiness she had been conjuring. So intense was her frustration at the idea of this ironic, unresolved threat that she came near to tears. With his mad, irresponsible schemes and behavior he had been nothing but trouble since his return. And now he had been metastasized into a murderer. The incomprehensibility of that still overwhelmed her. It was all so unfair, so unreal. If not for Paul she would never have known him, never been his friend—didn't he understand that? Her friendship had been with Paul, not with him, never with him. He presumed, he always presumed, so much and so wrongly; always wanting, demanding from her. She had even impetuously— under his badgering and importuning and insane scene-painting —agreed to his maddest idea of all—running away together. She must have been momentarily unbalanced, by pity, fear, anxiety. He would drag her down with him. His levels of existence were defined by wildness, failure, wantonness—and, now, murder. He had taken advantage of her, preyed upon her, seduced her into a most sordid and unnatural (and unwanted) relationship; exploiting her weaknesses, ignoring or mocking her strengths, her ideals. She had sunk to disgusting depths, achieving nothing, neglecting everything she believed in and had so long been working for. How had she ever allowed it? I felt sorry for him, she thought. Yes, that's what it was. And in feeling sorry forgot how reckless and destructive he was, had always been. *Oh, damn you, Frank, go away!* All it had taken was that one slip, that one lowering of her guard, and complete moral derangement had followed. From now on she would renounce that kind of self-indulgence. There were other things. She would return to her work, her sustaining ideals. And now there was Paul to care for. Perhaps Frank would leave her alone when he saw how devoted she was to his brother's welfare. She would offer him money, anything he wanted, if only he would go away and never come back. Because if he was reckless and unpredictable before, now it could only be worse, because now he was a fugitive, a murderer, with caution and prudence draining out of him by the moment. What was that remark about climbing in Scotland? What did he mean by that? What sort of menacing turns was his mind taking?

The first thing she did upon entering her house was to call his name. Her voice resounded into the empty house, and she found the unanswering silence ominous, mistrustful. She wandered about the house, again with that dread expectancy she had experienced outside in the dark of having him abruptly, threateningly appear. "Frank, where are you?" she asked aloud, moving from room to room, wanting him to be there now, to end the tension, break the spell; it was as if she sensed him there watching her, somewhere nearby, pitiless and sardonic. Wherever he had gone, she knew, it would not be far from this house. It could not be. As though sharing kindred sensibilities, she could feel his furious desperation, his entrapment in the night, his paltry and infuriating account of choices. And then she thought: he's doing this deliberately, deliberately taunting and frightening me; he's taking advantage again.—Again he was being presumptive and supremely self-assured, so certain he could boldly return and get from her anything he wanted. "*No you can't!*" she suddenly shrieked to the empty house, tears of rage starting to her eyes. In swift blurring seizures her resentment built to anger and then fury. "*Leave me alone!*" she shrieked again to the mute, sound-deadening house. It was too late for him, too late here, too late everywhere. He would interfere no longer. She had what she wanted now, and this meant that all else must be locked out.

She closed the downstairs light and went upstairs to her bedroom. She sat on her bed, spent, exhausted. Yes, she thought wearily, he's gone away. He'll never be back. He has too much to be frightened of, and there's nothing here for him. He knows that. He'll leave me alone. Of course. He must. After all, I know what he did. I have that over him.—The logic of this was like a tonic, it came lucidly out of the furies and made perfect sense. She had the advantage now and he was wise enough to know it. This was the last place he would want to come, she the last person he would want to see.

She lay down in the darkness with all her clothes on, fatigued by a long night of emotional turmoil. There was so much to think about, prepare for. She felt at once in the middle, the beginning and at the end of something. Unwilling, or unable, to contemplate the conflicts any longer, her thoughts began to assume a diminishing cogency. She closed her eyes for a few moments, then reopened them as they filled with a staring philosophical sadness. She gazed listlessly for several moments at the antic red glare on the wall, and then suddenly sat bolt upright, watching the pulsing light with transfixed and terrible fright, as though it were a looming premonition. Then she swung her legs to the floor and ran to the window.

"Oh, my God," she said, as she looked down at the bright red fire burning lustily in the garden.

FORTY

As he hurried from his brother's house Frank was appalled and horrified by what he had seen, unable to conceive what final thrust or impetus could have done this, knowing only that a host of enigmatic and threatening auras had long been hovering over Paul. *She has him now,* he thought bitterly of Charlotte, *has him the way she always wanted: helpless and dependent.* This finally achieved, she no longer had thought for Frank and his venomous predicament—that much he realized. She would now repudiate all that had occurred between them, and not only that, but doubtless repudiate too everything he had done in the name of the Movement, which she had always professed to be her life's interest and banner cry of her soul. The thought of that woman evanescing before his eyes was like an entrapped lightning bolt bounding against the walls of his head; it was suddenly as if he had done and risked everything for her, and now betrayal and ingratitude were balefully among the chaotic noises of his mind. And then again his heart was riven by the madhouse image of his brother; still he thought: *He'll realize that I had good reason for not staying. He'll understand.* And then he thought: *I'll have to worry about him later,* as with a sudden, irascible wrench of mind everything except his most overriding concerns took possession of him, like the precipitous influx of some furious coherence. He had the unnerving sensation of a situation moving with barbaric velocity toward its self-determining conclusion, propelled out of all control; the idea of something decisive and irreversible becoming more and more imminent was terrifying and he was driven by a kind of panic he had never known before.

He rushed through the empty streets, as yet without direction, without purpose, knowing only that he was utterly alone, the plaything of some gigantic inevitability which would not be deterred,

which was poised like some calculating feline to leap in his path
at its own chosen moment. The streets and houses of his boyhood
seemed dreadfully hostile and unfamiliar as he felt more and more
the wayward and abandoned victim, for the moment almost self-
righteously so, as though all of this were some monumental injustice. And this, too, built into his panic: it made no difference
which corner he turned, which street he chose—all of the night
was paved against him, in deadly silence, like an unholy sabbath.
There was nowhere left for him to go—no door, no room, no person; there was only himself, in menaced isolation, at once caught
and pursued, his every breath rippling the spider's web. He pulled
his key ring from his pocket and glared at it as upon a symbol of
his hopelessness: each key was for a door now forever closed
to him, for a place he could enter only at great risk. Cursing, he
hurled them pinging into the street. Then he stared off into the
night. How long was it since he left his brother's house? Five minutes? Ten? An hour? He had no idea, had absolutely no time
reference. He wondered, oddly, if that made him more, or less,
secure, since things good and bad could happen only in a time
structure. And then, as if to mock his disorientation, he heard
the soft rattle of an alarm clock coming from one of the darkened,
nearby houses. Perplexedly he gazed around, and as abruptly as
it had begun, the sound like ribald mirthless laughter ceased. He
looked up and the treetops seemed bending, though there was
no wind; and beyond that the watchful stars were in recession
from him, fading into night's drapery. And he had the pure,
cool, astonishingly serene thought that he was losing his mind,
that there could be no other explanation for the untroubled peace
of the night; he had the sickly sweet anticipation of unexpected
salvation, a surprise gift from out of perishing hope. He waited,
almost piously conscious of the content of his mind, waited for
some gentle release; and even as he waited he felt that cool Elysian
glade being once more darkly encroached, the eluvium rising and
reshaping itself, less with chaos this time and more with pressure.
He began walking again.

He stepped into the tavern not because he wanted a drink, not
because he wanted or needed companionship, but simply because
it was a place to enter, a thing to do; it was a sane, rational act,
a respite from the night and all its suggestive and malevolent

incursions. His face had a flat, fierce expression as he walked into
the crowded tavern. He went up to the bar, laid a dollar bill upon
its scarred and unpolished surface and ordered straight whisky,
then stood with his narrowed, mesmerized gaze fixed upon the
bar top, his lips sucked back into a grim line. He glanced up and
was surprised to discover himself in the back-bar mirror. He resented what he saw, as if suddenly confronting the stranger responsible for the convulsions in his life; studying the damnable
reflection and wishing he could detach from it, leave it frozen in
the glass and never have to see or hear about it again. With a look
of dumb, chastened pride he studied himself until the bartender
blocked the reflection and served the drink. Frank raised the shot
glass to his lips and drained it with a single swallow, then put the
solid-bottomed glass back down on the bar with a sharp knock.
Someone fed money into the jukebox and music poured forth,
gay and satirical to his ears, an incongruous flood of jarring sounds,
reinforcing more firmly his sense of isolation. He flattened his big
hands on the bar and leaned forward, his bowed face brooding. All
right, he told himself, as fragments of thought groped connectively: What now? Not much time. Think. There had to be paths
and exits, no matter the weight and size of the dilemma, the crisis:
the frailty of prayer, the coldness of confession, the sumptuous
emptiness of suicide, the grimness of hiding, the desperation of
flight. It was up to him to make something happen, wrest something from the arsenal of the fates and not leave anything to
chance . . . because there had never been anything like this before . . . a man lying dead in a hotel room with a knife hanging
from his body. He wondered how long before Kifner would be
found. He had that much time anyway . . . except that Kifner
might already have been found, and that room at this moment
crowded with policemen and photographers and newspapermen,
going through their obligatory ritualistic preliminaries before
spreading into the night to track him down. Seavery that son of
a bitch mole would burrow in somewhere and grow a beard or
shave a beard and emerge another persona, unafraid, unknown,
moving forth with that remorseless impunity which had enabled
him to plan murder in the first place. *I had no business being part
of it*. He shut his eyes for a moment and viciously expelled the
breath he had been holding. He opened his eyes and stared sul-

lenly at that pitiable mocker and derider in the mirror, then shifted
his eyes to the other reflections, to the detached and animated
people of the other world, the populated world of banal and unthreatened occurrences. He recognized most of the faces: small-
time neighborhood drinkers, secure and isolated in a world of pay
checks and Saturday nights. Goddamn bastards, he thought; clois-
tered and protected by their very banality, dimmed by prudent
and colorless life styles; not one of them would understand.

The music stopped and there was a gust of masculine laughter
as voices rose in noisy competition. He heard the steady pattern
of clicks from the shuffleboard table on the other side of the bar.
Again his lips rolled inward to shape a grim line of rancorous
despair. "Frank?" He looked up at the sound of his name. The
bartender was pointing toward the empty glass. Frank shook his
head and looked down again, still braced against the bar, feeling
the raging impotence in his muscles.

"How's your Commie girl friend, Frankie?"

He looked up, then turned around. Ed Slater was slouched at
a table midway across the tavern, long legs stretched before him,
staring dully, not smirking, a sullenly offended look in his face.
Two of his brothers sat with him, each with an inquiring gaze
for Frank. Frank turned back to the bar, his anger provoked not
by Slater's crudeness but by the unwanted invocation of Charlotte.
He had successfully driven her from his thoughts for several minutes; she was the last person he wanted to think about. And now
she was back, swarming through his head in an infuriating mon-
tage. *I don't want to think about her. I don't,* as if talking to some
whirling and autonomous source inside his head.

"Don't mind him, Frank. He's been at it all night."

The old man had moved up to the bar next to him. It was Pat
Slater, the patriarch of the clan, who had come to Capstone over
sixty years ago and achieved a terrific and prodigious spawning
which had produced thirteen children and, so far, more than fifty
grandchildren, with yet another generation beginning to copu-
late in beds and back alleys through the neighborhood; a
sprawling clan of drinkers and brawlers, all of whom still resided
in Capstone or close enough to be so counted, omnipresent in
bars, on street corners, in factories, behind the wheels of trucks;
glowering overseers of a community where they received the great-

est deference and respect. The patriarch was a small proud man
of dignified bearing despite a tough old face that looked as though
it had been twisted by strong fingers. He was wearing a short-
sleeved white shirt and had a cloth cap sitting on his white hair.
He had small blue eyes with a glint like mica, a broken nose with
a blue scar across the bridge, and a firm mouth with slightly extended underlip which seemed the seat of his pride, his dignity.

"Can I buy you a drink, Frank?" the old man said in a soft,
conciliatory voice.

"No," Frank said.

"My condolences for your father," Pat Slater said rather formally. "He was a friend for a good many years. I'm sorry he's
gone."

"Thank you," Frank muttered.

"He was a strange man," Pat Slater said wistfully, almost as if
to himself. "You're sure you won't have a drink?"

"Positive," Frank said. He was barely listening to the old man,
still braced forward against the bar, expelling his breaths through
his nose with terse audible noises.

"He was a very strong man," Pat Slater said. "Very powerful."

"And he killed himself," Frank said, leaving the irony for the
old man to work on.

"Frankie," Ed Slater called from behind, "you're too good for
that Commie bitch."

Frank turned his head several degrees, his eyes coming to rest
upon the twin blue glints in the old man's face. Pat Slater was
studying him now with a mild half smile, a curiously pleasant
disclaimer.

"I'm in no mood, Pat," Frank said quietly.

The old man nodded. "What you're saying actually," he said,
"is that you're very much in the mood. That's your point, isn't
it?"

Frank had to grin wryly. If there was one thing this old man
understood, it was violence, its sound, its odor, its glance.

"You don't have to pay him any heed, Frank."

"That's right," Frank said, feeling it building irresistibly through
his back and shoulders and arms and hands, to the very tips of his
fingers, a wanton surging force.

"He might not know you're in mourning."

"That's right," Frank said. He turned around and faced Ed Slater, who remained sitting in arrogant comfort, long legs extended, a stein of beer in his hand, which he raised in mock toast to Frank and then drank from, while his brothers smiled. The two, Frank and Slater, contemplated each other for a moment, and then Slater, without moving his eyes from Frank, put the stein down on the table.

When Frank moved away from the bar toward him Slater rose, his long legs sweeping in and lifting his tall, brawler's frame erect. He was a head taller than Frank, with long muscular arms hanging with limber menace from strong sloping shoulders. Frank knew how to fight a Slater—with a minimum of motion and maximum of muscle. His first blow, a left hook, caught Slater high on the cheek, knocking him several steps back against the table. The bartender shouted something and several astonished cries went up from the crowd as Slater, shaking away a look of surprise, came moving forward, fists raised now to high exacting familiar levels, an expression of utmost seriousness in his face. He swung out and with his superior reach his blow traveled over Frank's raised fist and landed with jarring force on the chin. *Boxing lessons from the old man in the back yard how many years ago Paul sitting on the grass watching with sour disapproval the old man dead now strong as an ox don't be afraid of getting hit Frank otherwise you'll always get hit.* Frank covered up and took the next punch on his shoulder, smelling Slater's panting beer-stained breath, saw the mean depths of Slater's flat soft-green eyes, then pressed forward and hooked into his midsection, took in return a barreling fist into his own middle which made him gasp. They locked for a moment in an awkward wrestle, each struggling to maintain his balance, Frank's fingers locked around one of Slater's humped-up biceps that felt like a living squirming thing in his grip.

Frank heard the old man yell "Sit down!" and knew this was for the two brothers, maybe for some cousins or uncles too; God knew how many of them were in the place, their mean green eyes lusting like fanatical voyeurs; but he wasn't grateful for the old man's sense of equity, because his fury had suddenly erupted over every restraint and he would have relished swinging out at that moment at a dozen different faces, including the old man's, knock-

ing that proud underlip back into his head, and maybe he would
too before this night was done.

He became aware of wild delusions, of incomprehensibly stimulating sensations—he was fighting free of every trap and hin-
drance—absorbing the incoming blows as though they were a
raucous pummeling from benevolent gods who were showing him
the way free. He kept his eyes riveted to Slater's intent and scrutinous face, advancing toward it and trying to break it as though it
were the last barrier to freedom. Now a somewhat baffled look entered Slater's eyes as he began to realize he was fighting something
more than he had bargained for, something he did not understand,
something that was coming at him as out of some ancient blood
feud instead of merely reacting to Saturday night banter. Frank
heard someone saying, "Why are they fighting? What happened?"
And then Slater, a closed and ignorant man, began responding
with blind anger to that which he did not understand and began
swinging harder, trying to stop the forward charge of his single-
minded antagonist. But he walked into an arcing left hook that
landed on his mouth and sent jets of blood spurting, and answered
with a bruising right hand to the side of Frank's head. Then they
weighed forward and stood head to head for a moment, each giving and taking a battering more ferocious than normally they
might have, each raising the fury of the other, and a barroom
brawl that would ordinarily have been stopped by this time now
held the onlookers enthralled as they watched Frank Dublin ex-
pending a rage that had no comprehensible source and Ed Slater
resisting it with the determined bitterness of a man who felt that
he had been somehow lured and trapped.

Slater moved around Frank, fists raised, tongue fixed between
teeth. Frank circled with him, the onlookers alternately moving
back and pressing forward as the two men defined and redefined
the area of combat. Slater lunged forward with a sweeping left
hand that Frank ducked under, but his retaliating right was short.
Slater's right fist came shooting in and bounced off of Frank's
chin; Frank staggered, felt his knees flexing. Son of a bitch, he
said to himself, as if realizing for the first time what was happening. As Slater came at him again Frank resisted the temptation
to charge and throw indiscriminately, but backed up, feeling the
rage bristling on the rims of his clenched fists, feeling the incred-

ible power there not merely to knock this man aside but to fight free of all trouble, past and present, the power to explode the mean and plotting forces of the night, the maliciously aligned fates.

Slater threw a left hook which connected on Frank's jaw, but instead of falling back Frank moved in and threw his own left, which Slater partially blocked, but then followed with a right hand thrown from inside, bringing it up to the point of Slater's chin, penalizing that experienced brawler for the amateurish habit of locking his tongue between his teeth, the blow forcing Slater to bite sharply and piercingly into his tongue. The impact of the blow and the sudden pain caused Slater to throw his head aside for a moment, his hair spilling brokenly across his face, and Frank put all his weight behind a terrific and pitiless left hook which exploded against Slater's face, knocking him off balance with jolting suddenness, sending him crashing backward into the round table where moments before he had been sitting with snide remarks on his lips. He went sprawling awkwardly across the rim of the table, which began tipping forward under his weight as his fists flew into startled fingers and big-handled steins went tumbling floorward with cascades of splattering beer. A moment later he dropped slackly to the floor, carrying the table with him, landing on hands and knees, dazed but not unconscious, his hair hanging over his eyes.

There was a moment of charged and expectant silence as Pat Slater advanced in a half crouch upon his son, the expression in his face at once curious and melancholy. Gently he tipped his son's head up by the chin, looked into the bleared and unfocusing eyes, then turned not to Frank but the others.

"That's enough," he said quietly.

Frank ran the back of his hand across his mouth. He was panting, glaring at the two brothers, who were watching him with contemplating uncertainty, still sitting in their chairs around the upended table and their fallen brother. He was anticipating their move, not that he expected it but that he had a perverse sense of wanting them to come at him. But they did nothing, remained sitting in gestures of arrested animation.

"Do y'want whisky?" Pat Slater asked his beaten son.

"Huh?" Ed said with a dumb, dazed grunt.

Without a word Frank suddenly walked out, already beginning to forget an episode which for those who had witnessed it would in the context of their lives assume quasi-mythic proportions; walked out and left behind him the crowd of still stunned spectators standing in the smoky light of their tavern, gazing with inarticulate awe upon the battered man and the upended table and the spilled beer, for them an event to be long remembered in its vividness and its enormity, while its chief architect and craftsman was already off into the night and halfway toward forgetting it had ever happened.

Now he was moving decisively; it was as if Slater's blows, or maybe the unbridling of his own fury, or combination of both, had cleared and demystified his thinking. Buoyed, exhilarated, decisive (again, not from the triumph, which every non-Slater in Capstone would have envied but which to him was not any kind of triumph, personal or otherwise, had simply been a clearing of his tangled path), he hurried through the night, ignoring the murmurous aches of head and rib where he had been pounded.

He went to Grant Avenue, passed the square and its modest granite remembrance to the dead of 1917–18, and continued on past the closed stores, walking faster now, a solitary figure on the quiet streets. Then he opened the street door to one of the connected four-story buildings fronting on the avenue, which were the closest Capstone came to apartment houses, and raced up the linoleum-covered stairs two at a time. When he reached the first landing he went hurriedly forward and pounded loudly on one of the doors, then withdrew his fist, staring puzzledly for a moment at the cuts and nicks across the back of his knuckles as if he did not understand how they had got there.

The door opened slowly and his sister appeared before him with a face at once so melancholy and lifeless it implied some profound and hopeless loss of self-contact and awareness. She appeared strangely unalarmed by pounding on her door at this hour of the night, dully uninterested in whom it might be, what it might mean, conveying a lassitude which neither the suddenness of abundant providence nor savage threat could have dispelled. Her hair was uncombed, the lines in her face deepened by the hallway shadows, her eyes soft with the muteness of a stilled heart. When she spoke it was in a faint, dispirited voice, her lips barely moving.

"What do you want, Frankie?"

"I want to know where it is," he said, his voice blunt, his mind so obsessively unidirectional he presumed instant understanding.

"Where what is?" Helen asked listlessly.

He entered the apartment, looking around with nervous agitation, as if what he was after would come immediately to view. She closed the door very slowly, then turned and followed him into the kitchen, the only lighted room in the quiet apartment.

"It occurs to me that it's here," he said. "She's back, isn't she? Then it's got to be here. This is the only place it can be, and I want it . . . right now. You have no idea how urgent this is . . . how important."

She walked past him to the stove where a pot of water was beginning to boil. She turned the gas higher, so that the blue flame reached up and around from underneath and embraced the bottom of the pot.

"What are you talking about?" she asked in a voice so drained and empty it seemed detached from brain, heart, effort, like a dumb, obligatory recitation.

His eyes darted around the kitchen, hoping to find what he was after without any further waste of time, to simply pick it up and get out.

"That money," he said. "The old man gave it to Lorana just before he killed himself. I know he did. He all but said it."

Not even that raised a show of interest. She stared with narrow, soulfully meditating eyes into the boiling water, watching the tiny bubbles beginning to blister the surface.

"Well?" Frank asked.

"I don't know," she said.

"What?" he demanded. "What don't you know? Tell me, dammit," he said, his voice rising.

Her mouth twitched, then she grimaced, as if some corner of her dulled and lethargic brain was making an effort to communicate. She ran her hand over her eyes for a moment.

"He gave Lorana money?" she asked, looking at him, the vexation of struggling with her recalcitrant brain bringing an almost pained expression to her face. "What money?"

"The money he stole all those years ago," Frank said impa-

tiently. "What the hell is the matter with you? Are you drunk or
something? Don't you see this is important . . . that I've got to
have it?" The conviction that the money was close at hand now,
and yet not in his possession, was near to driving him wild.

She left the stove and sat down at the table. She placed one
elbow up on the table, opened her hand and buried her face in
it. He watched her with excruciating, nerve-straining expectancy,
as if waiting for some word, some disclosure. But after several
seconds he realized that neither he nor his problem were anywhere in her thoughts, that she had simply sat down and ceased
to consider him. In furious exasperation he lifted the table at his
end, raised it several inches off the floor and then banged it down
with such force that she looked up, startled, for the first time a
flash of recognition passing through her eyes.

"What are you doing, Frank? What do you want?"

"Helen," he said, mustering all the self-control he could, "I'm
pleading with you."

"Frankie, what is it? What do you want?"

Suddenly he ran to the stove and lifted the pot of boiling water
by the handle and held it away from the flames.

"I'll put this on your head if you don't tell me," he said angrily.

Puzzled, amazed, she looked at his face, then at the pot of smoking water, then back to his face.

"Frankie, please tell me what it is you want."

"My God, how stupid are you?" he cried, trembling so with
rage that the water was shaking in the pot. "At long last, how
stupid and thick-headed are you?"

"Frankie . . ."

"That goddamned money," he said, making an effort to sound
sane, rational, lowering the pot of boiling water back upon the
flaming jets. "Where is it?"

"I don't know anything about it," she said tearfully.

"It's in this house. He gave it to her."

"Who . . . who? Who are you talking about?"

"Where is Lorana?"

"Asleep. They're all asleep. Keep your voice down, you'll wake
them up. Frankie, are you drunk? I'm making coffee . . ."

"She has it!" he cried, pounding the table with his fist so that a salt shaker jumped over and lay on its side. "He gave it to her . . . I was there . . . I saw it."

She gazed at him in utter astonishment, still not quite sure what he was saying, but frightened now, knowing only that she had been jarred from her depths, from her secret morbid anguish by something frightening and urgent that was beyond her understanding. Again he struck the table—"*Tell me!*"—the big fist coming down like a mallet, the impact rolling the salt shaker across the table top in a wide sweeping arc.

"You'll wake them up," she whispered.

"Wake them up?" he said. "You bet your ass I'll wake them up. I'll throw them all out of the window if I have to."

She closed her eyes for a moment and moved her head slowly from side to side. "There's no money here," she said, and then she said, in a strange, remote voice, "There's nothing here. If I don't die tomorrow, then I pray God makes me mad."

About to shout something, feeling the first rigid tremors of absolute, uncontrollable rage, he heard a sound behind him and whirled around. Lorana had emerged from the darkness of the inner rooms, in her pajamas, her eyes squinting querulously in the light, a red mark on her cheek from where her hand had been pressed in sleep.

"It isn't here," she said in a voice whose strength and clarity belied her appearance.

"What did you do with it?" he demanded. "Where is it?"

Her eyes shifted sharply to her mother for a moment, saw the inexpressible wail and lostness of that face, then fixed her uncle again.

"I don't have it," she said.

"Then who does? What did you do with it?"

With faltering courage she continued gazing into her uncle's eyes, her lips parted. She took a deep breath, held it, as if trying to contain with it the situation which she realized moment by moment was expanding beyond her despairing hope of persevering, then slowly, fatally, fully, released the breath.

"He gave it to me," she said.

"I know he did. He had no right to. He didn't know what he was doing. He was out of his mind. Don't you understand that?"

"No he wasn't," she said with sudden strength, her eyes filling with tears that glistened in the kitchen light.

"Where is it?" Frank asked.

"I gave it to my father."

"Your father?" Frank asked, his voice suddenly softening with incredulity. "Jesus Christ," he muttered, turning to look at Helen for a moment. "She gave it to . . ." Then he turned back to Lorana. "What did he do with it? Where did he put it?"

"I don't know. He didn't even know what it was . . ."

"You didn't tell him?"

"No."

"You simply handed him a fortune and ran away?"

"He needed it, he needed the money to help us . . . all of us."

"But what did he do with it?"

"He put it in his coat pocket," the girl said in slow, quiet, inflectionless tones, seeing the scene again before her eyes, handing the envelope to Philip, watching him put it in his coat pocket without thought or question as to what it might be; the scene frozen before her even as her eyes remained set resentfully upon her uncle's face. "He said he didn't have time . . . that he had to go somewhere."

"Where was he going?"

"I didn't know," she suddenly cried. "I didn't know what he was going to do."

"Don't tell me this was just before he set fire to himself?"

The girl said nothing, her answer inherent in her silence. Frank half turned, raising a clenched fist to his mouth and gnawing thoughtfully at one of his bruised knuckles. He felt now at the point of terminal despair; everything seemed shattering into a snickering insanity, a deranged archangel's diabolic joke. He studied the thin puffs of steam rising and evaporating from the boiling water, then looked at his sister's utterly vacant, self-consoling face.

"Helen," he said, bringing his hand down. "Philip's belongings . . . at the hospital . . . what did they give you? Did they give you the coat?"

"I don't know," she said listlessly.

"What do you mean you don't know? Jesus Christ, isn't anybody here going to help me?"

"The coat wasn't among his things," Lorana said. "I took notice."

"You took notice did you?" Frank said sarcastically, turning back to her.

"So much was burned," she said idly, wonderingly.

"You didn't ask about the coat?"

"I was worried only about my father, not some lousy money," she said, bitterly resentful, the tears shining on her lower lids for a moment, then coursing down her face. "I don't *care* about the money!"

"So where is the goddamned coat?" he asked.

"I don't know."

"It wasn't at the hospital?"

"I . . . don't think so."

"And you're sure it isn't here in the house?"

"If it were I would give it to you," she said contemptuously.

He looked into space for a moment. "Then it must still be at the union hall," he said aloud but to himself. "That's it. It's got to be there. He probably took it off before he . . . or maybe somebody got it off of him and threw it aside . . . that's logical . . . that makes sense, doesn't it?"

"Or maybe it burned in a heap," Lorana said spitefully.

"I don't think so," Frank said, again aloud but for himself. "It's still there. In all the excitement it was left behind. Nobody would have paid attention to his coat. That's what happened. Otherwise . . . somebody would have turned it in."

"You think so," Lorana said cynically.

"I'm going there," Frank said, moving toward the door, obsessed, unself-conscious. "That's where it is."

"The place is probably closed," the girl said. "How will you get in?"

"How will I get in?" he asked, and, as if to dispel any doubts about that question, gave a weary, sardonic laugh. Then he left.

FORTY-ONE

The union hall was a mile away and as he hurried there he had a lusty sense of excitement and anticipation. There was little hope of finding a taxi at that hour and the buses were so irregular that he had to walk, but he did not mind at all; in fact his conviction that the money was in the hall and that he would retrieve it was so powerful he almost needed this feverish expenditure of energy to give release to the excitement he could now barely contain, and he walked the distance in less than fifteen minutes.

The sight of the union hall in the darkness, the night, stirred his blood, as if it were a citadel to be stormed. The three-storied, unimaginatively architected building, standing on a quiet residential street just off of Queens Boulevard, seemed almost sinisterly replete with temptations and promises. Not until he was actually approaching the building did some very practical considerations occur to him: How would he get inside? How would he go about finding what he believed was there? But even these hard, demanding realities were almost immediately pacified by his believer's exuberance, by the absolute merit of his quest, and he felt as if every stride taken toward this building had created a momentum at his back which would prove irresistible.

A light was burning on the first floor of the building, a sort of faint, steady claim against the dark. Frank ran up the concrete steps and pulled at the chrome bar-shaped handle of the plate-glass door and was not surprised to find it locked. He pressed in close to the door and peered inside at the emptiness of the lobby and corridor, his excitedly expelled breaths clouding and fading on the glass; the light was coming from another corridor which ran perpendicular to the one he was looking at. Again he tugged at the chrome bar, with grim and obstinate resolve. Then he raised a clenched fist and pounded on the glass. There would

be a watchman, he was positive: after all, this was a union building, and one more job was one more job. He pounded on the
glass again, harder this time, knowing that in another moment
he was going to have to resist the impulse to put his fist through
it, and the last thing he wanted to do was make a commotion and
draw attention to himself. He stepped back, his frustration growing, fed by the sight of that light in the corridor, like an alluring invitation, a beckoning lover just beyond reach. A night watchman
in a union hall was surely asleep on the job—this went through
his mind with an irascible certainty, though he didn't know why it
should be so or why he should be so sure of it.

He took a coin from his pocket and with it began a sharp tapping on the glass. The keen, testy noises sounded inordinately
loud on the nighttime stillness. Then a man appeared inside,
wheeling around the corner from out of the lighted corridor, and
Frank's lips pressed into a tight, terse smirk of vindication: the
man was just buckling his trousers as he hurried forward in a burst
of busy quirky movements, making a poor job of stuffing in his
shirt: a man tossed and churned by the unexpected. He carried
the high years of his middle age on a short, rough-hewn body; a
man with the undeniable look of an ex-something—sailor, steam
fitter, carpenter—something manly and honest and not genteel.
He approached the front door with unabated celerity, as if impelled by some vague, nagging guilt, and then stopped short at
the glass as if suddenly confronted by a surprise barrier and peered
through at Frank with an expression on that ruggedly nondescript
face of at once perplexity and resentment, eyes pinched at
the corners, sternly scrutinizing the appearance of what he obviously considered a wholly unwelcome intruder.

"What do you want?" he asked, his voice distant and muffled
behind the locked doors.

"I want to come in," Frank yelled.

"The building is closed."

"I've got to come in," Frank said, pulling on the outside handle
as if to emphasize the urgency of his request.

"You can't," the watchman said, moving his head with its thatch
of disheveled gray hair from side to side.

"It's important!" Frank yelled.

"Are you a member of this union?"

"I'm the brother-in-law of the man who set fire to himself."

The watchman frowned, contemplating him now with a peculiar interest, as Frank struggled to contain himself, not wanting to alarm the man. Then the watchman spread his hands and again his voice came from behind the glass distant and muffled.

"But what do you want?"

"His coat was left behind; I've come to get it," Frank said, raising his voice to overcome the glass barrier, feeling now that in another moment he was going to drive his fist through and take this man by the throat: for suddenly this nameless and obstructionist person—like some accidental Citizen Drouet hurled across his path at the climactic moment—represented the last stumbling block between him and the money and the road to safety, and in this guise appeared to Frank as the most damnable, insolent, and loathsome person he had ever seen, one filled with infuriating malice and stupidity, one who was causing, inadvertently or otherwise, a maddening delay.

"His coat?" the man said, his voice inaudible but the words clearly upon his phrasing lips.

"The family wants it back," Frank shouted. "They sent me . . . asked me to get it."

The man pondered for several moments, then swung his shoulders partially around and stared back up the empty corridor for several moments more, then looked back to Frank, and even as he was unlocking the door was shaking his head dubiously.

Frank burst inside with a suddenness that startled the man.

"Where is it?" Frank demanded.

"What did you say it was?"

"His coat, his topcoat. It was left behind. Where is it . . . what have you done with it?"

The man gaped at him.

"I don't know."

"What do you mean?" Frank asked, taking a menacing step forward, his urgency manifestly more palpable now that he was inside.

The watchman shifted his eyes to the open door, almost as if questioning now the wisdom of having let this man in, as if wishing he could have the decision to make all over again.

"Listen," Frank said, as the watchman's eyes fixed warily upon

him, "I want his coat. He left it here and I . . . the family wants
it back."

The watchman nodded sympathetically.

"I understand," he said.

"So?"

"Listen," the watchman said, suddenly earnest, confidential,
"what made him do it? Can you tell me that much? The newspapers and all were around asking. Nobody seems to know what
made him do it, and especially here. It's given us a bad mark. Did
he have some kind of a grudge against us?"

"What's the difference why he did it?" Frank said angrily. "He
did it because he was crazy. The whole family is crazy. Now give
me that coat."

"I don't have it."

"Then who does?

"I don't know. I don't know anything about it. I was off yesterday and only came on at ten o'clock tonight. I don't know anything about a coat."

"Are you sure?" Frank asked with threatening skepticism, advancing toward the man, making him step back.

"I'm not lying," the watchman said. "Why should I lie?" he
asked indignantly. "I don't need his coat. I've got a coat."

"I'm not accusing you of lying," Frank said, trying to collect
himself, not wanting to offend this man (even as he felt like seizing him by the throat and squeezing out the information), hoping
to gain by tact what he was afraid he might lose by rashness.
"Please forgive me if I gave that impression . . . but we're all very
upset . . . you can imagine what a thing like this has done to us
all."

"I understand," the man said, not mollified however, still wary,
mistrustful, judging Frank by the charged expression in his eyes
rather than the forced amenity of his voice.

"But about the coat . . . I know it's here. I've got to find it
. . . the family wants it back . . . they're very sentimental."

The watchman nodded, trying to understand, trying many—
too many—things at once as he struggled with a conflict of wanting to look sympathetic and helpful at the same time he was
feeling dogged suspicion and apprehension. Again he looked at
the open door, this time not as if questioning the wisdom of hav-

ing opened it but as if contemplating the idea of escaping through it.

"Who would know about the coat?" Frank demanded, his perturbation now quite clearly evident in his voice. "Is there anyone else here?"

"Only the cleaning woman."

"The cleaning woman!" Frank said, his eyes lighting delightedly. "She would know, wouldn't she?—better than anyone else. Was she here yesterday?"

"I think . . . yes, yes, she was. But she wouldn't know anything," the watchman said. Now he leaned forward and in a confidential whisper said, "She's stupid. You'd be wasting your time," he added, shaking his head in negative, almost palsied movements.

"Where is she?"

"You can't see her . . . she's working."

Frank looked around the dark lobby for a moment, then began hurrying along the corridor (striding right across the place where Philip had set fire to himself), the watchman at his heels.

"Wait a minute, mister," the watchman said, a stern note of authority in his voice.

Frank stopped.

"The building is closed," the watchman said. "You can't go running around in here."

"I'm looking for something," Frank said. "It belongs to . . . to my family." Suddenly he gripped the man by the shoulders and shook him violently. The man, surprised, afraid, rattled slackly in the powerful grip. Then Frank released him and pushed him away.

"Why are you so thick-headed?" Frank cried.

"I'm only doing my job," the man said, digging his thumbs into his belt and hauling his trousers up over his billowing, ill-tucked shirt.

"Why didn't you do your job yesterday and stop that idiot from setting fire to himself?"

"I wasn't here," the man said with pained logic.

"But you're here now, and you won't help me."

"I'm trying to help you . . . but you won't believe me."

"Why should I believe you? Who the hell are you? I've never seen you before. What's your name anyway?"

"Jones," the man said indignantly.

"You listen to me, Jones," Frank said, jabbing a finger toward the man, "don't try to take advantage of a bereaved family. That's what you're trying to do. I know your kind—you're worse than grave robbers."

Jones listened attentively, nodding his head, as if he agreed absolutely with every word. The tip of his tongue appeared and deftly moistened his lips.

"But I never saw your brother's coat," he said.

"Brother-in-law! Brother-in-law!" Frank shouted savagely in a voice that echoed up and down the corridors. "What's the matter with you?" he shouted again as Jones glared at him, the watchman convinced now he was in the presence of a madman.

"Where is that woman?" Frank asked, and without waiting for an answer began striding along the corridor. He turned at the corner and began walking in the light, the watchman scuttling after him. Frank stopped at the sight of a mop and pail on the floor outside of a closed door, his eyes seizing upon them as upon the symbol of some terrific success, as though mop and pail indicated the final waystation of a long, excruciating and, now, triumphant journey.

"You can't go in there!" Jones cried, seizing Frank by the arm.

Furious, Frank whirled and would have thrown a punch—indeed, his fist was raised and poised—had not Jones read the message in his eyes and released the arm and jumped back. Then Frank rushed for the closed door, Jones running after him again. Frank opened the door with a momentum that carried him several steps into the room before he was able to stop, and when he stopped it was with an abruptness caused not by surprise but because he was trying to gather his wits for what he anticipated would be an assault upon further recalcitrance and obtuseness.

Sitting on the sofa in a small, cramped office that was lighted by a desk lamp was a woman in her late forties, fat, pink, and stark naked. At Frank's sudden and uninhibited appearance she clamped her knees together in a hapless, desperate attempt to hide herself, and crossed her arms over a pair of huge flaccid breasts which sagged down over a round protrusion of mid-section fat. She had bleached blond hair that stood away from her head in a mass of tiny curls. The expression on her face was of utter, ghastly astonishment, and then entreaty, as she set a pair of grieving brown eyes upon Frank.

"I'm looking for a coat," Frank said, moving toward her, her state barely registering upon his consciousness.

She continued to gaze up at him like a terrified child, her lower lip quivering.

"It belonged to the man who set fire to himself," Frank said impatiently. "Do you know what happened to it?"

She looked now to Jones, who was standing at Frank's side in abashed and helpless agitation, nervously flexing his fingers; then back to Frank, still hugging her breasts, her legs still clamped together like a threatened maiden's, the elastic marks from the top of her short stockings clearly visible in round indentations on her calves. Nearby on a cane-bottomed chair were piled her stockings and underwear and gray smock, topped by a pair of flat-heeled workshoes placed neatly, almost primly, together.

"Tell him, Irene," Jones pleaded. "That's all he wants, and then he'll get out of here."

Seeing her underlip quivering inarticulately, Frank again felt the compulsion of violence—the desire to slap sound, word, information from her.

"My husband sent you, didn't he?" she said in a soft, plaintive voice.

"No, no, no," Jones said, stepping forward. "He wants to know about the coat. That's all he wants."

"What happened to it?" Frank demanded.

"Tell him what happened to the coat," Jones said with almost inane simplicity, as if coaxing a reluctant child.

"The coat?" she asked.

"The man who set fire to himself," Jones said. "His coat. What happened to it?"

"I picked it up," she said, unable to lift her voice above a whisper.

"What did you do with it?" Frank asked.

"Was it damaged?" Jones asked.

Her eyes moved from face to face, still not quite comprehending.

"I don't think so," she whispered.

"But what did you do with it?" Frank demanded. "Where is it?"

"It isn't here," she said.

At this Frank was rendered so inarticulate that it was Jones who asked the final, decisive, culminating question:

"Where is it?"

"The police took it," she said. "They came in later and somebody said . . ." she took a deep swallow as her voice failed again for a moment, as she brought her round shoulders forward and hugged herself more firmly and pressed her thighs together more determinedly in an effort to hide her nakedness ". . . somebody said it belonged to that man and they picked it up and took it away."

Frank glared incredulously at her for several moments. Then, in a dull, hollow whisper, he said,

"The police took it?"

"There," Jones said buoyantly, smiling. "Now you know where to find it."

FORTY-TWO

Even before his hands and knees had risen from the tavern floor, Ed Slater knew what he was going to do next, a single infuriated maelstrom-thought awesomely free in his mind. Because of his pain and his humiliation—this latter not simply from having been beaten, publicly and decisively, at something he prided himself on doing well, but also because he had himself foolishly provoked it —he became instantly secretive, animated by the desire, the need, to balance the scales, his stunned, dazed mind swept clear by a bitter self-punishing anger. Even before he had made that first effort to push himself erect, still on all fours, cynosure of every eye in the almost reverently silent tavern, he was with terrible lucidity calculating the feasibility of the idea which was raging in his head like demonic inspiration; calmly twisting the irrationality of revenge into a pure and unassailable logic. There was a reason why he had been pounded to the floor, someone was to fault for this, for many things; and even as Frank had forgotten him in a matter of mere moments, so was Frank outward bound from Slater's thoughts during those same moments, as his mind groped toward the source of not only this but a thousand other antagonisms, great and small, real and imagined. What Frank Dublin had done to him was acceptable in that it was perfectly understandable, he himself had done it countless times to others; so his seething ire and malice was elsewhere directed, toward something that could never be acceptable, that was totally beyond understanding, and which therefore was the logical target for attack.

When finally he hove himself to his feet Slater appeared bereft of intellect but at the same time operating on an instinct, a reflex purer than thought. His tall powerful body rose with an air of brooding privacy, watched by the awestruck men around him. Grim-faced, he looked around for a moment, his sweeping gaze making eyes drop or shift away, his mind, his intentions fixed with secret and inviolable purpose, all of it characterized by the bitter stinging pain that seemed to be vibrating in his tongue. "You ought to take a whisky," his father said, looking at him with lingering curiosity. "No," he said, touching a handkerchief to his bleeding nose. He looked at the brownish stains on the handkerchief for a moment, then stuffed it back into his pocket. "Where are you going now?" his father asked, watching him stalk from the tavern.

With the unswerving purpose of a fired bullet, Slater headed into the night, with all the rigid resolve of one expecting a sect to collect at his back. His mind was actually very cool now, lucid and cogent with long-established responses to long and ongoing offenses, dangers. There wasn't even the question of justification; that, too, was of long and determined duration, defined by the nature of the offense, the danger—the longevity of which was in itself a forfeiture of its right to exist unmolested, for its very existence was a threat and an insult not merely against Ed Slater but against all that he believed in and all that was just and right in the world. There was no question in his mind about this, nor should there have been, given the unremitting, uncompromising flow of fact and propaganda to which he had been exposed all of his life; he had proved a fertile incubator for the doctrines accepted and passed along by the majority of his countrymen, disseminated not just in barroom conversations but in newspapers and books and magazines and on motion picture screens, from the lips of educators and clergymen and the nation's political leaders, all of it positive and unequivocal in its fervor, its absolute sincerity (except, of course, for the exploitative and demagogic, whose crude and subtle ways feasted ravenously upon fervor). In a society which had established arbitrary yardsticks for the measure of one's patriotism, this wasn't even paranoia—there clearly was too much on the record for that, too much acknowledged even by the informed and the objective, and even if a certain logic had been given a chance with him, there was no talking Slater out of what he had endured fighting Communists in Korea, where a piece of their steel had taken a measure of his blood. So he was no less fanatic than any participant in any holy war, nor any other recipient of a given dogma or piety, and so for whatever self-righteousness was worth, spite and malice were the less.

He stopped when he came to a bundle of wired-together news-papers resting on the sidewalk in front of a darkened candy store. He bent over and with a savage effort ripped one paper from the bundle, then went on, a stern and immutable frown upon his face, walking with a remorseless determination as if to liberate an arc of glowing truth from centuries-old bondage, an almost authori-tarian co-ordination between the unhesitating strength and ad-vance of his strides and the absolute terminus of his thoughts, the geometry of which was structured by the straight and simple lines of cause and effect. Being alone on the streets made ordained and ceremonial suggestions, solemnizing his sense of mission. As he walked under the still, leafy trees the shadows cast by street lights passed faintly over his face and fled down his white shirt. The folded newspaper in his hand swung rhythmically to and fro as he walked.

The sight of Charlotte Breitman's house finally introduced some turbulence into the equanimity of his thinking, stoking his rancor and incensing him still further. That proud, aloof house, dominat-ing the street from its elevated position at the crest of the upgrade, had always been like an affront, so cold and blatant, so imperious, from the lines of its roof to the solidness of its foundations, an arrogant fortress-symbol of all that was hateful and threatening. To his mind it was part and parcel of its scheming and seditious mistress: it was as if nothing associated with her could lay claim to innocence; everything was part of the infamous design—the house, the trees, the garden, all of it soaked and infected with the outrage of subversion, mocking and immoral, secure in the pro-tection of the very forces it sought to topple and destroy: and this was one of the baffling inconsistencies of this proud tough democracy: why that house and its occupant, whose avowed in-tention it was to bring a new and blasphemous authority to the land, should enjoy the protection of the institutions it was plotting against, which Ed Slater and others had shed their blood to de-fend—this was a philosophical weakness, inexplicable and inde-fensible.

He glared at the house as he passed it. A light was burning downstairs, and the very light itself seemed a further affront and threat, as if it were allied with the unspeakable cause within, a disdainful beacon of evil burning upon the unoffending and defenseless night. He walked several blocks and then sat on the benches outside of the children's playground, from where he could see the red signal lights pulsing languorously atop the Manhattan skyscrapers, as well as the lights within that most dubious institution—the United Nations. He smoked a cigarette, listening to the traffic rushing through Capstone on the expressway, below the sloping grass embankments. Sullenly he stared around at the sleeping houses as the fact of his aloneness in the night fed his righteous wrath, his inward monitors of conscience and obligation. Too many people were sleeping, too many were slack and remiss, too many were naïve and trusting, too many were lazily tolerant of that light burning in Charlotte Breitman's house, unaware of the subtle and insidious erosion occurring around them. It was a case of too many people being indifferent to the difference of others, and it was the fact that he was one of the few able to discern—and be concerned about—the dangers of that difference that angered him. Americans went to sleep too easily and slept too soundly, while that light in Charlotte Breitman's house burned through the night; Americans were inclined to forget the lessons of the past and ignore the threatening shadows of the present, lying innocently abed, while that light in Charlotte Breitman's house glowed luridly in the dark; too many Americans were content to let others guard their security, without so much as a thought for those guardians, while that light in Charlotte Breitman's house burned through the night.

Ed Slater was never less reckless or more solemn in his life; a sentry of the night, he felt like a hanging judge with a conscience. Love of one's country was a sentiment at once uneasy and humbling, at once a man's pride and vulnerability; and it was a sentiment of great expanse, seldom thought through in detail; it was a vague, almost abstract emotion of many temptations, of conscientious duty and unconscionable unrestricted license. Inevitably it was toned with a certain defensiveness and ambiguity, since one's country was an institution, an impersonal authority, existing not to be loved but rather to be advanced and bettered, and defended when necessary, and carefully observed always, since it was sometimes undeserving of bestowed love, a force of potential callousness and destruction, an unpredictable guarantor of nothing—returning in kind to its people whatever it received of them. A man's love for people could be demonstrated and expressed, but love of country was an indeterminate emotion with no truly fixed and passionate object to focus upon. So Ed Slater had little outlet for his national devotion, except to attack his country's enemies, as he perceived them to be—these enemies who in his mind provoked and defined that devotion, whose cunning and menace helped characterize the country and thus force that devotion with meaning and potency. A static, unthreatened country, one listlessly out of the competition, was hardly worthy of notice or respect, even by its own citizens.

He left the bench and walked again, retracing his steps, with stolid deliberation now, still carrying the newspaper. He had the streets to himself, and once more this seemed to add weight to the responsibility he felt incumbent upon him. Certain of these back streets were without sidewalks and he watched carefully as he stepped over the hard irregular ground, as though it were unfamiliar to him, as if he had not walked it a thousand times during the nearly forty years of his life. And then he lifted his eyes from the ground and waited for the house to come into view. This time the downstairs light was out and an upstairs one burning through the upper branches of the trees, the high, tapering branches like slender crackings across the rectangle of light. Coming closer, he paused and stood with deadly stillness in the shadows, studying the lighted window with the poised and stalking eyes of an avenging angel. Then he slowly moved forward. He stepped easily over a low rail fence that closed off the driveway, then went with soundless shadowless stealth across the grass to the garden. When he reached some of the flawlessly shaped hawthorn bushes he stopped and knelt on the grass, looking over his shoulder for a moment at the light through the trees above him. Then he lay the newspaper down, opened it to full spread and as quietly as he could lifted the centerfold page and crushed it into a wad between his hands and then pushed it into the shrubbery. He repeated this again and again with other pages, quietly reducing the centerfold level of the paper, jamming the balled-up pages into different shrub growths around the garden and along the side of the house too, arranging each piece with deft and precise firmness, pausing now and then for a quick and wary glance over his shoulder at the light in the upper floor.

When he touched the lighted match to the first wad of paper he stared fascinatedly for several moments as the fire took with small red gusts, causing the paper to expand inside the dark green-smelling hawthorn leaves; watching as the slowly awakening flames trimmed the edges of the paper and ate back into the wad with prim and undeviating course, like instincts released upon the air, already casting moist red shadows upon the surrounding leaves. Then, with an expression of ferocious exultation, he moved to his next target and inflamed that, and the next, as the glow from the first fire was already throwing an irascible red glare into the night. Fire after fire rose like glowing bouquets and spread with fierce and sudden independence. Slater drew back, a strange, sorcerer's gleam in his eyes, and then, with a prodigal burst of excitement, hurried from the garden. He went quickly along the street, then paused and looked back. After several moments he thought he could detect a slight, wavering red nimbus, like the hint of incipient dawn. Go, *man*, *go*, he whispered to the flames he had risen, and then turned and hurried on, leaving them to build into their own wild and voracious extravagance.

FORTY-THREE

"You say you don't think it was an accident?" the policeman asked. "What makes you say that?"

"I've been receiving a series of anonymous phone calls," Charlotte said.

"Threatening calls?" the policeman asked.

"Definitely of a threatening nature," she said with wry understatement.

"No idea, I suppose," he said, making a vague gesture with his hand, "who it is?"

"None whatsoever."

"Did he say he was going to burn your garden?"

"No. That was a pleasant surprise."

She was bored with the policemen—there were two of them, the other one was standing outside on the patio surveying the damage—and wished they would leave. The questioning one seemed reluctant to do so, seemed actually concerned about what had happened, or perhaps it simply was the nature of his job (or the nature of himself) to stand there at a lost and blurred hour of the night and ask what he thought were pertinent questions. He was young, with thick blond hair showing in short-edged bunches from under his hat. The fire department had arrived first, a fury of lights and sirens blatant and maniacal on the summer night, red flare lights sweeping the darkness with lurid spasms. Aghast, she stood and watched the aggressively equipped men invade her garden with axes and hoses and thick orgiastic streams of water. Furiously active and efficient with their satanic helmets and enormous boots, the fire-killers were like a swarming legion of the night, remorseless and irresistible. When finally they withdrew, with their water and their hoses and their sirens and their bells, they left behind a shocked and blistered atmosphere.

"You live here alone, Miss Breitman?" the young policeman asked.

"Yes," she said.

"Have you reported the phone calls?"

"To whom?"

"Well, the police, the phone company . . ."

"Not really."

"You ought to."

"Next time."

"We *can* help sometimes, believe it or not," he said with a self-conscious smile.

She was sitting on the sofa, trying wearily to maintain a polite interest in the conversation. The policeman was standing in the middle of the room, his attention occasionally wandering as his eyes made an intrigued and lingering appraisal of the room's affluent comforts, as if desirous of receiving a formal invitation to visit someday. The second policeman walked slowly in from the patio. He was older, with the rough skeptical face of the old-line cop, with a flat hard stare that seemed always focused just above the eyes, something at once menacing, stereotypical and doomed about him, a specter about to be relieved of his post by a moderating world and consigned to departmental history.

"The lady has been receiving threatening phone calls, Bill," the younger one told him.

"Yeah?"

"She hasn't reported it though."

"No?" the older one said. He folded his arms and stared moodily at her, with the unchallengeable dispensation of the law. He had two commendation ribbons over his shield.

"She lives here alone," the younger one said.

"I know."

The younger one shot Charlotte a quizzical glance, as if wondering why she should be known. She smiled ironically at him. Later, she knew, when they returned to their patrol car and the night the information would be exchanged: How come you knew she lived alone, Bill? And Bill: Don't you know who she is? Don't you know what goes on in that house? *A Communist? A Communist in Capstone?* Upholding the law could sometimes play havoc with a man's sense of justice.

"No idea who set the fire, huh?" the older one asked her.

"No," she said with a faint, whimsical smile. "There are lots of people around here who don't like me, I'm afraid."

"Doesn't give them the right to burn your house down," the younger one said.

"No," she said.

The older one was peering intently into the next room.

"Would you like to have a look around?" Charlotte asked him.

Caught at his thoughts, but nevertheless unflustered, he shook his head. He stared at her from the corners of his eyes—the look doubly menacing coming from under the visor of his cap. He thinks he's absolutely right in thinking whatever the hell it is he's thinking, she said to herself, looking back at him with a chill sense of fear.

"Some people from the fire department will probably be here tomorrow to have a look around," the younger one said.

"All right," she said.

"No way it could've started accidentally?"

"No way."

"You didn't have a barbecue or anything out there?"

She shook her head.

"An allegation of arson is very serious," the younger one said.

"Not half so serious as the arson," she said.

"Okay then," the younger one said as they prepared to leave. "We'll try to keep an eye on the place for you."

"I'm sure your partner has already thought of that," Charlotte said.

After they had left she walked out onto the patio. In the darkness she could see the garden was ruined, there was a grim, sullen look to it, the firemen's swift fury hovering inanimately over it. She would have to restore it as quickly as possible, make it warm and green again, for Paul; he liked calm and attractive places. Perhaps he wouldn't notice it now, the way he was; but in any event she would sit him to the rear of the house, where the fire hadn't reached. *Live here alone? No, I have a man moving in tomorrow . . . shocking, immoral Communist that I am.*

She locked the patio doors, turned out the lights and went upstairs. For the second time that night she lay down on her bed, fully clothed, and sought in the darkness for a healing sleep.

FORTY-FOUR

It seemed to Frank, during those first impetuous moments of intoxicating excitement, that the long quest was coming at last to a just conclusion. He was seized with a buoyant, vindicating joy, as though he had suddenly become the beneficiary of a providential intercession. These were his feelings as he hurried to obey his first instinct—to go to the police. As he raced from the union hall back into the night he had a vision of the coat lying up on the front desk in the police station, waiting for him to come dashing in to claim it. He, as the brother-in-law of the tragic man, would be received with great sympathy. There would be some nettlesome formalities, he would sign a scrap of paper and the coat would be released to him, for him to rush back with to the family for "sentimental" reasons. He accepted the fact that there could be complications if the police had found the money. What was your brother-in-law doing with so many thousands of dollars? Well, you see, it was his intention to burn it, to show his contempt for it; it was a symbolic gesture. ("He was crazy, don't you see? Absolutely off his head. Would a sane man do such a thing?") But where did he get it? He stole it from me. It belongs to me. But where did you—? It was given to me by my father, just before he died. (And it would have been, too, if the old man had not been out of his mind. The fact that he had given it to a sixteen-year-old girl proved he was crazy. But there was no point in belaboring that any longer.) They might not release the money that easily. There would be much debating back and forth. Perhaps Helen would have to be called, as the wife; but even that would be all right, for Frank would gladly settle for half. Paul needn't be included; he had never shown any interest in the money, and anyway he had that rich bitch caring for him now. Half would be fine, a bonanza, a way out.

That was when his excitement abruptly and soberingly vanished: a way out. Out of what? He knew very well what. And he realized this: the knife that had been driven into Stephen Kifner might as well have gone into him too, for all he could go to the police with any story, however artful. He was not running from his usual preposterous failures and misfortunes this time. Grimly sobered by the idea, by the abrupt cessation of his galvanizing excitement, he sat down on a bus stop bench, facing an empty street. He felt hopelessly circumscribed, ruined by a cycling of fates that was positively diabolic. Go to the police? Walk in and announce myself? *Jesus Christ, I must have been off my head.* It was almost beyond belief, to have lost perspective so totally at the very moment when his wits and resources were being faced with challenges greater than ever before. Walk into the police station? He shook his head ruefully at his naïveté. It was incredible what a momentary burst of hope could do, the blinding glare, the numbing and immobilizing impact. For all he knew one of those goddamn composite sketches of his face at which they were so fiendishly clever was already on the desk of every police station in the city. He had surely been seen by someone in the hotel; he didn't have to think back to be certain of that. The death of Stephen Kifner would not be treated as simply another New York murder; it was too ripe, too provocative, too *saleable*. This was a murder with a potent haunting factor, demanding to be aired in its every detail. Walk into a police station? (Dismay at his naïveté continued to dominate his mind.) And even if his momentum had somehow contrived to propel him into the police station, and even if his face had not been compositely re-created and was not lying on the desk —what in a million years made him think that the money would still be there? What made him think that it had not long since been discovered and divided by its finders? Yes sir, we have the coat. Money? What money? We found no money. Here, look for yourself. It probably fell out in the excitement, or maybe it got burned up, or maybe he didn't have it with him. You say he stole it from you? Do you want to press charges? This is very serious.—Serious? Frank thought. No, it's funny. The money is at this moment stuffed into the mattress of some goddamned cop, maybe even the one who is going to come by in the next five minutes and arrest me, and get promoted for doing it. A memo-

rable night for that man, who would probably begin to wonder
how he had ever managed without Frank Dublin.

His problems had posted themselves neatly at the four points
of the compass and were now advancing connectively one to the
other to forestall and obliterate him. It was a conspiracy of disparate elements united by a procession of sardonic accidents,
compounded by everyone from Arthur Seavery to his own father.
The situation was not entirely his fault; he had made an effort.
Calling Bennett had not been easy for him, but he was convinced
that it had been absolutely and unassailably the correct move. So
after that terrible grappling with his conscience he had done the
invited thing, the right thing, and made that unnerving call,
spoken to that glacial quasi-human on the other end of the phone,
making a terrific and irrevocable commitment. And nothing had
happened. He could not imagine what could have gone wrong; it
was inconceivable in circumstances of such a nature for something
to have gone wrong. He had the odd, deeply disquieting feeling
now that if he were to return to that massive impersonal downtown building there would be no office, no desk, no Mr. Bennett;
there would be only his own impression of the experience, and
that would not long remain trustworthy, for his situation was so
pierced by such unrelenting immediacy that there was little tolerance for anything not brutally realistic. Was it possible for them
(Them? They?—Who?) to be so cynical and cold-blooded to have
remained aloof and allowed it to happen, charmed by the idea
of one "enemy of the state" eliminating another? A true revolutionary would be only too anxious to believe that (though there
was precious little difference between the mind that accepted the
state's total omniscience and that which believed in its limitless
duplicity). If it were true, if they had deliberately ignored his call
and allowed the murder to occur, then he was the least guilty of
all involved. Even though such a conspiracy on the part of the
other side would at least exonerate him morally, it was the sheerest
of consolations and altered by not one degree the realities of his
situation. He found himself consciously resisting the idea of Them
allowing it to happen, while at the same time he was able to recognize the ingenuous source of such resistance—he did not want to
think that those in vested leadership could be capable of such
inhuman dealing; it depressed him with what was, under the cir-

cumstances, a very peculiar sense of disillusionment. But, with some stubborn and implacable loyalty to a trust, a presumption, he refused to believe such a thing could have been officially sanctioned. They had bungled it, that was the only reasonable answer. But either way, his own situation remained unchanged. Either way, they would hardly acknowledge having known him, spoken with him, received a telephone call from him. If he were caught, how could he tell such a story, to whom? Who would believe it?—only those who were willing to believe anything, those dissident paranoids who allowed themselves the obscene luxury of being subjugated by the most bizarre and implausible fables, eager to allow whatever fit the contours of their fantasies.

As he rose from the bench and began walking again through the night, he realized that Charlotte was the only one he could possibly go to now. He would restate his predicament in the bluntest, most direct way, almost letting it speak for itself. While he did not expect her to revert to her earlier agreement and go away with him, he would at least obtain shelter and financing, some measure of security while he planned what to do. She could renounce and disavow only up to a certain point before having to give him what he wanted. He would not again ask her to join him; that would be pointless, it would be rejected, and he was no longer sure he even wanted her to. She had proven too unstable and untrustworthy. It was best for someone eternally on guard to follow a solitary path. As he walked toward her house he began to soothe himself with the idea of vast, secure, disinterested places: Canada, Europe, South America. There were places and there would be time. All he needed were several unthreatened days, money to begin, and a plan to follow. Though his reappearance might alarm her, she would know that he could not stay, that he would soon be gone, soul and shadow, never to return. While he still did not know where he would go, nor specifically what he would do when he got there, of one thing he was certain: the insane pursuits and patterns of his life would become a secret history beyond resurrection. He would reverence his second chance, his new opportunity, and tolerate no repetitions of his disastrous past. Solemnly, he placed conditions upon himself, as if a sober new force had moved to possess him. He would live quietly and leave to casual reverie the things which had once been his very fuel and engine.

He was still young enough to find hope in renunciation. Suddenly he yearned for this new life, with all the strong and humble optimism of the homesteader looking beyond the challenge of river and mountain and ahead to his new home and his new beginning, and like the homesteader his trust would lie wherever the sun rose and fell, and his home would be in the cast of his shadow until the new beginning had outrun, outlasted the old unfulfilling endings. He felt the weight of time and error a crucible of learning translating now into wisdom, into a sort of penitence, defining with adamant strictures his new obligations. The force of all the things he had not yet done with his life began to dominate, like light upon dark, all that he had done.

With his growing sense of reprieve and renewal, he felt like running, but this idea brought sharply back into focus his immediate situation. A man running in the night was perilously conspicuous. Again he began to feel threatened, self-protective, moving through the placid side streets with an almost feline softness and alertness, watching with poised mistrust the occasional passing car.

What he saw when the house came into view drove him back into the shadows as abruptly as if he had been physically pushed. He positioned himself in an alley between the brick walls of two houses and with stunned incredulity stared through the deep soundless night at the police car outside of her house. Gradually his disbelief proportioned into resentment and anger as it came home to him what that car potentially represented—more than danger, more than betrayal, more than arrest and trial and conviction and unforgiving bars and concrete, but the effective and irreversible termination of life's forward surge, a meaninglessness of time and hope. *No,* he thought, *it has nothing to do with Paul. If it had to do with Paul then it would be outside of his house. It has to do with me.* All the time he had been walking steadily through the night celebrating his splendid vision of the future, his almost epiphanic revelations, that car had been there, waiting to intercept and subdue him: not sudden, not accidental, but forever and symbolic, responding to an ancient summons, pattern; and he felt like old complaining Job, wracked and infested in ways no human could have devised or inflicted; and he felt, too, as if his restoration into the new world of promise had been just another illusion, another cruel and bitter self-deception.

With an almost fatalistic calm he remained in the alley, feeling now the approaching peril of solid daylight which would in several hours lift the siege of night, and in which there would be no place for him. He could feel himself standing there, immobile, feel his very presence with sharp despairing awareness, saw himself with the most poignant and self-pitying compassion. He thought of himself as he never had before, as people seldom do, with the pure literalness of an objective observer: his name, his face, the weight of his body, his isolation in a world where he was not unlike other men. He was the hurt, brooding champion of Frank Dublin, who was guilty of certain offenses but undeserving of the penalties. His life had built to this banal climax—betrayal by a woman, a twist at once unexpected and unjust. And yet there was no sense of personal outrage. He felt he understood completely. He should have anticipated it. She had shown, earlier, an almost irrational fear of him, and now that fear had permeated the pleasurable view of her own future and shot panic into it. She suddenly had what she wanted, and a person so in possession could easily become pinched and narrowed against the merest hint of intrusion, flail against it with unreasoning and frenetic fury. Sometime during the evening, returning from Paul, her mind enraptured, she had remembered him, the last threatening outpost to be reduced, and so she had done it, probably impulsively, with hastily contrived rationale, motivated by her own impetuous instincts of survival.

And then his philosophic despair began to ebb. He understood what had happened, but he did not have to accept it. The pursued, the abandoned, the betrayed, had instincts of their own. He knew what had been done against him and that gave him advantages, as well as prior vindication for any move he chose to make. The widest latitude and most open license belonged not to the virtuous but the sinned-against. His mind leaped ahead now over every discretionary barrier, working in a series of cool, precise, counterplotting steps: get inside (the patio door was the most likely point of entry), find the money, slip away. He did not know how much money she had cached in the den, but she had indicated it was enough for two people to achieve a long forward step; so whatever it was, it would be a fortune to one man in desperation. Once he had that money the way ahead would be open. He would present himself to the underground of dissenters and fugitives, refugees from a system they abhorred, who would welcome another orphan with a tale to tell.

And then all of his plans and devisings were incredibly interrupted and blown into disarray by a telephone ringing with such loud and startling clarity it made him wheel and glare into the darkness. The sharp, incongruous noise sawed several times across the silence as he pressed himself against the brick wall as if trying to end or stifle the insistent sound. A light flashed out, falling in a yellow window-defining square almost at his feet, followed immediately by a sleep-baffled voice: "Hello? Hello? Who is this?" And hard upon this, virtually simultaneous with it, another voice, a woman's, with breathless concern: "Who is it? Who is it?" And then the first voice, the man's: "It's Mike. He says there's somebody standing in the alley." "In the alley?" the woman asked with ghastly fear.

But I'm not doing anything, he thought—a thought burning to rage into words. *I'm only standing here.* He glared furiously up at the window even as he listened to the stranger talking to another stranger about him. And then, abruptly, he moved out to the sidewalk and began walking, not afraid but angry, thinking: Some son of a bitch is looking at me, right now. Seldom in his life had he ever felt such righteous indignation. Fuming, he cursed bitterly as he headed away, walking with a stiff, self-conscious haste that damned caution. With a contemptuous look over his shoulder he turned the corner and continued for several blocks, then began circling back, approaching the house from another direction, with the sense of calculated risk now. When he was able to return again to a position of observation he saw that the police car was gone and the house all sides dark to the night.

FORTY-FIVE

The sounds rose soft and sinisterly allusive from downstairs and infiltrated that opaque zone in which she was lingering, which was neither sleep nor wakefulness, which was like a languorous indecision of consciousness; so that at first, out of both exhaustion and uncertainty as to from which side of that opaque zone the sounds were issuing, she did nothing, felt nothing, but merely lay there, in all her clothing on top of the covers. Her mind was too tired to shape a thought or accept a sensation, stubbornly resisting the idea that there could be any life left in this long night. It was as if what she heard was particles of noise left behind by the tumultuous fire engines and just now falling to earth. So when finally the sounds did indent upon her consciousness what she felt initially was something like a deep wailing inside of her as though she were enduring this on behalf of someone else, that it had nothing to do with her, but that she was going to have to rise and face it nevertheless. And then the fright struck her, pushing through that evanescing opaque zone like a chill wind in a locked room—as she realized that someone was in the house, was downstairs; that it was more than a telephone call and disembodied voice this time, more even than some lunatic on the outside with arson in his head: he was inside now, in her house, trying to achieve himself through the twin cloaks of darkness and quiet.

She sat up very slowly, drawing a tense, shallow breath, her suddenly alertly awake eyes searching the dark, which seemed possessed now by a gathering, tentative violence that was dreadfully personal. She stood up, her eyes fixed upon some dead unrevealing atom of darkness beyond the room, in the hall, listening for the sounds as if they would emanate from that spot; and then she moved with her own barefooted stealth across the carpet toward the bureau, herself soundless, the opposing shadow in this grim prebattle ballet of the specters. She slid forward the drawer with meticulous slowness, with a care for silence as though she were the intruder, her hand rummaging among cool fine underthings, finding the hard implacable pistol and lifting it out and fitting it into her hand. Thus armed, fortified, she turned on the sound-smothering carpet and moved toward the door, propped now by a sense of outrage and indignation, not at being threatened, not at the need to defend herself, but because of the presumption of whoever it was who had entered her home, her privacy, who was prowling downstairs now as if matching his will against hers, his presumption against her determination.

Taking slow measured consciously faultless steps she passed through the doorway into the hall, the pistol in her hand raised and held steadily but uncertainly as though it were her guide through realms of imperial night; feeling strangely weightless and invisible, as if dreaming her way through a stilled and unlighted arena, joined to reality solely by the lethal instrument in her hand, her fear free-flowing through her entire body, a motivating rather than inhibiting force. A casting from the street light outside came faintly through the trees, through the window with just enough pale filtering strength to dilute the darkness and delineate the moving figure below, whose motion was being carried out in utter stillness, who was so monstrously and unforgivably wrong there. She leveled the pistol and swung it several deadly degrees across the darkness.

"Stop," she said, not loudly, the single word startling and peremptory upon the silence.

He did stop, arrested by the word, the unexpectedness.

"I need *money*," he suddenly cried from below, from within the faint veil of light.

She would tell herself later, sometimes with conviction, sometimes not, that she did not recognize his voice, that the cry and the emotion had strained it beyond recognition, and that it was out of excusable fright and panic that she had pulled the trigger *But six times? Emptying it into him after he had fallen with the first shot?* startled by the explosive report, the flashing glare, the shuddering recoil: her finger on the trigger with frozen reflex, emptying the chambers with mindless savagery, icy with the im-

periousness of regal decision. It was understandable, even reasonable. But why then, she asked herself, did I run halfway down
the stairs screaming his name?

*Oh, damn you, Frank, why did you come back? There was
absolutely no reason for you to come back.*

FORTY-SIX

1

Groping for an analogy he thought the lay mind could understand, the doctor said it was like a piece of fine china that has been
dropped on concrete. "Think how difficult it would be," he said,
"to put all of those pieces not only back together again, but to
make the piece as good as new." Paul's mind, he said, had shattered into countless fragments of infinite shapes and colors and
distances and intensities. "It's going to take a lot of time, a lot
of patience," he said, as they walked across the grass toward the
parking lot. The doctor, psychiatrist, was a comparatively young
man, wearing a tweed suit in the mild October sunshine. He was
smoking a small thin cigar, which he had lit the moment they left
the hospital.

"You couldn't have handled this by yourself, Miss Breitman,"
he said. "You ought to have known that, particularly in light of
your own . . . tragic experience. It was a noble try, but far beyond
your capacities."

It had, in fact, been Helen's idea, insistence, that Paul be sent
where he could receive constant, and expert, professional care,
and Charlotte had finally agreed, though for her own private reasons. "You can't help him," Helen told her. "You don't know
what's wrong. You can't help him. You can't." And then she added
coldly, "He doesn't even know Frank is dead." And Charlotte:
"That was an accident. You know it was." "I'm not saying it
wasn't," Helen said sullenly, adding, "I don't know. I wasn't
there."

Paul had lain abed in her house for two weeks, not quite a
catatonic but in a state of ineffable passivity, staring and taciturn. He ate, he slept, he occasionally responded, but he did not

change, day after day. It was after she had called the men back for a third time to clean the carpet that she realized she could no longer cope with the situation, that she agreed to have him institutionalized. After the second cleaning the men insisted the bloodstains were out; but coming down the stairs one morning she thought she could detect, because of the way the light was hitting the carpet, a certain cloudy patch where Frank had fallen. And even if no one else could see it, she could, and the thought of Paul walking across it time after time when he was well again was too much for her to bear; and not even the idea of having that carpeting picked up and replaced by another could placate her, because if it existed in her mind then its invisible cloud would surely reappear, and if this was happening to her then she was in no fit state to care for someone in Paul's condition.

"His responses are still vague and incoherent," the doctor said as they crossed the driveway and headed for the parking lot. "He knows now that his brother is dead—though not how he died," he added with a sidelong glance at her, "but he hasn't seemed quite able to absorb it. Were they very close?"

She thought for a moment. "No one was close to Frank," she said.

"He occasionally refers to his father, but mostly he talks, when he talks at all, of his wife."

Deliberately, self-consciously, with a distinct feeling of resentment, Charlotte said nothing, looking straight ahead as they walked.

"He says she whispers to him," the doctor said.

"What does she say?" Charlotte asked dryly.

The doctor puffed several times on his cigar, then removed it to his hand.

"Look," he said, "he quite seriously believes this. There apparently is a residue of guilt over her death that he's never been able to dislodge."

"That's nonsense," she said curtly.

"A lot of things are going to sound nonsensical at this stage, I'm afraid. He should have had help months ago. This long period of morbid introspection that you've described certainly indicated something was wrong."

"He seemed to be coming out of it, even after his father's death. I thought he withstood that very well, all things considered."

"Obviously not. He's been having a breakdown for some time, and been resisting it. In fact, he's still resisting."

"I don't blame him," Charlotte said. "So would I."

"Why?"

"I can't conceive of placing my mind into someone else's hands." The doctor laughed lightly.

"You don't seem to have much faith in psychoanalysis."

"This is hardly an age of faith, Doctor."

"What kind of age is it?"

"Look," she said as they reached the parking lot and walked toward her car, "Paul has an extremely fine and sensitive mind. I'm . . . I'm concerned."

"You have every right to be. And that's why you brought him here. We're trying to help him, believe me."

"That expectation is basic," she said; "I want you to do more."

"Miss Breitman," the doctor said as they reached the car, "you're writing the checks; you know the cost of this place. I can assure you the care and treatment he's getting are commensurate with the cost."

"Sometimes I wonder if he wouldn't have been better off staying with me," she said, a wistful note in her voice.

"You know better than that," the doctor said, opening the car door for her.

"I don't know," she said. "Perhaps one man's normality is another man's psychosis."

She received a bland, noncommittal stare.

"It's the age of slogans, Doctor," she said getting into the car.

2

The blazing flashlight penetrated his sleep and brought the youth suddenly, alertly awake. He got slowly to his feet, raising one hand to blot out the light. He was able to distinguish the man, the policeman, behind the bright explosive glare, saw the bulky leather jacket, the cap and visor.

"What are you doing there?" the policeman asked, holding the light steady.

"Just sitting," Seavery said, his hand still raised against the light.

"This bungalow is private property," the policeman said. "Didn't you see the no trespass sign?"

"It's boarded up, I figured nobody would mind. I wasn't doing anything."

"You live around here?"

"No," Seavery said. "I live in Florida. I'm walking there."

The policeman, the bulky menacing figure behind the enormous blazing flashlight, said, his voice testy and humorless,

"You want me to run your ass in?"

"No, sir," Seavery said quietly.

"Then get the hell to moving and don't let me see you around here again."

The light followed him as the youth came down from the porch and walked along the slanting wooden path to the sidewalk. He stood there and watched the policeman return to his prowl car and drive slowly away.

He walked a little way, passing a row of small, nailed-up bungalows. Then he turned and cut across the dunes, heading for the ocean, his feet driving through the soft yielding sands.

In the windy autumn night he sat alone upon the open, empty expanse of the Jersey shore, gazing pensively out at the dark ceaseless Atlantic waves. A strong cool sea wind was blowing in. The sands were cold, abandoned to the massive sweep of the changing season.

Idly he picked up fistfuls of sand and let them sift down across his palm. His thoughts reverted. He was disappointed at what had happened, or, more accurately, what had not happened. The students, the Movement people, everyone, had failed him. He had given them their opportunity, their justification. And they had let it slip away. There had been a few angry editorials, a few speeches, a few memorial meetings, and the ghost of Stephen Kifner passed quietly to the shadows.

My fault, really, Seavery thought, watching a tall, foam-veined wave rise boldly from the timeless Atlantic and crash onto the beach. He had timed it wrong. America was a country that slept

on Sunday. Committing the action on a Saturday night had allowed it to be deadened by Sunday lassitude, a tactical mistake.
By Monday, when the country had wakened from its weekend,
there had been other news. The moment had been lost. But no
matter, the youth thought as he smoothed the cold sands with the
flat of his hand. It was trial and error. Experience would prove
trustworthy. Next time it would be called on a Monday or a Tues-
day or a Wednesday . . .

He lay back on the sand now, possessed by a feeling of profound
tranquillity, of communion with things outside of his soul. He lay
with his hands folded behind his head, listening to the ocean's
soothing roars and whispers, gazing intently at the flood of stars.
Then he closed his eyes and fell asleep, under those stars that were
forever watchful over this wayward orphan, this planet, this earth,
this striving and radiant vessel of soil and leaf and stone and
water, whose thundering kings and priests were doomed to threads
of dust, consumed by time and prey to the wild wind.